Part One

Return to Maricopa County

Chapter One

It had been a cruel and vicious winter on the coasts of Ireland and England. The waters of the Atlantic Ocean challenged the sea captains and their ships who boldly dared to challenge such a force. But the ones who did succeed were making a fortune.

Still, the most seaworthy captain can play his luck one too many times, and such was the case with Captain Steve Lafferty. There had always been that cocky, self-assured air about Lafferty that made him dare to venture one more trip against all odds. He'd shrugged off the pleas of his beautiful auburn-haired wife that he shouldn't go this time, for, she reasoned, they had plenty of money to last until spring came and the seas calmed.

And this time Lafferty's ship, *Lucky Lady,* did not win the battle with the powerful winds and tempestuous seas.

None survived the shipwreck of the *Lucky Lady,* and the sad news was delivered to Lafferty's pretty young wife that her husband and his crew had died off the

Irish coast. There was no one in Ireland to give her comfort, for all her friends and family were across the vast ocean, back in Arizona territory, in Maricopa County.

Gillian Browne Lafferty had come to Ireland as Lafferty's young bride less than a year ago. Making friends had not been easy for her, since the little cottage with its thatched roof was in a remote area, and the nearest neighbors lived far away. This had not mattered to Gillian when she'd first arrived in Ireland, though, for she was so in love with Steve Lafferty that the only thing that mattered to her was being with him.

When they crossed the ocean to come to this little enchanted cottage Steve had purchased, their plan had been that Gillian would accompany him on his jaunts in his fine, sleek schooner, for she loved the sea and his ship. But those romantic dreams had been shattered after they'd arrived in Ireland. Gillian had lost the baby she carried, and she was not able to accompany him when the time came for him to leave Ireland on his schooner. So Steve had left her behind.

Gillian found herself alone at the cottage for several weeks before Steve returned from his voyage, but the cottage became an enchanted place once he was home to share it with her. They shared romantic nights, and glorious days of roaming around the green country-side, or going down to the beaches to watch the ships sailing and the tides lapping at the beaches. Gillian would pack baskets of food and they would sit there, plotting the dreams of the future they would share.

Oh, they dreamed such beautiful dreams, and Steve comforted her that they would certainly have a child soon. This time she would not miscarry. He blamed the

8

crossing they'd made after they'd married, back in Arizona territory. They'd sailed to Ireland as soon as his contract with the railroad was fulfilled, when he'd delivered all the rails and equipment.

But the miscarriage had left Gillian frail and weak, so Steve had insisted that she remain at the cottage when he left on his next voyage. In the first six months of their marriage, Steve was away from the cottage almost five months.

Gillian had to admit that it was not exactly the life she'd envisioned for herself and Steve when they'd married. More and more, she found herself lonely for her family and friends back in Arizona.

If it had not been for the little Irish lady, Nora Kelly, who lived about a mile away, Gillian didn't know what she'd have done during those lonely weeks when Steve was away on the *Lucky Lady*.

Nora Kelly had kept her from going over the edge, the day she received the news that her handsome husband was dead. Never more would his strong arms hold her or his sensuous lips kiss her. Never again would she know the savage fury of his hot-blooded Irish passion. He was dead!

Gillian found this almost impossible to accept. She was so young, and so was Steve. They had not yet celebrated their first year of being man and wife. It wasn't fair! How could life be so cruel to them?

For almost two weeks after she received the horrible news, Gillian existed like someone in a foggy maze, roaming aimlessly around the grounds of the cottage.

Nora Kelly understood the anguish of the pretty girl, and her heart went out to her. She also knew that Gillian could not remain there, for she would never shake off the ghost haunting her. She was far too young and pretty to wither away. Nora did not want to see it happen, so she decided to do something about it.

The next day she went to the Lafferty cottage and, as she and Gillian sat in the kitchen enjoying a cup of tea, Nora told her, "Gillian, my dear—I think you should leave Ireland. I think you should go back to Arizona and your dear folks, the Fosters, who you've talked so much about. I really do."

"Funny you should say that, Nora. I've been thinking about it lately. I'm so lonely to see them, and there's nothing to hold me here now," Gillian admitted sadly.

"Then get busy booking yourself passage on the next ship, Gillian."

Gillian reached out to pat Nora's hand as she declared, "Nora, I've said it before and I'll say it again: I don't know what I'd do without you. You're right, and I'll get busy making my plans tomorrow. I'll need to have a talk with Mr. Callihan, Steve's solicitor, about his property here."

"Dearie, everything was left to you—remember? What you do with this land and cottage is your decision. Should you want me to try to take care of it for you, if you don't wish to sell it, you know I would," Nora assured her. But Nora Kelly knew that if she left Ireland to return to Arizona, Gillian would probably never come back here, for she was far too young and beautiful to remain a widow for long.

Poor dear, Nora thought to herself. It was a terrible thing to be a widow before she'd had her twentieth birthday.

A visit and chat with Nora Kelly was always an

uplifting and pleasant experience for Gillian. She found that the night did not seem so long and lonely after Nora had left and Gillian had fixed her dinner. To make dinner for herself and eat alone was nothing new to her, but she didn't enjoy it.

As she ate, she reflected that something about the climate here in Ireland had not agreed with her, since the minute she'd arrived. Her miscarriage had left her weak and drained, but that had been many weeks ago. Gillian should have felt stronger than she did now. She missed the warming heat of the Arizona sun, and the dry climate.

Sitting in her little parlor, she thought about the bright sun that beat down on the Foster ranch where she had lived. She used to wander in Nancy Foster's garden, which was filled with brilliantly blooming flowers, and look across the distance to see the mountains sprinkled with snow.

It would be magnificent to behold that sight again, after all these months, she thought, as she sat in the rocker by the small stone fireplace.

A child might have made a difference, but she had also been denied that, Gillian mused. A baby would have been someone she could have loved and cared for when Steve was away for weeks at a time. It could have helped fill the void of so many hours when time had hung so heavily. For as much as she had enjoyed puttering in the little cottage, she still couldn't spend the entire day keeping it clean and in order. There seemed to be so many rainy days when she could not take a stroll down the little country lane, or do some chore out in her yard.

Being in this reflective mood tonight, she thought

about the nights when Steve was home after one of his spells at sea. No woman could have wished to be more ardently loved than she was. Those had been the wonderful times for Gillian, and she cherished the sweet, romantic memories. But most of the time she'd slept in their bed alone, and as a new bride she had found herself resenting it more and more as the weeks and months had gone by.

The truth was, she had been very vexed with her husband when he had left her for his last, ill-fated voyage. She had talked until she was blue in the face to try and persuade him not to go. But the happy-go-lucky, headstrong Lafferty figured his pretty wife's spitfire temper would have cooled by the time he returned home, and he tried to cheer her up when he kissed her farewell.

"I'll buy you anything your little heart desires, my sweet Gilly. We'll go into the city and have ourselves the wildest shopping spree," he'd called back to her, as he was walking down the path that would take him to the harbor where his *Lucky Lady* was moored.

She'd been so angry when she turned around to go back into the house that she gave the front door a mighty slam, and muttered, "What I desire, Steve Lafferty, money can't buy!"

She had no idea that it would be the last time she would see his handsome, grinning face.

Brian Callihan felt a deep compassion for Captain Lafferty's pretty little bride. It wasn't easy to be in a strange country, with all her family and friends across the ocean, and to be all alone.

"If you want me to try to sell the property for you while you're away, and send the money to you in Arizona, then you just leave me the details of where you'll be."

"I do think that would be best, Mr. Callihan. I can't ask Mrs. Kelly to take on the burden of looking after the place if I just leave it vacant. I—I am not sure about my plans right now. I might decide not to return here."

Brian Callihan nodded his head, and told her that he could understand that. A pretty young lady like her should not allow herself to wither away in that secluded cottage, even if it was in a very picturesque setting.

Gillian opened up her reticule and handed Callihan a slip of paper that gave him all the information he would need to get in touch with her after she was gone.

"I'll be leaving in two weeks, Mr. Callihan. I booked passage on the *Morning Star* before I came to your office. Other than my personal possessions and a few small items, I shall be leaving all the furnishings there. And there are some things I'll give to Nora."

"That's just fine, Mrs. Lafferty. I'll attend to all that for you. In fact, I have a young couple in mind who might be interested in the cottage and remaining furnishings. I might even be able to settle this for you before you leave. I'll be in touch in a few days, if they are interested and would like to have a look at the cottage and property."

"Oh, I thank you, Mr. Callihan." She rose and extended her dainty hand to him. Callihan shook it and bade her farewell, thinking what a cruel trick fate had played on such a likable couple as Captain Lafferty and his beautiful lady.

Gillian felt much better about everything after her

visit to Brian Callihan's office. With her passage booked, and the property in the capable hands of Steve's solicitor, she had nothing left to do except her packing.

There was a childlike excitement churning within her about going back home, and she suddenly realized she had not felt this happy for a very long time.

Chapter Two

When Gillian Browne Lafferty boarded the *Morning Star* to go back to the States and leave the coast of Ireland behind, the winds were not so fierce nor the air so cold and harsh as they had been just two weeks ago. Yet there was enough of a breeze, as she was guided across the deck, for the long skirt of her gown to billow out. Her richly colored blue cape clung to her as she was walking toward the steps that led below to her cabin. Her matching blue bonnet was tied securely under her chin, so that her thick auburn hair would not be tousled by the breeze.

It was a relief to reach her cabin and begin to settle in. Taking off the bonnet, she took a long look at herself in the small mirror on the wall of the cabin. It seemed to her that the Gillian reflected there was different from the one she used to see.

Actually, it was only Gillian who would have seen this change. The face was still the beautiful face of the romantic young girl Gillian Browne had been a year ago. That same glorious crown of copper-colored hair flowed generously around her petite shoulders. The bright blue eyes were flashing with life and excitement again, despite all the tears that had been shed when she'd learned about Steve's untimely death.

But she was thinner, and she could already imagine Nancy Foster and her good husband, John, gently admonishing her and telling her that she needed to put some meat on her bones.

Oh, how wonderful it was going to be to see those dear people again! She'd often wondered what would have happened to her if they had not taken her into their home and their hearts after her parents had been killed by the Apaches.

At least she was not returning to Maricopa County penniless. Steve might not have been a wealthy man, but he did leave her with enough funds to take care of her needs until she could decide what to do with her life. And when Callihan sold the property, she would have even more to sustain her for a while.

For the first hour she was in the cabin, she got her valise unpacked and her toilet articles put in the small chest's drawer. The rest of her luggage, she left packed. Then she sat down by the porthole and gazed out at the turbulent waters by the dock, allowing her mind to wander over the previous two weeks.

Her only regret about leaving Ireland was dear Nora Kelly. She had insisted that Nora take all the good linens and coverlets from the cottage, as well as much of the kitchenware. For three days, Gillian had emptied out her cupboards and loaded the articles into her buggy to take to Nora's cottage. She also gave almost all of Steve's clothing to Nora for her husky nephew, Terrence, holding back only a couple of Steve's favorite shirts as a keepsake.

The little Irish lady was stunned by Gillian's generous gift of china and glassware. She sighed, "Mercy, child, that is more than I'll need in my lifetime!"

"Then you find someone who might have need of it," Gillian laughed.

It had been a very busy time for Gillian these last two weeks, but by the time she left she had the cottage exactly as she wanted it for Mr. Callihan. All that was left was the furniture. All personal belongings had been removed; nothing of Steve's or Gillian's was left behind. As she closed the front door behind her for the last time, she had felt strongly that she was closing a chapter of her life.

If Gillian had any doubts that life had changed her, they were gone after a couple of days aboard the *Morning Star*. Most of the time she stayed within her cabin. She found nothing relaxing about roaming the deck of the ship to gaze out on that desolate, endless sea of gray-green water. It had been those vicious, churning waters that had claimed the man she loved. It was strange now to remember how intrigued she'd been by that same sea when she and Steve had sailed toward Ireland after they'd left Arizona. She'd loved strolling on the deck of the *Lucky Lady,* and standing by the railing in the moonlight with her new husband.

But now, when she tried to take a brief walk around the deck of the *Morning Star,* all she could think about was that the authorities had never been able to find Steve's body, or that of his first mate, Harry Driscol, on the shipwrecked *Lucky Lady.* Gillian had become very fond of Harry when she'd made that first crossing with Steve, so she felt a deep sorrow about his death, as well as her husband's.

And it was with such sad thoughts as these that she occupied her days, reading quietly in her cabin or simply replaying the past and wishing things had turned out differently.

For the first few days the *Morning Star* was at sea, Captain Glover figured that the reason he never saw Mrs. Lafferty strolling around the ship was that she was still in mourning over her husband's recent death. He had shivered when he heard about the tragedy, for like any sea captain, he accepted that this could be his fate, too. The sea was treacherous.

His path had crossed a few times with Captain Lafferty's, and he knew that Steve had had a reputation around various harbors as the best. They called him Captain Lucky, because he'd safely ridden out many fierce storms at sea. But for whatever reason, he hadn't managed to ride this one out.

Out of courtesy, and respect for her husband, he decided to invite Gillian to join him in his cabin for dinner the following night. It might do her good to get out of that cabin she was spending so much time in. He sent his young cabin boy, Artie, to her with his invitation.

When Artie knocked at her door, Gillian invited the young boy inside the cabin to wait while she read the message. A warm smile came to her face, and she told Artie, "Tell your captain I will be pleased to have dinner with him tomorrow night."

"Yes, ma'am, I'll tell him," Artie said, and he hastily prepared to go out the door.

Gillian smiled again as he left, and wondered how old the boy was. He hardly looked old enough to be away from his mother. He was a cute little tyke, with hair a brighter shade of red than hers, and a generous crop of freckles across his nose and cheeks.

She found herself wondering about Captain Glover and if he was a married man. He had to be in his forties, and she thought about Steve, who was just in his mid-twenties. Dear Lord, she didn't know if she could have endured life with him going to sea for twenty-odd years. Obviously, some ladies learned how to live with it and, when she had married Steve Lafferty, she had not had any qualms that she could, too.

But she had suddenly begun to realize, after she arrived in Ireland, that she would not know with Steve the joys and shared pleasures that John and Nancy Foster experienced on their ranch back in Maricopa County. The Laffertys' interludes of paradise were brief indeed, compared to the togetherness the Fosters shared.

She spent a pleasant evening with Captain Glover. He had come to her cabin to personally escort her down the passageway to his cabin at the appointed hour. His thick, graying hair was worn long, touching the collar of his shirt. He was a tall, stoutly built man, and he had a warm, friendly way about him as he told her what a treat it was to have her as his guest for dinner. "I get tired of always eating alone, and I'd noticed you had been keeping to your cabin, so I thought it was about time we share a dinner together. It's a pleasure for me to get to know you. I knew your husband, ma'am."

19

"You knew Steve?" Gillian echoed, as he ushered her through the door of his cabin.

Politely he led her over to the table, assisting her as she took her seat. "Couldn't say I knew him well, but then I guess the only people who get to know sea captains very well are their crew and their first mates. That's who they spend most of their time with."

He poured a glass of wine for each of them, and sat down in the other chair. He spoke about the few times he'd had a chance to meet up with Lafferty and talk with him. Gillian could believe that a ship's crew would know their captain better than even his own family. Steve's first mate, Harry Driscol, had obviously been his best friend, and knew him better than anyone.

Harry had spent a lot of time at their cottage when the two of them were not at sea, and Gillian had come to know him quite well during the last year. She had liked him as he had liked her, from the minute Steve had introduced her as his new bride, when they'd boarded the *Lucky Lady* to come to Ireland about this time last year.

Once she'd even pleaded with Harry to use his influence to discourage Steve from making those runs out in the vicious waters. Driscol had told her, "Tried it already, Gillian. We're dealing with a hardheaded Irishman. Myself, I'd rather stay in port a few more weeks."

Sitting here in Captain Glover's cabin brought back bittersweet memories, for it reminded Gillian so vividly of the cabin she'd shared with Steve aboard the *Lucky Lady*. She tried to be gracious to the captain, for the meal was delicious and Glover was quite a conversationalist, but he had a keen sense of perception, and he knew that the pretty lady was preoccupied with her own private thoughts. Since the meal was over, and both of them were at the point of finishing their wine, he asked if she might enjoy a stroll around the deck before he escorted her to her cabin.

"Oh, a short stroll would be very nice, Captain Glover, but I think I will then be ready to go to my cabin and retire. It was a delicious meal, and the wine was so fine that I feel pleasantly relaxed."

"Well, that's nice to hear. I find that the night breeze from the ocean has that kind of tranquilizing effect on me."

The two of them left the cabin to go out on the moonlit deck of the ship. Captain Glover had that same fatherly air about him as John Foster had.

As they walked, he talked about his family, back in a little seaport on the Irish coast. He had sons and daughters who were about Gillian's age. Gillian enjoyed hearing about his family, and she knew that they were very dear to him from the way he spoke so lovingly about the children and his wife, Anna Lee.

"She must miss you terribly, Captain Glover," Gillian remarked.

"Anna Lee is a very independent lady. She told me from the first that she wasn't going to sit home waiting around for me to make port, and she never has. She tutors youngsters and teaches piano."

"So the lonely hours are filled?"

"Anna Lee never allowed herself to be lonely, and she knew that the sea was a fever in my blood. When a man is afflicted by it, he loves the sea as fervently as he does a woman."

He noticed that she became very quiet and thoughtful when she heard this, and without saying a word he turned around to guide her toward her cabin.

21

They said goodnight, and Gillian thanked him again for a most pleasant evening. Captain Glover walked back to his cabin occupied with his thoughts. He hoped that his words about his love for the sea might help her in her grief.

He had indeed enlightened Gillian, and she thought about what he'd said as she was putting on her nightgown. After slipping into the matching wrapper, she sat down on the bunk. She realized that the sea would always have been her rival—and how would she have fought that? She could have fought for Steve's love if it had been with another woman, but the love for the sea was different.

Suddenly, Gillian realized that she would never have found true happiness, for the sea would always have come between them. That honest nature of hers had to confess that resentment and bitterness had already started to fester in their marriage.

She just was not like Captain Glover's Anna Lee, which meant that she had not been the right woman for Steve Lafferty. The day she'd married him had been planned as her wedding day with another young man, but when the dashing Lafferty suddenly appeared, she forgot everything as he swept her up into his strong arms.

Perhaps she and Steve had been doomed from the start. Theirs had been an illicit and tempestuous love affair—perhaps they were being punished. And with this gloomy thought, Gillian went to bed and fell into a troubled sleep.

Chapter Three

From the moment Gillian left the *Morning Star* after it docked in New Orleans, and even more when she hired a carriage to take her to a nearby hotel, exhilaration began to consume her. She knew she should never have left this country where she was born and raised.

She had been quite sorry to leave Captain Glover, having found that his genuine concern about her endeared him to her. He was worried about her traveling alone to Tucson, but she assured him that she would be just fine. And she had no doubt that she would be.

She spent only one night in the busy port city before starting the long overland journey to Tucson. She boarded a train the next morning and spent a restful, if impatient, few days watching endless scenery pass. The railroad was noisy, but she enjoyed the change of being on land instead of rolling sea. When at last they arrived in Phoenix, she went directly to the stagecoach office and booked a seat.

The only passenger on the stagecoach with her was

an elderly lady going to see her daughter in Tucson. Gillian was very tired, and at the stopover that night she barely made conversation over dinner, and retired early to her room. But she awoke the next morning feeling refreshed and very excited, for she knew that today she would, at last, be home.

The sight of the golden-red canyons and the high mountains in the distance thrilled Gillian. She was getting so close! The vast flatlands and the tall saguaro cacti were a very familiar sight, and she had envisioned them for so many weeks now.

Already the Arizona sun was warming her, and she removed the wool jacket she was wearing over her light woollen gown. She was thinking that by the time she got to Tucson, this gown was going to be far too warm. She must have forgotten how hot it could get, for in Ireland this gown would not have been enough to keep her warm. How her life had changed when she went with Steve to his homeland.

Pensively, she also removed the rich blue velvet bonnet from her head and ran her long, slender fingers through her hair. It felt good to let her hair flow around her shoulders, loose and free.

As the stagecoach rolled along the rutted road toward Tucson, she thought about what she was going to do once she got to the Fosters'. She had no intentions of staying there with them too long. After all, she was no longer their responsibility. That had ended when she had left them to marry Steve.

She could always buy herself a ranch nearby, for she would have the money to do it once the cottage was sold. Or maybe she could buy herself a house in

Tucson. She had some very fond memories of the city and the people she'd known there. She was looking forward to seeing the Old Pueblo Inn, where she was planning to stay until she could leave to go to Maricopa County, and the Fosters' ranch near Rock Springs.

When she was so far away in Ireland, she could never think about Maricopa County without also thinking of the wonderful Solange and her son, Hawk. Solange's cabin up in the mountains, near the Fosters' ranch, had been Gillian's refuge so often when she had needed to talk to the older lady. What a fountain of wisdom she had been!

But Gillian knew that the last year had changed Solange's life as well as her own. Solange had left her mountain cabin when she married the French-Canadian trapper who'd entered her life shortly before Gillian had left Maricopa County as Steve's wife.

Gillian wondered if Solange had ever come back to visit the cabin, as she'd told Gillian that Gaston had promised her they would.

Of course, she also wondered about Solange's handsome half-breed son, Hawk! What had happened to him during this last year? Perhaps he had found himself a wife, and still lived in the little cottage that had been his and Solange's home for so many years.

Or maybe Hawk had left Maricopa County after his mother and Gaston had gone to Canada. Gillian thought how much she would like to see him—but maybe it would not be pleasant. There was no doubt in her mind that Hawk must hate her for what she had done to him; for she'd married Steve Lafferty on the very day she was supposed to have become Hawk's wife.

She couldn't blame him if he did hate her. Hawk had been willing to marry her, even though she had admitted to him that she was carrying Steve's child. But when she'd promised to marry Hawk, she had given up hope that Lafferty would return to marry her, as he'd promised.

On the day of her wedding, everything had happened so swiftly. She and the Fosters were boarding the wagon to go to the little church where she was to wed Hawk, when suddenly the indomitable Lafferty had returned to claim the lady he loved. Nothing was going to stop him. So it was Lafferty who had stood there in the church with her that day, instead of Hawk.

Neither of them ever knew that Hawk had been riding his horse, Tache, down the ridge of the mountain on his way to the church, at the same time as Lafferty came galloping up to the Fosters' wagon. All his black eyes had to see was Gillian rushing into Lafferty's arms to know that this would not be his wedding day. He had reined Tache around to go in the opposite direction, and ridden away.

All that mattered to Hawk was that Gillian was happy. He had worshiped her for years, and he knew nothing would ever change that. Long before she knew he even existed, he had thought she was the prettiest creature he'd ever seen. From afar, he'd sat on his horse and just gazed down into the valley at the fourteen-year-old girl, with her copper-colored hair flowing around her shoulders as she roamed through the pastureland picking wildflowers.

Fate had finally allowed them to meet, but to Hawk it seemed that almost immediately fate had stepped in again to take her away. There was a period of time when he felt very bitter, but not about the sweet Gillian.

Instead, his bitterness was directed toward Lafferty and that damned Irish luck of his.

By the time Gillian's stagecoach was pulling into Tucson, she could see through the window one of those spectacular Arizona sunsets, its glorious shades of purple, rose and gold spanning the sky.

The streets looked very familiar, and when they arrived at the stagecoach station, she asked the driver about the Old Pueblo Inn.

"Oh, yes, ma'am—going stronger than ever. That where you're heading?" the driver asked her, starting to unload her luggage.

"Yes, I'll be there until I can get on up to Maricopa County." She laughed as she surveyed all the luggage she had brought with her from Ireland. It was more than she'd realized, so she was going to have to hire herself a buggy or carriage to get it all to the inn.

The middle-aged driver saw her predicament, and he took pity on the pretty little lady. "If you wouldn't mind riding in my flatbed wagon, I'll get you and all your stuff to the inn. You just have yourself a seat up on the porch while I check in, and we'll be on our way."

Gillian was grateful, and she offered to pay him for his services, but the driver quickly told her, "Ain't about to charge a nice little lady a fee, when I'll be going right past the inn on the way to my house. Now you just make yourself comfortable on that bench over there, and I'll be with you in just a minute. I'm eager to get myself home, too."

A short while later he returned with the wagon and got all her luggage loaded, then came around to the side of the wagon to assist her up into the seat. He gave her a friendly smile as he declared, "Have you at the Old Pueblo before you know it, miss."

"Well, I certainly appreciate your kindness. May I ask what your name is?" she asked with a smile.

"Sure can, and I was just about to ask you the same thing. It's Will Fowler, ma'am. And yours?"

"Gillian Lafferty."

"Well, it's a pleasure to meet you, Miss Lafferty, and like I told you, we'll be at the inn real soon. It's just a short hop from the station."

Dusk was settling over the city by the time she entered the lobby of the inn, Will trailing behind her with his arms laden with her luggage. It was only when he'd seen that she'd gotten herself a room that he tipped his dusty old felt hat to bid her goodbye.

He was rewarded by her lovely smile and her thanks. How obliging he'd been, she thought gratefully.

A strange feeling was washing over her by the time she had got settled in her small suite of rooms, which had a small sitting room adjacent to the bedroom. It seemed like nothing had changed since she'd last been here. Right here, at this inn, Steve Lafferty had made love to her one stormy summer day, when he was staying here on an assignment for the railroad.

Once she had unpacked a few things and enjoyed the luxury of a warm bath, she found herself too exhausted to dress to go to dinner in the dining room. She knew that a dinner cart could be wheeled to the room, and this appealed to her tonight. She rang the bellpull and, when a maid appeared, ordered a simple meal. She was glad she had decided to stay in her room. She was just not in the mood for an encounter with Melba Jackson or Helen Clayton, who ran the inn. Much as she liked both ladies, tonight she could not face telling them about Steve's death at sea.

She left her bedroom to go into the small sitting room, dressed in one of her silk wrappers. She had only to open the door that led out onto a small patio off the sitting room, and feel the dry, gentle breeze, to know that her health was going to improve now that she was back in Arizona. The warmth felt so good to her when she recalled the chill at this time of night back in Ireland.

When her dinner was brought to her, she ate every delicious morsel. When she had finished she smiled wryly. If she continued to eat like this, she would quickly gain back all the weight she'd lost over the last few months.

Now the only thing left to do was get to the comfort of that inviting bed in the next room, and sleep. Gillian didn't care if she slept through the next day, for now she was back in Arizona.

If she didn't leave for Rock Springs for a few days, it didn't matter. Tucson was so much closer than Ireland, and now she was not so far away from her family and friends.

Now, she did not feel so lonely and desolate.

Melba Jackson still tried to make the rounds of the inn just before closing time every night. She liked to check with the desk clerk in the lobby that all was in order, and take a survey of the vast dining room. But like an old plow horse her legs were going, and lately she'd been using a cane to support herself. This was not to her liking at all, but she figured it was better than falling flat on her face. So she ignored her vanity and pride, and resentfully started to use the cane.

29

Business had never been better than in the last year, since the railroad had extended to Tucson from the East. When she looked at the ledger, she saw that they had a full house at the inn again tonight.

Suddenly, one name from the ledger leaped out at her like a bolt of lightning. She turned to her clerk, Cecil.

"Cecil, this guest—Gillian Lafferty—did you sign her in?"

"Yes, Miss Melba. She was one of the first I signed in after taking over from Jack at six."

"Tell me about her."

"Very attractive lady, I must say. Finely attired, if you know what I mean. A genteel lady, Miss Melba, I'd swear."

All this didn't matter to Melba. "What color of hair did she have, Cecil?" Melba knew few ladies had the glorious auburn hair that Gillian Browne had.

"I'd call it dark red, Miss Melba." Cecil was feeling a little perplexed about his boss's intense interest in this guest. But right now, Melba didn't wish to enlighten him. She left the counter and went out of the lobby toward suite 101. However, when she came to the door of the suite, there was darkness under the threshold, so she decided not to knock. Turning around, she went back down the hallway to her own private suite.

But for the longest time after she had retired for the night, Melba found herself speculating about her guest. If this was the beautiful little Gillian Browne who'd married that handsome Irish man, Steve Lafferty, what was she doing here by herself?

Melba slept the next morning until noon, as she usually did. For Melba, this was why having Helen Clayton as her partner was such an advantage, for

Helen Clayton was a morning lark, and Melba was a night owl. It was the best deal Melba had ever made for herself, bringing Helen into the inn as a partner. With business booming as it was, Helen had been worth her weight in gold.

Gillian, too, slept through the morning. The sixteen hours of sleep did wonders for her. She awoke eager to leap out of the bed and get dressed, and soon she was ready to go to the spacious dining room to enjoy a late breakfast and get herself awake with some coffee. It felt good to dress in one of her light muslin frocks with short puffed sleeves, and to know there was no need for a wool shawl over her shoulders. She wore her long hair loose, and free to hang over her shoulders.

She slipped her feet into black leather slippers, and in her black velvet reticule put a couple of articles that she did not wish to leave in the room while she was away. She made a very attractive figure in the muslin frock, with its cream background and black sprigged design. Black velvet lacings wound up the front of the bodice to a scooped neckline. Gillian emerged from her room and jauntily walked down the hallway, swinging her reticule back and forth. She was feeling very gay and lighthearted this morning.

Today, she felt like that young wistful girl she'd been all those months ago, and she liked the feeling.

Today, she felt younger than springtime, and she suddenly realized that it *was* spring, here in Arizona!

Chapter Four

The inn's kitchen was a beehive of activity this morning. Helen Clayton was so busy that she'd not looked out through the door once to survey the dining room and the diners eating their breakfast. If she had, she would have immediately recognized Gillian's familiar pretty face.

Melba had not had a chance to tell Helen about finding the name of Gillian Lafferty on her guest ledger late last night, since Helen was already in bed while Melba was making her nightly rounds of the inn. It was usually at midday that they encountered one another.

Gillian had caught the eye of most of the diners when she'd strolled in alone and taken a table. The auburn-haired beauty drew curious stares from some of the gentlemen when no one had joined her by the time the waiter came to her table. She was far too lovely not to have some man by her side, most of them were thinking.

But Gillian was oblivious to the interest she aroused. It had been a long time since she had indulged herself with such a hearty breakfast, and she enjoyed it.

When she left the dining room she went through the lobby and on out the front entrance, instead of turning to go down the hallway to her suite. A stroll around the magnificent grounds of the old inn would be delightful, for she remembered all the beauty of the various tropical plants and flowering shrubs. The stone pathways that led around the grounds were edged with flowers that were already blooming profusely.

Also, she thought, a brisk walk would surely do her good after the huge meal she had just devoured. She was used to having just a cup of coffee and toast spread with jam, her daily breakfast back at the cottage in Ireland. Only when he had been home did she go to the trouble to fix eggs and ham, and the fried potatoes Steve had so dearly enjoyed.

Thinking of Steve saddened her, and she walked somberly into the grounds. But she had gone only a short distance down the stone pathway before she encountered a couple of gentlemen who gave her broad smiles as they tipped their hats. One tried to strike up a conversation with her, but Gillian politely excused herself. "I'm on my way to meet someone. A good morning to you, sir." And she walked on in the opposite direction. But an amused smile was on her lips. It seemed like a lifetime ago that she was that carefree young girl whose bright blue eyes twinkled flirtatiously when she encountered a handsome young man. But she was, a single lady again. She no longer had a husband or any other man in her life.

She had to admit that it was nice to know that men still found her attractive. She was certainly convinced of it by the time she was headed back to the inn. There seemed to be a number of male guests there who had no wives accompanying them, and they had all seemed to be in the grounds smiling at her!

By the time she got back to the suite she was ready to sit and recover in the sitting room, with her feet propped up on a footstool. For the next hour, as she sat there resting, she wrote Nora Kelly a letter, to tell her about the voyage and her safe arrival in Tucson.

She heard the little clock in her suite chiming two, but she felt no need for any lunch, so she continued to write the letter to Nora.

Later, she planned to check the schedules at the station to see when she could set off for Rock Springs. But as anxious as she was to see the Fosters, she didn't mind delaying her departure from Tucson for another day or so. It was good to relax for a while, and it would give her time to see Melba and Helen while she was here in the city.

At one o'clock, Melba was sitting in her office waiting for Helen to join her, as was their routine each day, so that they could share lunch and discuss business.

Helen Clayton came bustling through the door and greeted Melba with a laugh. "I tell you, Melba, if business keeps up like this we're going to have to hire more help. Lord, I'm working those poor gals in the kitchen to death!"

Melba smiled. "Sit down, Helen—you look beat yourself." Helen had worked like a dog that morning, because one of her cooks was sick. Eagerly, she sank down in the chair and took a sip of the coffee that was waiting for her, declaring how good it tasted.

Melba allowed Helen to catch her breath and have a few bites of food before she brought up the subject of the guest who had signed in yesterday evening. Melba had gone again to suite 101 before coming to her office, and no one answered her knock, but as soon as she and Helen parted company after lunch, she was going back to the suite.

"Helen, a young lady signed in, by the name of Gillian Lafferty, late yesterday. Suppose it could be our little Gillian Browne? That's such an unusual name, I figure it's got to be her—but there's no man with her."

"Lord, Melba, you reckon?" Helen looked surprised.

"Gonna find out this afternoon. I'm going back to the room after we have lunch. Went by a while ago, before I came to the office, and no one was in the room when I knocked. She must have been out. Dang, it's sure got me curious, though!"

It had Helen Clayton curious, too. If it *was* Gillian, why was that Steve Lafferty not with her? She could not imagine him allowing his pretty young wife to travel alone all the way from Ireland. Helen's sister, Nancy, always kept her posted about any news from Gillian in Ireland, and she felt that somehow, Gillian wasn't too happy living in Ireland. Of course, Gillian hadn't written that to Nancy; it was just something Nancy felt, knowing Gillian so well.

After half an hour of resting her tired feet and eating lunch, Helen excused herself to get back to the duties waiting for her. "If it *is* that sweet Gillian, give her a kiss for me. Tell her I'm anxious to see her," Helen called back to Melba as she was rushing out the door.

Melba wasted no time after Helen left before leaving the office to go back down the carpeted hallway.

Once again, she rapped on the door, leaning on the support of her cane. This time she heard feet coming to the door, and when it opened, there was the pretty Gillian, who stood silent for only a fleeting second before she gave out a delighted sigh. "Oh, Melba! Melba, how good to see you again!" Warmly, she embraced the older lady, noticing that she was now using a cane. "Come on in."

"Oh, I just knew it was you when I checked that ledger late last night! My stars, honey—I think I'm in a state of shock!" Melba exclaimed.

Gillian smiled and, taking Melba's hand, led her to an armchair. They chatted for a while, and then Melba asked about Steve. "I know he isn't with you—the clerk said you checked in alone. Where is that handsome devil, eh?"

By now, Gillian thought she had cried all the tears left in her, but her blue eyes swam. "Steve's ship was caught in a terrible storm about two months ago, Melba, and he was killed."

For once, Melba Jackson was struck dumb. Steve Lafferty was a fellow everyone considered invincible, and Melba found it impossible to believe that he was dead. When she did finally speak, she, too, had tears in her eyes. "Oh, honey—I'm—I'm so very sorry. I don't know what to say," she stammered.

Gillian reached out to pat her hand. "There's nothing to be said, Melba. It—it was a mean winter in Ireland. Most of the captains were waiting out the fierce storms, and I pleaded with Steve to do the same, but there was no talking him out of leaving."

"Oh, men can be such a stubborn lot sometimes," Melba declared, shaking her head. "Well, I'm glad you came back from Ireland. It's here that you belong, Gillian."

"Yes, I'm staying here where I belong, Melba. I never wish to cross that ocean again as long as I live. I hate the very sight of that endless, ugly water."

Melba nodded her head understandingly. She saw and heard a bitterness in Gillian, and the older woman sensed that the beautiful young girl had not found the happiness she'd expected to find when she'd left Maricopa County. So very young, she was, to be a widow!

"Well, Helen is sure going to be thrilled to see you, and the Fosters will be overjoyed. I'm sure you're heading there next, aren't you?"

"Oh, yes. I can't wait to see them, either. I've missed all of you back here," Gillian confessed.

"Well, you're back now, honey, and there's no reason why we can't see each other often," Melba told her.

The two of them sat talking for another hour, for Melba was anxious to know if she had any plans to settle back in with the Fosters, or if she might be considering living in Tucson. Now that she was Lafferty's young widow, she was not penniless, as she had been when the Fosters took her into their home when she was only fourteen. Melba thought it would be a shame for such a lovely young lady to bury herself out on a ranch so isolated and far away from everything.

When she did finally take her leave from Gillian's suite, Melba had offered the services of her buggy and driver to take her to the station and make her arrangements for the trip to Rock Springs. "You just take the buggy whenever you like, Gillian, as long as you're here. I don't do that much gadding about any more. This damned leg puts a cramp in my style."

"Well, that's awfully nice of you, Melba, and I thank you," Gillian said as she walked her to the door.

Melba insisted that she join her for dinner that evening, and Gillian was happy to accept the invitation.

There might have been a few bigoted individuals who called Joe Hawk a half-breed Apache and made their smirking remarks behind his back, but they were in the minority.

Most people who knew Hawk now respected him as much as Warner Barstow learned to when Hawk came to work for him as a scout for the railroad. But that was over a year ago, and now Hawk was an agent for the Southern Pacific Railroad. He worked in the office part of the week, and the rest he rode the route and reported back to Warner Barstow.

Joe Hawk liked the job Warner had offered him about a year ago. Most of his time was spent in Tucson, but on his days off he always went back to Maricopa County, to the mountain cabin where he'd been raised and had lived until a year ago.

He was feeling especially happy this wonderful spring afternoon, for Warner had given him a raise in salary as well as ten days off, for he had been working constantly for the last six months. He was looking forward to spending this much time up at the cabin and visiting with his old friend, Troy. He would enjoy fishing in the mountain streams and hunting in the woods, and there was that good old brown dog, Little Bear—he was going to have some romping good times with him for the next ten days.

Little Bear was no fuzzy little brown pup any more, though, for now he'd reached his full size and weighed almost forty pounds. Little Bear had gone with Hawk's mother, Solange, and her husband, Gaston, when they left for Gaston's home in Canada, but Little Bear had not been happy in his new home. So when Solange and Gaston returned to her mountain retreat for a few weeks, she'd left Little Bear back in the mountains where he liked to roam. Solange's and Hawk's lifelong friend, Troy, looked after him when Hawk was in Tucson.

When Solange had married the French Canadian Gaston Dion, it was understood that while she would agree to live in Canada, they must return to her mountain cabin from time to time, for she dearly loved it up there in the mountains. Gaston loved her so much that he would have promised her anything, just to get her to agree to marry him.

No one was happier than Hawk that his wonderful mother had found a man who loved her so devotedly. The last year had been a gloriously happy time for her, and her letters to Hawk reflected that.

For Hawk, however, it had been a bittersweet year. All his energies were applied to his job and making a future for himself. He felt great pride in how he'd advanced himself in the last twelve months. Barstow had helped him acquire a small piece of property at the edge of Tucson, and there was a nice little house and small barn on the land. There was enough room for his horse, Tache, to run and exercise. The house was small and nothing fancy, and there were only a few acres of land, but it was enough to satisfy Hawk right now.

He'd thought about bringing Little Bear back to Tucson with him, but he worried that the dog wouldn't be content there either, so he left him in Troy's care. Besides, he figured, the big dog was company for his friend.

Only one thing marred Hawk's joy in returning to the mountain cabin, and he'd come to terms with that by now. When he returned there from Tucson, the memory of Gillian Browne always haunted him, and he realized it always would.

For a brief period of time after she'd married Steve Lafferty and left Maricopa County, he'd thought he might be falling in love with Troy's pretty cousin, Shawna. In fact, he'd damned well convinced himself of it after Gillian had been gone several months. Every time he'd come back for a few days' visit to the mountains, he'd courted her, and he was about ready to ask her to marry him when fate stepped in.

Shawna had never heeded Troy's warnings to not roam too far into the dense woods surrounding their cabin. She had disobeyed him once too often and fallen prey to a hungry mountain lion.

Hawk was in Tucson when the tragedy happened, and he had not learned about it until he'd returned to the mountain on a few days' visit. By that time the pretty little Shawna had been buried. With Troy, he'd visited her grave at the back of the house. Troy had enclosed it with a wooden fence and put flowers on the mound of earth. Unashamed of the tears flowing down his face, Troy had cried, "Damnit, Hawk—I miss her! The cabin seems so empty now without her. You know how I resented it when I found myself saddled with her—I feel so guilty about that now."

"I know, Troy, but it was inevitable you'd feel that way. You'd always had the cabin to yourself. Having a young girl like Shawna under your roof had to be uncomfortable at first," Hawk said gently, trying to comfort him. Somehow his own grief seemed less important than his friend's.

"Now I've got to get used to being here alone again, and I'm going to find it just as hard, I guess."

It was then that Hawk figured Little Bear just might prove to be a good tonic for Troy, under the circumstances. A few weeks later, Hawk could see his idea had worked. Troy and the dog roamed around the woods together and became constant companions. Hawk had returned to Tucson reconciled to the fact that it had not been his destiny to marry Shawna, as he'd thought it was.

The short-lived interlude with pretty, black-eyed Shawna faded from his memory as the weeks went by, and he poured himself into the job he was doing for Warner Barstow. But the same was not true about his haunting memories of Gillian Browne. He wondered if he might be wiser to never take himself a wife, for no woman could receive his complete love and devotion, as Gillian had. Perhaps it would not be fair to any woman, for she would forever be fighting with a ghost.

Whenever he was at the cabin, he would hear the soft, gentle breeze echoing through the pine trees and be reminded of Gillian's soft, lilting laughter. The dancing, swaying flames in the fireplace brought back to him the swaying length of her auburn hair. The blue wildflowers recalled, but were not as beautiful as, her

41

sparkling blue eyes.

By now Gillian would have had the baby she was expecting when he offered to marry her, even though he knew it was Lafferty's child. That had not mattered to Hawk when he'd asked her to marry him. A part of the child would be Gillian. He figured that baby must be a few months old by now, at least.

To Hawk, Gillian seemed hardly more than a child herself when he recalled how he had towered over her when they were together.

Twilight descended over the countryside as he and Tache traveled northward toward Rock Springs. He couldn't explain it to himself, but the vision of Gillian was so vivid that he felt he could reach out and touch her lovely face. But he sighed wistfully, for he knew he could never expect to see her again.

Chapter Five

Everything seemed very much the same as it had when she left as Gillian traveled around the streets of Tucson. It had taken her only an hour to arrange her trip to Rock Springs and make one hasty stop at one of the little shops, before asking Melba's driver to take her back to the inn.

She got back in plenty of time to rest awhile and have a leisurely bath before she dressed to have dinner with Melba and Helen. She still felt tired from her traveling, but since she would not be leaving Tucson until two the next afternoon, she could sleep late in the morning if she wished to. This was just as well, for knowing Melba Jackson, she expected it to be late before they said goodnight. She took out the gown she would wear to dinner, and also hung out the outfit she planned to wear to travel to Rock Springs. Everything else, she packed back into her valise. It was then that her eyes surveyed the vast amount of luggage that had been piled up in the closet, and she wondered how in the world she was going to manage it all. She had no need to take everything to John and Nancy's ranch, for she had already decided that she would only be staying with them for a week or two.

Gillian had realized that wherever she settled, whatever she did, it would be on her own. She would not be satisfied to live with the Fosters, as she once had. Time had changed all that.

She figured that she could talk to Melba this evening about storing some of her belongings here until she made a decision about what she was going to do with her life.

But deciding to leave some of her luggage here changed things. For the next hour she was busy rearranging her clothes so that her more casual outfits, like divided skirts and simple cotton tunics, were in the large bag she would take with her to the Fosters'. By the time she had made all the switches, she was ready for a relaxing bath.

At the appointed hour, Gillian emerged from her room to go and meet Melba in the lobby. She looked very lovely. Her frock was the color of cornflowers, and her long auburn hair was pulled back from her face and held with a large mother-of-pearl comb splashed with bright blue brilliants.

Melba was there waiting for her when she came into the lobby, so she witnessed the impact the breathtaking woman stirred among the guests there.

Gillian seemed to not be aware of the sensation she was causing as she came to join Melba, but the proprietress of the Old Pueblo Inn didn't hesitate to compliment her.

"Lordy, you look stunning tonight! I could use you around here every night to spark some excitement in this place," Melba laughed, as she led her toward the dining room. "Helen will be joining us just a little later, Gillian."

Most of the diners in the spacious dining room recognized the familiar Melba Jackson, but the beautiful young lady with her was the one they were curious about. Melba wore an amused smile on her face as she and Gillian sat down at the table Melba had chosen for the three of them. It was given some seclusion by a huge palm tree, which shielded them from the crowded room.

The sight of Helen Clayton coming to join them gave Gillian a pleasant surprise. A year of working at the inn with Melba had given her a completely different image. Helen dressed with more flair now, and her frock was much more fashionable than the ones she'd worn when Gillian had first met Nancy's younger sister.

She and Gillian embraced one another. Helen had already been informed by Melba about Steve's death. She'd liked Gillian from the first time her sister, Nancy, had brought the young girl to Tucson with her on a visit. That was when Helen was still Kent Clayton's wife, and was selling her pastries to Melba Jackson to earn money to dress her daughter, Melissa, in the pretty clothes she wanted to provide for her.

Helen was thinking, as she took her seat at the table, how both her and Gillian's lives had changed in one short year.

Melba motioned to the young waiter to bring a bottle of champagne to their table, for it was a night to celebrate.

Helen patted Gillian's hand. "You are prettier than ever, and I'm so glad you're home. Lord, Nancy's going

45

to be tickled pink to see you again."

"It's good to be back home again, Helen. Ireland was too far away," Gillian confessed. She knew that Melba had told her about Steve and that Helen was hesitating to bring up anything that would make her feel sad. She appreciated the sensitivity.

They talked and laughed like three carefree girls for the next half hour, then Melba finally suggested that perhaps they should have their dinner.

And a delicious dinner it was, for Melba had left special orders with the cook. After one more glass of champagne, Helen knew that she was never going to be able to make herself get up in the morning when she usually did, if she didn't leave shortly.

"How long before you will be leaving us to go to Rock Springs, Gillian?" Helen asked her.

"I leave tomorrow at two, Helen."

"Oh, honey—that soon?"

"Oh, I will be back to see you again, Helen. In fact, I was going to ask Melba if I could leave some luggage here. I can't see taking all my things there until I know where I'm going to be settling."

This remark got Melba's immediate attention. "Of course you can, honey. You know that. So . . . you aren't considering the Fosters' ranch for your home now?"

"Oh, no, Melba. I'm a lady on my own now, and Steve left me enough funds to take care of myself for a while. I also arranged for his solicitor to sell the property in Ireland for me—I never intend to return there."

"I see," Melba drawled. The wheels in that busy head of hers were already beginning to turn with ideas. She

46

would mention some of them to Gillian, and she could consider them in her spare time with John and Nancy.

As Gillian had anticipated earlier, it was very late when she finally returned to her suite, for she and Melba had gone to Melba's quarters to continue talking after they'd left the dining room. In fact, it was past two in the morning when Gillian had finally undressed and crawled into bed. But it was a good feeling to be back home among friends who cared about her. Now she did not feel so lonely. After the offer Melba Jackson had made her tonight, she had no qualms about what the future held for her.

Melba had told her there was a position waiting for her, if she wanted it, after she'd had her visit with John and Nancy. Gillian was thrilled; she had never expected to be this lucky when she'd left Ireland.

Joe Hawk knew that whatever the future held for him, however high he might climb to attain what he wanted in this life, there would always be a certain magic for him when he stepped inside this little mountain cabin. It was here that his beautiful French mother had raised him. There was no woman he admired as he did his mother. Solange had been taken captive by Cochise and his Apache warriors, but she had survived long months at his mercy, and Cochise had sired Hawk. After his birth, her babe in her arms, she had fled the Apache camp and lost herself in the woods. He knew no woman as brave as Solange. A woodsman by the name of Tim McGrath had been in the woods the day she made her long, frantic flight from the Apache camp, and he took her under his robust and protective wing, bringing her with her little baby to this cabin. It was the only home Hawk had ever known. When Tim had died, Hawk and his mother had continued to live in his cabin in the mountains. Apparently Cochise must have given Solange up for dead, because the chief never came to find them.

Everything about this cabin spoke to Hawk of his beloved mother and her complete devotion to him. As young as she had been when this horrible experience had happened to her, she had dedicated her life to raising the son of her captor.

She had told him the story of her past. When Cochise had taken her as his captive, she was the only one of her group not killed. She had been the mistress of one of a number of young French noblemen who were taking a tour of the territory when the band of Apaches swarmed down on them. Back in France she had led the life of a pampered coquette, taken at the tender age of sixteen, because of her outstanding beauty, by this French nobleman to be his mistress.

Seeking adventure their party had come to the territory, and it had ended in tragedy. Solange survived, but for months she endured a hellish torment she'd never known before. Still, she had lived.

Nothing in her background had prepared her to live in the primitive, isolated mountain cabin where fate had placed her. By the time Hawk had become a young man he admired tremendously his mother's bravery and courage. Never had he known a day of going hungry or not having a roof over his head, and one petite lady had done it all for him. By the time he was sixteen he already towered over her by a foot, and he assumed a very protective attitude toward Solange.

Perhaps he could not have accepted Gaston Dion entering his mother's life, had he not found himself in love with the beautiful Gillian Browne at the same time. When the huge French Canadian had stumbled to the cabin door, injured, and Solange had taken him in and nursed him back to health, she thought he was a trapper who'd had the misfortune to step into one of the traps in the woods. But, as it would later be revealed by Gaston, he was a very wealthy gentleman, and he found himself hopelessly in love with the lovely Solange.

Hawk was happy to know that, when she married Gaston, Solange could at long last have the leisurely life she was meant for. She had waited her entire life to know such a love as she felt for the rugged Gaston, and he loved her in return with gentle tenderness as well as an overwhelming passion.

But Hawk had to admit, when he entered the cabin after his journey from Tucson, that it seemed strange to not find her there. The essence of her lingered with the aromas of her herbs, which hung from the rafters. He figured that she must have put them there when she and Gaston were visiting a few months ago, for they were all dried now.

He smiled as he threw his saddlebag on the chair, then roamed around the cabin to see that everything was in order and no intruder had taken advantage of finding it unoccupied. Troy came by to check on things every few days, but one could never be too sure.

Before he took the time to unpack, Hawk threw some kindling in the old cookstove and started a fire so that he could brew himself a pot of coffee. Once that was done, he quickly put his things away. Hawk didn't bring that much here from Tucson, for he had left some old, faded shirts and pants here. The food supplies he'd brought, he took to the kitchen to store in the small pantry and cupboards.

The fresh-brewed coffee tasted wonderful, and when he had drunk it he felt refreshed after the long trail ride. Looking out the window, he saw that the sun was setting and it would soon be dark, so he decided to take a walk around the grounds before nightfall.

He had only walked down the two front steps and into the yard when a massive hunk of brown fur came surging toward him. He gave out a deep, hearty laugh. "Well, Little Bear—how are you?" The dog reared up affectionately, and Hawk grabbed his huge paws and rubbed his face against Little Bear's head. "Good to see you, fellow," Hawk told him, rubbing the thick fur with enjoyment.

Very soon his old friend, Troy, appeared out of the woods and walked into the small clearing around the cabin. A broad grin came to Troy's face when he saw Little Bear rearing up against Hawk's tall, strong body.

They greeted one another with gusto, and it didn't take much persuasion on Hawk's part to convince Troy that they should enjoy the evening together.

Troy was still lonely without his cousin, Shawna, living with him in his cabin, so the two men put an evening meal together there at Hawk's cabin. Little Bear curled up in his favorite spot, by the hearth in the small parlor, as though he was happy to be back in what he considered his home.

It grew late as the two of them talked after supper, so

Troy ended up spending the night at Hawk's cabin. Early the next morning Troy left to go home and attend to his chores, but Little Bear stayed with Hawk.

Troy understood the dog's feelings, so he did not urge him to come with him. Hawk's cabin was Little Bear's home, and nothing was ever going to change that.

But, Troy wondered as he walked through the woods toward his own cabin, didn't Hawk feel the same way as that big brown dog? Surely he did. That cabin was always going to be home to his friend, Hawk.

Chapter Six

During the next two days, Hawk fished in the mountain stream and caught a fine string of fish, which he and Little Bear enjoyed for their supper, along with some cornbread cakes Hawk fried in the cast iron skillet. Everywhere Hawk roamed, the big dog was by his side.

It was at times like this that Hawk had the yearning to remain on this mountain for the rest of his life and never return to Tucson; but he knew that it was not possible. Despite how happy and contented he felt there, he had to earn his living.

As his mother would have done if she had been there, he took out some cold cornbread cakes after dinner and crumbled them up to throw out to the birds. They would enjoy the feast.

As he thought about his mother while he and Little Bear sat out on the front steps of the cabin, he also thought about Gillian. He knew that this mountain cabin was so dear to him partly because it held memories of the beautiful Gillian. He recalled how he'd brought her here when she had been thrown from her horse, and his mother had tended her until she was able to ride back to the Fosters' ranch down in the valley.

It was the first time they had actually encountered one another, although he had watched her many times from the high plateau as she wandered in the meadows down in the valley around the ranch. It was thus, from afar, that he had fallen in love with Gillian Browne, even though she did not even know then that he existed.

Sometimes all this seemed like a lifetime ago, but today, here where his memories were so vivid and clear, it could have been yesterday.

Time went by too fast, Hawk thought to himself, as he and Little Bear sat watching darkness steal over the mountains.

Two days after Hawk returned to his cabin, Gillian arrived back at the Fosters' ranch. It was a joyous and tearful reunion for all of them, including John Foster. He didn't try to restrain the tears flowing down his weathered cheeks, for he was too happy to worry about shedding a few tears.

As had been the case with Melba and Helen, Gillian had to tell the Fosters why she was returning alone. Sadly, she related to them how Steve had met his untimely death at sea. As she did so, she realized she was going to be glad to have no one else to tell.

"Well, let's get ourselves cozy, honey, 'cause we've got ourselves a lot of talking to do. We're awful sorry about what happened, but now you got yourself back here where you belong," Nancy declared, as she led Gillian over to the settee to sit down beside her. John went over to sit down in his favorite chair.

Both of them watched Gillian's blue eyes scanning the entire room and a slow smile appeared on her face. "It looks just like it did the day I left. Oh, Mother Foster, I—I sure wished many a time to just sit like I'm doing now and talk with you!"

"We felt the same way, Gillian," John Foster told her. "Ireland was too far away. Nancy and I feared we'd never get to see you again." He looked at his wife and gave her a warm smile. She was busily wiping the tears from her cheeks with the bottom of her apron. Few times in his life had he seen her give way to tears, so he knew how overcome she was to see Gillian again. It had been a long year without the girl here in the house.

A broad smile broke out on her plain face as she remarked, "John, this is the first day of spring, and our Gillian is back. Had you thought about that?"

"Sure hadn't, dear, but you're right." He turned toward Gillian and smiled. "It was the perfect time for you to come back home, honey."

"Oh, this good warm sun feels good to me. I felt like I was always cold over in Ireland, and there was so much rain," Gillian told them.

Nancy excused herself to go to the kitchen and put her coffee pot on the stove. She remembered that Gillian enjoyed a good cup of coffee, and she figured they would all find it refreshing.

Their gathering finally broke up when John had to go to the barn to attend to some chores, but first he carried Gillian's luggage back to the bedroom she'd always occupied.

"You just go in there and get yourself settled in,

honey. You'll find it pretty much as you left it. Take a rest and get yourself unpacked, while I see what I want to start for supper," Nancy told her.

Maybe it was because she had finally reached her destination, ending the journey that had been started so many weeks before, but as soon as she had unpacked her luggage Gillian lay down to rest, and quickly she fell asleep.

When Nancy came to the door and saw that she was sleeping so soundly, she moved away quietly and went out to the barn, where John was still busy doing the evening chores.

"Poor little thing is tuckered out, John. She's sound asleep." She sat down on a wooden milking stool and told John that she didn't like the way Gillian looked. "Oh, she's as pretty as ever, but she's too skinny, John. I've got to get that girl fattened up now that she's home."

John smiled and nodded his head. Knowing what a mother hen Nancy could be, he had no doubt that she would do just that. He knew that Gillian would always be to Nancy the daughter she had never had.

He came out of the stall and, in that quiet way of his, told his wife, "I think it has been a hard year for Gillian."

Nancy had a blunt way about her. There was never any need to guess how she was feeling, for she blurted it right out. "So you don't think our little Gillian has been too happy in Ireland with Steve Lafferty?"

"No, Nancy, I'm not saying that, but I *am* saying that this last year has drained her. First she loses the baby she was carrying, and then she loses her husband, all in a year's time."

"As usual you're right, John. She has a right to feel drained. Sitting here thinking about things now, John, I must say that maybe Gillian would have been better off if she'd just married Hawk, as she had planned to do that day."

"We'll never know that, will we, Nancy? Well, I got to get busy again." And he began to walk away.

Nancy got up off the stool and started to leave the barn, but she stopped to call out, "Supper may be a little later than usual tonight, John. I'm going to let that child have a good, long nap if she wants it."

"That's just fine, Nancy," he told her, as he scooped up a pail of grain from the bin.

Supper was indeed an hour later that evening. Nancy just let the beans and ham hocks simmer on the back of the stove until an embarrassed, sleepy-eyed Gillian came stumbling into the parlor, apologizing for having slept so long.

"It will be good when we eat it, Gillian," Nancy said with a chuckle.

The long rest gave Gillian a very hearty appetite, or perhaps it was just Nancy's good cooking. She ate the beans with relish, and then had a very generous piece of blackberry cobbler.

Later, when they had retired, John gave Nancy a hug, declaring, "If that girl keeps eating as she did tonight, she'll put back any weight she's lost in a week or two."

Nancy gave a pleased, contented sigh. "Oh, it seems just like old times again, doesn't it, John?"

"Sure does, Nancy, but it's not to say that Gillian is planning on staying here. She could be only visiting us. You're going to have to bear in mind that she's a young widow now, and not that helpless young girl we took in, Nancy."

"I know that, John." She kissed her husband goodnight and turned over on her side to go to sleep. But she couldn't drop off, because she was thinking about what John had pointed out to her. She had not admitted it to him, but she had assumed that Gillian had come back to the ranch to live with them again.

Well maybe John was right and this was just a visit Gillian was paying them, but Nancy could at least wish for it to be a long visit.

The fresh air of the countryside and the warm rays of the Arizona sun seemed to do wonders for Gillian. She went to bed early and slept late, and it seemed she needed this much sleep. When she woke up in the mornings, she always felt ready to have one of Nancy's hearty breakfasts, and so she didn't need a midday meal. But she certainly ate supper as though she was famished.

She swore to Nancy that her clothing was becoming more snug on her after she had been there four days. Nancy laughed. "Well, good! You'd got yourself too thin, Gillian."

Gillian did not deny that, for she knew she'd lost a lot of weight over the last few months.

She greatly enjoyed the leisurely hours she spent talking in the house with Nancy or puttering around in the kitchen. It was also pleasant for Gillian to roam around the barnyard with John, and she helped him with the chores sometimes.

Gillian did not think that it was her imagination

when she looked in the mirror and saw that her cheeks had a new rosy glow. And she could have sworn that there was a new glossy sheen to her auburn hair after she had washed it in the crystal clear spring water that John carried in pails up to the house.

It was wonderful for Gillian to roam the pastureland and pick the wildflowers she loved, or to help Nancy gather up the eggs daily. But as she roamed around the grounds and the pasturelands, she found that her eyes kept looking up to those mountains where Solange and Hawk had lived.

She wondered, now that Solange had married that nice French Canadian, if Hawk was still living up there alone.

Gillian could not deny that she felt guilty about the way she'd treated Hawk. He'd been nothing but kind and caring to her since the moment they'd met.

So far, she had not asked Nancy and John about Hawk. They obviously were not going to mention his name if she did not wish to speak about him. But both the Fosters had wondered why she'd not spoken of him. Nancy had figured that it was because she was embarrassed about jilting him.

News about Hawk had drifted back to them from various sources, mostly from their rancher friends. But there was also news about him from Helen. The Fosters were pleased to hear that the young man was doing quite well for himself with the railroad in Tucson during this last year.

John Foster could never forget that it was Joe Hawk who'd killed two renegade Apaches, right in his pastureland, to save Gillian from becoming their captive. Gillian, who had been only sixteen at the time, had had no inkling that she was being stalked by the savages.

The truth was—and John had never mentioned this to his wife—it was his opinion that the young half-breed had finer qualities than Steve Lafferty did.

That night, as the three of them ate supper, Gillian asked John if she might take the roan out for a ride tomorrow. "I've not been on a horse for such a long, long time," she remarked.

"I wondered when you were going to get around to taking a ride, like you used to love to do." John smiled. "You take her out anytime you want, Gillian."

"I think I will go tomorrow morning."

Nancy laughed. "She'll enjoy kicking up her heels again, Gillian. You used to give her a good run often, and I'm sure she's missing it. John rides her into Rock Springs once in a while but he usually takes the wagon to bring back supplies."

Later, as they sat in the parlor after Nancy's fine supper, John tried out the new pipe Gillian had bought for him in Ireland. The weather was so mild that Nancy had opened the door to allow the gentle breeze to come into the parlor.

Gillian finally gathered the courage to ask them about Hawk and what had happened to him. It was Nancy who told her. "He's done real well for himself, so we hear. Works for the railroad and lives in Tucson. I think you knew that his mother was marrying that French Canadian and going to live in Canada."

"Yes, I knew that," Gillian replied. "Well, I'm happy to hear that Hawk is doing so well. I know I was hardly fair to him."

Nancy saw the look on Gillian's face as she spoke,

and she tried to console her as best she could. "That's all in the past, Gillian. Things just happened the way they happened, and you did what you thought was right."

"Thank you for saying it that way, Mother Foster." Gillian gave her a weak smile. For the rest of the evening, as she sat there in the parlor with them, she was occupied with her own private musings.

More than once, Gillian had wondered if she had been punished for taking her chance for happiness with Steve Lafferty and for not honoring her promise to marry Hawk. Maybe she had lost her baby and Steve because she had done Hawk wrong. Maybe she had been denied her happiness because she had denied Hawk his.

Chapter Seven

It was a wonderful spring morning, and Gillian felt happier than she remembered as she dressed in her dark blue riding skirt and light blue tunic. To keep her long hair away from her face as she rode, she braided it in two long braids, and tied blue ribbons on the ends of them.

As she galloped away from the ranch, she gave John a farewell wave of her hand. He watched her gallop away, and swore there had been an improvement in the pretty girl in just five days' time. He was happy about the change he saw in her. The paleness was gone, and the sparkle of life had come back to her bright blue eyes.

Gillian knew where she was heading when she rode out of the ranch. Even though she expected to find no one there in the mountain cabin, something urged her to ride there, as she had so often in the past.

It would feel strange to see Solange's cozy cottage not stirring with life, and standing vacant. Gillian knew that she would find it hard to go there and not find the lovely French woman there to greet her. But it was a part of her past she wanted to revisit.

She had always felt a certain kind of magic when she left the valley to ride up the mountain. The trail was surrounded by dense forest on either side, and there always seemed to be a stronger breeze blowing as she rode to a greater height.

Gillian was so enthralled by all the old familiar landmarks she was seeing as she guided the little roan up the trail that she was unaware that she had gone around the last bend before the cottage.

Suddenly, there it was, right ahead of her. For Gillian it seemed time had stood still. But there was no smoke whirling out of the chimney today. Solange had always been cooking something in her kitchen. And by the time Gillian had dismounted and tied the reins to the hitching post, she saw there was something else missing. How strange it was not to see the little lady, with her long graying hair in braids, gathering up the herbs she loved to grow in her yard.

Slowly she moved toward the house as she allowed herself to absorb what she saw. She wondered if Hawk's friend, Troy, was taking care of the place, for the yard was well tended, and there were no weeds taking over Solange's gardens.

Suddenly, before she could realize what was attacking her, Gillian felt a mighty thrust at her back. It was like a bolt of lightning, and she felt herself plunging face first to the ground. Somewhere behind her, she heard a harsh, deep voice calling out, "No, Little Bear!" Right now she was slightly addled, but she did feel the dampness of a huge beast licking her face, almost smothering her. A massive mountain of brown fur was hovering over her.

As Hawk had emerged from the woods with Little Bear trailing beside him, the breathtaking vision of Gillian came in sight for him at about the same time Little Bear spotted her. For one fleeting second, Hawk figured he was only imagining it, but Little Bear's reaction told him different. Unfortunately, he could not keep up with the huge dog as he dashed toward Gillian.

He ordered Little Bear to move away, and he bent down to scoop Gillian up in his arms. Her lovely face was smudged with dirt, and her thick lashes fluttered in disbelief as she gazed up at his bronzed face and his piercing black eyes, felt his strong, powerful arms holding her. Stammering, she exclaimed, "Hawk—Hawk, it's you!"

A slow smile came to his face. "Yes, Gillian, it is me. And the monster who attacked you is Little Bear."

"Oh, Lord—that—*that* is sweet Little Bear?"

By now Hawk was moving toward the cabin with her in his arms. "That is sweet Little Bear. He is still sweet, but he's just got to his full size."

Gillian gave a soft little laugh. "To think that I used to cuddle him in my lap."

Hawk was thinking that time had surely stood still, for here he was, once again carrying little Gillian into the cabin, just as he had done when she was thrown from her horse. So many things had happened to both of them since that time, but to Hawk, she was that same beautiful girl with her hair of fire, as he always thought of it. She felt just as petite and helpless in his huge arms now as she had back then.

He didn't release her until he had placed her on the

settee in the parlor. Little Bear ambled up to her to have his head patted, and Hawk could have sworn that he remembered her. After she had made a fuss of him he was content to curl there by the settee at her feet.

"I understood you were working in Tucson, Hawk," she remarked as he was going to the kitchen to get a cloth to wipe the dirt from her face.

"I am, but Warner—my boss—gave me ten days off, so I came here, as I always do when I can. You know how I feel about this place, Gillian."

By now, he was gently cleaning the smudges from her forehead and cheek. Gillian inquired about his mother. Hawk told her that Solange was very happy, and why she had brought Little Bear back here. "Seems he didn't like his new home, so when they came here a few months ago to spend some time in the cabin, she left him here. Troy looks out for him when I'm back in Tucson."

Gillian had expected to feel very ill at ease when she encountered Hawk again, but she felt completely relaxed as they talked. She saw a self-assured air about Hawk that she liked. Obviously, his life was going as he wanted, and she was happy about that.

"I'm glad to know that Solange is so happy, Hawk. And you seem happy, too. I gather you have a job you like?"

"Yes, Gillian, I do like my job." By now he had taken the damp cloth back to the kitchen and returned to the parlor to sit down opposite Gillian. His penetrating eyes were looking into hers when he asked her, "And how about you? What brings you back to Maricopa County? A visit with the Fosters?"

"Yes, I'm visiting the Fosters for a little while. I'm

not exactly sure what I'm going to do after that."

Hawk knew Gillian well enough to know that she had not revealed the real reason she was back. He wondered about the child she had been carrying when she married Lafferty.

"What did you have, Gillian? Was it a daughter or a son?" His black eyes were warm and tender as they gazed at her.

Her blue eyes looked back at him as she shook her head in reply. "I lost the baby, Hawk. Perhaps it was the ocean crossing. I just don't know. It happened a week after I arrived in Ireland."

"I'm sorry, Gillian. I'm really sorry."

"I know you are, Hawk. I, of all people, know what a kind, understanding heart you have," she told him. Hawk saw the warmth in those blue eyes. As it had always been between him and Gillian, there was a bond of honesty.

He studied her lovely face as she was talking to him, and in it he saw something of the pain and hurt she'd known since he had last seen her. Compassion welled in Hawk for this lady he'd always loved.

Soon he was to learn, as Gillian told him about Steve's death at sea, why he saw a different girl than the one he'd known a year ago.

"Well, Gillian, you are back home again with people who have always loved you. I know you must have felt that this was where you needed to be, or you would not have come all this way back to Maricopa County."

Gillian nodded her head in agreement. It was always easy for her to talk with Hawk, and so it was this afternoon, as the two of them sat there in the cabin drinking the coffee he'd brewed. Gillian forgot about time, she was enjoying herself so much.

It meant a great deal to her that Hawk didn't hate her for what she'd done to him. It put him many notches ahead of most men, but then she'd always thought that he was a rare treasure of a man. Today she was convinced of it.

When she finally announced to Hawk that she had to be leaving, he quickly replied that he was going to ride with her, to the foot of the mountain at least. What he didn't tell her was that he wanted to linger with her as long as possible. Already, he was feeling regret that he had only a few more days left before he would have to return to Tucson. Now that he knew she was back, departing from this mountain was going to be even more painful than usual.

A short time later, Gillian mounted the little roan, Hawk leaped up on Tache, and they rode down from the mountain top. In an easy, bounding lope, Little Bear trailed behind them.

Gillian asked Hawk how long he would have here before he had to return to Tucson. "It was so good to see you, Hawk, and I hope I'll get to see you again before you leave."

"I'll see you again, Gillian."

They rode along at an unhurried pace, for the sun was a long way from setting. There was another hour before twilight would settle over the countryside.

Just before they reached the base of the mountain, Gillian told him something he was very pleased to hear. She remarked quite casually that she, too, might be coming to Tucson after she finished visiting with the Fosters.

She saw the pleased smile on his face as she told him

the news. "Well, I can hardly live with the Fosters now as I once did, Hawk. I'm a widow now, and I've a life to make for myself. In Tucson, I could work for Melba Jackson. She offered me a position at the inn. In fact, I left most of my luggage there with her when I came here."

"I—I guess I never thought about it that way, Gillian." He gave a light laugh, playfully teasing her. "I guess I still look on you as that sixteen-year-old girl. Be patient with me, Gillian."

Gillian laughed. "Ah, Hawk—I wish I *was* that sixteen-year-old girl you're talking about, but I'm not. That seems like a long, long time ago."

Hawk smiled, saying nothing. Riding beside her like this, he could almost believe it was that spring day when he'd escorted her back toward the Fosters' ranch, after she'd been thrown from her horse.

After that first visit to Solange's cabin, as the weeks had gone by and Gillian had returned to the cabin to see them, Hawk's mother had become very fond of the girl. In fact, Hawk knew that nothing would have pleased her more than having Gillian as her daughter-in-law.

Just as he had that day, Hawk told her farewell at the foot of the mountain, but he remained there to watch her ride safely to the Fosters' ranch before he reined Tache around to go back up the mountain.

As he watched her long, auburn braids toss to and fro, he knew that she would forever be that sweet, innocent, sixteen-year-old girl.

Chapter Eight

For the rest of the evening, Hawk went around like a man in a blissful daze. He had to admit that he was glad Troy didn't come over that evening, for he would have been poor company for his old friend.

It was as if he had been dreaming this wonderful fantasy and then had stepped right into it, to live it out. Gillian had walked back into his life when he had least expected it; they had actually talked, and he'd ridden by her side. And it was no dream!

He couldn't deny to himself that the news that she was a widow had encouraged him to have hopes. Now that she was no longer Steve Lafferty's wife, she was free to marry again if she wished to. Hawk could not help thinking that maybe destiny still meant for the two of them to be together. He wanted to believe it was meant to be. He also thought about Solange and what she, with all her wisdom and instincts, would be saying if she were there.

He wished that she was there. He needed to have one of those talks they'd had so often in his life.

Until he went to bed that night Hawk was engrossed in thoughts of Gillian and the past. Solange had always told him to reflect on the past to know how to go into the future. He knew of no one wiser than his mother, and he admired no one more than her, not even Warner Barstow.

He slept deeply when he did go to bed, and he was not really ready to crawl out of bed the next morning when Troy came rapping on the cabin door and calling out his name.

He stumbled to the front door, brushing his tousled black hair away from his face. Little Bear was giving out excited barks, recognizing Troy's voice on the other side of the door.

"What the hell brings you here so early, Troy?" Hawk grumbled as he opened the door and Troy came dashing through.

"A deal too good to pass up, but I don't have the money to make the deal. Thought you sure might want to hop on it, though."

Hawk was still dazed by sleep, and Troy's excited chattering was not registering with him.

He ran his long fingers through his hair as he mumbled, "I'm not even awake, Troy, so I'm hardly in a mood to talk a deal to anyone."

"You don't have to be wide awake to know this is a deal and a half, Hawk, knowing how you and me have both always admired old Carlos's red stallion, Fuego. He says to me that he's got to sell it for a hundred to get his wife back to her father, for he's dying."

Hawk's black eyes got more alert instantly. "A hundred dollars, you say?"

"That's what I said, but I didn't have it, so that's why

I came racing over here and left old Carlos cooling his heels at my place."

Hawk didn't have to think twice about such a deal, sleepy though he may have been. "Carlos has himself a deal." Hawk had that much money, and more, since he'd just been paid before he left Tucson. The only thing he'd spent any of his pay on was the few supplies he'd brought here with him. He ambled back into the bedroom to get the money out of a leather pouch. When he returned to the parlor, he handed the money to Troy and said, "Go make that deal for me, Troy, and I'll treat you to a fine dinner tonight."

A broad grin broke out on Troy's face as he eagerly accepted Hawk's invitation. He made a hasty departure from the cabin, and Hawk went immediately to his kitchen to fire up his cookstove and fix himself a pot of coffee.

He and Troy had long admired that red stallion of Carlos's, and they'd often speculated on where that old Mexican had acquired such a fine horse as Fuego.

Now, for the price of a hundred dollars, the horse was to be his!

Both the Fosters were becoming very anxious about how long Gillian had been gone on her jaunt around the countryside that day. In his calm manner, John had pointed out to Nancy that she wasn't exactly their little girl anymore. "She's a grown lady, Nancy. She's traveled all the way from Ireland, across an ocean, all on her own, so you just quit fretting. She's all right."

He had left his wife there in the house to go to the barn and start the evening chores. As he'd predicted, a half hour later Gillian came riding up the road.

As she leaped off the mare and greeted John, he could see that she was very excited about something. She quickly announced to him why she was so late in returning to the ranch. "I rode up to the mountain, and Hawk was there! Oh, it was so good to see him again. We talked and talked, and I lost track of time."

"So Hawk's back on a visit, is he? I heard he came back to the cabin from time to time," John responded.

"Seems he's doing just fine, Father Foster. We had such a nice visit. You wouldn't believe what a huge monster that Little Bear has become!" There was a girlish enthusiasm about her as she was talking to him and leading the mare up to the barn. John Foster was glad that she seemed in such a happy mood after her encounter with Hawk, since it meant that Hawk harbored no hard feelings toward Gillian for what she'd done to him.

She took the mare to the stall, removed the saddle, and fed and watered the mare before she went on into the house.

When she entered the kitchen, she related her news to Nancy as she had to John a few minutes ago. Helping Nancy in the kitchen, she told her about Hawk and all the news about him.

Nancy felt as John had when he observed that Gillian seemed in such high spirits. Nancy couldn't be irritated with her for being so long on her ride. A year ago she would have been gently admonishing her for being gone so long and causing them concern and worry, but she couldn't do that now, she told herself. Gillian was her own woman now. She was not theirs to tell what she could or couldn't do.

71

As they sat that night at the kitchen table, having the dinner Nancy had prepared for them, each of them had some private thoughts of their own. Gillian was thinking that she had been here for almost a week now. Perhaps it was seeing Hawk today that made her realize she was ready to get on with her own life. This ranch was what Nancy and John loved, and their lives revolved around it. But it couldn't be her world. She wanted more than this. She could see no future for herself here.

After dinner, as they were sitting in the parlor, she felt it was the time to start preparing them for the fact that she would be leaving very soon.

"It's been marvelous for me here at the ranch again, being with you two," Gillian said, by way of introduction to what she was about to tell them.

"It's been wonderful for us, too, honey," Nancy replied, sensing that Gillian was leading up to something.

Her eyes searched Nancy's face, then John's, and she knew she was being scrutinized carefully. "But you know, I've a home to make for myself, and Steve did leave me the funds to do it. I can hardly run a ranch, but there are some things I can do. They just wouldn't be here, at Rock Springs. I've been offered something in Tucson, and I'm considering settling there and buying a little house. Melba Jackson has made me a very tempting offer, and being a widow now, I think I should give it a try. I'm sure you can understand my feelings."

John Foster was the first to speak up. "We can understand, can't we, Nancy?"

Nancy gave a nod of her head, not trusting her voice.

She was not expecting Gillian to make this announcement this evening. While she could not expect a pretty young thing like Gillian to want to settle here permanently on the ranch, with only her and John for company, her visit had been such a short one.

Later, when Gillian was lying in her bed and replaying the conversation, she realized that Mother Foster was more startled by her news than her husband had been.

Knowing that she was going to be leaving in another few days, Gillian spent the next day in the house, wanting to share that time with Nancy. But the day after that, she intended to ask for the loan of the mare again, to ride into Rock Springs and make arrangements to go back to Tucson.

Just before noon she started out from the ranch. From his vantage point on the high plateau that overlooked the valley, Hawk spied her riding away from the ranch. Instantly he spurred Tache into action, knowing that he could catch up with her quickly. She had not gone a mile from the ranch when she heard the galloping hooves of a rider coming up behind her. When she turned and saw that it was Hawk and Tache, she pulled up on the reins to bring the little mare to a halt.

She greeted Hawk with a smile. "And what brings you this way, Hawk?"

"You, Gillian. I was coming to the ranch to see you, when I saw you riding away."

She explained to him where she was heading. A slow smile came to his face as he told her, "There's no call for you to be riding into Rock Springs, Gillian, when I can personally see you back to Tucson. I'm going there myself. My ten days are up, so I must get back there."

"But Hawk, you're going to be riding Tache, aren't you?" Surely he couldn't expect her to ride all the way to Tucson along with him on Tache.

"Of course I'm going to be riding Tache, but I've another fine horse you can ride. Come to the cabin with me and see for yourself," he urged her. She had a quizzical expression as she looked at Hawk's bronzed face. The thought of riding back to Tucson with Hawk excited and appealed to Gillian. She gave no thought to the fact that the Fosters would not approve of it.

"All right, Hawk. Let's go." She gave a lighthearted laugh.

Together they rode toward the mountain trail, and in a short time they were arriving at Hawk's cabin. He leaped off Tache and rushed around to help her down from the mare. When Gillian felt herself pressed against the firm, broad chest of Hawk, something stirred in her that she had thought was dead. Hawk was very much aware of her reaction, but tried not to show it as his dark eyes met with hers.

They walked in silence up the pathway toward the house, both of them shaken by what had happened back there when he was helping her off the horse.

"Come on, we're going to the barn. Like I told you, I've something to show you, Gillian." He smiled. By now he and Gillian were both feeling more relaxed.

When they were inside the barn she immediately spied the horse Hawk was talking about. A fine beast he certainly was. She saw him move back and forth restlessly in the confining stall, and knew he was full of spice and ginger.

"Oh, Hawk—he's magnificent! Where, when did you get him? You didn't mention him to me day before yesterday when I was up here."

"I didn't have him then. Just got him yesterday. Do you like him, Gillian?"

"Do I *like* him? Why, I'd have to be crazy if I didn't! Look how shining his coat is, and what a beautiful color. What will you call him, Hawk?"

"Oh, he already has a name. Meet Fuego, Gillian."

"Well, Fuego—you are a most handsome fellow," she giggled.

She reached over the top of the stall to brush her hand along the silky mane. Hawk watched her for a few minutes before he said anything. "Do you think you'd like to ride that handsome fellow back to Tucson?" There was a devious twinkle in Hawk's eyes.

"Oh, Hawk—do you think I could handle him?"

"I'm sure of it, or I wouldn't want you to try it, Gillian."

"Well, when do you have to leave?" She turned around to face him.

"I've got to leave no later than midafternoon tomorrow. I would have left today, but I wanted to see if you would like to go back with me. With two high steppers like Tache and Fuego, it would take us one afternoon and the next day."

For a moment she stood there with a thoughtful look on her lovely face, and then she looked up at him, those blue eyes sparking with fire and excitement. "I'll go with you, Hawk!"

"I was hoping you would say that."

"But if I am to leave with you tomorrow, then I've got to get back to the ranch, right now. This is going to take the Fosters by surprise, as it has me." She did not hesitate a minute more, but started to walk toward the barn door, with Hawk trailing slightly behind her.

Once again the two of them rode down the mountain, and when they said goodbye, Hawk told her he would arrive at the Fosters at two the next afternoon. Gillian turned back to wave to him as she was galloping away.

Gillian resolved, as she rode on to the ranch, that this time, Hawk would find her waiting. This time, she would keep her promise to him.

Neither John nor Nancy Foster approved of Gillian's plans to ride across the state with Hawk, as she'd told them she was going to do tomorrow. Nancy had to bite her tongue a couple of times during the evening to keep from voicing her opinion.

John was well aware of his wife's restraint. She didn't hesitate for a moment to speak her mind to John once they were alone in their bedroom that night.

"I'm inclined to agree with you, Nancy, but Gillian is no sweet, innocent virgin. She's been married, miscarried a baby, and traveled alone around the world, so she is her own woman now. We have nothing to say about it."

So they didn't protest the next morning, and when Hawk came riding up on Tache, leading Fuego behind him, the Fosters greeted him cordially.

Gillian gave them each a warm embrace, and promised that she would write them once she was settled in Tucson. Hawk gave her a hoist up onto the huge red stallion, then mounted up on Tache.

The Fosters watched the two young people ride down the drive that led away from their ranch house.

They made a striking pair—Gillian atop the huge red stallion whose coat was an almost exact match to her own long tresses, Hawk riding beside her, an impressive figure of a man, his mane of hair as black as Tache's.

John Foster was thinking to himself that life had had many strange, unexpected twists to it. A year ago, he and Nancy had seen Gillian riding away with another man. Today, she was riding away again, with a different man. It made him wonder what the next year held for the young girl so dear to his and Nancy's hearts.

Chapter Nine

The two of them had been galloping along the dirt road at a fast pace, but when Hawk slowed his pace, so did Gillian. Hawk asked her, "Do you like your fellow, there?"

"I surely do," she declared.

"I told you that you'd handle him just fine."

Gillian smiled and gave Fuego an affectionate pat as they rode along slowly. "You've got yourself a fine horse here, Hawk."

He couldn't resist any longer saying what he'd wanted to tell her yesterday. He had not bought Fuego for himself—he had himself one fine horse in Tache. He had bought Fuego for her.

"No, Gillian—you have yourself a fine horse. Fuego is yours. I got him for you."

"You bought Fuego for me, Hawk? Oh, I can't let you do this," she protested.

He gave a deep, throaty laugh. "I've already done it, Gillian. He was meant to be your horse, and if you are going to settle in Tucson you'll have Fuego to go out for a ride on from time to time. Perhaps you'll want to get a little gig later."

"Oh, Hawk! What can I say to you?"

"You can say thank you for Fuego," he teased her.

"I do thank you, from the bottom of my heart. But I have no place to stable Fuego when I get to Tucson."

"I do, Gillian. Don't you fret about that," he assured her.

The two of them rode on for another two hours before they stopped for the night at a small hamlet, Guadalupe. Five hours of riding had left Gillian more than ready to seek the comfort of the lodging house and a soft bed. As soon as they had eaten a hearty meal in the small dining room, Gillian went to her room to retire for the night.

As soon as her head hit the pillow, she fell into a deep sleep. It was Hawk's deep voice calling her, as he rapped on her door the next morning, that roused her from that profound slumber.

Hawk had insisted that she have a hearty breakfast, as he intended to, before they mounted up to ride that morning. Later, she was glad she'd listened to him, for the small towns were far apart and it was long after midday when they finally came to a place where they could have a bite to eat and refreshing couple of cups of coffee. The meal revived her.

Hawk could tell that Gillian was becoming very weary by late afternoon, but they were so close to Tucson that he hesitated to suggest they stop over somewhere for the night, so he remained silent. But his eyes kept darting back to her, and he saw how exhausted she was. He knew that he was pushing her.

"We're not too far out now, little Gillian. You're not going to the inn tonight—you're coming home with me to rest up before you worry about settling in there," he declared, in a most authoritative voice.

She did not argue with him, for she was in no mood to greet Melba or Helen after this long day's ride. She saw that twilight was already falling, and there was still no sign that they were reaching Tucson.

But when Hawk told her that his place was just ahead, Gillian remembered that he had told her he lived on a small acreage outside the city.

When they rode up to the hitching post, Hawk dismounted from Tache and rushed over to help Gillian down from Fuego. But he did not lower her down to the ground. His huge arms scooped her up effortlessly, and he carried her into his house.

Darkness was descending over the countryside as well as inside Hawk's house, so he placed her in a chair in the parlor, by the front door, while he went to light a lamp.

"Now you just sit there and rest, Gillian, while I bring in our gear and get the horses settled in," he urged her. He took time to light the kerosene lamp in the parlor before he left her.

She sat there in Hawk's front room, now brightly lit by the lamp, and she could see that although it was a small room, it was comfortable. There was a small stone fireplace, with comfortable chairs placed on either side of the hearth. A small settee was further back, in front of the fireplace, and she recognized one of Solange's woven rugs lying in front of the hearth.

By the front door, where he had placed her in a huge, overstuffed chair, there was a square oak table upon which the lamp was placed.

She took off her boots and got up to stretch her stiff legs. It felt good to walk around the room in her stockinged feet. She found herself curious to explore the rest of Hawk's house, but she didn't dare venture into the dark adjoining rooms.

Hawk entered the front door shortly afterward to find her pacing back and forth across his parlor. He wondered suddenly if she even reached the height of five feet.

"Glad to see you're making yourself at home, Gillian. I got the horses cozied into the barn for the night. I think they're glad to be off the trail."

"I know I am! That was a long ride, Hawk," she declared.

"I realized that I probably shouldn't have suggested it to you after we started out today. I fear I was being selfish, Gillian. I'm sorry."

"Oh, I enjoyed it—but I can't deny that I am tired. And I know there's not a selfish bone in your body, Hawk."

"Don't be too sure of that, Gillian. I am just human enough to be selfish at times." He walked out of the parlor to go into the kitchen and the other rooms of the house, as he usually did after he'd been away. He carried Gillian's luggage into the back bedroom, and flung his saddlebag on the bed in his bedroom.

When he came back into the parlor, after he'd gone through the house lighting lamps in all the rooms, he invited her to tour his humble little cottage. She followed him around, and after they had gone over the house she said teasingly, "Well, Hawk, for a man, you keep a very neat house."

"I thank you, Gillian," he said, and laughed.

An hour later, with Gillian pitching in to help him, Hawk had put together a simple meal which they both ate with relish, as though it were a grand feast. Both of them were aware of how relaxed and at ease they could be together. It was a nice feeling.

While they were sitting at the table enjoying one last cup of coffee, Hawk became quite serious. "Don't be in too big a rush to go to the inn. My house is yours as long as you want it to be. Rest a day or two. You've come a long, long way to get to the Fosters'. Now, the two of us have had a long ride. I'll be going to work tomorrow, but the house is yours to do what you want with."

Gillian reached out and took his hand in hers. Her eyes were warm with the feelings engulfing her. "Oh, Hawk, you are so good to me, and I thank you. I will accept your offer to be lazy tomorrow, and maybe another day, if that is all right. My—my health has not been the same since I lost the baby. Spending so many months in Ireland didn't seem to agree with me, but this warm Arizona sun is helping."

"Give it time, Gillian. You will get back to normal in time. You'll be fine!"

"I know I will, Hawk."

Hawk looked on her lovely face, her blue eyes looking back at him in her very honest way. He wanted to say so many things to her, but he knew that this was not the right time. He was a patient man, and for Gillian, he could wait as long as it took to convince her that no man could ever love her as devotedly and constantly as he did.

Together they cleaned up the kitchen, for Gillian refused to allow him to do it alone as he wished. When all was in order, the two of them were leaving the room, the lamp had been dimmed, and Hawk spoke to her in a fatherly manner. "Now, you go to your room and get yourself into that cozy bed, for a good night of rest, Gillian."

She looked up at him with a smile on her face. "Yes, sir!" But before she left him, she paused for a moment. Standing on tiptoe, she reached up to plant a kiss on his tanned cheek. "Goodnight, Hawk. Thank you for being there when I needed you so desperately."

Before he could respond, she marched out of the parlor and into the back bedroom. He was glad that as long as she needed or wanted him, he would be there.

For the next hour, Hawk kept busy around his house by unpacking what he'd taken up to the cabin, and then he made a fast trip out to the barn to check on Tache and Fuego. The house was quiet when he returned, so he figured that Gillian was sleeping soundly. That was good, for she surely needed it.

He went to his own bedroom, folded back the covers on his bed, and got out his clothes for the next day. He would be making an early departure from the house in the morning.

But before he retired for the night he decided to light one of his cheroots and sit in the parlor for a quiet moment. His head was still whirling with what had transpired since the afternoon he'd left Warner's office to take his ten days off.

If anyone had told him that Gillian would be coming back into his life, he would have called them crazy. But she had, and the powerful effect she had on him was there with just as much intensity as it had been when she had married Steve Lafferty and run off to Ireland. But any bitterness about the past was swept away for Hawk now.

As he sat there in his bare feet, his shirt removed, Hawk felt weary from the long trail ride, but he was filled with a serene contentment. He was back in his little house here in Tucson, ready to go back to his job

83

in the morning. The lady he loved was here in his house with him. Hawk could ask no more from life.

The clock was chiming eleven when Hawk took his last puff on the cheroot and rose to dim the lamps in his parlor.

He went into his bedroom, where the lamp was low, and removed his pants, preparing to crawl into bed. His hand had just dimmed the wick of the lamp, and he had flung the coverlet back on his bed, when he heard a bloodcurdling scream coming from his back bedroom. He rushed into the dark room to find Gillian fighting the covers as she tossed and turned in the bed.

He did what his instincts guided him to do. He sank down on the bed beside her, took her into his arms to try to calm her. Her screams did not cease for the first few moments that his strong arms held her, but he kept whispering in her ear that everything was all right. "Oh, Gillian—Gillian, I won't let anything hurt you," his deep voice assured her.

"Oh, Hawk! Hawk, hold me!"

"I'm holding you, Gillian," he soothed her. He wondered what this horrible nightmare was—it seemed so vivid.

His huge body curled around her petite one to assure her that she was safe and secure. She snuggled closer to him, and he held her as though she were a frightened child. But Hawk was only human, and as he was holding her, there was nothing about Gillian that was childlike. He felt the soft mounds of her breasts and the firm round curves of her hips. A savage passion erupted within him when her arms reached up to encircle his neck, and she gave a soft moan of pleasure at the nearness of him in bed with her.

Suddenly, before either one of them was aware what

was happening, Hawk found himself buried between her silky thighs. Gillian's arms were clinging around his neck, urging him closer and closer. Never could he have refused her anything. He gave her all of himself, as he never could have to any other woman. But as intense as his passion was for this young woman he was making love to, there was a gentle tenderness in him that Gillian had never known before. She found herself carried to a height of ecstasy that she had never known with Steve Lafferty.

Hawk's strong arms continued to hold her long after they had made love, and she was glad that he had not asked her what she was dreaming. Rarely did that nightmare return, as it had tonight. She knew why she had had it, but she did not want to confess this to Hawk tonight. Perhaps, sometime, she could. But not tonight, when she'd known a rapture like nothing she'd ever known with Steve Lafferty. Steve had been the only man she'd ever given herself to with such abandon, until now, and she had considered Lafferty the most exciting man she'd ever known. But Hawk had carried her to a higher plateau of passion tonight than she'd ever experienced before.

She was content to just lie in his huge, strong arms, and a quietness fell over them. Hawk was content just to hold her, her soft body was encircled by his.

Before long, sleep consumed them.

Chapter Ten

Hawk was very reluctant to free himself from Gillian's entwined body when the sun came streaming through the window of the back bedroom. Quietly, he left the bed and went to his own room to get dressed and ready to go to work.

But before he left the house he took time to write a note, and left it on the nightstand so that she would find it when she woke up. It was a note that spoke straight from Hawk's heart, for it told her that if such a night as last night never happened again, it would be enough to thrill him for a lifetime.

Hawk had never felt as happy as he did this morning as he and Tache rode away from the house.

Gillian woke up asking herself if it was true that she and Hawk had actually made love, or if it was just a dream. It seemed to be mingled in with the nightmare. From time to time she dreamed of when the Apaches had attacked the wagon train with which she and her parents had been traveling through Arizona. It was a trauma that would live with her forever, and she had the nightmare periodically. She never knew what would cause it. But last night something had, and she questioned what had made her wake up screaming like that. She supposed that it could have been because Hawk was part Apache and the son of the fierce Apache chief, Cochise. Somehow, she would have to come to terms with that fact.

Gillian got up and dressed unhurriedly. She spied Hawk's message to her, read it once, and then read it again. She knew that he wrote from the heart, and what he said meant everything to Gillian, but she had to convince herself that she was worthy of such worship from Hawk. He was a different kind of man from any she'd known before. There was a sensitive side to Hawk that she'd never seen in a man.

She felt a glimmer of understanding for the turmoil Hawk had endured and fought all his life—the turmoil of knowing that he had been sired by the fierce Apache warrior, Cochise. Despite the fact that he was nothing like that savage, he could not shrug aside his heritage, and the truth was, Gillian found she couldn't either. How could she ever forget that it was Cochise's renegade Apaches who'd attacked the wagon carrying her and her parents? For a girl of fourteen to witness the brutal murder of her parents was something from which she would never recover.

When Steve Lafferty had entered her life she was so naive and innocent that she never gave any thought to the possibility that she could become pregnant, when she so willingly surrendered to his fierce lovemaking. Last night she had given herself equally eagerly, but she knew now how easily she could become pregnant with Hawk's child. And that child would have Cochise's blood flowing in its veins.

Now, in the morning light, she didn't know if she could accept that. She didn't regret what had happened between her and Hawk, but as for bearing a child who would be Cochise's grandchild . . . why, the babe's face would haunt her! No, she could not have Hawk's child.

All day while Hawk was away at his job this thought gnawed at her, and she knew if she remained here under his roof they would surely make love again. It would be inevitable. But she did not know what she should do, for she didn't want to hurt Hawk's feelings. He'd been so kind to her.

She knew Hawk loved her, and she believed him when he told her he always had. And after lying in his arms last night, she knew that her feelings for him went much deeper than she'd realized—but that didn't ease the torment nagging at her.

By midafternoon, she'd decided what she must do. It would give her the opportunity to think things through, until she could come to some decision.

She changed into her divided skirt and tunic, and packed her nightgown and wrapper along with her toiletry articles.

Then for the next couple of hours, she made herself at home in Hawk's kitchen, preparing him a good dinner to have ready when he returned to the house. After they'd eaten, she was going to ask Hawk to take her to the inn. For both their sakes, it was the best thing to do.

Now that she had made up her mind, she felt more relaxed as she puttered around the kitchen. An hour later there was a pie baking in the oven, and she had selected the other ingredients for their dinner.

She set the table and went out into the yard to pick a fresh bouquet for the table. Hawk obviously did not have much time to devote to his yard and flowers, with the hours he worked at the railroad office, but she did find enough for a small arrangement.

Dinner was simmering on the stove when Hawk came bounding through the front door with a boyish enthusiasm on his face. As he entered, calling out her name, he smelled the pleasant aroma coming from his kitchen and knew Gillian was preparing supper for them.

Her lovely face wore a warm smile as she came out of the kitchen to greet him. She looked refreshed and rested and this pleased Hawk.

He sauntered up to her and gave her a gentle kiss on the cheek, unsure what she might be feeling about last night. He wanted to believe that she would be feeling as he felt, but until he knew, he dared not be so bold as to grab her up in his arms and kiss her soft lips. Just the sight of her, standing there in her deep green skirt and cream tunic was enough to set off a savage passion within him.

His black eyes gleamed down at her. "I can tell you got your beauty sleep—you look very beautiful."

"I don't dare tell you how late I slept," she laughed. "But I do feel fine now, so I know it did me some good. I was really tired. Now you go wash up, Hawk, and we'll have our supper. It's all ready."

"My goodness, I'm a lucky fellow tonight." He smiled and went off to do as she requested. It was nice to come in from work and not have to cook his own meal. As he'd expected after being away for ten days, there had been a lot of things to attend to in the office, and if he had not had Gillian at his house this evening he would probably have worked on for another couple of hours, to have gotten more of his work cleared away.

A few minutes later, Gillian had bowls of steaming hot vegetables and a platter of meat on the table, ready for them to eat. By the time Hawk had finished the generous piece of pie she'd served him, he was feeling completely sated and very lazy.

"A man could get very spoiled by all this, Gillian."

She gave him a smile as she rose to start clearing away the dishes. Now came the time she was dreading, for she did not know how he would take her announcement, nor how convincing a liar she would be. It wasn't her way, but she knew she must lie to save Hawk's feelings.

When she had washed the last dish, she took a deep breath and, as he was sitting at the table puffing on his cheroot, began casually, "Hawk, it is early yet—just beginning to get dark. I'm going to get on over to Melba's tonight so that I can get settled in. I've got a lot of things to sort out in all that luggage I left with her. Better tonight, than in the morning when you've got to get to your job."

Her back was turned to him as she spoke, so she did not witness the stunned look on his face. Her words were the last thing he'd expected to hear this evening. It took him a moment to find his tongue. "I—I had no idea you'd be leaving tonight, Gillian."

She gave out a forced laugh. "Well, Hawk, I had no idea when I left the Fosters' that I'd not be going directly to the Old Pueblo Inn last night. But then, I didn't know how weary I'd be after that long ride."

"You—you know you can stay here as long as you

like, Gillian. I told you that."

"I know, Hawk, and that is very sweet of you, but I've got to get busy making a life for myself. You can surely understand that."

"I guess so." Hawk realized that he'd assumed what happened last night would have changed Gillian's mind about her plans. But now he knew he was wrong. "I'll take you to the inn whenever you are ready to go, Gillian."

"We'll be on our way as soon as I finish here in the kitchen. That way, you can get back home early enough to relax for a while before you go to bed."

"Yeah. Well, I'll get the horses ready while you finish up." He ambled slowly out the kitchen door.

By the time she had dimmed the lamp in the kitchen and gone to the back bedroom to gather up her things, Hawk was coming through the front door to tell her that Tache and Fuego were at the gate when she was ready.

"I'm ready now, Hawk," she told him. Hawk thought she seemed very anxious, and eager to be on her way, so he did not try to talk her into spending another night here with him, as he yearned to do.

They left the house and swung up onto the horses. The brief ride to the inn gave them little time to talk much, and all too soon they were dismounting. When they reached the walled garden surrounding the inn, Hawk took her arm to halt her. "I'm going to say goodbye here, Gillian. You know where I am when you want to come and see me. Fuego is there when you want to go for a ride, or until you find out that he can be kept here."

"Oh, Hawk, I'll be pestering you sooner than you

think. Thank you for everything." She reached up on tiptoe to meet his lips in a kiss. "I'll come to you very soon."

But Hawk did not allow his lips to linger too long in the kiss, for he knew that if he did it would spark a flame that might never be put out.

"Goodbye, Gillian, and take care of yourself," Hawk told her, as he took a couple of steps backward and prepared to leave.

"Goodbye, Hawk. I'll be seeing you soon," she called out to him as she watched his tall, towering figure walk away from her.

Swiftly, she turned and walked up the pathway to the front entrance of the inn. She inquired at the desk in the lobby where she might find Melba Jackson, and the clerk told her that she was in her office.

"Would you please tell her that Gillian Lafferty would like to speak to her?"

The young clerk returned shortly to tell Gillian to go into the office. Carrying her valise in her hand, Gillian marched into the office to announce to Melba that she was back, and ready to accept the position she'd been offered before she left for Maricopa County.

"Well, young lady, I was hoping you'd be coming back here. In fact I was hoping so hard you'd tell me yes that I reserved one of our nicest little suites for you. It hasn't been occupied for over a week now, and all your belongings have been stored there."

"Oh, Melba," Gillian laughed, "you must have felt sure I would be returning here, then!"

A knowing grin came to the older woman's face. "Just couldn't see a pretty young thing like you wanting to isolate yourself on that ranch of the Fosters'—not now that you've been a married lady."

"No, I realized that after a couple of days, Melba. I think even the Fosters understood that it couldn't be the same as it was before I married Steve and left."

"Have you had your dinner, honey?" Melba asked, as she slowly got up from the chair where she'd been sitting, at her desk.

"Yes, I have."

"Well then I'll show you to your suite so you can get settled in, and we'll talk business in the morning. All right?"

"All right, Melba." She followed the owner of the inn out of her office and down the carpeted hallway. When they entered the suite, Gillian knew she was going to feel comfortable there. "Oh, Melba, this little sitting room is so pleasant and cozy looking. The colors are all my favorites," she exclaimed. She walked around the room and saw that just outside the sitting room was her own secluded little patio, with tropical plants growing on either side. There was her bedroom, adjoining the sitting room, the bed covered with a soft blue coverlet, and with an armoire and a large chest in which she could store all her clothes. By the window was a mahogany dressing table and a stool covered in blue velvet.

Melba could tell that she had picked out the perfect suite to please Gillian, for her blue eyes were flashing excitedly as she surveyed the rooms.

"I want you to be happy here, Gillian, so that you'll stay to help me out—which you certainly can. Helen is marvelous in the kitchen and tending to the running of the dining room, but she is no good at the books or keeping accounts. That is where I need your sharp mind. Oh, by the way, in case I didn't mention it to you, all you have to do if you want something from the kitchen is request it. Your meals are furnished, and coffee or a late night snack is included in that."

"Oh, Melba, you've made me a most generous offer. Food and lodging, along with a salary! It's very agreeable to me, and I'll just try to be worthy of it for you."

"You will be, Gillian. I know it, or I would not have offered it to you. Now, I'm going to leave you to get cozied in, and I'll see you at noon tomorrow." Melba turned to leave Gillian, but as she got to the door, she turned back and smiled. "Now remember, if you want a carafe of coffee or a snack before you turn in, don't hesitate to ask for it. I'll be letting the staff know that you are now working for the Old Pueblo Inn."

"I'll remember, Melba," Gillian assured her, as she followed her to the door. After Melba had left, Gillian locked the door and got busy unpacking her belongings.

It was a good feeling for Gillian to have her clothing all put away in the armoire and the high chest in the bedroom. She felt this was a place she could call home, and after all her traveling she was ready to be settled in for a while. She was ready to have some order to her life again and to know what to expect when she woke up each morning.

Tomorrow she would start a new day and a new life, here at the Old Pueblo Inn.

Chapter Eleven

The streets were dark as Hawk rode toward his home, leading Fuego behind him. Most of the stores and shops were closed for the day and the shopkeepers had left for their homes, so the city was quiet and deserted. It did not take Hawk long to ride the short distance to his little house.

By the time he'd got the horses stabled in the small barn and entered through the back door of his house, the clock in the kitchen was chiming eight. Most evenings, Hawk was just sitting down to his supper by now, having got in from the office and cooked it.

Finding some coffee still hot on the back of the stove, he helped himself to a cup. It seemed lonely tonight, with Gillian gone. Ambling into the parlor, he brightened the lamp that had been dimly burning and sank down into a chair. He had not been planning on sitting here alone tonight, for he had expected Gillian to be here with him.

Had he assumed too much, just because Gillian had allowed him to make love to her the night before?

Obviously, he had. Perhaps she had had every intention of leaving tonight all along, but he could not help wondering if her sudden impulse to get to the inn was because she didn't want to be here with him again tonight.

He had every reason to believe that Gillian had found pleasure, as he had, when they'd made love. If she hadn't, she had damned well fooled him! But if she had, he reasoned, surely one more day and night before her arrival at the inn would have made no difference.

He had no idea of the financial state Lafferty had been in when he died, but he guessed that even if he wasn't a wealthy man, he wasn't a poor one either. So Hawk was sure Gillian must have returned from Ireland with enough money to provide a comfortable life for herself for a few months, whether she worked or not.

But a lot had happened to Gillian while she was away. She was not the same, and he could understand that. She still had the same lovely smile and glorious auburn hair, and there was a sensuous air about her that Hawk felt she was still not aware of, any more than she had been when she attracted the Irish sea captain. But the difference was there, deep within her, Hawk sensed. So he had decided, as he was riding back home, that he would give her some time and not push her. In the meanwhile, he had a job to keep him busy. He'd just wait until she wished to come to see him.

After all, he knew what an impulsive little creature she could be.

Before he retired, he remembered the pie she had baked for their supper, so he went to the kitchen to get himself another piece of it and a glass of milk. Nothing could have pleased him more than having Gillian right here in his kitchen every night, cooking their supper and sharing his life. In fact, he was ready to offer to marry her once again, for now he could support her. But he wasn't sure she was ready to accept his proposal, and Hawk had his pride, too. It would devastate him to be refused.

So the next morning, as he went to his job at the railroad, he told himself to forget that Gillian was just a few miles away, getting herself established in her new life.

By the time the day was over and he was back at home, puttering around in his kitchen to get some supper ready, it felt as if his life had settled back into the usual routine from before Gillian had suddenly come back into his world.

It was only when he lay in bed that night that his thoughts were consumed by the lovely vision of Gillian. It seemed that her sweet fragrance lingered on the pillow.

Gillian found her first day at the Old Pueblo Inn very stimulating and exciting. She enjoyed the constantly changing parade of people in the lobby and dining room. It seemed that they came from everywhere to stop at the inn on their way to different parts of the country.

By the end of the day, Gillian was engulfed by a feeling of satisfaction that she was going to play a role in, and be a part of, this establishment.

She had met Melba promptly at noon, dressed in one of her modest gowns of deep blue with a small white lace collar and cuffs. Melba gave her an approving look as she entered her office, for she had dressed perfectly for the role Melba intended her to have here.

After they had shared a light lunch, she urged Gillian to pull up a chair beside her and watch how she posted in the huge ledger last night's receipts from the inn and dining room. When she was half way through the pile, Melba allowed Gillian to take over, while she observed her.

After the stack of receipts was done, Melba laughed. "Well, you're so good I can take tomorrow off. You seem to have the hang of it." Melba explained to her that at the end of the evening the dining room receipts were brought to the desk in the lobby and turned over to the clerk in charge. "When I come to the office, I pick them up on my way. As you can see, this takes about an hour. Now, Gillian, the main job I have for you, which I used to do with grand style, if I do say so myself, is mingling in the lobby, greeting my guests and making them feel at home here. I've not been able to do this for months, because of this danged leg."

"So you wish me to greet the people out there, and extend to them our wishes that their stay at the Old Pueblo Inn will be pleasant?"

"Exactly! I think you can make a very attractive hostess, Gillian. There is a touch of class about you, in case you don't know it."

"I guess I never thought about it, but I'm pleased that you think so," Gillian confessed.

"Well, I saw that air about you the first time we met, and I see it even more now. I used to spend a couple of hours in the lobby every afternoon, and in the evening I would do the same thing in the dining room. I'd roam around the tables and stop to chat with the guests dining there. People like being noticed, Gillian, and I know all this paid off for me. It's why my guests return constantly. But damnit, I can't do it now."

"Well, I'll try to do a good job for you, Melba. I can certainly be your legs, but I may not have that Melba Jackson charm!" Gillian smiled.

"Oh, child, you've got your own charm, and I might tell you that you've dressed exactly as I would have wanted you to this afternoon. But tonight you must get yourself up in a fancy gown."

Melba saw a concerned look coming to Gillian's face. She confessed to Melba, "I don't have any fancy gowns, Melba. Most of my clothes are simple, basic frocks and riding skirts. I can manage with what I've got for a while, at least for the afternoons, but I fear I won't look the way you want me to for the evenings."

"Well, we'll just have to remedy that. It's not yet two, so why don't you take my gig and make a fast trip over to Denise's Dress Shop. Tell her you are my new assistant manager. Get yourself two gowns, if she has some already made up, and tell her to bill me, honey."

"Oh, Melba, you're so kind to me," Gillian sighed, shaking her head in gratitude at this woman's generosity.

"It's a good investment, Gillian. Now be off with you."

Gillian did as she was told, taking the time to go to her suite first to get her reticule, and soon she was guiding Melba's gig to the dress shop.

Two hours later she was returning with her purchase of two lovely gowns. One had fit perfectly, and the other had been given a quick alteration by the seamstress to make it fit Gillian's tiny waist. The clerk had called the shade of one of the gowns delphinium, but Gillian just knew it was the prettiest shade of blue she'd ever seen, and that the color suited her auburn hair and blue eyes. It had a pretty scooped neckline—which displayed no cleavage—and fitted sleeves, with a soft flowing skirt of silk. Gillian knew it was exactly the type of gown Melba wanted her to wear.

The other dress was a soft pastel pink, with a sweetheart neckline edged with white lace. Gillian had also bought herself some stockings and a pair of soft white leather slippers, with the feeling that she was probably being extravagant. She knew she should fashion her hair in a more sophisticated style for the evenings, so she bought a small cluster of pink silk flowers to pin in her hair and two tortoiseshell hair combs with blue trim.

She felt like an excited child as she returned to the inn. As soon as she had neatly hung up her gowns and put her other purchases away, she left her suite to seek out Melba. But Melba was not in the office, and the desk clerk told Gillian that she had gone to her rooms to rest. The young desk clerk, Tommy, handed Gillian a note telling her, "Miss Melba said to give this to you when you returned."

"Thank you, Tommy." Gillian read that she was to go to her room and rest, for she would begin her evening of hostessing in the dining room at six. The note said Melba would meet Gillian in the lobby at that hour.

So Gillian returned to her room, realizing that it would not be all that long before she would have to start getting bathed and dressed to meet Melba at six.

She felt excited and nervous at the prospect of beginning her first real job. What would the first evening hold in store?

A little later on, Gillian was relaxing in the cast iron tub. The sweet scent of lilac bath oil permeated the room. When she finally emerged from the water, she slipped into her silk wrapper and sat down in her sitting room to eat the light meal she had asked to be brought to her room. She had realized that she would have no time to eat dinner tonight, so she had decided to eat her evening meal at five o'clock and then, if necessary, have a snack before bed.

When she had finished eating, Gillian went and sat at her dressing table to see how she might fashion her long tresses in a becoming arrangement for the evening.

For a half hour she tried various styles until she finally decided on the one she felt was the most flattering on her. She looked at the back of her hair, holding the mirror in her hand. Her auburn curls were hanging down her back, pulled tightly at the sides with the hair combs she'd bought this afternoon. Soft wisps of curls were clouding at her temples, and on her ears she wore pearl earrings. She was now ready to slip into the lovely blue gown. When it was on and fastened, Gillian was pleased with the image she saw in the full-length mirror.

Before going down to meet Melba in the lobby she dabbed some lilac toilet water behind her ears and at her throat, and took one final look in the mirror before going out the door.

On the way to the lobby she encountered some guests coming down the hallway, and the stares she received were enough to boost her ego. She had a smug smile on her face as she continued. She did look very attractive tonight, and she knew it.

Knowing this, she felt very self-assured by the time she made her entrance into the brightly lit lobby, which was buzzing with guests ready to go into the dining room. Some were staying at the inn, and others were people living in Tucson who enjoyed coming to the elegant dining room at the inn.

Many eyes were drawn to the auburn-haired beauty strolling into the lobby dressed in the rich blue silk gown. Melba watched her moving gracefully toward her and knew that that blue gown was worth every dollar it would cost her. Gillian was going to be worth her weight in gold around the inn.

Proudly, Melba went up to greet her. "Well, honey, you look stunning tonight. You've got everyone's attention just by walking into this lobby."

"Do you like the gown, Melba?"

"Like it? It's gorgeous, and so are you, Gillian. Come with me. I've got some people I want to introduce you to." Melba led her over to an elegant looking couple.

"Mr. and Mrs. Humbolt, I'd like you to meet my new assistant manager, Gillian Lafferty. When you can't find me, you just ask for Gillian," she said, leading Gillian up to meet them.

Gillian gave the couple a warm smile as she greeted them. "It is a pleasure to meet you."

Herman Humbolt was certainly impressed by the beautiful young lady and responded quickly. "Well, Melba, you've picked yourself a very attractive assistant. Miss Lafferty, I shall certainly seek you out without hesitation."

102

"It's a pleasure to meet you, Miss Lafferty," Ernestine Humbolt told Gillian. "Herman has always had an eye for a lovely lady. I tell you so you will be warned!" Giving a jovial laugh, she turned to Melba, remarking, "Ah, Melba, our son, Eric, will never want to leave the Old Pueblo once he spies Miss Lafferty, here."

"Is Eric with you this trip, Mrs. Humbolt?" Melba inquired. She was genuinely interested. Ernestine was an easygoing, good-natured lady, and there was not one snobbish bone in her body—unlike most of the wealthy matrons coming to the inn.

"Yes, but I don't know what has happened to the scamp this evening. He was due to join us for dinner, but Eric is not known for his promptness."

Melba figured that it was time they moved on to some of her other guests, so she took her leave of the Humbolts, telling them to enjoy their meal. "You'll find your favorite wine waiting at your table," Melba added, as she ushered Gillian along with her.

The scene with the Humbolts was repeated a couple more times with other guests before Melba told Gillian she needed to sit down. When they reached a small table in the back corner of the dining room, Melba urged Gillian to sit down with her. As Gillian took a seat, Melba asked her if she got the drift of what she wished her to do.

"I think so, Melba. I can't see that I'll have any problems being nice to people like the Humbolts."

"Well, all of them aren't that nice. That son of theirs can be obnoxious—I just thought I'd warn you, before I let you go out there on your own. A handsome devil he is, and he thinks he's God's gift to women."

103

Gillian gave her a reassuring smile. "I married a cocky Irishman, remember, Melba? I think that I can handle Eric Humbolt."

"Go to it, then, Gillian. I'm going to sit back here this evening and allow myself to be perfectly lazy." Melba smiled and gave her a wink.

Gillian made her first stop at a table near where Melba was sitting. The older woman could hear as she greeted the guests and asked if they were enjoying their dinner. She was impressed by Gillian's ease, immediately enlightening the diners as to her name and position.

Melba's one concern had been that her lady diners would resent the beautiful girl and that their husbands would be completely entranced by her. But Gillian made a point of turning her attention to the lady at this table to compliment the gown she was wearing. Gillian sounded very genuine as she remarked, "It is absolutely stunning!"

A smug grin came to Melba's face when she saw the woman smiling up at Gillian and thanking her. When Gillian moved on, Melba heard the woman remark to her husband, "Wasn't she charming? This is such a nice place, Henry. We must come here more often."

The other pleasing thing that Melba observed was how Gillian made a point of noticing each newly arrived couple and going immediately to greet them. By now, Melba felt that she could relax and order her own dinner.

Helen slipped out of the kitchen a few minutes later to see how Gillian was doing. She bent down to whisper in Melba's ear, "Is she managing all right?"

"Take a look at her."

"Lord, isn't she pretty tonight, Melba!" Helen exclaimed.

"She sure is, and she's a natural for this job, Helen. In fact, I'm ready to have dinner myself. Gillian will do fine."

By the time Melba had finished her beefsteak there were no more people entering the room, which was just as well, for the tables were all filled. However, some diners were beginning to leave the room.

It had been a busy couple of hours for Gillian, but she had enjoyed meeting and talking to the various people in the dining room.

She was feeling very happy that she had handled everything so smoothly this evening. Obviously Melba had felt so too, for she had quietly left the dining room to retire for the evening.

Gillian had a brief moment to speak to Helen, as the evening had now calmed down. Helen told her eagerly how well she'd handled herself tonight. But while they were talking, Gillian noticed a displeased look coming to Helen's face. "What's the matter, Helen?" she asked.

"Oh, it's that Eric Humbolt coming in at this late hour. His folks were just ready to leave, and now he'll expect a meal, but my stoves and ovens are cooling."

"What have you got left, Helen? Any of that rib roast, and the little roast potatoes?"

"Yes, we have that."

"All right, let me see what I can do." Gillian left to greet him, and Helen went back to her kitchen.

When Eric Humbolt spotted the gorgeous girl walking directly toward him, in her brilliant blue gown, it wasn't exactly an appetite for food that consumed him. He ogled her shapely figure and lovely face.

"Good evening, sir."

"Well, good evening to you, ma'am. I'm Eric Humbolt. I wish to join my parents," he told her.

Gillian gave a nod of her pretty head and a warm smile. "Follow me, Mr. Humbolt."

A devious glint sparked in his eyes. "Oh, gladly! I'd follow you anywhere—but tell me, my lovely, who you are?"

"I'm Gillian Lafferty, the new assistant manager."

"Well, well! The Old Pueblo Inn becomes more interesting a place, I must say."

By now they had joined the Humbolts, and Eric took a seat. Ernestine Humbolt was very vexed at her son, and made no effort to conceal it. Harshly, she admonished him, "You can hardly expect to have dinner now, Eric. It's far too late."

Eric, undaunted by his mother's comments, turned to Gillian to ask her, "Is that right, Miss Lafferty?"

"I fear your mother is absolutely right about most things on the menu, but we at the inn try to accommodate our valued guests. Would you perhaps enjoy a succulent slice of rib roast and tiny roast potatoes?"

"Ah, that sounds grand to me!"

Gillian smiled. "I think we can manage it for you."

She hurried back to the kitchen, where Helen was waiting for her. All the help had gone for the evening, except for one of the waitresses.

Eric Humbolt was served his dinner quickly, and the kitchen was shut down. Gillian insisted that she would wait to close down the dining room and take the receipts to the desk clerk. For that, Helen was very grateful.

The Humbolts were embarrassed to be the last ones in the dining room, but they were very impressed by the new assistant manager. Herman Humbolt told his wife that they should do something the next day to show their appreciation to the young lady. She had been very gracious about their irresponsible son causing her to linger another hour in the dining room.

"I wholeheartedly agree with you, Herman. Whatever we buy, take it out of Eric's allowance. Maybe that will make an impression on him!"

Eric left the dining room with his hunger sated, but his interest in the lovely auburn-haired young lady he'd encountered tonight was gnawing at him like hunger. His passion had flamed the moment he had seen her walking toward him, and he vowed that she was going to be his next conquest.

Chapter Twelve

It had been an interesting twenty-four hours for Gillian. This was a new, exciting kind of life for her, after having grown up on the ranch with the Fosters. And it was certainly a different life from the one she'd lived as the wife of an Irish sea captain in Ireland.

She was still bubbling with excitement when she got to her suite shortly before midnight. She took great care as she removed the new blue gown and carefully inspected it before hanging it up. Tomorrow night she would wear the pink gown.

Before she went to bed, she picked out the afternoon frock she'd wear for the daytime duty tomorrow. There was no question about it, she was going to have to spend some money on her wardrobe.

On the other hand, there was no reason to think about purchasing a house with the nice living arrangement she had here at the inn. Her quarters were very comfortable and her meals were furnished, so there was no reason she could not afford to buy a few new afternoon gowns with the money Steve had left her.

On her first day off, she would go on a shopping spree to Denise's Dress Shop and purchase a few things she needed.

Although she had retired so late, Gillian was still able to have a good night's sleep and a few hours to spare in the morning before she went to the office.

By the time she joined Melba in the office at noon, Helen had already informed Melba about events in the dining room, and how capably Gillian had handled the late arrival of Eric Humbolt.

Once again, Melba was impressed with this young girl's shrewd thinking, and she told Helen so. When Gillian appeared in the office, looking refreshed and cheerful in her cotton frock the color of buttercups, she was like a breath of springtime.

As they had done the day before, Gillian and Melba shared a light lunch, with Helen also joining them. But today, Melba abruptly handed the receipts to Gillian and announced that she had some business to attend to, so she was going to leave Gillian to handle them.

"By the way, young lady, you did a grand job last night. Helen told me how you handled that rascal, Eric Humbolt. That's why I'm going to leave you in charge, while I take care of some business I've been long overdue in getting to."

Gillian immediately got busy going through the billings that were piled on the desk. By the time the office clock was chiming two, she was finished and had put the ledger away.

She was preparing to leave Melba's office when the young desk clerk came rushing into the office, carrying a huge wicker basket of flowers. "These were sent to you, Miss Gillian, from one of our guests. You must

109

have made an impression on the Humbolts last night."

Gillian thanked him, delighted with the basket of flowers. Before she went to greet the guests in the lobby, she took the flowers to her suite, thinking that it was certainly a strange, different world she was living in, here at the inn. She could not deny that she found it very thrilling.

At four that afternoon, Gillian returned to her suite to rest for a while before having a bath and dressing in her fancy new gown.

Because she wanted to present a proper image as the hostess, Gillian took special care again tonight as she dressed. She styled her hair in the same fashion as the previous night, and pinned the little cluster of pink silk flowers at one side of her pulled-back curls.

She'd never owned such fancy gowns as the ones she'd worn the last two nights, and they had suddenly made her very conscious about the rest of her attire. Her wardrobe had always consisted of simple muslin gowns, and twill riding skirts worn with cotton tunics. When she had married Steve, she had taken the same clothes, with the addition of a couple of gowns he'd bought her in New Orleans before they left to sail away to Ireland. He had also brought her some lovely wool shawls and a warm cape on one of his voyages at sea, but in this warm Arizona climate, she would have to leave them packed away.

During the last two days, observing all the finely attired ladies and wearing her fancy gowns had ignited the desire in her to own pretty things that she'd never given any thought to before.

By the time she left her room this evening, she had decided definitely that with her first pay from the inn she was going to buy herself a nice selection of new clothes.

When she arrived in the lobby, Melba was there to greet her as she had been last night. Gillian saw that Melba's being able to have more time to rest had done her a world of good. She was glad to think that she had enabled Melba to rest more.

She made a point of telling Melba how well and attractive she looked in her emerald green gown. "And you look like a beautiful pink rosebud, dear. It would seem, from all I've observed so far, that this is going to be a very busy night. The dining room is already filling up."

"Well, that is good for business," Gillian said with a smile.

Melba had already decided that she was going to give Gillian a new challenge. "Tonight, Gillian, I shall stay in this part of the lobby. You start around there in the alcove, and I'll leave it up to you when to leave the lobby to come on into the dining room."

"All right, Melba. I'll see you later," she agreed, and started to move out in the lobby on her own.

Gillian knew that Melba was testing her, so she lingered in the lobby only as long as she felt necessary. Some of the guests were enjoying the pleasant setting of the lobby as a place to visit and chat, but the dining room looked very busy, so she moved in there quite soon. The room was full and she could not spot Melba in her vivid green gown. She wondered if her boss had left.

Tonight, when Herman and Ernestine Humbolt entered the dining room, their son Eric was accompanying them. When Gillian greeted them, Eric handed her a small package. "This is my way of saying I'm sorry I came to dine so late last night, Miss Lafferty," he told her, giving her a disarming smile.

Gillian could see why Melba had warned her about him, for he did have a great deal of charm with his handsome features, blonde hair and flashing blue eyes.

His broad shoulders and narrow waistline reminded Gillian of a picture she'd once seen of a Greek god.

Gillian thanked him. "But you didn't have to do this. It is my job to make all our guests here at the Old Pueblo Inn happy. Thank you so very much for sending me the flowers, Mr. and Mrs. Humbolt. It was a most kind gesture." She could feel Eric's eyes on her as she led the trio to their table. He was burning with the desire to spend some time with this beautiful creature.

Once the Humbolts were seated, Gillian told them who would be their waitress that evening. Before moving on she said, "I hope you enjoy your dinner—and thank you very much for your gift, Mr. Humbolt."

She didn't get the chance to open Eric's gift for the next hour or so, but when she did she found an exquisite, delicate fan edged in lace with etchings of gold. On the end of it was a woven silk cord with which to hang it around her wrist. She'd never owned a fan, and she was very pleased with it.

When the Humbolts were preparing to leave the dining room Eric was unable to speak again with the lovely Gillian, as he had planned, for Melba Jackson had returned to the dining room and she and Gillian were engrossed in a conversation at one of the back tables.

But Eric Humbolt was not a young man to be denied

what he desired. He did not accompany his parents back to their suite, but with that arrogant air of his, he intimidated the young night clerk into telling him the number of Miss Lafferty's suite.

As huge a crowd as it had been that evening in the dining room, most of the guests seemed to leave at about the same time. Gillian realized there was no predicting a routine. She was able to get back to her suite much earlier than last night.

When she arrived there she found a note that had been slipped under her door. It was from Eric Humbolt. He expressed his desire to take her out to dinner, but said he knew that this was impossible. However, he would leave the Old Pueblo Inn very disappointed if he could not entice her to accompany him on an afternoon jaunt around the city or countryside before he left Tucson. He also made a point of stating that he and his parents would be leaving in a couple of days.

Gillian could not deny that she was very flattered by Eric's invitation. Melba had told her that the Humbolts were very wealthy. Mr. Humbolt actually owned a great deal of land in the state, and they called him "the Baron." He and Ernestine were of German descent— Melba had heard that Ernestine was the granddaughter of a German nobleman who had established himself as a big landowner in Texas. The community there was dominated by German immigrants, as it had been for many years.

Gillian knew not how she could possibly accept Eric's invitation, though, for her hours at the inn left her only two or three hours free between her midday duties and the evening hours.

But Gillian could not know the tenacious nature of Eric Humbolt. He was a young man who'd never done a day's work in all his twenty-one years of life, but he would work vigorously to woo and win a lady he had his heart set on.

The next morning, when Gillian got up and dressed to go to the office at noon, she was still unsure about how she should handle Eric Humbolt's invitation. She decided to seek out the sage advice of Melba Jackson.

When she opened the door to leave her suite she saw a massive basket of flowers waiting for her, and she knew before she picked up the envelope in the basket that the flowers were from Eric. What she was not prepared for when she opened the brief note was to see a sparkling sapphire set in gold and hung on a delicate gold chain.

Quickly Gillian returned into her room and placed the flowers on the table in the sitting room. Eric's message was brief. He'd written that when he saw the gem it had reminded him of her lovely eyes. Gillian knew that such a piece of jewelry did not come cheap; now she was faced with another problem to discuss with Melba.

The burden Gillian had lifted off Melba's back was already making the owner of the Old Pueblo Inn feel a lot less tired. But Melba also knew that she had to let the young girl have some time off. The best days for that, because they were quiet ones around the inn, were Sunday and Monday. Melba decided that those were the days off she would give to Gillian.

This morning Melba had some more personal

business to attend to, so today would be another test for the young lady. Melba would not be there to share lunch with her at midday, and Gillian would have to carry the load entirely alone.

Gillian carried off the midday shift by herself, and quite effectively, but she was disappointed not to have her talk with Melba, as she'd planned.

When she was preparing to return to her suite at around three, she stopped by the desk to inquire of the desk clerk, Tommy, if Miss Melba was back at the inn yet.

"No, ma'am, she isn't."

So Gillian went back to her room and followed the routine she had established during the last two afternoons. After her rest she laid out her clothes for the evening. Tonight, she would wear the blue gown again.

As she was taking her bath, she found herself curious about what Melba had been up to today, with such a long absence from the inn. She had just emerged from the tub, dried herself off, and slipped into the silk wrapper when she heard a knock on her door.

She expected it to be her meal, but it was Melba, holding a most gorgeous lavender gown. Its color reminded Gillian of the hyacinths that bloomed in the spring in Nancy Foster's front yard. Melba marched into the room telling Gillian that she had seen the gown and could not resist buying it for her. Underneath the folds of the gown, Melba was holding a pair of dainty satin slippers of the same shade.

"You will look quite striking in this, Gillian."

Gillian had never seen such pretty slippers, and as Melba said, they matched the gown exactly. Gillian gave a sigh of delight as she took the gown and held it up against her. "Melba—oh, Melba! I feel like Cinderella, and you are my fairy godmother."

Melba gave a hearty laugh. "I can't think of anything nicer than being a fairy godmother, Gillian." Then she bade Gillian farewell, for she knew that it was time for Gillian to eat her meal and get dressed.

Gillian was unaware that nothing happened at the inn without Melba knowing about it. She knew about Eric Humbolt's gift to Gillian last night, and she knew about his making the young desk clerk give him Gillian's suite number. Melba had already given the clerk a harsh reprimand about it, and warned him to never make that mistake again. She also knew about the basket sitting outside Gillian's door, but she didn't know about the expensive pendant that had been hidden in the basket of flowers.

And something else that neither Melba nor Gillian knew was that Warner Barstow would be coming to the dining room tonight, and that among his guests would be Hawk.

Chapter Thirteen

Hawk knew there was part of him that would always be a loner, enjoying the quiet solitude of his cabin in the dense forest far more than the busy, bustling city of Tucson.

He was not thrilled that Warner Barstow had invited him to join him and his friend, Howard Curtis, in dining at the inn tonight. Accompanying them would be a young man Curtis had brought to Tucson, whose name was Brett Harrison.

The thought of seeing Gillian made him happy, but getting dressed up in those fancy clothes he'd finally bought some months ago didn't appeal to Hawk, nor did dining in that elegant dining room. His simple dark twill pants and cotton shirts were the clothing Hawk felt comfortable in, but tonight he was wearing his new gray pants and darker gray coat with a new white linen shirt. He felt very uncomfortable. The one item of attire he was enjoying was the brand new black leather boots he'd purchased that afternoon.

Tonight he was riding Tache to the inn, since he'd

ridden Fuego to work that day. He liked to be sure that both of the spirited horses got some exercise. The run of his corral was a small area, and Hawk was already making plans to expand it.

He arrived at the inn promptly at seven. He saw Warner going in through the entrance as he was walking up the path from the front gate.

Hawk had not realized that Howard Curtis and Brett Harrison were guests there at the inn during their brief stay in the city. By the time Hawk had walked to the front door of the inn, Curtis and his young friend Harrison had seen Barstow arrive and gone to join him.

Hawk saw them but he held back, his black eyes surveying the huge lobby for some sight of Gillian. With the exception of Warner and his party, there were few guests remaining in the lobby. Just a few moments ago, Gillian had gone into the dining room for the rest of the evening. Once again, Melba had left it to her to decide the right time to make that transition.

As it happened, the Humbolts arrived just as she was starting into the dining room, so she accompanied them.

Eric's eyes were devouring her as she walked along with them, and Gillian noticed that they went to her throat to see if she was wearing the exquisite pendant. She wasn't, for she hadn't yet decided whether she should accept it, and she'd never had the chance to speak to Melba and get her opinion.

But the last thing in the world she wanted to do was offend the Humbolts, so she did acknowledge his generosity by saying, "Your gift was far too extravagant, Mr. Humbolt." She gave him a friendly, warm smile.

"Ah, Miss Lafferty, I am crestfallen, for I expected to see my gift draped around your lovely throat tonight," Eric remarked, with a devious gleam in his eyes. He was feeling quite desperate this evening, for his time here was growing short, and this urged him to speak so boldly. His remark drew a displeased look from his mother, who was walking directly behind him, and she glanced at her husband with a look that told Herman she was tempted, as she often was, to slap Eric's mouth. She was wondering what he had taken the liberty to send that nice Miss Lafferty. As much as she loved her only son, he caused her embarrassment at times.

To fill the slightly awkward silence, she remarked to Gillian how beautiful she looked tonight in her pretty gown. Gillian thanked her, and complimented Mrs. Humbolt's gown in return.

With the Humbolts seated at their table, Gillian turned around to see who her next guests were to be. To her amazement she found herself watching Hawk and three other gentlemen entering the dining room. Never had she seen Hawk dressed so handsomely. His tall figure towered over the other three gentlemen, who were strangers to her. She assumed that they were men Hawk worked with at the railroad office.

This was a different Hawk than the one she'd known, and she found him very intriguing. She also found herself stirring with sensations, recalling the night she'd lain in his arms and Hawk had made love to her.

She walked up to greet them. Hawk's eyes were devouring her as he watched her coming closer. Dear God, she was so beautiful that she took his breath away!

"Good evening, gentlemen. Allow me to show you to your table," she said in greeting. She managed to move to Hawk's side as she was guiding them to the table. "It's a pleasant surprise to see you, Hawk," she said very softly as she smiled up at him.

A slow, easy smile came to Hawk's face. Being so near Gillian made Hawk look forward to the dinner he was to share with the other gentlemen. "You're looking quite beautiful tonight, Gillian, and it's good to see you again, too."

By now they were at their table. Gillian told Warner Barstow and his guests she hoped they would enjoy their dinner, and then she excused herself.

The minute Gillian had left the table all the men's eyes turned in Hawk's direction. Howard Curtis said teasingly to Hawk, "I think you've been holding out on us, don't you, Warner?"

Warner just gave a lighthearted laugh. He had always figured that there was some young lady in Hawk's life, but the young man talked little about his personal life, and Warner figured it was his business.

But Brett Harrison was more outspoken. He declared, "She is a most beautiful lady—the prettiest one I've seen in Tucson." Then he suddenly realized that Curtis might not take too kindly to him praising the charms of this young lady when he was engaged to marry Howard's daughter this summer. So he said no more, but it didn't stop him from thinking or looking.

All of them had to agree that she was most beautiful. A surge of pride shot through Hawk, as if these gentlemen were praising his wife.

For the next hour Hawk was mesmerized by the sight of Gillian gracefully floating around the dining room, stopping at the tables to speak to guests. Hawk had never seen this sophisticated side of Gillian. Just as she had been intrigued by the sight of Hawk coming into the dining room in his fine attire, he found himself entranced by the aspect of Gillian he was observing this evening.

They had almost finished their main course when Brett Harrison made an observation. He'd been glancing around the room and said the impulsive remark before stopping to think. "Hey, Hawk—it seems the beautiful Gillian has another admirer. That blond-haired gent sure seems taken with her."

Hawk's attention had been on the juicy steak he was enjoying and he had not noticed the attention Eric Humbolt was giving to Gillian. He had touched her arm to detain her as she passed their table, and had kept her talking for longer than he should.

Ernestine was vexed at her son's antics tonight, and as soon as Gillian had moved away from their table, she had let him know exactly how she was feeling. "Eric, you are being too brash tonight, and I think you are making that nice Miss Lafferty feel ill at ease." Folding her napkin and laying it to the side of her plate, she turned to her husband to say, "Herman, we're all finished, and I'm ready to leave before this obnoxious son of ours does anything more to make himself look foolish."

Eric, feeling full of devilment tonight, sought to cajole his mother. Usually it worked for him, but tonight, it didn't. "You had no business, Eric, sending her an expensive piece of jewelry. You have placed her in an embarrassing position."

"Oh, Momma! I've sent other girls expensive gifts

121

like that before, and it never seemed to ruffle your feathers," Eric said, trying to soothe her.

"Oh, I know all about your flamboyant ways, Eric, but I happen to think Miss Lafferty is a very genteel young woman. Are you ready to leave, Herman?" Ernestine's tone was enough to tell Herman he'd better get up from his chair to escort her and Eric out of the dining room.

Reluctantly, Eric got up to leave with his parents, and Hawk's black eyes watched him leave the room. Warner noticed that Hawk's mood had become very somber since Brett had called his attention to the blond-haired young man across the room. Hawk had all the symptoms of a man who was jealous, Barstow thought, observing the tense look on Hawk's face.

As for Gillian, she was glad to see that the Humbolts had taken their leave. She made her way back toward the kitchen to have a final check with Helen. All the guests had now been served their dinner, and the dining room was clearing out.

When she went to speak to Helen, she counted only two couples left, plus the Barstow party. But when she came out of the kitchen, the dining room was empty— all the guests were gone. Gillian was very disappointed that she'd had no opportunity to speak with Hawk again.

Quickly she ran out of the dining room and into the lobby, in the hope that he would not have left the inn yet. But there was no sign of him. Gillian gave a dejected sigh and strolled out the door for a breath of fresh air. It was a quiet time around the inn, and she could afford to take a couple of minutes for herself.

She stood in the doorway looking toward the wall

122

that surrounded the grounds of the old inn. Only a few young couples were still strolling around the courtyard gardens.

Hawk had bid Warner, Curtis and Harrison good-night and walked out the gate, but he had not yet mounted up on Tache. Something had urged him to go back inside the garden. When he saw Gillian quickly dashing through the front door of the inn, he was glad he'd come back, and he started walking back up the walkway.

When he got within a few feet of her in the darkness, he called out her name. A delighted smile came to her face as she rushed down the steps toward him. "Oh, Hawk, I was afraid you were gone, and I wouldn't even get to say goodbye."

"That is why I lingered, Gillian." He smiled down at her and his hand took hers.

"It was so good to see you tonight, Hawk. You—you looked so handsome!"

He laughed. "It's nice of you to say that, Gillian. I can tell you that I've never seen you so beautiful as you looked tonight. Every man in the room had his eyes on you."

"Did I really look that pretty, Hawk?"

Despite all the sophistication he'd seen her display tonight, she was back to being that sweet little Gillian he'd first known and loved. There was a childlike innocence about her now as she stood there with him.

"Don't you know it, Gillian? Just look in the mirror," he teased her, as his finger playfully brushed a straying wisp of hair away from the side of her face.

"Hawk, can I come to see you and go for a ride on Fuego on my first day off?" she asked him.

123

"You can come to me anytime, you know that. Like I told you the night I brought you here, Gillian, you know where I am if you need me," he told her.

"It—it gives me a good feeling knowing that, Hawk. Well, I guess I'd better say goodnight, or I'll be too late to get myself a snack in the dining room. I've not had anything to eat since this afternoon."

He bent down to give her lips a tender kiss, and then his husky voice urged her, "Then be off with you, Gillian. It's long past time that you ate. I'll be expecting you in a few days." Slowly his hand released hers, and she turned to go back into the inn. When she had gone, Hawk also turned on his heels to leave the courtyard.

In the cover of the thick tropical plants, Eric Humbolt had been observing them. A smirk was on his face as he, too, turned to walk away.

The genteel Miss Lafferty, as his mother called her, was no different than other women he'd conquered, Eric was now convinced. He would have her!

Part Two

Turmoil in Tucson

Chapter Fourteen

It was not difficult for Eric Humbolt to figure out which of the little private patios was the one leading off Gillian's suite, since he knew her room number. He moved through the shrubs and plants until he spotted the patio he figured was Gillian's. But there was no gleam of light visible behind the pulled drapes. Her quarters were in total darkness.

He had thought she would have come directly to her room after the full evening of work she'd just done, and the brief encounter with her gentleman friend out there in the dark courtyard a few moments ago.

He was disappointed that he was not going to get to carry out his plans. It seemed that Gillian Lafferty was an elusive little butterfly where he was concerned.

But Gillian's only delay was getting a small tray of food and a generous glass of milk to take to her suite for a late night snack.

Once she had entered the suite and set her tray on a small table just inside the sitting room, she locked her door. Then she went into the bedroom to make herself comfortable in her nightgown and wrapper before lighting the lamp in her sitting room and enjoying the snack. This new gown was so beautiful, and she didn't want to soil it the first night she wore it.

The lamp in her bedroom was not visible from the patio, so the disgruntled Eric, who was still sitting out there, didn't know that she was in her suite. But he came alive when he saw a gleam of light coming from the sitting room.

A devious grin came to his face and he leaped up from the ground to go to the patio door and knock. It startled Gillian, who had just sat down to take the first bite of her food. She got up and went to the door to see who was knocking at this ungodly hour, but she stopped before she turned the lock, remembering Melba had told her that occasionally one of the guests would have too much to drink and go to the wrong door.

"Never open your outside door, Gillian, until you look out the window to see who it is," she'd cautioned. So Gillian peered through a small opening in the drapes, and there was no question about who it was standing there. The bright moonlight shone on his blond curly head. She wondered if Eric might have had too much to drink—if not, how could he have the audacity to come to her door so late?

After a moment she went back to her chair and, ignoring his repeated knocks, started to eat, for she was famished. The door was secured, so there was no way he could enter the suite. Sooner or later he would surely leave, she kept telling herself.

But then she heard the mighty thud of his boot slamming against the door. That was enough to make her stop eating. She put down the tray, ready to dash out into the hallway should he break down the door. To her great relief, he kicked at the door a couple more times, and then stopped.

After there had been a few moments of silence, Gillian tiptoed to the draped window to peer outside, and she was glad to see that he was no longer there. She went back over to the chair, sat down, and finished her meal. She was looking forward to the comfort of her bed; for the last five hours she had been on her feet, and her legs were aching. She had to admit that she was soon going to be ready for a couple of days of rest from the job.

As she lay in bed drifting off to sleep, Gillian reflected that she was going to feel very tense the next time she encountered the Humbolts and Eric. But she was too tired to linger on those thoughts too long. Soon she was asleep.

It was a nice surprise for Gillian, when she walked into the office the next day at noon, to find Melba there at her desk. She looked up from the papers she had been going over. "Hello, dear. Thought I'd earn a little of my keep around here today. Having you to do all my work is making me lazy," she added with a laugh.

"It isn't going to hurt you to be lazy for a few days, Melba." It suddenly struck Gillian that she might not be doing the accounts as Melba wanted them done. "I've not done something wrong with the ledger, have I, Melba?"

"Oh, no, honey," Melba replied quickly. "I'm going to sit here at the desk and do the receipts while you use your beautiful legs running some errands for me. I have a deposit I need you to take to the bank. Ask for Mr.

Bentworth. And this envelope, I want you to take to my attorney, Sawyer Lewis. This other envelope goes to Denise Lasone at the dress shop. If you take them for me, I figure it'll save me a couple hours of very strenuous effort."

Gillian gladly agreed, and then they sat down to lunch together. When Gillian was preparing to go and do Melba's errands, she hesitated at the desk for a moment. "Melba, I—I hope I am doing a good job for you here. I'm trying, but . . . well, I guess I just want to be sure that I'm not failing you in any way."

"Oh, Gillian, you are doing a grand job! You can't realize how many hours' work you have taken off my back already. Why, since you came I have enjoyed more hours of rest and leisure than I have in years. Now don't you fret your pretty head for a minute about that."

That was all Gillian needed to hear.

That Melba had eyes and ears observing and reporting to her from every corner of the inn was what she credited for having been able to run this inn so successfully and for so long. She knew who checked in and who checked out, as well as which guests dined in the dining room during the evening. If anything out of the ordinary happened in the inn or around the grounds, Melba was informed.

She knew of Eric Humbolt's bold behavior in the dining room last night and his outrageous antics outside Gillian's patio door. Melba's cunning mind had decided that she'd beat young Eric at his own game, but without ruffling the feathers of the older Humbolts,

130

since they were leaving tomorrow. That was why she sent Gillian on errands for the afternoon.

For an hour that afternoon it was Melba who roamed around the lobby, speaking with the guests milling around there. By the time the clock was striking three, Melba was on her way to her room to rest for the afternoon.

Half an hour later Gillian returned to the inn and went to Melba's suite to tell her she had made all the stops. She gave her the envelopes her banker and lawyer had sent back to Melba.

Gillian was in for another surprise when Melba told her she didn't have to work tonight. "Several guests checked out today, and the dining room will be slow tonight. Hardly any local people have made reservations for this evening, so I'm going to let you enjoy being lazy tonight, dear. I'll take over and let you rest—for tomorrow night is going to be the busy night."

Gillian did not question for one minute that Melba's reasons for giving her the evening off were anything but the truth.

Once she got to her room, Gillian found that she was relieved not to have to dress up in a fancy gown tonight. She spent the free time washing her hair and sitting around in a leisurely fashion in her silk wrapper. It was the first time she'd given any thought to the fast pace she'd been going at since she'd arrived at the inn. Once her day started, it lasted for well over ten hours, and she had little time to herself.

This afternoon she took the opportunity to write John and Nancy a long, newsy letter about what she had been doing. The time went by swiftly, and Gillian was not even aware that the sun had gone down and

131

darkness was settling over the courtyard garden just outside her patio.

By now, she would usually have been dressed in one of her fancy gowns and ready to leave her suite. Tonight she did not miss it at all. Tonight she was going to request that her dinner be brought to her room, and she might just spend the rest of the evening in her comfortable silk wrapper. She ordered herself a grand feast for dinner, along with a bottle of wine.

At seven, one of the young waiters from the kitchen wheeled in a cart bearing delectable food, which Gillian intended to enjoy thoroughly.

The meal and the wine were delicious. Only the thought of Eric Humbolt kept her from going out to her patio in the moonlight, to sit and enjoy the lovely spring night. There was a bright full moon shining down on the courtyard tonight, but she wanted no unpleasant encounters, so she stayed in her room.

Since Melba had not had to get herself dressed up for a few nights, she found it rather exciting tonight as she dressed in her finery. She knew that as long as she breathed, she would want to do exactly as she was getting ready to do tonight. It was her life. To sit around idle was like a slow death. Still, it was nice to have Gillian carrying the load she could no longer carry.

Tonight she felt like being the old Melba, and she was looking forward to the next few hours. It annoyed her that she would never last for four hours, but her legs would not allow it.

There was a certain conceit about Melba Jackson.

132

She would have been the last person to deny it. She knew by the time she left her suite that she could still be a most striking figure of a lady, in her dark red gown and with ruby earrings dangling from her ears. On her finger she wore a magnificent ruby ring circled with diamonds. Melba had learned a long time ago that her guests were impressed by the exquisite gems she wore.

Regally, she made her entrance into the lobby a few minutes after six. She had a wonderful hour there with her guests, and all of them seemed to be delighted that she had appeared to greet them.

She realized suddenly that her flamboyant air was not something Gillian could acquire overnight. It took time. It had taken her a lifetime.

And there was something else Melba was to realize, after she had spent an hour in her lobby. She and the Old Pueblo Inn had become a legend in Tucson, and as beautiful and exciting as young Gillian was, she could not replace Melba Jackson, proprietress. Melba could not deny that this gave her an overwhelming feeling of satisfaction. It was what made all these years worthwhile.

Only one party entering the lobby seemed slightly disturbed when she, instead of the lovely Gillian, greeted them. It was the Humbolt party.

Ernestine Humbolt was the first one to inquire about Gillian. "Oh, I was hoping to see her tonight, since this is our last night here. She has been so lovely to us, Melba. I must say that I'm very disappointed," Ernestine said with a pout.

"Well, Ernestine, I felt Gillian needed an evening off after the busy afternoons and nights she's worked. But I agree, she is a lovely person, and that's why I want to keep her here at the inn." As Melba directed her conversation to Eric's mother, she darted a couple of glances in his direction. She was confident that neither of his parents had any inkling of what Eric had done after they'd left the dining room together the previous night.

Melba would have wagered that young Eric would make an early departure this evening from the dining room. In hopes of sparing Gillian a repeat of last night's scene, she told Eric a little white lie. As they were taking their seats in the dining room, Melba remarked that she had moved Gillian into a different, and nicer, suite. "So she has had a rather busy day getting settled in her new quarters." Melba then excused herself to go to greet some new arrivals who were coming through the archway.

Once she had these guests seated, Melba was ready to take one of the back tables and sit down to rest. Helen came out of the kitchen, for everything was running smoothly in there and her services were not needed for a while. Melba urged her to sit down and share a glass of the white wine she was drinking.

"Damnit, Helen—I can't do it! I just can't get through a three- or four-hour evening on my feet any more," she complained dejectedly.

"Well, Melba, don't do it then. I think that little waitress, Lisa, could work into a hostess to give Gillian a break on her off nights. That way she could keep serving the tables, and every now and then stand in for Gillian."

"You might just have come up with a good idea, Helen. That's Lisa waiting on the Humbolts, isn't it?" she asked. She watched the pretty black-haired girl moving efficiently around the table. She was attractive enough to be holding Eric Humbolt's attention.

Helen finished her glass of wine, ready to go back into the kitchen. "Go on to your suite, Melba. There aren't any more guests coming in. I've got to where I can tell when the night's winding down."

"I think I'll do just that. I'll go through the kitchen, so I won't have to stop to talk to anyone else tonight," Melba declared, as she reached for her cane and pushed up from the table.

Helen watched her move through the kitchen and felt a grave concern about her dear friend. She seemed to get more feeble all the time. If something happened to Melba Jackson, Helen wasn't sure what the future would hold for her.

A few years ago, when Melba had offered her a partnership in the inn, it was the best thing that could have happened to her. She was finally able to get rid of her wastrel of a husband and start a new life for herself. It had been a good life she'd had here at the Old Pueblo.

But Helen knew she would not be able to run the inn without Melba. She just was not a smart business woman like her friend. But at least, she thought, she had been able to save her money, now that Kent was not around to run through her wages. Her daughter, Melissa, was married now, so she did not have to support her.

At long last, Helen had only herself to worry about.

Chapter Fifteen

Gillian welcomed the news that the Humbolts had left the inn, for now she would not have to worry about Eric pestering her. But she still had the pendant, having not had the chance to return it to him as she felt she should.

When she finally got to talk to Melba about it, Melba told her not to fret. "Young Eric throws his money around like crazy, but then he's never had to soil his hands to earn a cent of it. Wear it and enjoy it, honey. That's what I'd say."

So Gillian did just that, with the fancy blue gown that night. It was a very busy evening, but the next night, Sunday, was slower, and Gillian was grateful for that.

She was delighted to hear Melba tell her she didn't have to work Monday night. She would have all Monday and until noon on Tuesday to do whatever she wished. Well, she knew exactly what she was going to do with part of that time: she was going to Hawk's to take a ride on that magnificent stallion he'd given her.

All the time she was working in the dining room on Sunday evening, she found herself anticipating the free time and a change of scene. Gillian was already finding that the glamour of wearing a fancy gown every night and roaming around the inn to greet guests was not quite as exciting as it had been those first few nights.

In fact, after one week, she was finding it to be rather predictable. She realized just how much Melba must love this place, to have spent so many years doing the same things day in and day out.

Gillian's duties were all too consuming; they left her little or no time for herself. She was beginning to realize that she wasn't sure just how long she could carry out her role.

When the night was over, and she went into the kitchen to get her usual snack before she went to her room, she was already planning the wonderful day she was going to spend tomorrow. She gave Helen a goodnight wave of her hand as she rushed out of the dining room to go to her room.

When she had finished eating her food, she went to the armoire to get out her dark green divided skirt and cotton tunic to wear tomorrow. When this was done, she decided to go to bed so that she could get up earlier than she usually did. She didn't want to sleep until ten, as had become her habit since she'd come to the inn.

A bright ray of sunshine coming through her window woke Gillian up the next morning. She got up immediately and got dressed, then decided not to have breakfast. She had a carafe of steaming hot coffee sent to her room and drank it quickly, then she left the inn.

In Melba's borrowed gig, she rode through the city

137

streets toward the outskirts of the city. Already the city was alive with people going about their daily routines.

She would have sworn, when she came to the open countryside beyond the city limits, that the air smelled fresher and the gentle breeze seemed cooler.

She knew that Hawk would not be home when she arrived, for he was at work, but he'd told her that his door was never locked. Hawk didn't need to be there for her to take Fuego out of the barn and go for a ride around the countryside.

It seemed that she had been driving only a short time after she left the city when she found herself at Hawk's house. She leaped out of the gig, hitched the reins to the post, and ran through the gate and up the path leading to the front steps. As she expected, the door was not locked, and she walked inside. She saw that everything was in order, and it occurred to her that it must have been his mother, Solange, who had trained him to be this tidy. Oh, she'd love to see her again someday!

Gillian could not remember more pleasant days than those she'd spent up in that mountain cabin talking with Solange. More than once, she'd got herself in trouble with the Fosters because she'd stayed there too long.

She roamed around the rooms, thinking of that first night she'd arrived in Tucson with Hawk, when they'd made such passionate love in that back bedroom. The nightmare she'd had that night had not occurred again.

Leaving the house, she went out to the barn to take that ride on Fuego. A ride would be the tonic she needed right now. The truth was, Gillian found herself in turmoil as to what she truly wanted out of life now. She just could not decide what direction she wanted her life to take. She'd known that she did not wish to remain in Ireland, so she'd left there to come back to the place she'd known as her home. But a week at the Fosters' ranch had found her discontented, and ready to come to Tucson and accept Melba's offer of a job. As much as she loved Nancy and John, she knew that she could not live with them.

And now that she had been at the Old Pueblo Inn for a week, she was feeling that same feeling of discontent settling over her. This disturbed Gillian. She'd been so excited when she'd arrived there, but now she wasn't so sure that the Old Pueblo held the answer for her and what she wanted out of life.

But if she didn't stay there with Melba, then where was she to go to find the happiness she was so desperately seeking? She did not know.

To her relief, all these troubling thoughts left Gillian as she saddled Fuego and the two of them galloped over the open country for over an hour. He seemed to remember her, much to her delight. Lovingly, she patted his silky mane and promised that she was going to come out to see him more often.

When they returned to Hawk's barn, a most pleasant exhaustion washed over her. The spirited Fuego also seemed ready to go into his stall after the fierce run she'd given him.

Hawk's house seemed cool and comfortable after the brisk ride, and she helped herself to a light lunch from Hawk's cupboards. Afterward, she found herself becoming very lazy, so she sank into one of the overstuffed chairs in his parlor, laid back languorously and closed her eyes, to just rest awhile. She had no intention of taking the two-hour nap she took.

When she woke up she heard the clock chiming four, and she was amazed that she'd slept that long. She got up and went to Hawk's kitchen to pour some water in the basin. Splashing the cool water on her face revivified her.

She figured it would be nice to surprise Hawk when he arrived home by having a meal waiting for him. She took a survey of his pantry to see what she might fix, but there was not enough time to prepare a tasty pot of stew or beans.

Still, she could fairly quickly fix some cornbread cakes and a skillet of fried potatoes. Some nice thick slices of ham would go nicely with that. She began to work busily in the kitchen so that it would all be ready when Hawk arrived.

As Hawk rode down the country lane on Tache and spotted a gig in front of his picket fence, he wondered if he dared hope that it was Gillian. She had, after all, promised to come to see him as soon as she had a free day.

A boyish eagerness was exploding within him as he led Tache into the corral and removed the saddle to take it into the barn. He could hardly wait to get into the house to see if it was Gillian waiting for him.

The minute he rushed through the door, he smelled the aroma of food cooking, and hopefully he called out, "Gillian?"

She came to the door with that lovely smile on her face. "Yes, Hawk, it's me. I'm just making myself at home—I hope you don't mind."

His black eyes surveyed her, from the top of her head

140

down to her dainty feet, which were shod in brown leather boots. How different she looked this evening from when he had last seen her, in that fancy silk gown. But with her long auburn hair flowing around her shoulders, and her simple riding clothes, she looked to Hawk just as beautiful as she had been that night. It was not the clothes that made Gillian beautiful or exciting to him.

His eyes gleamed with adoration as he moved across the room toward her. "You know I don't mind. I can't think of a nicer surprise than finding you here, Gillian. I presume you had today off."

"I did, and I came here first thing this morning. I had a lovely ride on Fuego, and I think he liked it, too. Oh, Hawk, he is such a fine animal!"

He smiled as he took her hand in his. "That was why he was meant to be yours, Gillian. Some things are just destined to be, in life. I really believe that, so I knew Fuego was meant for you."

"I believe that, too, Hawk."

His eyes moved slowly over her lovely face as she looked up at him. She was such a tiny little thing—he was always more aware of it when they were standing together as they were now. He was a full foot taller than she was.

He was fighting the urge to take her into his arms, as he yearned to do, when she shrieked, "Oh, Lord, I think our potatoes are burning!"

Hawk gave a deep laugh. "Well, honey, we don't want *that* to happen!" He watched her rush back over to the stove and lift the lid from the cast iron skillet. Everything seemed to be all right, for she said, "Get yourself ready to eat, Hawk. They're almost ready."

"Yes, ma'am—I'll be ready in just a minute." He took some papers he'd brought home with him to look over tonight and deposited them on the chest in his bedroom. Then he washed his hands in the basin before he went back to the kitchen to join Gillian.

By now she had the platter of ham and the cornbread cakes on the table. She was busily scooping the fried potatoes from the skillet as she asked him, "Coffee or milk, Hawk?"

"I'll get it. I know you want coffee, and so do I."

It felt right to Hawk to have her sitting there across the table from him tonight. More and more, Hawk believed that a man needed a woman to feel whole. Now that he was older, he realized what a devoted mother he'd had in Solange. All those years while the two of them lived alone, she must have been a lonely woman with only him for company most of the time. A son was not the same as a husband.

Hawk might have resented Gaston intruding into their life at first, but as he got to know the French Canadian he came to like him very much. Now Solange had a loving husband, even though he'd come along after she was middle aged. But then Solange would be forever young, Hawk figured.

He looked across the table and reflected that Gillian would be like that, with her childlike nature. "This is mighty tasty, Gillian," he told her, with a warm smile on his face.

"I'm glad you think so. It feels good to me to eat some food like this, after my rushed lunches and the snacks I grab after I quit working. Somehow it just isn't the same as this, if you know what I mean, even though the food is wonderful at the inn."

"I think I know what you mean, Gillian. However good the food is, it isn't like a homecooked meal. I know I wouldn't want that every day."

She smiled. "Melba wouldn't be very happy to hear us, for she takes great pride in the food served at her inn."

"She has a right to feel that way, but it's still not like the food cooked in a kitchen at home," he said, rising from the table to pour another coffee for himself and Gillian.

"You looked awfully fancy the other night, Gillian."

"Did I? Well, I enjoy dressing so well, but you know, Hawk, it seemed nice to get into these simple riding clothes this morning."

Hawk was observing her expressive face as she spoke, and he sensed that Gillian was not completely content with her life at the inn. He listened as she talked about how she was finding she had little time for herself, with the way the days as well as the evenings were taken up with the shifts she worked.

"It isn't an easy life, I guess, Gillian. Maybe it isn't the life for you, but then you will only know that as time goes by."

"Well, if I should come to that conclusion, Hawk, I can always leave. But for now, I have to give it a chance after the faith Melba had in me. She needs me, I know that. She isn't a well lady, so I do the things she can no longer do."

Hawk gave her an understanding nod of his head. Taking a sip of coffee, he remarked to Gillian, "Melba Jackson has to be a very wealthy lady. There could come a time when she will be forced to step down completely, and pay someone else to run the inn, whether she likes it or not."

"Oh, Hawk, I think that would kill her."

"We all have to learn to accept what we can't change, Gillian. Melba is not the exception."

"I suppose you are right." Pushing back her chair, she rose from the table, declaring that she had better get busy doing the dishes. Looking out the window, she could see the darkness gathering quickly now. She had to think about getting Hawk's kitchen in order before she prepared to leave.

It had been a most pleasant day for Gillian, having a ride on Fuego, a relaxed nap in Hawk's parlor, and sharing dinner with him this evening. But now, she knew, she should be thinking about getting back to the inn, for she had to start work tomorrow at noon.

Hawk helped her clear the table, and as she washed the dishes he dried them. As Gillian was drying her hands and Hawk was hanging up the dishtowel on the peg, he said, "Surprise me again like you did today, Gillian. I've enjoyed having you back here at my house."

"I promise to do just that, Hawk, but I guess I'd better get started back to the inn now. Melba will be sending the sheriff after me for taking her gig and being gone so long."

Hawk reached out to take her hand and his dark eyes danced adoringly over her face. "I wish you didn't have to go back. If I had my way, you'd just stay right here with me, Gillian."

"Oh, Hawk—I—I can't do that," she stammered. There was a part of her that did want to stay right there in the cozy comfort of Hawk's house. Being there with him all evening had been so relaxed and serene that she did not want to return to the beehive of activity at the inn.

But Hawk knew he was expecting too much to hope that she would be willing to stay with him. He did not try to force the issue. "No, I suppose you can't, Gillian." But he did insist on accompanying her back to the inn, so he went out the kitchen door to go and get Tache out of the barn.

He returned to the house after he'd secured Tache to the back of the gig. They made the trip from Hawk's house to the inn all too quickly, and Hawk leaped out of the gig to untie Tache after he and Gillian had said goodnight.

But when Gillian was standing by the walkway, Hawk boldly took her into his arms and held her close to him. He took a kiss from her honey sweet lips before he released her, and he felt her eager response as his arms enclosed her and his lips met with hers.

He was encouraged by her response to believe that Gillian did care for him, but little did he know that there was a savage passion surging through her, as it did in him.

Chapter Sixteen

Hawk's strong arms holding her, and his sensuous lips kissing her, made Gillian reluctant to break away. But she made herself do it, and walked slowly up the flagstone walkway and into the inn. She lingered only long enough in the lobby to ask the young desk clerk to get the stable attendant to come for the gig and bay, out at the hitching post.

Her casual attire did not exactly fit in with the way the guests were dressed, but there weren't that many in the lobby this evening, and Gillian left hastily to go down the hallway before she encountered anyone she knew.

Entering her suite, she lit the lamps and went directly into the bedroom to get into her nightgown and wrapper. She was more than ready to relieve herself of her boots and slip her feet into her soft little slippers. As she removed her skirt and tunic and was padding around the bedroom in her bare feet, Gillian suddenly realized what was lacking in this suite of rooms. There were no personal touches to make it seem like home. As small and humble as Hawk's cottage was, it was more pleasant to be there than in this expensively furnished suite.

Perhaps, she thought glumly, she had been too impulsive in rushing into the job Melba had offered her. It wasn't as if she was penniless. She would not have had to think about working for a while. A nice little cottage like Hawk's would have been more to her liking than these two rooms. How nice it would be to have her own little kitchen to putter around in. She could grow her own flowers and herbs, as Solange always had. She also thought about Little Bear—to have such a loving companion as him would give her many hours of pleasure and joy, but that would not be possible here.

The luster of the Old Pueblo Inn faded even more during the next three weeks. She could not seek haven at Hawk's cottage, for he had had to leave Tucson to go on an extended inspection tour for the railroad. Still, she did go over a couple of times on her days off to take Fuego out for a ride. But there was something lacking with Hawk not being there to spend time with. Gillian found that she was missing him very much.

There were some things to brighten Gillian's spirits during those three long weeks. She had a letter from her dear friend Nora, back in Ireland, and also a letter from Steve's solicitor informing her of the sale of the property. To Gillian, it seemed a very handsome price he'd gotten for the land and cottage, and she was thrilled to receive the bank draft he sent.

But the long, newsy letter from Canada that Solange

had written was the one she read over and over again. Hawk had written his mother telling her that Gillian was back in Arizona, and Solange was obviously thrilled to hear the news. She wrote that she was looking forward to seeing her when she and Gaston came down from Canada to spend some time in the cabin. They tried to come there for a week or two every six months, and they were already planning a return there in two or three months' time. Gillian found this gave her something to look forward to, and eagerly anticipated seeing her again.

It was very consoling to Gillian to have such a nice sum of money in the bank in Tucson. She knew it was her security, but also it gave her more options in life. The only extravagant thing she did was go on a shopping spree at Denise's Dress Shop, to buy herself some gowns and undergarments. She felt she could afford them, now that she had come into such a substantial sum of money.

Gillian had never owned so many gowns or pairs of slippers as she now did. She felt rich to have five fancy gowns hanging in the armoire, along with five attractive afternoon frocks. It was all very exhilarating to the pretty auburn-haired girl who'd worn muslin gowns all her life.

Melba saw the changes in Gillian, and knew that her employee was not spending her time in the inn when her duties did not require that she be there. There was nothing she could fault the young lady for, because she played her role as hostess to perfection, but something was different. Gillian went out in the mornings, returning to the inn just in time to come to the office at noon. When she finished in the lobby at three in the afternoon, after visiting with the guests, Gillian did not retreat to her suite as she used to, but left the inn for a couple of hours.

Melba had become most curious about what she was doing during those hours away from the inn. When the two of them were together, Gillian was the same sweet little charmer she'd always been. The whole thing left Melba very perplexed.

She did ask, "Are you happy here, Gillian? I'm not working you too hard, am I?"

"Oh, no Melba. I have no complaints at all. I just hope you are satisfied with me," Gillian had responded.

After this unenlightening exchange, Melba was still in the dark. But Gillian realized that Melba sensed something. Melba was one clever lady, and very perceptive, so Gillian realized that she was soon going to have to tell her what she'd been up to.

It had been merely by chance that Gillian had been traveling down a side road near the inn a few days ago. She had spied a wiry little gentleman hammering a sign onto his picket fence announcing that the place was for sale. She was immediately prompted to stop and inquire about it. It was a small, but very attractive, little cottage and she had only to look at it to know that it had been given devoted care by its owner.

She pulled up the gig and called out to the man, "Good afternoon, sir. Is this your cottage?"

"Sure is, young lady. Been my place for many a year," Arthur Dennison told her.

"And you want to sell it?"

"Nope, I don't want to sell it at all, but I got to, since I'm going to live with my son and his wife," he told her.

By now Gillian had got out of the gig and walked up

to the gentleman. He was no taller than she was. "Might I have a look around, then? You have a pretty yard here." She smiled at him.

"You like flowers too, eh?"

"Oh, yes."

"So do I. Guess that's why there's so many here. Well, you just come along with me, miss, and I'll show you my place. Are you looking for a house?"

"I've been thinking about it."

"How long have you and your husband lived here in Tucson?" Dennison asked her as they were walking up the front steps and across the small porch.

"Not long, and I have no husband. I'm a widow." She introduced herself and said that she worked at the Old Pueblo Inn, just around the corner.

In turn he told her his name and ushered her through the front door. Gillian found herself standing in a very pleasant little parlor with a small stone fireplace, and with windows that allowed the sunshine to come in from the south and east. "This is very nice, Mr. Dennison."

"Well, come along, miss, and I'll show you the rest of it." He led her first into one bedroom and then into the second. From there they went into the kitchen, which was actually roomier than the parlor and also had windows on the south wall. Blue and white checked gingham curtains hung at the windows and matched the tablecloth on the square table.

When he saw her looking at them he boasted proudly to her, "My wife made them. Real handy with a needle, she was."

"Well, she's a grand seamstress," Gillian replied.

"She was, yes, ma'am. I lost my little wife a couple of

years back. Have you been a widow long?"

"No, Mr. Dennison—only a few months now."

Gillian finished inspecting the pantry and back porch, and she was enchanted by the house. She saw no reason why she could not have a nice little place like this and still work for Melba. Why, it was so close she could walk to the inn.

There was a vegetable garden out in the small backyard, which was also something she would enjoy, she told herself. After only a moment's consideration, she asked Mr. Dennison what he was asking for the house.

"Well, miss, I'm not one of those wheeling-dealing fellows. I'll hit you with a figure for just the house, and I'll also tell you what I'm asking if you take the house and all the furniture."

He named his price and she calculated that, after receiving the money from Ireland, she could afford it comfortably. And the furnishings were a bonus.

"I think we have ourselves a deal, Mr. Dennison. I want the house and the furniture. May I ask when you will be leaving to go to your son's?"

"At the end of the week, whether I had sold the house or not. I'd have had to leave it for a good friend to handle for me."

They shook hands on their deal, and Gillian promised him she would return tomorrow after she had been to the bank. A pleased Arthur Dennison went out to the gig with her when she left, to remove the sign he'd just put up.

Gillian returned to the inn in the highest of spirits. She decided not to say anything to Melba tonight when they met in the lobby, but she did tell her that Steve's property had been sold. She knew Melba must be curious about the new gown she was wearing, so she confessed that she had gone on a shopping spree at Denise's shop to purchase some new gowns.

"Well, good for you!" For a moment, Gillian's news calmed Melba's curious nature. She figured that this had to be why the young lady had been acting different lately. Perhaps she was spending her spare time on shopping jaunts.

Now that Gillian had been with her for over a month, Melba realized that she would be hard to replace. She wondered whether Gillian's windfall would make her stop working, but decided that was unlikely. And it was just as well. The young waitress Lisa could step in occasionally, but she had a long way to go to be the kind of hostess Gillian was.

At the end of the week, Gillian made her deal with Mr. Dennison, and by the weekend the little cottage was ready for her to move into. Not only was Gillian left with all the furnishings, but he'd left her the pots, pans, and dishes in his cupboards. He left a note saying that he had no use of them now, so she might as well have them.

What a nice man he was, Gillian thought as she sat there in her own kitchen reading the note. She went through each of the bedrooms and found them emptied of his personal belongings, but he had left all the linens and quilts for her.

Unfortunately she did not have long to linger, for she'd left the inn at three and had to be dressed and back in the lobby by six. But tonight she must tell Melba, for tomorrow, on her day off, she would be moving her things into her own house. She was looking forward to getting this evening behind her, so that she could spend tomorrow and Monday settling into her new home. Until noon on Tuesday, she could enjoy the pleasant surroundings of her own house.

She rushed back to the inn for she had less than an hour to bathe and dress. For the first time since she'd been working at the inn, she did not take the time to style her hair as she usually wore it. Instead, she left it to flow loose and free around her shoulders. She wore the second new gown that she'd purchased last week. It was a most flattering shade of daffodil yellow, with a squared neckline and ruffled sleeves to her elbows.

There was no jewelry adorning her ears or neck, and yet she was glowing and radiant as she entered the lobby this evening, with nothing to detract from her own natural beauty. She was the vision of spellbinding simplicity, and Melba was not the only one to be impressed as she watched Gillian strolling across the lobby to meet her. Young Jake Harmon was standing with Melba, for she and his father had been talking for a few minutes. Jake did not hesitate in asking her, "Damn, Miss Melba—who is she?"

Melba gave a soft laugh. "She's my hostess, Jake, and you'll be meeting her in a few minutes, if you behave yourself." She looked over at his father and gave him a wink of her eye. She'd known Sam Harmon and his boy for years, which she felt gave her the liberty to talk as she had to the twenty-two-year-old son.

"She is a beauty, Melba," Sam declared, as he, too, watched the young lady approaching them.

As soon as Gillian joined them, Melba made the introductions. She saw that Jake was entranced by Gillian Lafferty. As always, Gillian was warm and

153

friendly as she greeted the Harmons, who had come into Tucson to meet with some cattlemen and purchase some livestock for their vast ranch, just outside the city.

Melba had not seen the Harmons for months, so she had enjoyed chatting with her old friend, Sam. She was going to see that they got the best table in the dining room, and the best waitress.

Gillian left Melba with the Harmons while she excused herself to go and greet some of the other guests who were coming in for Sunday night at the inn.

But as she moved around the lobby, Gillian's mind was not on her work, and she was hoping that the evening would be a short one, as it usually was on Sunday nights.

It was late in the evening before Gillian found a moment to be alone with Melba, and finally got to tell her about having bought her house. "I'll be able to walk here, Melba. It's just down a little side road very nearby." She added that she would be moving into the house tomorrow, on her day off.

All this was a startling blow to Melba. She sat there absorbing it all, telling herself that Gillian was not saying she would leave the job. She would just be living away from the inn.

But she confessed to Gillian, "I guess you really stunned me, honey. You obviously weren't content to just have a suite and meals here at the inn, eh?"

"No, Melba. It would never have worked for me. I like my own kitchen, and a place to call my own. I like the idea of my own little yard, instead of a courtyard garden that everyone roams around. Can you understand that?"

"I guess so, dear." But the truth was, she didn't. This

inn and its courtyard garden had been the only surroundings Melba Jackson had known for over forty years. She knew no other way of dining than here in the inn's dining room. She had not lived in a house for so long that she wouldn't have known how to exist where there were not people milling around constantly.

Listening to Gillian talk so excitedly about her new house, and seeing the brilliant gleam in her blue eyes, Melba suddenly realized that she would never find anyone who'd feel the same as she felt about her Old Pueblo Inn. It would be asking the impossible. No one would have the fever in their blood, as she had, for this place. It was not even in her partner, Helen, to feel as she did.

Melba was also to realize, as she sat there talking with Gillian, that her whole life had revolved around this inn. And the inn had revolved around her. Without Melba, the inn could not last.

Chapter Seventeen

Gillian could be perceptive, and she realized that her news had not been received by Melba with any enthusiasm. She thought she knew why. Later, when she had gone back into the kitchen and had a moment to talk to Helen, she had been far more thrilled to hear that Gillian had found herself a house nearby.

"Oh, Gillian, I'm happy for you. You'll probably be a lot happier. I have to admit that I miss having a little place to call my own," Helen confessed to her. She went on to say that she had a secret that she would share with Gillian, as long as she kept it to herself.

"I promise, Helen."

"Well, I don't intend to live the rest of my life here. I've been saving my money. I don't want to go to my grave working this kitchen. Melba's been good to me, so I have a lot of paying back to do, but she can't keep running this place much longer, Gillian, and I couldn't do it for her."

"I know, Helen, nor could I," Gillian said. But she had to get back to work. Peering out the kitchen door,

Gillian looked back to tell Helen that they would all be leaving very soon, for there was no one left in the dining room except the Harmons.

But Gillian also saw that Melba was at their table with them, and she wondered if she should stay nearby. She moved back into the kitchen to ask Helen what she should do. "They seem to only be talking, Helen. Do you think I should stay?"

"No, you go on, honey. You've got a busy day tomorrow. I'll tell Melba I told you to leave. You don't want to get yourself mixed up with that Jake Harmon. He's a spoiled rascal. Let Melba handle them. Sam's her friend and he's nice enough, but that son of his is a wild piece of work."

Gillian took Helen's advice and left through the kitchen door. Helen wished she could close down the kitchen and get on to her quarters. She rarely felt irritated with Melba, but tonight she did. The dishes had been cleared away from the table long ago, and yet they lingered there, sipping wine. It was not like Melba, either, to drink so much.

Sunday night looked likely to be a lot longer and later than Helen found it. Vexed, she grumbled to herself that if Melba wanted to have an endless visit with her old friend, Sam, and his son, she could have invited them to her suite.

When Helen's usually calm nature had reached its limits, she no longer cared if she riled Melba by leaving the kitchen. The three of them were having a good laugh about something when she reached the table, and she suspected that they had all had a little too much to drink. She patted Melba on the shoulder and asked, "Melba, is there anything else you need from the kitchen before I leave?"

Melba turned around to look up at her. "Where's Gillian? I was going to ask her to join us."

"She was through for the evening, Melba, so she's gone. I've already let the kitchen help go, too."

"She left?" Melba frowned.

"I told her she could."

"Then you go ahead, Helen. Me and Sam have got a little more talking to do." Melba spoke in a blunt tone, with a disgruntled look on her face.

"I was planning on it, Melba," Helen replied in just as curt a tone. She figured it was time she tested out this partnership she had here. A partner did not take orders; a partner shared the responsibility and the work. Helen figured that she had given more than her fair share of work tonight.

When she got to her room, it felt wonderful to sink down on the edge of her bed and slip out of her shoes. Her feet and legs were aching. Wearily, she struggled to get up after a while, and put on her nightgown. For a while she just lay there in bed so tired she couldn't get off to sleep. There were some things on Helen's mind, even at this late hour. Gillian's telling her about the little house had ignited a desire in Helen to live in her own cozy little cottage again, as she had when she was married to Kent Clayton.

Like Gillian, she had found it exciting and stimulating to work here at the inn, but as time had gone on Helen had found it to be not her life, but a job, and a very demanding one, too. Melba could be a very hard taskmaster, for her beloved inn was her all-consuming passion. But nobody else could ever feel about it as Melba did.

The best thought in Helen's mind, as she finally found her eyes growing heavy with sleep, was that she did not have to return to the kitchen until noon tomorrow.

Long before Helen or Melba were awake, Gillian had all her belongings packed and had summoned the stableboy, Barry, to bring the wagon to the gate. He and Gillian had a full load in the bed of the wagon when they left the inn.

She left a note for Melba at the desk with Tommy, just to say that she had gone. In less than an hour, all her luggage was unloaded and Barry was heading back to the inn in the wagon.

The day went by fast for Gillian as she worked steadily unpacking her belongings. There were chests, but no armoires in either of the bedrooms. However, Mr. Dennison had installed a pole in each room, enclosed with a ruffled panel of bright floral chintz. It was enough space to hang up all her gowns neatly.

One thing she had not thought about was stocking her cupboards with some food. In her anxiety to get moved into her new house she had forgotten all about that.

By the time she realized about the empty pantry, she was too tired to think about dressing to go over to the inn and dine there. Suddenly she remembered the little garden out in the backyard. She knew she had seen some salad ingredients growing there. At least there would be something to fill her empty stomach.

Since Mr. Dennison had moved out so recently, she wondered if he could have left some food behind. On a careful survey of the pantry, she found that she was certainly not going to starve tonight, or have to make do with just radishes, lettuce, and green onions. She found half a slab of bacon and a basket full of potatoes and dried onions.

In a side cupboard in the kitchen, she found a half loaf of bread and a jar of jam. But the crock of coffee she found was the most welcome discovery. Without wasting another moment she fired up the cookstove so that she could brew herself a pot of coffee.

A couple of hours later, Gillian was sitting at her kitchen table enjoying the feast she'd prepared for herself, with the lamplight glowing in her blue and white kitchen. On her blue and white gingham tablecloth was a nice platter of slices of ham and a couple of boiled potatoes. Next to it stood a delicious bowl of crisp lettuce leaves, radishes, and green onions from her very own garden.

It was the most delicious meal she'd had since eating with Hawk at his house. What a surprise she would have for Hawk, she thought, when he returned from his tour of inspection for the railroad.

The rest of the evening was as busy for Gillian as the day had been, but she was enjoying herself as she made a careful survey of the house, jotting down a list of things she should pick up at the store in the morning before she went to work.

She was grateful to Mr. Dennison for all the things he'd left for her. There were a broom and a mop, but she did need oil for the six lamps. But most of the things she had to purchase were food supplies for her pantry.

She was soon very tired, and she prepared to go to bed in the front bedroom. It was much earlier than she usually went to bed, but she wanted to get an early start in the morning. She hoped young Barry didn't forget to come and take her to run her errands, as she'd asked him to do. She had quietly placed some coins in his hand before he left, to help him remember to come for her in the morning.

But Gillian did not have to worry about Barry forgetting to come to her house the next morning. He considered her the nicest and the prettiest lady he'd ever seen. He would have done anything for her, even if she had not been so generous as to pay him for helping her move. No one was as kind to him as Miss Gillian and he appreciated that she took the time to talk with him when he took her out in Miss Melba's buggy from time to time.

So he was there at the appointed time. Gillian came out of the house, greeting him with her usual friendly smile. "I need to go to Nelson's General Store, Barry."

"Yes, ma'am," he replied as he helped her up and urged the horse to move away.

It took her less than an hour to make all her purchases. When they got back Barry helped her carry everything into the house. "Nice place you have here, Miss Gillian," he remarked, as he was taking the supplies into her kitchen.

"Well, thank you, Barry. You'll have to come over some evening and have dinner with me."

"Could I, Miss Gillian? Golly, I'd like that!" His young face lit up with excitement.

"Well, you are invited, Barry. Do you like fried chicken?"

"Oh, yes, ma'am, I sure do!"

"Well, we'll have ourselves some fried chicken the

next night Miss Melba gives me an evening off."

"Do you like fresh-caught fish, Miss Gillian?" he asked.

"I love it, Barry."

"I'll bring you some next time me and my friend, Ross, go fishing. I always catch a good line of them," he boasted.

"Well, I'd be delighted to have a nice mess of fish."

Barry was so elated about being invited to dinner by Gillian that he awkwardly slammed into one of the kitchen chairs as he prepared to leave.

"You—you need me to come and get you at noon, Miss Gillian?"

"No, Barry. I think I will walk over, it's such a lovely day. But I might ask you to bring me home this evening, if it isn't too late for you."

"It won't be too late for me, Miss Gillian. You just send word with one of the kitchen staff when you're ready, and I'll be there at the front entrance for you."

"Well, thank you, Barry. Thank you very much for all the help you've given me in the last two days. I don't know how I'd have managed without you," she told him.

"Glad I could be of service, ma'am. Well, guess I'll be going. See you this evening," he declared, as he dashed out the door.

Gillian watched the young lad drive away and then turned her attention to getting the goods stored away in her pantry. She'd only purchased one impulsive item. It was a parasol in a bright shade of scarlet, like the ones she'd seen the ladies carrying as they strolled around the courtyard gardens in the midafternoon. She'd never owned a parasol before, but she was in the gayest spirits today, so she had given way to the impulse to purchase it.

When she had finished her work, she found she still had time for a leisurely bath before she dressed to go to work. It seemed the perfect day to wear one of the new afternoon frocks she'd purchased last week. The skirt of the gown was black and white striped taffeta, and the bodice was white with a high neck and a lace jabot. The sleeves were full and puffed, buttoning at her wrists with small pearl buttons.

Gillian was very pleased with how she looked when she was all dressed. She pinned a bright red velvet flower on the jabot at the neckline. She could not help thinking how much better she was dressing now than she used to. It was nice to feel that her life was beginning to fall in place, after so many months of turmoil. Now she had a place she could truly call home.

Dressed in her new taffeta gown and carrying the new parasol Gillian left her house, making sure she locked the front door before she went on down the steps.

The bright noonday sun was hot as she started to walk down the road, and she could see why the ladies carried parasols to shield themselves from it as they strolled around the gardens.

As Gillian turned the corner to go up the street that led to the inn, she thought that it was such a short distance that she would not be fearful to walk home, even at a late hour. When she was almost at the gate, she heard a male voice calling out her name. Turning around, she saw that it was Jake Harmon, riding up on his horse.

"Tarnation, Miss Gillian—you're too pretty to be allowed to walk the streets alone," he called, with a devious grin on his face.

She gave a soft laugh. "Oh, come now, Mr. Harmon."

Quickly, he moved his horse up to the hitching post and leaped down before her. "I mean exactly what I said. And please don't call me Mr. Harmon, it makes me feel old. My name's Jake, all right?"

"All right, Jake." She smiled up at him. "So you and your father are still here in Tucson?"

"Leaving tomorrow to get back to the ranch. Now, I'm inviting you to come out to the ranch for a weekend and let us show you some good old Harmon hospitality. You'll never eat a better barbecue than we fix out there."

"Well, thank you, Jake, but I never get a weekend off from the inn."

"Are you serious? Well, I think I'd better have old Sam talk to Melba about that! A lady needs a weekend off, every now and then. She's just working you too hard."

She smiled, and told him he would have to excuse her, for she was due to start work. He tipped his hat and smiled. "We'll see you tonight. Now don't you run off so soon this evening."

Gillian went on through the gate with an amused smile on her face. She could certainly believe what Helen had told her about Jake Harmon. He was a happy-go-lucky rascal and he had a very smooth tongue. It was obvious that he usually got his way. There was something about the way his eyes twinkled when he talked that reminded her very much of Steve Lafferty and those devious green eyes of his.

Melba did not appear at noon, so Gillian took care

164

of all the ledger work alone. There was not as busy a crowd in the lobby as usual, and by two o'clock she had spoken to most of the guests who were sitting in the lobby or coming out of the dining room.

Unsure whether to leave yet, Gillian made her way back to the kitchen to seek out Helen. She told her, "It's a small crowd out there today, Helen. Melba hasn't appeared yet."

"She made it too long a night last night, Gillian." The tone of Helen's voice prompted Gillian to ask her if she had left too early last night.

"Maybe it bothered Melba a little, Gillian, but then I made it worse. I went out there and complained that I was ready to fall on my face, waiting for the three of them to leave. I can't stay in the kitchen that late and still be in here early the next morning. Melba has got to understand that."

"I'm sorry if I caused you a problem with her," Gillian said.

"Oh, no, honey. Don't you worry. Did you get yourself settled in yesterday?"

"Yes, Helen, and I love the little house already," Gillian said candidly. "You will have to come over and visit me."

"I will, Gillian, gladly." Once again, Helen decided to exert her authority as a partner of the inn. "Honey, if you've gone around the lobby and greeted everyone, there is no point you wasting any more time here. Go and enjoy your new home until six."

Gillian could not exactly pinpoint it, but she knew Helen was upset about something, and it had to do with Melba.

As she went back through the lobby she surveyed the

area carefully and saw that the guests lingering there were the same ones she'd already chatted with. Therefore she felt no qualms about doing as Helen suggested and leaving to go home.

She was home before the clock in her parlor was chiming three, and she felt serenity washing over her as she entered.

Now that she was home she wished she did not have to leave again in a few short hours to return to the inn. This only added to her feeling that she would not be working at the inn with Melba for too long a time. Wanting to make the most of her afternoon, she decided to take a brief stroll in her yard.

Seeing the garden and the flowers, she was reminded of Hawk's mother, and how she loved the wonderful things growing there on her mountain. How wonderful it would be to see Solange again.

But the afternoon flew by, and all too soon she had to think about dressing and getting back to the inn. She felt dispirited. Walking down the street in her fancy gown would be more tedious than doing so in an afternoon frock. She did not want to feel conspicuous. Also, she was not looking forward to tonight, for she knew that she was going to be encountering Melba's friends, the Harmons. She didn't want to do anything that would offend them or Melba, but Gillian did not intend to grant Jake Harmon special liberties just because he was Sam Harmon's son!

With this thought, she checked her hair in the mirror and prepared to leave her house.

Chapter Eighteen

As she closed her door behind her and locked it, she noticed Melba's carriage in the street. Barry was there, waiting for her with a broad grin on his face. "Evening, Miss Gillian. Couldn't see you walking to work in that fancy gown."

Laughing, Gillian allowed him to help her up into the seat. "This is awfully nice of you, Barry."

"Ain't much trouble for me, and besides, I figure you're going to be a busy lady tonight, the way buggies are starting to roll in."

A few minutes later, Gillian saw what he was talking about when he let her off by the gate. When she walked into the lobby she recognized the familiar faces of several local people, so she was detained for a while before she could make her way over to where Melba was sitting on one of the settees at the far side of the lobby.

When Gillian finally got over to greet her boss, she did not think Melba's reply was exactly cordial. There was a bluntness in her tone when she looked up at

Gillian and said, "Running a little late, Gillian?"

"I was here at my usual time, Melba. I stopped to talk to several local people over there when I came in. I'm just trying to do my job. I guess you didn't see me come in, Melba," Gillian replied, with a bit of an edge to her own voice.

"I guess I didn't. Well, I heard you got all moved out."

"Yes, I did. I've settled in nicely." Before their conversation could go any further, one of the lady guests called out to Gillian. "Excuse me, Melba, but it seems Mrs. Bradford wishes to speak to me."

When she left Mrs. Bradford, Gillian was slightly relieved to see that Melba had moved off in another direction. She figured that it was just as well. Melba was in a huff tonight, and Gillian didn't know whether it was because she'd moved out or because she'd left early on Sunday night without saying goodnight to her and the Harmons. But Gillian did not feel she had done anything wrong.

After a moment, Gillian noticed, coming through the front door, the man who had brought Hawk to dinner a few weeks ago. For a brief moment she hoped Hawk might be with him again, but she soon saw he wasn't. It was just Mr. Barstow and another middle-aged gentleman.

They walked directly into the dining room, so Gillian didn't have a chance to speak to them. Finally, most people in the lobby either went in to dine or left, so Gillian turned to go into the dining room.

The minute she entered the dining room she spotted Melba, already at the Harmons' table. Somehow, she'd missed them entering the lobby.

As she moved further into the dining room, she heard someone addressing her and saw that it was Warner Barstow. "Nice to see you again, Miss Lafferty. I must tell you how much my guests and I enjoyed our meal here a few weeks ago." Then he introduced her to the gentleman sitting with him.

"Well, I hope you will both enjoy your dinner this evening. It is a pleasure to meet you, Mr. Arnold." And with that, she prepared to move on around the tables.

"I'm sure we will. Oh, by the way, Miss Lafferty, Hawk is due home tomorrow," Warner told her, for he figured she would be pleased to hear the news.

"That's nice to know." She smiled as she began to move away, purposely heading in the opposite direction from where the Harmons and Melba were sitting.

It was obvious to Gillian that she was playing the role of hostess entirely on her own tonight, for Melba was sharing dinner with her friend, Sam.

Finally, Gillian could no longer linger on the east side of the dining room, so she began to move around toward the Harmons. She wished she could just sit down at one of the tables to rest her tired legs. Getting up so early to go on that shopping spree with young Barry was taking its toll on her tonight, for she was used to sleeping later.

She tried to be the gracious hostess Melba would wish her to be when she walked over to their table to greet Sam and Jake Harmon.

The elder Harmon greeted her first, while Jake allowed himself to survey her beautiful face and figure. "You are one mighty fine young lady, Miss Lafferty, and I'm glad we're getting to see you again before we leave tomorrow."

"Well, I'm glad I got to see you too, Mr. Harmon."

"Sit down, Gillian, for a minute. You've put in a busy night," Melba urged her, with a more friendly sound to her voice.

The carefree Jake taunted Melba by saying, "I think you work this little lady too hard."

But having known young Jake since he was knee-high to a grasshopper, Melba flippantly tossed back to him, "Work never hurt anyone, Jake. You might try it sometime."

This brought an explosion of laughter from Sam Harmon. He had always genuinely liked this earthy, gutsy woman. He would probably have been offended at anyone else speaking so bluntly and candidly to his son, even though he knew that Jake was shiftless and lazy.

"I couldn't even ask Miss Gillian to go on a buggy ride with me, with all the shifts she works," Jake told her.

"Well, Jake, don't pout, and the next time you and your father come to town I'll try to have Gillian working less hours," Melba promised lightly.

By the time Gillian had got to their table they had finished eating their meal, but Sam had ordered a bottle of champagne for this their last night at the Old Pueblo. While she had been sitting at the table sipping a small glass of it, several of the diners had left, among them Warner Barstow and his friend. Although she felt a little guilty at not saying goodnight to these guests, Gillian could not deny that she had enjoyed just sitting down for the last fifteen or twenty minutes. She hoped that Barry would be waiting to take her back to the house.

Before Gillian had come to the table, Melba had invited her friends to come to her suite for a nightcap before they went to their rooms. She knew she would not be up as early as Sam always left. Melba had gathered that Helen had been vexed by them lingering so long at the table and delaying her from leaving the kitchen, and she did not want to cause the problem again.

Now that the bottle of champagne was empty, Melba suggested that the three of them go along to her suite. This pleased Sam, for she always kept his favorite whiskey in her liquor cabinet. That suited his taste far better than the champagne he'd drunk tonight.

Knowing it would please Jake, Melba invited Gillian to join them, if she liked, after she had finished in the dining room. Jake got up from the table reluctantly, for he was enjoying being with her at the table, but he could hardly refuse to accompany his father and Melba.

"See you later," he told her, as he finally began to follow his father out of the dining room. Gillian, who had not actually accepted Melba's invitation, merely smiled, nodding her head to Jake as he was leaving the table.

To her delight, a short time after Melba and her friends departed, the last two couples also left. Gillian was finally free to be on her way home. She stopped to talk to Helen for a few brief moments, then headed quickly for the door.

As she had known he would be, Barry was waiting to take her home. Ten minutes later she was inside her quiet, cozy parlor and exhaustedly slipping out of her shoes.

It was into her own kitchen that she went tonight to fix her late-night snack before she headed for bed.

She had no reason to get up early in the morning, she reminded herself with relief as she dimmed the lamps in the kitchen and parlor.

The comfort of her bed was enough to make her drift off to sleep quickly. She slept soundly until a sudden loud noise made her sit up, alert in her bed.

Someone was beating at her door and calling out her name. Swiftly she leaped out of bed to go through the dark bedroom to the parlor. She recognized the voice as that of Jake Harmon. His speech was slurred and he was demanding she let him in.

"Go away, Jake. It's late, and you're drunk," she told him.

"You're right I'm drunk! I'm stinking drunk! You didn't come to say goodbye," he mumbled.

He kept hammering on the wooden door, and Gillian did not know what she would do if the lock didn't hold.

"I'm going to stay here and beat at this door until you open it, Gillian Lafferty!"

By now, Gillian was feeling very desperate. How could she handle Jake? Then out of this desperation a wild idea flashed through her head, and she dared to try it. "Jake, I've a gentleman friend in my bed who has just gone to sleep. If I wake him and tell him what you're doing, you'll regret it! You'd better walk away from here, while you're able."

She stood there holding her breath and hoping her lie would work. At least he'd quit slamming at her door. Then she heard him muttering, "Gillian Lafferty, you're a little red-haired bitch!"

After a moment of silence, Gillian went over to the window to see if he was still standing there at her door. To her delight she saw him stumbling down her two front steps. In a staggering gait, he moved down the path and out the gate. But she remained there at the window until she saw him stumble out to the road in front of her house and start in the direction of the inn.

It took her a while to calm down, after she crawled back into bed, but before long sleep claimed her again.

It had been three long weeks, and Hawk was glad to be arriving back in Tucson. His thoughts had often been on Gillian as he rode the many miles of his inspection over the last weeks. He found himself very eager to see her and know that everything had gone well with her while he was away. He realized that he would always feel this very protective concern for Gillian. It seemed like a natural thing for him to do.

Not even her brief marriage to the handsome Irish sea captain had changed Hawk's feelings. The interlude when he'd tried to convince himself he was in love with Troy's pretty cousin, Shawna, had not swept Gillian out of his thoughts. Her beautiful face had still been the one that haunted his dreams at night.

He and Shawna could not have been completely happy if he'd married her, for he could never have given his all-consuming love to her. Oh, he would have been a good, faithful husband, but sooner or later Shawna would have known the truth.

It was good to get to his house this late afternoon and go to the barn and corral to see Tache and Fuego. He had paid a neighbor's boy to come in to feed and water

173

them, but both of them seemed glad to see him, and vied for his attention. Hawk had to laugh, and one of his huge hands patted Tache while the other stroked the mane of Fuego.

Since the sun was still high in the sky, Hawk walked down the lane to the neighbor's house. Charlie Christy, who was fourteen, was a good boy, and although Hawk didn't need to make the trip over to his house, he wanted to go and say he was back. The half-mile hike was invigorating, for Hawk felt he had been sitting too much as he rode the railroad routes.

An hour later, Hawk was puttering happily around in his own kitchen to fix himself some supper.

Sitting at his table alone, eating his supper, Hawk thought again about Gillian in her fancy gown at the inn. It might be all glittering and exciting to her for a while, but he knew his Gillian. He might just know her better than she knew herself. She was not going to be happy and content there for very long. He remembered the pretty girl who loved to roam around the meadows picking her flowers, and riding her little mare about the countryside. He also recalled her removing her boots to swish her feet in the cool creek waters.

He knew that there would come a time when the Old Pueblo Inn would not allow her free-spirited ways the room they needed to express themselves.

And when that time came, Hawk knew he would be there to offer her the life she really needed.

Chapter Nineteen

The first thing Barstow said, when Hawk arrived at the office the next morning, was that he'd seen that pretty Miss Lafferty last night when he'd taken a friend to the inn to dine.

Warner had only to notice the bright gleam in Hawk's black eyes to see that he was more than fond of that young lady, and he could certainly see why. She was strikingly beautiful. He had watched her last night as she talked graciously to the various guests there in the dining room. She certainly had a touch of class about her that old Melba had never possessed, Warner considered.

The truth was, having known Melba for years and years, he'd found her in a rather strange mood last night. She had seemed to have no time to give to anyone except Sam Harmon. While Warner liked Sam well enough, he had no use for that hell-raising son of his. Jake was a little bastard who needed to be put in his place. Warner had made a point of observing how he acted toward Gillian when she sat down at their table.

However, he said nothing to Hawk about it.

At the end of the day, Warner gave Hawk his wages for this last month. In turn, Hawk counted out enough of it to give back to Warner, to settle the last payment he owed him for the small house and acreage Hawk had acquired over a year ago.

Hawk laughed. "Well, I can now actually consider that house and land mine, Warner. It's bought and paid for."

"Well, Hawk, I never expected you to pay it back this soon," Barstow told him. He knew that the young half-breed spent little money on any luxuries. Most of his salary from the railroad was saved, instead of his squandering it as most young men his age would have done.

Hawk had always seemed to live a very quiet life. Warner knew that there was a part of him that remained on his beloved mountain in Maricopa County. Warner also had no doubt that he would return there someday.

But he could not fault him for that, for it was wonderful for a man to feel that way about a place.

Warner had realized from the first time he'd met the young half-breed that he was no ordinary man. He knew some people found Hawk hard to understand, but somehow, he and Warner had enjoyed a camaraderie from the first. Hawk always seemed willing to talk to him. Some of the men working around the railroad expected Hawk to be quiet and reserved, so they didn't try to get to know him.

When Hawk left the office that evening, he was

feeling very happy. It was extremely satisfying to know that he'd paid his debt to Warner Barstow. He wished that he could have celebrated with Gillian, for he was feeling in such a grand mood, but he knew that she would be working tonight.

As much as he wanted to see her, he did not intend to go to the inn and sit at a table alone, just to see her and talk to her for a moment or two. That was not the kind of contact he wanted with her. He rode Tache toward the house that he now owned, and once he arrived there he began to get busy in his kitchen to prepare himself some supper.

By the time he was washing up the dishes, he had decided that there was nothing to stop him from going to see Gillian when she finished her shift for the evening. He could wait in the lobby for her to come out of the dining room on the way to her suite, and they could take a late-night stroll in the courtyard gardens for a while. So instead of going to his parlor to spend the evening reading, as he usually did, Hawk changed into a clean shirt and brushed his thick, black hair. By nine, he and Tache were riding away from the house on their way to the inn.

When he arrived he knew that it was too early to expect Gillian to be through for the evening, so he roamed around the courtyard aimlessly.

It would have been a great comfort to Gillian to know that Hawk was so close this evening, for it had been a very tense day for her, from the time she'd arrived at noon for the afternoon shift.

It seemed that the desk clerk, Helen, and her helpers had all been the victims of Melba's foul mood, even before Gillian had arrived in the office. Gillian was not to be spared, either, when she encountered her. She witnessed a side of Miss Jackson's personality that she would once have found hard to believe, as the woman had been so kind and generous in the beginning of their association.

Without so much as a hello, Melba informed Gillian that she had already had her lunch and was going to get started on the receipts from the night before. Gillian, sensing she was out of sorts, told her, "I'll do them, Melba. It won't take me long to have a little lunch."

"No, I'll do it!" Melba muttered.

So Gillian said no more, but left the office and went into the kitchen to get a tray of lunch. Helen immediately rushed up to her as she came through the door, and said, "Oh, Gillian, let me warn you. Melba is a holy terror today."

"I know, I've just been in the office. She acts like she's mad at me and the whole world. What's the matter with the woman lately?"

In a low voice Helen said, "I can't talk now, but I'll try to run by your house after you get off this afternoon. Will about four be all right?"

"Yes, I'll be there then," Gillian told her, as she filled a cup with coffee and picked up one of the little meat pies with its thin, delicate crust.

She couldn't say that she enjoyed her lunch, or the coffee, as she sat in the office with a sullen Melba Jackson. When she had finished eating, she pondered what she was supposed to do, since Melba was doing the ledger. There had not been any guests in the lobby when she had come through there just a few minutes ago. Gillian had noticed that the midday crowd had decreased lately, and she wondered if that was what was bothering Melba. Gillian figured that a new tearoom in the city could be pulling some of the lunch crowd away from the inn.

But she had no intention of sitting staring at the walls and waiting for Melba to say something, so she asked, "What would you like me to do, since you're working on the ledger? I can go out to the lobby and roam around, if that's what you'd like, but there are no guests there except those little ladies from suites 110 and 114."

Melba closed the ledger and looked up at Gillian. "Maybe we should talk, Gillian. I get the feeling that your interest in working here has faded lately. You aren't as sociable to my guests, and you've chosen to move out of the inn."

"I would think my moving out would be to your advantage, Melba, for now you can rent my suite to a guest. And I thought I spent a rather busy night being sociable to all the guests here, last night."

"You certainly avoided the Harmons like the plague. They are not only dear friends of mine, but they spend very extravagantly when they are at the inn. They stay here many times during the year."

So *that* was what this was all about, Gillian thought.

"I did not think you would have wished me to neglect the rest of the people here, even so."

"But you didn't even come to my suite after I'd invited you, Gillian. I felt that was an insult." Melba's eyes flashed angrily as she spoke.

"It was not meant as an insult, Melba. I was tired when the evening was over. I've been working to get moved, and I was up early to buy supplies for the house that morning before I came to work. I didn't want a

179

nightcap after I was through in the dining room; I wanted the comfort of my home and bed."

"And the comfort of the man in your bed?" Melba smirked.

Now it was Gillian who was angry, and she snapped at the older woman, "What in the hell are you talking about?"

"Come on, Gillian. Jake came back here and told us you threatened him that if he didn't leave, the man in your bed would beat him up."

Gillian gave a roar of laughter. "Oh, what a poor excuse for a man he is! There *was* no man in my bed. I lied to him because I had no intention of inviting him into my house. I'd been asleep for an hour and besides, he was so drunk he was slurring his words, Melba. You can believe me or not, as you choose."

"Most young ladies would be fawning over the likes of Jake Harmon, and he has taken a shine to you."

"Well, I didn't take a shine, as you call it, to him. But I think we had better come to an understanding right now, Melba. If I *had* had a man in my bed last night, that would have been my business. The Old Pueblo Inn doesn't own my personal time. I'll put a hard eight hours in, here at the inn, but my time away from here is to do as I wish. That's all I can give, and I'll wager that's all you'll find anyone else to give."

Gillian turned sharply around to go to the door. Before she opened it, she looked back at Melba sitting at the desk, and her blue eyes were fired with anger. "I'm going to the lobby, Melba, in the hope of earning my wages!"

Long after she had finished the ledger, Melba sat at her desk staring at the wall. It had been a most frustrating few days for her, and it had not helped to know that Sam and his son had left the inn with a foul taste in their mouths.

From the moment Jake had arrived and spotted the beautiful Gillian, he had wanted to add her to his list of conquests. It certainly had not sat well with old Sam when his son had returned to the inn to tell him that she was too busy with another man to open her door to him. This just wasn't done to the Harmons.

Melba was wondering if they'd even come back to the inn when they made their next trip into Tucson. It was one time that her magic touch had not worked. Nothing she could say had seemed to soothe Sam's ruffled feathers when he marched out of her suite late last night.

As she'd expected, they were checked out by the time she got to her office this morning, even though she was there an hour earlier than usual.

The last thing she had needed to hear when she first came in was Helen's whining that she might have to leave for a few days to go to Maricopa County because her sister, Nancy, was ailing. Melba had not been too sympathetic, and had flatly informed her that her first responsibility was here at the inn. Helen had been so distraught that she'd turned away from Melba in tears. Melba had marched out of the kitchen, but she had not failed to notice the disapproving looks she'd received from the kitchen help, who were so loyal to Helen Clayton.

When she did finally leave her office, it was not pleasant to see her lobby so quiet at two in the afternoon. She spotted Gillian over in the alcove, talking to some of the ladies gathered there, as she

181

moved on slowly through the lobby.

Melba was dejected as she went to her suite this afternoon. She had managed to offend so many people, it seemed, in the last twenty-four hours. She was beginning to wonder if she was fighting a losing battle to keep this old landmark open and running.

Whether it suited Melba Jackson or not, Gillian considered it a waste of her time to just linger in the almost empty lobby, as she had been doing for the last hour. As the clock was striking three she was walking toward her little house. The first thing she did once she was home was to start the fire in her cookstove so that she would have some coffee to serve to Helen when she came by around four. Once that was done, she removed her slippers to pad around her house in her stockinged feet, as she loved to do.

By the time Helen arrived, Gillian had a pot of coffee steaming on the stove and a tray of little spice cakes baked and ready to serve her.

Helen had hardly entered the front door before she started praising the house. "Oh, Gillian, it's so nice! It makes me want to have a little house again."

Gillian took her on a grand tour of the house, and the backyard with its little vegetable garden. It was only when the two of them were back in Gillian's parlor, having a cup of coffee and munching on the spice cakes, that Helen told her about her encounter with Melba this morning.

The news that Nancy Foster was ill was very disturbing to Gillian. That dear lady had been like a mother to her. Helen was obviously very upset, too.

"Oh, I don't know, Gillian, I—I thought the inn was the answer for me, but lately I've been wondering about it. It just seems to take all of me, and there is never time for anything else in my life. Melba expects us to feel that way, I've decided," Helen declared to Gillian.

"Well, I told her today that it would not be that way with me. But I think I have a solution for both of us, Helen. It will be our little secret until I decide to tell Melba. After all, I owe the Fosters so much. They took care of me when I needed help, so it is only right that I go to take care of Mother Foster, if she needs me."

"Oh, Gillian, how sweet and kind you are!"

"But could I get you to come here to my house and look after it, while I'm gone to Maricopa County, Helen? Would you do that? I'd hate to think it was neglected, for I love it so."

"Gillian, it would be a joy for me to live here and look after the place while you're gone," Helen said, with a radiant glow on her face at the thought of spending time here instead of at the inn.

"Then we have ourselves a deal, Helen." Gillian smiled. "I'll start making arrangements tomorrow."

"But Gillian, do you know that Melba will be so angry that you will probably no longer have a job at the inn?" Helen asked.

"It doesn't matter to me, Helen. Steve left me some money, so I won't starve. My little house is bought and paid for. Don't you fret about that," Gillian assured her.

It was a very happy Helen Clayton who returned to the inn late that afternoon. Gillian realized that she would barely have time now for a bath and to get dressed so that she could return to work for the evening. More than ever, she realized now that this was not how she wanted to spend the rest of her life.

That evening, she went around thinking that there was no luster left. To wear a fancy gown every night did not excite her anymore. The thrill of it was over.

She was just glad that the evening went by without any problems, and that Melba did not appear. By ten she was ready to leave the dining room, and she went back into the kitchen to tell Helen goodnight. She could see that Helen was in much better spirits this evening than she had been when she'd come to her house this afternoon. This made Gillian very happy!

She was feeling in a much more lighthearted mood by the time she was leaving the lobby for the front entrance. It did not surprise her to spy the gig, and young Barry sitting there waiting for her to come out.

But it was a wonderful surprise for Gillian to see the tall, dark, handsome figure of Hawk standing there in the shadows. She rushed to him with an eagerness that thrilled him. "Oh, Hawk, I'm so happy to see you!"

She meant it, Hawk knew, and it thrilled him.

Chapter Twenty

Gillian told Barry his services were not needed tonight, for Hawk was going to see her safely home. The boy looked crestfallen, but cheered up when she thanked him warmly. Hawk and Gillian both laughed as she sat in his saddle in that fancy gown. She could hardly sit astride the saddle, so rode sidesaddle, with Hawk's strong arms holding her securely from behind.

He had to admit that he had been surprised to hear that Gillian had purchased herself a house so soon, but it only confirmed to him that the allure of the inn would fade after a while.

When they reached her house he helped her down from Tache, and her hand clutched his as she led him up the pathway to the front door. "There's a vegetable garden in the backyard, Hawk," she told him.

He heard the enthusiasm in her soft voice and knew she was very happy about this little cottage. When she had guided him through the front door and the lamp was lit, he could see why this would suit Gillian much more than a suite at the inn. She showed him through the house as she had done with Helen this afternoon.

She offered to make some coffee, but Hawk refused it. "I just wanted to see you, Gillian, and let you know I was back in Tucson. I've—I've thought about you a lot while I've been away."

"And I missed you, Hawk," she declared with that air of candor that had always endeared her to Hawk.

A broad grin came to his face. "Well, I'm glad you did. I want you to miss me when I'm away from you."

"I'm especially glad that you came to the inn tonight, for it gives me the chance to tell you that I'm going to have to leave Tucson for a while. I'll be going in a day or two, to the Fosters."

"Why are you doing that, Gillian? You've just bought this house, and what about your job at the inn?" He was puzzled.

"I feel I must, because Mother Foster isn't well. Helen had a letter from Mr. Foster yesterday. We talked this afternoon, and Helen's going to look after my house while I go see what I can do for Mother Foster. After all, you know what they did for me when I needed help."

"I know, Gillian. So I understand why you feel you have to go to them."

"I've not told Melba yet, and I expect she's not going to take it too well. But then she hasn't been in too good a mood, lately," Gillian told Hawk. She confessed to him that right now the Fosters were much more important to her than her job.

Hawk would have expected her to feel this way, or she would not have been the lady he loved so much. He only wished that he could travel back to Maricopa County with her when she went.

He knew that there was no point in asking her how long she would be gone, for she couldn't know yet. This news was not what he'd expected to hear, anymore than the news that Gillian had bought herself a house.

"Well, since you could be gone awhile, you'll have to come over before you leave so we can take Tache and Fuego out for a ride. I really want to see you before you leave, Gillian," he told her, his hand reaching out to take hers.

"And I will certainly want to see you too, Hawk. Yes, I will come over, when I know exactly when I'll be leaving."

Hawk was reluctant to go, even though he knew it was late and he needed to be riding back home. She was probably more than ready to retire after working this evening at the inn.

Slowly, he forced himself to rise from the chair with his hand still holding hers. "I'd better go, Gillian. You need to get to bed, and so do I, or I'll never make it to the office in the morning."

Gillian stood up from the chair she was sitting in. She knew that Hawk was going to kiss her even before his head bent down to let his lips meet with hers. She saw it in his black eyes, and she also saw a fire of passion flaming there.

Her arms went up to circle his neck as his firm, muscled arm closed around her and pulled her closer to him. With his sensuous lips searing hers, Gillian forgot about all the things that had troubled her after she'd made love with Hawk at his house. The fact that he had Apache blood in his veins didn't matter to her right now. He was a handsome man who was stirring wild, savage sensations within her, and she felt her own passion mounting as his lips lingered on hers.

She gasped breathlessly when he finally released her. He, too, gave a husky gasp as he murmured, "Oh, Gillian, you must know how much I love you. I don't intend to stand by and let any other man ever take you away from me again."

"Oh, Hawk—there's no other man. There never will be."

She felt the fierce pounding of his heart in his broad chest, and liquid fire seemed to be consuming her as he bent down to kiss her again. This time, both Gillian and Hawk knew that kisses would not satisfy the hunger washing over them.

There was no doubt in Hawk's mind that Gillian wanted him to make love to her as much as he wanted to. He let his arms sweep her up and he took her into her bedroom.

Sitting down on the bed with her on his lap, his long, slender fingers worked impatiently at the numerous buttons at the back of her silk gown. Gillian was soon to realize that her gown had been slipped down, for Hawk's lips were working with tantalizing effect on the sensitive tip of her breast. She gave a moan of pleasure, which was enough to urge Hawk to free her of all her clothing and then undress himself.

Flinging the coverlet away from the bed, he came back to her, letting himself entwine with her. Their bodies moved and swayed as though they were fused together. The ecstasy heightened, sweeping them to the loftiest heights.

Gillian let herself soar, for she wanted to be with Hawk completely. She did not care if she never came down from that peak of rapture she was experiencing.

So violent was the quaking of their bodies that Gillian thought she might faint. She gave a last, deep shudder. Hawk, similarly enraptured, finally sank down by her side, and his hand went to Gillian's face to brush away the thick hair draped over it.

Tenderly he whispered in her ear, "I'll never love a woman as I have you tonight, Gillian." He felt her snuggle in the circle of his arms.

A moment later, he heard her softly purr, "I love you, Hawk." He knew she was falling into an exhausted sleep, so he slipped out of bed to go back into the parlor and dim the lamp that had been left burning there. Then he crawled back into bed beside her, for he had no desire to get dressed and ride back to his house. Right now he, too, was ready for sleep.

He slept soundly until almost six the next morning, then leaped out of bed to get dressed. After he had written Gillian a note and left it on the nightstand, he dashed out of the house, feeling a pang of guilt about poor Tache. For the first and only time, he'd neglected his horse. The animal was still outside the house, looking rather dejected, but he perked up at the sight of his master. Hawk was thankful that there seemed to be no one up yet in the street where Gillian lived; her neighbors might question a fellow like him leaving at this early hour.

He had time to get back home, brew and drink a pot of coffee, and get himself shaved and dressed before saddling Fuego to ride to the office. He figured that Tache deserved the comfort of the stall this morning.

Warner would never have guessed that Hawk had lost sleep last night, for he seemed very alert and in fine spirits this morning.

The same could be said for Gillian. When she awoke she gave a lazy stretch there in her bed, and looked over to the pillow where Hawk's head had lain beside her last night. A slow smile creased her face.

Finding herself lying in bed nude was enough to make her recall how fervently Hawk had made love to her last night. When she got up and slipped into her wrapper, so that she could go into her kitchen to start a fire and make a pot of coffee, she was feeling in a very grand mood. The thought of facing Melba and telling her that she was going to be leaving Tucson did not bother her this morning.

Gillian enjoyed a leisurely bath and got dressed for work. She planned, when she left the inn this afternoon, to have Barry take her to make her arrangements to travel to Rock Springs. It occurred to her that it would probably be best if she didn't say anything to Melba until this evening, for she didn't know how her boss would react. She might just dismiss her on the spot, and if she did that, young Barry would not be taking her anywhere. A few hours' delay in informing Melba would not matter anyway, she concluded.

When she arrived at the inn and went into the office to find Melba not there, Gillian had to confess that she was glad that she was alone to have her lunch and bring the ledger up to date. When she had finished she left the office to go to the kitchen and seek out Helen, so she could tell her that she wasn't going to say anything to Melba until this evening. "I want Barry to take me to make my travel plans before I say anything," Gillian confided to Helen.

"I can't blame you for that, because she's going to be

190

madder than a wet hen. I can assure you of that!"

Gillian smiled. "I don't care, Helen! I really don't."

Helen gave her an affectionate pat on the shoulder. "You're a nice person, Gillian. No wonder Nancy and John love you so, and I love you too, for what you're willing to do for my sister. You can be sure that little house of yours will be taken care of while you're gone. Melba probably won't like that either, but she can't complain about it as long as I'm here for my shifts."

"Well, Helen, I don't think it would bother most people, but I've come to a conclusion about Melba: I think she feels that the people working here have to exist for the place. They must have nothing else in their lives but the Old Pueblo Inn."

Helen smiled and nodded her head. Gillian was far quicker than she had been, for it had taken her a year to see the light about Melba Jackson. She was not exactly the generous lady Helen had thought her to be, for the first months she had worked here. The title of partner that Melba had offered to her had not ended up being that at all. Poor Helen had not realized it until she had been here over six months. But the money she'd received for running the dining room had been so much more than Helen had ever earned before that she did not openly question anything.

But in the last few months, Helen had slowly but surely come to realize how demanding and overbearing Melba could be with the people working for her. Helen had little or no time to spend with her old friends or even her daughter.

She had to say that she admired Gillian's spunk, to be willing to stand up to Melba as she would be doing this evening.

Conscientiously, Gillian made a point of greeting and talking to the few guests who were in the lobby, but there just were not that many people there this afternoon.

Wondering why there was still no sign of Melba, she prepared to leave. It seemed ridiculous to linger at the inn when there was absolutely nothing to do.

When she and Barry were driving away from the inn, he told her that he had been taking Miss Melba around the city today. "She wanted to go to this new tearoom, to check them out, she told me."

"And what did she find out, Barry?"

"They had a big crowd of people there, so I don't think she was too happy by the time I brought her back to the inn, Miss Gillian."

"No, I guess she wouldn't be." Gillian could well imagine the mood she would be facing this evening at six.

It took Gillian less than an hour to make her arrangements to go to Rock Springs, and then she had Barry take her back to her house. She walked in through her front door just as the clock in her parlor was chiming four.

She realized again how little time one had for oneself when working for Melba Jackson. In two hours she was expected to be back at the inn to put in an evening's work.

She found herself rushing around her house just to be able to be ready by that appointed hour of six. It was insanity to live this way, and she didn't want to do it any more. She had a bath and laid her gown out on the bed, along with her undergarments and slippers. Then she dressed in her wrapper to go into the kitchen and have a glass of milk and some spice cakes, for by then there was certainly not enough time to cook a proper meal.

Now that she had her own little house, she had anticipated doing more cooking in her kitchen than she'd been able to. This lifestyle really was impossible. She had just been fooling herself about it, except when she had the entire day off from the inn. There was another thing that had not come to pass as Melba had promised: that she could have two days off together after working five straight days.

When she had dressed in her gown and her hair was fashioned, she glanced out the window to see if young Barry was there yet. There was no sign of him, so she picked up her black velvet reticule and started out the front door. It was getting too close to six for her to wait for him, so she would just have to walk. This wasn't like Barry, for he was usually as faithful as an old hound dog.

The sun was still up, so she didn't mind the short walk, but she was curious about why he'd not shown up.

When she had reached the inn and was just about to go through the gate, she heard Barry's voice calling to her anxiously. She stopped to look for him, and spied him rushing out from behind the trunk of a huge tree. "Miss Gillian—I didn't mean to let you down this evening, but Miss Melba ordered me to not take her buggy out any more. After I got back from taking you out this afternoon, she called me into the office and gave me orders to get her permission before I left these grounds."

Gillian felt sorry for Barry, for she could see that he

was very upset. She gave him a pat on the shoulder and assured him that he must do as Miss Melba ordered him, and not worry. Her next words surprised even her. "I won't be needing you to come for me anyway, Barry. I'm going to leave the inn tonight. I won't be working here any longer—but that doesn't mean you can't come to see me when you wish. I am going to be out of town for awhile, but I'll be back."

"Oh—well, I will come to see you, Miss Gillian," he promised her as they parted.

As Gillian walked up to the entranceway, her mind was made up. What Barry had told her had made her decision for her. She was going to tell Melba she was quitting her job, instead of asking for some time off to go to Rock Springs.

She spotted Melba immediately across the room. She had a smug smile on her face, and was obviously gloating that Gillian had had to walk to the inn, since Barry's services had been denied her.

Well, thought Gillian smugly, before this evening was over, *she* would be the one gloating!

194

Chapter Twenty-one

Several of the guests in the lobby knew the beautiful Gillian Lafferty by now, and they found her warm and friendly nature always a pleasure when they came here to dine in the evening. So tonight, she stopped to talk to a number of ladies and gentlemen. There was no reason why she should rush over to Melba's side. Let her do her socializing alone, Gillian thought.

As she slowly moved closer to where Melba sat holding court, Gillian was thinking that this would be her last night in the role as the hostess here. For that reason, she tried to be most gracious and charming to everyone she talked to.

It gave her some satisfaction to know that, when she was gone from the inn, there would be many guests who'd be asking Melba where she was, when she was not here in the lobby in the evenings.

When she finally walked up to Melba, after some of the guests were beginning to leave the lobby to go into the dining room to their tables, Melba looked up at her with a sly grin on her face. "Well, Gillian, you're quite the little charmer tonight."

"Why, thank you, Melba. It's nice of you to say so." Gillian was not going to react to such a comment. It was best to be as friendly as possible. Since most of the guests were now exiting the lobby, Gillian asked Melba, "Shall we go into the dining room?"

"I suppose so."

Gillian had been tempted to take this quiet moment to tell her of her plans, but decided against it. She was glad later that she'd postponed telling Melba.

All the guests had arrived about the same time that evening, and as sometimes happened, it seemed they were all going to leave about the same time, too. There were no late diners tonight, as there sometimes were.

Gillian had caught sight of a nervous Helen Clayton peering out of the kitchen door a couple of times. She knew exactly what Helen was concerned about.

By ten, Gillian and Melba were sitting at one of the tables alone, and Gillian knew that the moment had arrived. But before she could say anything to Melba about her decision, Melba spoke out about something that was on her mind.

"Gillian, I don't mince words about things. It was your decision to move away from the inn, but I can't allow Barry to be constantly trotting after you. I told him this afternoon he could no longer do it. When you were residing here at the inn, the use of my buggy was yours, but things are different now."

"Well, that's all right, Melba. I'll have no need of Barry's help after tonight. You see, I must leave Tucson to go to Rock Springs. Mother Foster is ill, and I'm going there to help them out, as they helped me when I needed them. I was planning on telling you this evening that I think it's best that I quit my job, because I don't know how long I'll be gone."

"What?" Melba cried, a stunned look on her face.

"I'm quitting, Melba. I think we both know that it was not going to last too much longer, even if I'd not received word about Mother Foster."

A snarl came to Melba's face, and she hissed, "Why, you ungrateful bitch!"

"Oh, ungrateful bitch, am I? I have worked long and hard for you, Melba, but you expect someone to exist for this place, to eat, breathe, and sleep in it, and I'm not going to do it!" Gillian rose from the table, for she was not going to sit there and take a tongue-lashing from this woman.

"I laid out a lot of money on two fancy gowns for you, but obviously you've forgotten that."

"Well, I shall return them to you, Melba, or you can keep my salary for this week's work. Let's say that I owe you nothing, and you owe me nothing."

"Well, Gillian Lafferty, your gall amazes me! Your salary would not cover the price of those two gowns."

"I beg to differ with you, Melba. I have bought myself two gowns very like the ones you got for me, and from the same place, so I know exactly what you paid for them."

Melba had never met her match like this, and she was rattled. "You—you were obviously able to buy yourself some fancy things, then, from your salary. I didn't ask you to work for nothing."

"No, Melba—you are wrong again. I could never have bought all the things I got at Denise's on the salary I make here. It was the sale of Steve's house in Ireland that enabled me to buy my house and get myself some clothes."

"So *that's* what this is all about. You've come into some money, so you don't need me or the inn anymore," Melba snapped.

Gillian suddenly felt very sorry for this lady sitting at the table, who was looking up at her with so much anger in her face.

"No, Melba, it's not that at all. I don't think I could make you understand, so I won't try. If my salary won't cover the price of those two gowns, I will pay you the difference. I wish you and the Old Pueblo Inn well, Melba, but I won't be back tomorrow."

Gillian's blue eyes contemplated Melba's face with great intensity. Gillian could not know their effect on Melba as she slowly left the table and the dining room. Her parting remark to Melba was, "I want more in my life than the Old Pueblo Inn."

Helen knew that Gillian had left the dining room, but she dared not go out to Melba. The old woman sat alone, looking very downcast and desolate.

Gillian did not mind that she had to walk to her house in the darkness. She suddenly felt so free, knowing that she did not have to go back there tomorrow. The whole day was hers to do whatever she wished. That was a glorious feeling!

By the time she entered the house and locked the door behind her, she felt as if she had had a heavy burden lifted away from her. She knew that she owed Melba Jackson nothing, and it did not matter to her that she would receive no salary for her last six days' work at the inn.

Well, tomorrow was hers, and she knew who she wished to spend it with. She knew that Hawk would be thrilled to see her at his house when he got home from the office tomorrow afternoon.

So that this last day before she left Tucson would be free for her to spend with Hawk, she packed the things she wanted to take with her to Rock Springs. She packed simple clothing—her divided riding skirts and tunics, and a few of her old muslin frocks. The fancy gowns and the afternoon frocks had no place out there on the Fosters' ranch.

By the time she was ready to go to bed, she was eager for tomorrow. Gillian sensed that her life was going to take a new direction now. She did not know where it was going to lead her, but she was ready to go.

Across the miles that separated them tonight, Hawk's and Gillian's spirits were entwined as their bodies had been last night in Gillian's bed. She was just as much on his mind tonight, after he left the office, as he was on hers after her packing was done.

Feeling in such a frivolous mood, and not caring that it was so late, Gillian kindled up her cookstove to scramble herself a skillet of eggs. She ate them with relish, along with a slice of bread.

Sleep, when it came, was sweet for Gillian that night!

But sleep was not sweet for Melba, for Gillian Lafferty had made her face a stark reality she had refused to face for years now. She had no husband to warm her bed at night, and she had no children to comfort her in these older years of her life. The truth was, she had no dear, close friends. Oh, she knew a lot of people, but that didn't make them friends. And she'd never known what it was like to live in a house of her own. The only home she'd ever known was the Old Pueblo Inn.

Now she was too old to have any of these things, she told herself as she sat in her suite tonight. The person Melba could most nearly call her friend was Helen Clayton, but she had sensed lately that Helen was not as enamored of the inn as she was, and it had caused some tension between them. Perhaps it was as Gillian had told her tonight: no one else could exist only for the inn. Perhaps Melba was the only one who could feel this intensity.

For the longest time after she went to bed that night, Melba lay there staring at the ceiling and thinking. Perhaps the best thing she could do for the inn and herself was to torch this place, and let it all go up in flames. That would solve all her problems.

Helen Clayton's sleep did not come too quickly tonight, either. She had known that Gillian had had her talk with Melba, and she had been curious about how it had gone. But she had not known about Gillian's impulsive decision to quit. She was to hear that from an enraged Melba before she marched out of the dining room that evening. Helen let her fume and fuss, but said nothing. She dared not tell her that she was going to be staying at Gillian's while she was away. It would be best to wait a day or two, Helen considered.

*   *   *

The next morning, at a very early hour, Gillian was awakened by knocking at her door. Sleepy-eyed, she opened the door to see Helen standing there. "I apologize, honey. I know I woke you up, but I had to get here early if I wanted to talk to you before I had to get to the kitchen," Helen told her.

"Oh, that's all right. Come on in, Helen. Is something wrong?" Gillian brought her into the parlor as she tied the belt of her wrapper.

"I guess that's what I came to ask you. Melba said you've quit the inn, and I wanted to hear your side of the story. Lord, she was in a frenzy, Gillian."

"I know, and I hadn't exactly planned it that way, as you know. But I'm glad it happened as it did." Gillian told her about the little episode with Barry. "I wouldn't have thought Melba capable of those kinds of petty antics. I guess I just decided there and then that I didn't need Melba, or her inn, if she was going to act like some kind of tyrant."

Helen shook her head in disbelief and sighed. "Mercy, how childish that was of her! I know Barry didn't mind the short trip over here for you, and it was certainly no inconvenience to Melba."

"No, it was a matter of showing me that she was the boss, and any favors I got came from her. She was taking my privileges away from me. It was just as simple as that, Helen."

"Poor Melba—she is her own worst enemy, I fear. She's losing one of her best desk clerks today, too. He told me he was quitting yesterday afternoon. Tommy is a real nice kid."

"He certainly is. I like Tommy, and I'm sorry he's going. But this is just an inn, Helen, not a kingdom.

Melba can't rule people's personal lives."

Gillian offered to get a pot of coffee brewing, but Helen told her she had no time for any coffee. "You go ahead and get it started for yourself, though."

"I think I will. Come on into the kitchen, and we can talk while I get the fire started," Gillian suggested.

Helen sat at the table as Gillian worked around the cookstove. She assured Gillian that she'd come over the day after she left for Rock Springs. "I may tell Melba, and I may not. Actually, it isn't any of her business, as long as I'm doing my hours at the inn. If I tell her she'll probably have another fit of temper. She'll have one today when she finds out about Tommy. I pity him when he tells her."

Gillian laughed ruefully. "I know what you mean."

Helen realized she should get up from the chair and prepare to leave Gillian's house. Somehow, she loathed the thought of going to the inn and its kitchen today. She was seriously thinking, as she walked out of the gate and down the road, that her days at the inn might also be numbered.

Gillian looked out her kitchen window to watch Helen going down the road, and her heart went out to her. She, too, was finding the inn an unhappy place to work.

Gillian had also concluded that Melba was a frightened lady. Perhaps it was because her health was failing, or that business had fallen off drastically. But perhaps it was because she had given her whole life to something that could never enfold her lovingly in its arms and comfort her. It was nothing more than a structure of stone and timbers.

Chapter Twenty-two

It was strange but wonderful for Gillian not to have to rush around or look at the clock to see what time it was. Unhurriedly she strolled around her house to see if there was anything else she wanted to pack in her luggage before she started to dress.

It was not until she was sitting at her dressing table fixing her hair that she realized she couldn't have young Barry take her to Hawk's house. She burst out laughing about her dilemma. Well, there was nothing to keep her from walking to the railroad office, where Hawk would be working.

As she left her house, she reminded herself that it would be nice to take the stroll from her house to the office, for it was a delightful day.

It took her about a half hour to walk to Hawk's office, and it was an unexpected and pleasant surprise for him to look up and see her lovely face smiling at him as she walked through the door. He leaped up, declaring, "Gillian! What did I do to deserve this?"

He was glad that Warner Barstow had gone out of

the office to have a talk with one of the men, because he didn't have to hesitate to take her in his arms and kiss her.

She told him what had taken place since she'd last seen him. He was glad that she had quit the inn. Hawk had always known that Melba could be an overbearing, demanding woman, and that Gillian would not tolerate it too long.

After they'd talked for a minute, she told him how wonderfully free she felt to have the whole day and night to do whatever she wished.

Hawk smiled. "I'm glad for you, Gillian. I'll tell you what: you take Tache to the house and do whatever you'd like there. About five, ride Fuego back here and lead Tache. What about that?"

"Do you think Tache will mind me riding him?"

"I'll give him orders to behave himself, or I'll have his hide," he laughed.

Warner chanced to enter the door, then, to find the two of them laughing. "Well, Miss Gillian—what a pleasure to see you again."

"It's nice to see you, too, Mr. Barstow. I was just about to leave so Hawk can get back to his work," she told him.

"Now don't let me rush you off."

"No, really, you aren't, Mr. Barstow." Gillian started to move toward the door, and Hawk followed her, telling his boss he'd be back in a minute.

"Take your time, son," Warner said, with a sly grin on his face. He went and sat down at his desk. He'd wager his wages that those two young people were in love. It showed on their faces. They made quite a striking couple, Warner thought, as he got himself comfortable. The tall, dark, handsome looks of Hawk were a nice contrast to the little auburn-haired beauty, with her flawless, fair skin and flashing blue eyes.

Outside, Hawk helped her up on the huge Tache, and gave him the command to behave himself with his lady riding on him.

"I'll be here at five, Hawk," she said, urging Tache into motion. Hawk watched her go galloping away before he turned to go back into the office.

As he went to his desk to get back to the papers he was working on, Warner commented, "She's a mighty pretty lady, Hawk, and seems to be a very nice one."

Hawk grinned, "She is that, Warner."

"Well, she's certainly a charming attraction at the Old Pueblo Inn—and I happen to know that Melba Jackson isn't the easiest person to work for."

"Actually, Gillian has quit the inn, Warner." He explained that she was going to Rock Springs to help the family who'd given her a home after her parents were killed.

"I knew she was a fine young lady. She'll certainly be missed around that inn. She has a touch of class that old Melba never had. The guests I've observed when I've dined there liked her genteel manner."

"Gillian has always been a kind, gentle person. I've known her since she was fourteen," Hawk told him, before he finally turned his attention back to his work.

"Well, you have my permission to see her off at the station. Use my buggy if you'd like it, Hawk."

"Oh, thank you very much. It would be terrific to have your buggy to get Gillian and her luggage to the station. I know she will appreciate your kindness, too."

*   *   *

It was exactly the kind of last day Gillian had hoped to spend in Tucson, before she left for Rock Springs and the Fosters. She'd ridden Fuego and led Tache back to the office, and had got many stares from the passersby on the streets where she rode. They were both very powerfully built horses, and people probably questioned her ability to handle them, but neither had posed a problem.

Hawk had come jauntily striding out the door of the office at five, and together they had ridden back to his house. Warner had left the office at the same time, and once again he had admired the fine-looking couple they made, riding away together.

When they arrived home, Hawk had taken charge of the horses and Gillian went on into the house to fire up the cookstove and start the evening meal.

Gillian reveled in how much more pleasant it was sitting here in the lamplight of Hawk's kitchen, feasting on their simple meal, than it would have been in the elegant dining room back at the inn.

Later, they did the dishes together and talked. Hawk told her of Warner's generous offer of his buggy tomorrow, and added, "I'm getting time off to see you to the station, Gillian. Don't ask me to take you back to your house tonight. Stay this last night with me, for we may be parted for a while and I'm going to be very lonely without you."

Her hands went up to caress Hawk's face. "I had no intention of going home tonight, Hawk. I want to stay here with you."

There could have been no sweeter music to Hawk's

ears than that reply. They went to sit in his parlor, and his black eyes looked into the blue pools of hers as he told her, "I know that you must go to the Fosters', Gillian, but when you have done what you must do for them, I want us to never be parted again."

"I hope we won't have to be, Hawk," she told him, and turned her face up to his for a kiss.

It was a most savage passion they surrendered to, on that last night together. It would be many days and nights before they would see one another again. Afterward they lay together, Hawk's strong arms encircling her as they slept.

The next morning he took her back to her house, his arms were still around her as she rode with him on Tache. Leaving her to get herself dressed and ready to leave, he rode Tache to the office to exchange him for Warner's buggy.

All too quickly he had returned, and Gillian found herself sitting in the buggy, traveling toward the station. Before she knew it she was leaving Tucson. Hawk found himself alone in the buggy, going back toward the office. He had the strongest desire to ride after her and go with her back to Maricopa County.

He vowed that, some day, he would leave Tucson for good, and return to Maricopa County for the rest of his life. He would build a castle for himself and his ladylove, right there on that mountaintop he loved so much.

Hawk had spent many hours dwelling on what he wanted his mountain castle to be like. He had also dreamed about the beautiful lady who would share it with him. It had always been Gillian. He could not imagine any other woman sharing his life.

There was a reason for him saying what he'd said to her last night about never wanting them to be parted again. He never wanted her to feel the anxiety she'd felt when she discovered that she was pregnant with Steve Lafferty's child and did not know whether he would return to her. He remembered that frightened young lady very well. Should she be pregnant with his child, as she certainly could be, after the two nights of ecstasy they'd shared this week, she would have no cause for concern about his intentions.

He wanted Gillian to know that he worshiped her, and that nothing could make him happier than to learn that she was to have his son or daughter.

Like his mother, Solange, Hawk had very strong instincts, and he felt sure that his seed had been planted in his beautiful Gillian. He figured that the passage of a month or two would prove whether he was right that Gillian carried his child.

Gillian's last day in Tucson might have been glorious for her, but it was a miserable day for Helen Clayton, just as she had expected. For Melba Jackson, it proved to be a day that led her to the brink of insanity. She had gone into the office knowing that Gillian would not be there to assist her, and that was enough to make her unhappy. But when her desk clerk, Tommy, told her he was quitting too, she had to gather all her willpower to stay in control. She found herself quite unable to cope with things like this, as she would have done a few years before.

It seemed to Melba that everyone was deserting her and her inn. The only one who might give her some sympathy and understanding was Helen Clayton. But she found that Helen wasn't that comforting when she told her about Tommy.

By the time she left the lobby to go to her suite in the afternoon, she was exhausted and drained. For the first time, Melba felt the impact of the demanding hours of this place. She wasn't eager to get dressed in a few short hours to go back into the lobby at six. How sorry she was that Gillian would not be there tonight.

After that first evening she decided to pull the pretty young waitress, Lisa, in to play the role of hostess, but it was obvious from the outset that she could not fill Gillian's shoes. There was an outpouring of regret and commiseration from her guests when they learned that Gillian was no longer there. Melba soon realized what a jewel she'd had in her.

Young Lisa went into the kitchen every night to cry on Helen's shoulder. She was not happy trying to carry out the duties of hostess, and Helen felt very sorry for the girl. She became so distraught after the first three nights that she did not appear for work the next day, and so Helen lost one of her best waitresses. Lisa had enjoyed the work as a waitress, but trying to be the hostess had made her just quit and get a job at the new tearoom.

In one week Gillian, Tommy, and Lisa had left the inn. Three members of staff were too many to replace in a few days, so their duties were put on those who remained.

Melba had to take it upon herself to greet her guests, but she lingered no later than two o'clock in the lobby, after she'd worked in her office since noon. And once she had milled around the lobby from six to eight in the evening, she went to her suite and had dinner served there.

She already blamed Gillian for deserting her, and her guests were constantly whining because she was no longer there. Melba was sick of hearing Gillian Lafferty's name.

She was yet to learn that Helen Clayton was staying over at Gillian's house. So far, Helen felt, there had really been no reason to inform Melba, and she was never around when Helen left the kitchen in the late evening.

Helen had to just pray that something didn't happen to cause her hard-working Maria to quit. This capable woman was now managing the kitchen from early in the morning until two in the afternoon, so Helen came in then and stayed the rest of the evening.

She had enjoyed the last few days at Gillian's, with the little yard to roam around in. She had helped herself to some of the fresh vegetables from the garden. It was fun to putter around the little kitchen and to fix just things for herself. It had been a long time since Helen had had her own kitchen, and she allowed herself to pretend that Gillian's little house was hers. She gave it as much care as she would have done if it had been hers.

Each day, she went to the suite she occupied at the inn to gather up a few more of her clothes to take over to Gillian's house. Soon she would have enough over there that she wouldn't have to bring any more.

Helen had not even told the people she felt closest to at work about her new arrangement, for she knew how easily a tongue could slip.

But each day, when she came to her quarters to get a

few more things out of her armoire, and to look around
the two rooms to see that everything was in order, she
realized anew what a cold place this was, when she
compared it to the warmth she felt in Gillian's little
home. Oh, the furnishings were finer here than the ones
at Gillian's house, but there were no personal touches
in the two rooms of her suite. Now that she thought
about it, even in Melba's suite, where she'd lived for
well over twenty years, there was nothing to say that it
was her home.

Helen thought that was very sad.

Chapter Twenty-three

Once Gillian got to Rock Springs, she still had a few miles to go to get out to the Fosters' ranch, but there was a livery in town where she could hire herself a gig. But as it turned out that wasn't necessary, for as she stood under the shelter of the station, with her luggage by her feet, she heard someone calling out to her. "Miss Gillian—Miss Gillian, is it you?"

She turned to see a tall, lanky young man approaching her with a broad and friendly smile on his face. "You don't remember me, I can tell, but I sure knew you the minute I saw you standing there," he said in greeting.

Gillian was a little embarrassed. "I'm sorry, but I have to be honest. I don't know who you are."

"That's all right—the last time you even saw me was over two years ago. I'm Zack Morrison. My dad has the ranch close to the Fosters'."

"Oh, Zack, I do remember now. Guess you just grew a lot taller in the last two years," she said, and smiled up at him.

"Yeah, I did that. Heard you'd come back from Ireland . . . I'm sorry to hear that you lost your husband."

"Well, thank you."

"You headed for the Fosters'? If you are I'll give you a ride. Got my wagon right over there. Had to come into town to get some supplies for my folks. It'd be my pleasure to take you, Miss Gillian."

"Well, it would be my pleasure to accept your offer, Zack. I've just come from Tucson."

Zack picked up her two pieces of luggage as if they weighed nothing, and she followed him to his wagon. As they traveled out to the ranch, Zack told her what he knew about Nancy Foster's ailment. "She and John got caught in a bad storm going home from town, a couple of months ago, and Mrs. Foster took ill with chills and a bad chest cold, so my ma said. She just hasn't come out of it, and seems to get weaker and weaker all the time."

"But Mother Foster was always so hale and hearty! I would have suspected John to get ill from something like that, not her," Gillian protested.

"Yeah, I know what you mean, Miss Gillian."

Before long they were pulling into the driveway of the Fosters' ranch. John Foster happened to be out in the barnyard, and he spotted the flatbed wagon rolling up his drive. He stopped working to take a better look at who was riding in it, but he had only to see that flaming hair to know it was Gillian, being driven by young Morrison. He was overcome with joy as he started to rush toward the gate. As he was rushing out to greet them, he thought how happy his Nancy would be to have Gillian here. Who knew but that Gillian's

213

presence wouldn't work the miracle of getting Nancy well again!

He was by the wagon when it came to a halt, and helped Gillian down. "Oh, honey—it's so good to have you home!" he told her as he gave her a warm embrace.

"I had to come when I heard that Mother Foster was ill," Gillian said, hugging him back.

"Well, you'll be the best medicine she could have, Gillian dear." He went over to shake Zack's hand and thank him for bringing Gillian out to the ranch.

Zack did not feel he should tarry any longer, so he told them he'd be going. "Tell Mrs. Foster hello for me. It was nice seeing you again, Miss Gillian."

"Nice to see you, Zack, and thank you again for the ride," Gillian called as he turned to get back up into the wagon.

As Zack's wagon rolled back down the drive, John picked up Gillian's luggage and the two of them walked to the house. As soon as they got inside, John urged her to come with him to the bedroom to see Nancy. Gillian found it hard to imagine that robust, stout lady lying in bed instead of going around the house busily doing the daily chores as she had always done.

The lady she saw lying back on propped-up pillows was pale, and Gillian did not have to see her standing up to know that she had lost a lot of weight.

"Nancy," John called out softly as they went through the door, "Nancy, our Gillian is home."

Nancy turned her head and immediately looked more herself. Gillian rushed to the bed and lovingly embraced her, exclaiming, "Oh, Mother Foster, it is so good to see you."

"And it's wonderful for me to see you again, dear."

As they embraced, they both had tears streaming down their cheeks. John, standing there watching them, found himself ready to give way to tears too, so he turned to walk out of the room and allow the two of them to have their reunion in peace.

He went to the kitchen to put some kindling into the cookstove. Gillian would welcome a good cup of coffee after her long trip from Tucson. Maybe she would be able to get Nancy to have a cup with her. He was lucky these days to get her to have one cup in the morning, and with a sigh he remembered the woman who had kept her coffee pot going throughout the day.

Gillian could feel how frail Nancy was, and she vowed silently that she was going to get her back on her feet, no matter what it took.

For the next half hour they talked, and Gillian told her all the things that had happened in her life since she'd left to go to Tucson. Gillian feared that she might be tiring her out, but Nancy insisted on knowing what she'd been doing.

When John brought their coffee, it was pleasant for him to see how easily Nancy accepted the cup he handed to her and started to sip the coffee.

When Gillian had finished drinking her coffee, she rose out of her chair to say that it was time she got herself settled in and left Nancy to rest. "We'll talk some more later, Mother Foster."

For the next hour, Gillian unpacked her luggage and put away her things in the back bedroom she'd always occupied. When she had finished, she went into the kitchen, where she knew she would find John Foster preparing their evening meal.

She insisted that he allow her to take charge of the kitchen while he attended to the evening chores, even though he protested. "You must be tired, Gillian. You shouldn't have to cook dinner on your first evening here."

"I'll enjoy it, Father Foster. I've missed having the time to do a little cooking. You go and do whatever you have to do in the barn, and I'll get us a meal put together."

"You'll find a beef roast already cooked—I was going to add some potatoes to it."

"Then I don't have much to do, do I?" she replied with a grin.

"All right, young lady, you take charge and I'll get out of your way. Maybe, just maybe, you'll be able to get Nancy to eat some of that rich beef broth. I couldn't get her to eat at all last night."

Cockily she told him, "Oh, I'll get her to eat some of the broth, *and* some beef and potatoes."

She was determined to do as she said. She put on one of Nancy's aprons, then started to peel some potatoes to add to the cast iron pot where the roast was already simmering. To that she added two onions, quartered, remembering how Solange had told her that onion helped ward off colds and chills. "I put chives and onions in almost everything I cook," she had told Gillian.

After she had a pan of cornbread ready to place in the oven, Gillian began to set the table. When that was done there was nothing else to do in the kitchen, so she slipped quietly into the parlor to light the lamps and then went to check on Nancy to see if she was sleeping.

To her amazement she found her sitting up on the

216

side of the bed, and Gillian rushed into the room to see if she needed help.

"No, honey, I'm just testing myself, that's all."

"Well you call me if you need me, Mother Foster. I've got to check my bread. Father Foster is out in the barn."

"I'll let you know, Gillian, if I need you," Nancy assured her. Gillian was unaware that Nancy Foster had not been so alert for many weeks now, and had certainly shown no interest in getting out of bed.

Once Gillian had left, Nancy made a big effort and stood up, holding on to her bed. There was no denying that she felt weak, but she made herself keep standing. When she had done this for a few moments, she was encouraged to become bolder, and she took a few steps along the side of the bed. And when she had managed to do that, she knew there was nothing to keep her from trying to walk into her kitchen tonight and sit at the table with John and Gillian to have her evening meal.

There was a very nice aroma coming from the cast iron pot on the stove by the time John Foster entered the kitchen almost an hour later. He was thinking how nice it was that the sun was just now setting—usually it was long after dark when he returned to the house from doing the chores, since Nancy had been so ill.

It was comforting for John to see Gillian in the kitchen tonight. He did not know how long she was going to be there with them, but each day would be a blessing.

As John poured some water from the pail on the stand and washed his hands, he told Gillian dinner was sure smelling good.

"It's ready for eating, Father Foster," she told him. John dried his hands and reflected that it would have been the perfect evening, if only Nancy could have been able to sit here in their lamplit kitchen to share the meal with them.

Neither John nor Gillian could know the effort Nancy Foster demanded of herself to put on her wrapper and, very slowly and nervously, attempt to walk from the bedroom to the parlor. Having done that, she knew she could make it to the kitchen. It had been a long time since she'd been there, and she could think of no better night to try to be there again. Gillian was home! The thought of sitting at the table with her was enough to inspire Nancy to try.

Both Gillian and John were taken by surprise to see Nancy walking hesitantly into the kitchen. There was a happy smile on her face despite the effort the walk was costing her. Anxiously, John rushed to help her into one of the chairs, for he didn't want her to fall.

"Lord, Nancy, why didn't you let me help you?" he said as he took her arm.

"I wanted to try to do it myself, John," she declared in her old independent tone, which John had not heard for many weeks. Secretly, he hoped she wasn't pushing herself too hard, just because Gillian was here. He knew Gillian would not want her doing that, and it would not do for her to overtire herself.

But he was happy to see her eat some food. Hopefully it would make her gain some strength. He was also glad when Gillian spoke up as they were finishing their meal. "Now, Mother Foster, you've had a good dinner, and I want you to get back to bed and rest, or else you're going to make me feel guilty. I'm not going to allow you to overdo things just because I've arrived."

"I will, if you'll come in after you and John clean up the kitchen," Nancy replied. "I want to talk some more."

"That's a promise." Gillian smiled and looked over at John Foster, who gave her an approving nod.

While he was helping Nancy back to bed she began to clear the table. When he returned she was already washing the dirty dishes, so when the kitchen was in order John insisted that she go into the parlor and rest awhile, before she went to talk to Nancy.

"You haven't had a minute to catch your breath since you got here, Gillian. I know you're tired," he said firmly as he dimmed the lamp in the kitchen and accompanied her to the parlor.

And indeed, Gillian found as she sank down into one of the parlor chairs that she was weary. She told him that she would rest for just a minute before she went in to talk to Nancy. "But I won't stay with her long, for I'm about ready to go to bed myself."

John sat down in the chair opposite her and lit his pipe. The two of them were content to just sit there and relax quietly together. Gillian had to make herself get up, for she knew that if she didn't she was going to lean her head back in the chair and fall off to sleep.

"I'm going in to Mother Foster now, before I go to bed," she told him as she got up from the chair.

But when she went into the bedroom she found Nancy sleeping soundly, so she tiptoed quietly out of the room to go back to the parlor and inform John that she was already asleep. She bent down to kiss him goodnight, and went off to bed.

219

After she had left the room, John sat for a while, thinking. He was pleased that he'd seen Nancy back up on her feet and eating with more relish than she had in a long time. If Gillian's coming back had brought this about, then he hoped she'd stay with them for a long time. The girl seemed to have worked some kind of miracle!

Chapter Twenty-four

Gillian's remedy for Nancy Foster was very simple. She knew that to gain back the weight and strength she'd lost she had to be encouraged to eat, so Gillian insisted that she eat three meals a day. She also insisted that she walk around the house for a short time every day.

With Gillian taking charge of the house and of Nancy, John was free to catch up on things he'd had to let go, like going into town for supplies and mending some fences around the ranch. Having Gillian there for a week had been a tremendous help for him, and he finally felt like he was getting his ranch back in good order.

But more wonderful for John was the change in Nancy. Her face was not so pale now, and he knew that it was not his imagination that she had put on a few pounds. He knew that Gillian was walking Nancy around the house several times a day now. It was grand, when he returned in the wagon yesterday from his trip for supplies, to spot the two of them sitting out in the swing on the front porch, absorbing the warm afternoon sun.

There had actually been a rosy flush on Nancy's face when she went back into the house! He could tell that Nancy's spirits were lifted and she was encouraged. She had to be feeling the strength growing within her. He knew what a robust, strong woman she had always been, so he could appreciate what it had done to her to find herself so helpless.

Gillian was also feeling very pleased with Nancy's progress, and she set a new goal for next week. By then, she and Nancy would stroll around the yard together each day.

It boosted Nancy's morale to be able, at the end of the week, to sit in the kitchen and chat with Gillian while she worked. She would sit in a chair and snap beans or peel potatoes. Each day that she made a little more progress thrilled Gillian.

As Nancy's health slowly improved, Gillian was finding herself with more free time, so she sat down after supper one evening to write letters to Hawk and Helen. She had enjoyed telling Hawk how much she missed him, and she knew Helen would be pleased to hear her sister had improved so much. The next day John had taken her letters into Rock Springs when he'd gone to pick up some cattle feed.

As she had stubbornly determined, Gillian did have Nancy walking around the yard by the next week. The two of them gathered up a colorful bouquet of flowers and took them into the house, where Nancy arranged them in a couple of vases. One was placed in the parlor and the other in the center of the kitchen table.

Nancy sat down in the kitchen and let out a sigh.

"Oh, Gillian, honey, you've brought me back from the dead. I really thought I would never be any good to myself or John again. I blame myself for part of it, for I just got the don't cares after I had that bout with the chest cold, or whatever it was that hit me so hard, and I didn't even try to get better."

"Well, that's all over now. You're getting better and better every day," Gillian reassured her happily.

"Yes, you bet your boots I am! I'm going to surprise John tomorrow, and bake that sweet man of mine an apple cobbler that he loves so much," she told Gillian.

The next afternoon Nancy kept her promise by going into the kitchen to make the cobbler, filling a deep dish with sliced apples and topping them with her special batter. She looked up proudly at Gillian and asked her to put the baking dish in the oven.

That night, when John came in from the barnyard and he smelled chicken stewing and saw the fresh-baked cobbler on the table, he knew things were most assuredly getting back to normal around the place.

As the three of them sat around the table that night it was as if time had rolled back. Nancy was laughing and in a lighthearted mood, and so was Gillian. It reminded John of those wonderful years when Gillian had lived there with them, before Steve Lafferty had come into her life.

It had been a long couple of weeks for two people back in Tucson. Hawk was finding life very lonely now that Gillian had been gone for so long. The wonderful ecstasy they'd shared before she left Tucson made him hunger even more for her.

He found himself very discontent in the evenings once he'd come home from the office. He recalled vividly that last night she'd stayed there with him, when they'd dined together in his kitchen and later, she'd shared his bed and they'd made wild, wonderful love.

He had to fight the urge to take off for Maricopa County to see her, for he felt she needed some time alone with the Fosters.

Across town, Helen Clayton was as miserable as Hawk. She was anxious to hear from Gillian, who had promised to write once she got there and found out exactly how Nancy was. She was also worried that, sooner or later, Melba would find out that she was spending her nights away from the inn. Nothing went on at the inn that didn't get to Melba's ears.

For almost a week after Gillian had left, Helen had managed to keep her secret, but she had not given a thought to the possibility of Melba coming to her room to have a talk. That was what happened.

For a couple of hours one evening, Melba had sat in her suite sipping on some wine and feeling blue. Finally, looking at the clock, she figured that Helen should be out of the kitchen and in her quarters by now. She felt the need to talk to someone, and Helen was about the only person left she could talk to.

So she'd left her suite, dressed in her nightgown and frilly silk wrapper, to go down the hallway to Helen's suite. When she knocked and knocked on the door, and there was no answer, Melba marched back to the desk to get a duplicate key to Helen's room so that she could see for herself if something was wrong.

When she entered the dark room and found no signs

of Helen there, she was very perplexed about just where she could be.

She took the key back to the desk and quizzed the new desk clerk about whether he'd seen Helen. He told her that he had seen her leave the inn. "She told me she was going to spend the night away from the inn when I asked her where she was heading so late. I was sort of teasing Miss Clayton, I guess."

This perplexed Melba even more, and she felt concerned about Helen. "Did she mention where she was going?"

"She just told me that it was a lady's house she was going to, and said I shouldn't get any wrong ideas. She knew I was just joking with her."

"I see. Well, leave a message for the morning clerk to tell Miss Helen that I wish to speak to her as soon as she arrives at the inn." She turned to go back to her suite, feeling irritated. She had it figured that Helen was spending the night over at Gillian's and that they were enjoying one another's company. She had forgotten that Gillian had told her she was leaving Tucson.

The next day, when Helen came to the inn, she went to the office, where Melba was sitting at the desk doing the receipts. All Helen had to do was look at Melba's face to know that she was in one of her dark moods again, as she had been so often lately.

"Sit down, Helen. I want to talk to you. I needed to discuss something with you last night, but I found that you were not at the inn."

"No, I wasn't, Melba. I spent the night over at Gillian's house." She went on to explain that Gillian was in Rock Springs taking care of Helen's ailing sister.

"So you're going to watch over her house while she's

gone, eh?" Melba asked.

"Well, I figure that's the least I can do, after what she's doing for my sister. Wouldn't you feel that way about your sister, Melba?"

"I couldn't tell you, since I never had one, Helen," Melba said tersely. Rising from the desk, Melba remarked casually, "Well, get along to your job, Helen, and I'll do the same."

"All right, Melba. See you later," Helen replied, and she turned to walk out of the office. As she made her way toward the kitchen, she felt relieved that Melba's manner changed. When Helen had walked into the office she'd looked very annoyed, but for whatever reason, Melba had seemed to mellow during the conversation. At least it made the day easier to get through.

Helen's conversation had made an impact on Melba, and she thought about many things after she'd left the lobby and was alone in her suite that afternoon. Helen Clayton was a wealthier woman than she was, when she thought about it, for Helen had a sister and a married daughter, Melissa. All Melba had was her inn, and now that her health was failing she was finding that the inn wasn't enough for her any more. Maybe a family could be important, after all. Through all these years, Melba had been so busy with her inn that the thought of growing old alone someday had never dawned on her.

She found herself too weary to fight for the business she'd been losing lately. The coming of the railroad to Tucson was making a lot of changes and bringing in a lot of new people. A new hotel was being built with an elegant dining room, and already new tearooms had made the numbers at her lunches and dinners fall off over the last few weeks.

There were vacant rooms at the inn that would have been occupied this time a year ago. Why, she used to have to turn people away at this time of year.

Melba figured that there was only one solution. When the Old Pueblo Inn died, she would too. It would be better that way.

Being in this bleak mood, Melba made herself face some other unpleasant truths. It had been over a year and a half now since she'd made Helen Clayton a partner, but she had never given Helen her fair share of the profits. And now she couldn't, for last year's profits had been swallowed up by the recent losses.

But she did need to ease her guilty conscience. The meek, gentle Helen had never brought the subject up, or approached her about the agreement they'd made in the beginning, when Helen had arrived to live and work at the inn with her. God knew, Helen had kept her end of the bargain and worked very hard.

So the next day she set about righting the wrong she'd done Helen. She had young Barry drive her to Harvey Featherston's Jewelry Store and wait for her as she marched into the store with a small leather case in her hand. When they were in the privacy of Harvey's office, she amazed him by telling him she wished to sell all the pieces of jewelry she had brought.

"Melba, are you sure of this? My God, some of these pieces are exquisite. I should know, I sold you some of them," he said, with a quizzical look on his face. He wondered if she was selling them to keep the inn open.

"Well, Harvey, I've enjoyed all this for years, but I wear very few of them now. I got my money's worth, shall we say. Now I've decided that I'd rather have the money. Besides, I'm getting older, and I've not one living soul to leave this stuff to." Her mood seemed too lighthearted for Harvey to believe she was in dire straits financially. Perhaps, as she had no family, she was smart to do what she was doing.

"All right, Melba, but you know that when I quote what they are worth to me it won't be what they cost you," he pointed out.

"I've never doubted for a minute that you were making yourself a nice profit, Harvey. That's why you've been in business for so many years," she said with a chuckle.

Harvey Featherston looked across the table at her and smiled, then he turned his attention back to the contents of the leather case.

After several minutes of taking out each piece and jotting down figures on a pad of paper, he looked up and announced what he would pay her for the entire lot.

Melba told him, without batting an eyelash, that she would take him up on his offer. Harvey found this surprising, because he would have expected her to haggle with him. But he was not about to argue, and ten minutes later they had concluded their business.

With a thick roll of bills in her reticule, Melba boarded the buggy to go back to the inn. She was pleased with the trip to the jewelry store, for it had brought her enough to pay what she owed to Helen Clayton. Knowing how frugal Helen was, Melba thought it should be enough to take care of her nicely for quite a long time.

Young Barry found Miss Melba much nicer this afternoon than usual. He was taken very much by surprise when, as she left the buggy, she placed some bills in his hand. "I think it's time I gave you some days off, young man, for you've been working quite steadily. You're free as of now to go visit that brother of yours for the weekend. I shall be staying in the inn, so I won't need you to take me anywhere."

"Oh, thank you, Miss Melba! He's got a new colt I've been waiting to see," Barry exclaimed excitedly.

"Well, off you go and see him and that colt. I'll be just fine until next Tuesday—that will give you four days to visit with your brother."

"Oh, I surely thank you, Miss Melba," he declared, a big grin on his face.

Melba smiled as she started up the walkway to the inn. Perhaps, before this day was over, there would be two people, at least, at the inn who would think kindly of her when they remembered Melba Jackson.

She walked unhurriedly into the lobby and greeted the new desk clerk there. For once, she did not look carefully at the guests milling around the lobby. As she went on down the hallway toward her suite, she could not have said how many people there had been there, nor who they were.

The truth was, Melba didn't care this late afternoon. She wouldn't rush to be in the lobby at six this evening, but when she did appear, she was going to be wearing one of her grandest gowns. She took the gold brocade out of the armoire and gave it a good shake, then hung it on the doorframe.

She also got out the jewelry she was to wear tonight, along with two other pieces, and laid them out on her dressing table.

Only then did she sink into the comfort of her big old armchair and lay her head back against it.

Chapter Twenty-five

Melba knew she was still a most attractive lady when she was dressed in her gold brocade gown, with the emerald earrings dangling from her ears. Before she went into the lobby, she went to the kitchen to tell Helen that she wished her to come to her suite before she left the inn.

"I'll be there, Melba. You sure look grand tonight, Melba," Helen told her. She'd never seen her wear this lovely gown before.

"Well, thank you, Helen." As Melba left the kitchen, Helen mused how pleasant it was to be around Melba when she was as nice as she was this evening. It was good to see a smile on her face, for a change.

As Melba went on to the lobby, she saw that once again there were not many guests there tonight. She did not let this upset her, though, and she played the role of gracious hostess beautifully as she greeted them.

It did not even disturb her, when she checked with her desk clerk, to learn that the entire east wing of her inn was unoccupied this evening.

By eight the lobby was deserted, for all the guests had moved into the dining room to eat. Melba followed them, took herself a table at the back, and ordered a fine meal. She made no effort to circulate around the tables to talk to anyone, for it was a sea of strange faces she gazed upon tonight. She realized that when Gillian had come to the inn, she had stopped making the effort to get to know new guests.

By nine o'clock the only people left in the dining room were two young couples, who were not guests of the inn, and herself at the back table.

She got up and went to the kitchen to tell Helen to start closing it down. "It's over for tonight, Helen. I'm going to my suite, and I'll see you there as soon as you're through in here."

"All right, Melba. I'll be there as soon as I can," Helen told her.

Just before ten, Helen was at the door of Melba's suite. She didn't know what to expect from Melba tonight. Was she to find another change of mood in this very complicated lady?

Melba was still dressed in her gold brocade gown, and there on the table by the settee were two glasses and a bottle of white wine. "I thought we should have ourselves a treat before you go to Gillian's house. You are going back over there tonight, aren't you?"

"Yes, I'll be going over there just as soon as I go to my rooms to get myself some extra clothing," Helen answered cautiously.

Melba poured each of them a glass of wine and took a seat in her chair. Taking a sip, she told Helen, "My reason for wanting you to come here tonight was to tell you what a marvelous job you've done here at the inn.

231

I've decided it's high time I divided the profits for the last year with you. I will give your share to you tonight before you leave."

"Well, thank you, Melba! I know business has not been good lately, but it isn't because of the food in our dining room. I wish I knew something that would help."

Melba smiled, for she appreciated Helen's sincerity. "I have no solution for it either, Helen, so let's just not worry about it. Anyway, this is your share of the profits." She handed an amazed Helen an overstuffed envelope containing the money she'd collected from Featherston this afternoon. "I've two other things I'd like to give you tonight. One of these little boxes is for you, and the other one is a little gift for Gillian, just to let her know that there are no hard feelings as far as I'm concerned."

"Oh, Melba—that will make her very happy. And I thank you for your generosity," Helen said gratefully, as she took the boxes.

"I hope you're right about Gillian. I can't deny I was very angry with her when she left, but all of that has passed now."

"I'm glad to hear you say that, Melba, for Gillian is such a nice young lady. She really is. She just couldn't cope with living here at the inn, where she had no breathing room. You and I being older does make a difference, but Gillian is so young and full of life. She's a free spirit, and I think she was missing having time to herself when she happened to find this little house. Its front yard is filled with flowers and the backyard with a vegetable garden—it was everything Gillian wanted."

"I understand, Helen. Truly I do. I have come to

terms with the fact that no one could possibly care as much about this place as I do. So: with all that said, I am going to suggest that we say goodnight now. You get on over to Gillian's, before it gets any later. I know you are tired."

Helen agreed that she was exhausted as she stood up. But the glass of wine had been enough to make her feel pleasantly relaxed, and she was reluctant to move from the comfortable settee.

"I'm glad we had this talk, Melba. Thank you for everything."

Melba told her that she was glad, too, as she walked with her to the door.

"Goodbye, Helen," she said, her voice unexpectedly emotional.

"Goodnight, Melba," Helen responded, and walked pensively down the hallway to her room to gather up a few more things from her armoire. She found it hard to believe Melba had given her so much money—she wouldn't know until she counted it how much was there, but it sure felt like a lot. When she got to Gillian's she would have to do some thinking.

The clock was chiming eleven when she entered Gillian's house, and it was not until she had undressed and got comfortable in her nightgown that she opened her reticule to pull out the thick roll of bills. She began to tremble, for she had never had so much money in her possession. It was just as well she had not known how much was there when she'd walked here in the dark, for she would have been frightened. She promised herself that she would take all this money to the bank first thing in the morning.

Now, her curiosity was whet_ about the two small

boxes Melba had given her. She opened the one that was for her, and inside rested a brooch of sparkling diamonds. Helen had never seen the likes of it before, and to think that Melba had parted with it left Helen dazzled.

She could not resist opening the other box to see what Melba had given Gillian. When Helen gazed down at the sparkling blue fire of the sapphire teardrop earrings lying there, she thought immediately of Gillian's blue eyes and how they could twinkle with just as much splendor. She could see why Melba had picked this piece of jewelry to give to Gillian. But what was more important to Helen was the message Melba was sending with it to Gillian. She felt filled with compassion and forgiveness for Melba tonight.

Helen was thinking that things would be different around the inn than they'd been in many weeks. She wouldn't make any hasty decisions about what to do with her money. Maybe Melba would be a little kinder to her help now, and things would improve.

When she went to bed that night, she felt as if a very heavy burden had been lifted off her chest. As she fell asleep she knew nothing about the golden-red glow that was lighting up the black night skies just a short distance away.

After Helen had left her suite that night, and because she knew young Barry had left to go to his brother's farm, just outside the city, Melba's tormented mind told her that she had paid her dues to the people who deserved them. She knew the kitchen and dining room were empty for the night. There were only a few guests left in the inn, and with them in mind Melba went back into the lobby, which was deserted. The desk clerk was sitting behind the counter with his head cradled in his hand, drowsing off to sleep. Before she woke him up she checked to see which rooms the guests were in.

"Arthur—Arthur, wake up long enough to get yourself home. We're not going to have any more guests coming in at this late hour. Go home and go to bed."

Arthur's head snapped up and, bewildered, he mumbled, "Go home? Are you saying I can go on home, ma'am?"

"I'm saying exactly that. Billy is on the next shift, and it's not too long before he'll be coming in," she told him as he slowly got up from the chair. She'd never before let a member of her staff go home almost two hours early, but he certainly wasn't going to argue with her. He grabbed his cap from the rack and went toward the front door, calling back to her, "Goodnight, Miss Melba."

"Goodbye, Arthur." She watched him going out the front entranceway, then she turned to leave the lobby. It was an ideal night for a moonlight stroll in the courtyard gardens, so Melba indulged herself in a brief walk there. She pondered how many couples had roamed these gardens of hers, over the many years the Old Pueblo Inn had been open, and how many romances had begun when young lovers met by the fountain.

She took the time to sit down on one of the little benches by the fountain, feeling in a very reflective mood. Life was crazy, she suddenly realized, as she sat there in the darkness all alone. She had loved these gardens and this inn so much that she'd allowed herself to forsake everything else in her life. Oh, there had been men who'd courted her over the years, but she'd never had any time for them, except to sit in the dining room at a table or take a brief walk in her gardens. Most of the gentlemen who had come into her life became good friends—like Sam Harmon.

But sooner or later, any man who'd been attracted to her had tired of competing with the inn, and had faded out of her life.

So the inn became her husband, her child, her friend. But it gave her no warm embrace, no kiss on the cheek or amorous lovemaking. And tonight she sat there hating the inn, because in the end it had robbed her of everything. Damn, she hated it tonight with as much passion as she'd once loved it!

She wanted to destroy it, as it had destroyed her. For the last two days she had plotted that destruction, and now the hour to do it, before Billy came in for his shift.

She went to the wing of the inn that was completely unoccupied and unlocked one of the rooms. When she had taken two kerosene lamps, emptied their contents on the bed, and fired it, she stood back, amazed how quickly the flames mounted to catch the drapes. By the time she reached the door the entire room was circled in dancing, savage flames, which she knew would move quickly into the next room, and then the next. So she tarried no longer, but left to go to the west wing.

By the time she managed to get to the west side of the inn, the entire east wing was aglow with blazing flames. She wasted no time banging on each door and screaming that there was a fire, and to get out immediately. When she reached the end of the long hallway, she could see doors flying open and the guests scurrying toward the entrance, clutching valuable belongings to them.

She stood and watched the exodus. As she saw the last couple rushing madly down the carpeted hallway, a trail of smoke began to enter the lobby, for the kitchen and dining room were beginning to flame. She heard the sounds of cracking glass from the mirrors and crystal chandeliers echoing down the hallway, but Melba began methodically to inspect each of the rooms she knew had been occupied. She was pleased to find them all empty, but by now the smoke was becoming thicker and thicker.

The guests huddled outside in their nightclothes were awestruck by the spectacular sight of the burning inn. They could hear the sounds of falling glass inside, and they all knew that if anyone was left inside, it was now impossible to rescue them, for the lobby filled with demonic, orange-red flames. They stared mesmerized by what they saw.

No part of the building was untouched by fire now. The Old Pueblo Inn was a luminous inferno.

Melba had to struggle to make it back to her suite, for she found herself overcome by the smoke, and her breathing was labored and difficult.

But when she got to her room she smiled, and even gave a little chuckle. She'd found the solution, for the old inn and for herself. She sank down into a chair near the door. There were strange sounds, like explosions, erupting on all sides.

Smoke was now billowing under her door. When she was giving in to the smoke with her last deep gasps, there was a pleased smile on her face. She'd done it her way, and she'd done it all herself. But no one had paid with their life—she'd seen to that. All her guests were spared, all her help was gone for the night, and young Billy was not due to arrive for a while yet. She felt no guilt.

She had been more than generous to Helen Clayton. The truth was, the inn had been losing money for the last two months. Helen's just dues would not come to half as much as she had given her, but Melba had known she could take nothing with her when she left this world tonight.

And as for Gillian, she hoped that she would think kindly of Melba Jackson when she wore the teardrop earrings.

Little did she know that this night, the inn and Melba Jackson would become a legend in the city of Tucson. The tale would be told over and over again, for years to come. Had she known, this would have delighted her.

Chapter Twenty-six

Tucson was stunned by the devastating news of the fire that had destroyed one of the landmarks of the city. The Old Pueblo Inn had been in existence for all of some people's lives. The curious passed by to see the ruins that were still smoldering in the morning and the news spread over the city as quickly as the fire had spread over the inn.

There were some mourners—Helen Clayton and Arthur Norton among them—who came and stood at the courtyard gate when they learned about the terrible tragedy. The young desk clerk, Billy had arrived for his shift to find the inn ablaze and guests wandering aimlessly around the courtyard. He could not make himself go home, so for over seven hours he'd just stood there and looked beyond the gate in disbelief.

Helen felt sorry for the emotional young Billy, and she knew there was nothing they could do there now, so she suggested, "Why don't you and Arthur come to Gillian's house with me. I'll make us a pot of coffee, and I have some rolls we can eat. There's nothing more to do here."

"That sounds like a good idea, Miss Helen," Arthur agreed.

"I could use your company right now, too," Helen admitted.

"Well, we'll go, won't we Billy?" Arthur urged him. He realized the tremendous impact it must have made on Billy to witness the horrible inferno. He and Miss Helen had been spared that, and Arthur was glad.

"I—I guess so," Billy stammered. He allowed Arthur and Helen to take him over to Gillian's house, and for the next two hours the three of them sat in the kitchen sipping coffee and half-heartedly nibbling on the little cinnamon rolls Helen had served.

Dejectedly, Billy complained that he didn't know what he'd do now that he didn't have the inn to work for. But Arthur had an idea. He suggested that Billy go with him tomorrow when he applied at the railroad company for a job. Billy accepted his offer.

"You know, Miss Helen—it's rather funny, now that I've had some time to just sit back and think. Miss Melba came to the lobby, I guess after you and her parted company last night. She caught me napping, and she told me to go on home. She'd never done that before."

Helen reached over to pat Arthur's hand and told him, "Oh, Arthur dear—let's just say that a guardian angel was sitting on your shoulder."

"Yeah, Miss Helen, that's what I'm going to figure it was. I would have been there, otherwise."

"That's right, you would have been, Arthur," Helen agreed.

A while later, the two young men left the house. Helen insisted that they must keep in touch with her, since none of them would be going to the inn anymore, and they vowed that they would.

After they left Helen was left alone with her thoughts. She came to the startling conclusion, especially after what Arthur had said, that Melba had set the fire herself. That was why she'd told Arthur to leave early. She had known exactly what she was going to do, and that she must do it before Billy arrived. That was also why she'd given her the money last night, along with the two expensive pieces of jewelry.

Yes, Melba knew what she was going to do, and she'd carefully planned it all in advance. It was also the reason she was nicer yesterday, and why she'd dressed up for that last night to be the hostess at the inn. And Helen also became convinced that nothing could have prevented the tragedy, for Melba was ready to die and had wanted to take her beloved inn with her.

Knowing Melba as she did, Helen could understand why she might have felt that way, now that her health was failing and there was no family for her to call on to help her. The inn was her whole life, but with business falling off she no longer had the stamina to fight back, as she once would have done.

Helen spent the rest of the day quietly in the house, for there were things she had to think about now that she would no longer be working for Melba and the inn.

She realized the unpleasant fact that she could not carry through with the plans she'd made last night to deposit all the money Melba had given her. It was too large an amount to deposit all at one time, or the finger of suspicion could be pointed at her. She knew there would surely be speculation as to how the fire had started. Helen was convinced beyond any shadow of a doubt that Melba had done it herself. And if that was her wish, Helen would accept it. Knowing that made some of her sorrow lift away.

In fact, accepting that Melba had shaped her own destiny lifted Helen's spirits, and by late afternoon she had turned her energy toward preparing herself some supper. There was no beef with which to make a tasty pot of stew, but she did gather enough vegetables from the little garden to start some vegetable soup simmering on the stove. And an hour later she had mixed up a bowl of meal, eggs, milk, and some bacon drippings, and baked herself some cornbread.

Then Helen sat in the kitchen wondering what to do about all this money in her possession. It made her nervous, for she had never had that much in her entire life. She decided that she would go to the bank to deposit the amount of her salary, as she'd done so often in the past. It would take a long time to get it all in the bank that way, but she knew no other way to do it. Of course the bank staff would know she was no longer working at the inn, but she would say she had found some other employment.

As she sat there at the table, Helen thought how grateful she should be to Gillian that she had a place to stay, now that the inn was reduced to smoldering ashes. She was also grateful that she had brought most of her clothing here to Gillian's house.

As she looked out the kitchen window and watched the sun setting, it struck her that there would be no Old Pueblo Inn for anyone to go to tonight. It was gone forever, and so was Melba Jackson, and a wave of sadness swept over her.

Suddenly there was a sharp rapping on the door, which brought Helen out of her reverie. When she opened the front door she saw a very handsome young man, with bronzed skin and a thick mane of jet black hair that reached below the collar of his shirt. There was a friendly smile on his face as he introduced himself. "I'm Joe Hawk, Mrs. Clayton. Gillian told me you would be staying at her house while she was gone, and when I heard about the inn I felt I should come to see that you were all right. I know how fond Gillian is of you."

"Oh, Mr. Hawk, how nice of you! I guess I don't have to tell you how fond I am of Gillian, too. Please, come in," Helen replied.

Hawk entered the parlor, thinking that Gillian would be happy to know that Helen was safe and secure. He'd ridden by the horrible sight of what used to be the inn, and he was relieved that Gillian was in Maricopa County and had not been here last night.

"I'm glad to see that you are all right, Mrs. Clayton," he told her as he accepted her invitation to sit down.

"And I, Mr. Hawk, am very happy that I have Gillian's house to stay in until I can make other arrangements."

"Well, ma'am, I'll help you in any way I can if you need my services. I'm sure that you can stay in Gillian's house for as long as you need to, but if there's anything else I can do you have only to let me know."

"Oh, thank you, Mr. Hawk," said Helen, thinking what a kind young man he was.

"Please, why don't you just call me Hawk, as Gillian does?" Helen returned his warm smile. She had met the young Irishman who'd swept the beautiful Gillian off her feet and stolen her heart so swiftly, and there had been no denying that the dashing sea captain was a man who could make any young lady lose her heart. But this young man was a different sort, more dependable, and

Helen liked him very much. There was a warmth in his black eyes, and obviously he had the capacity to care deeply—she could see it in his face, as easily as she could see that he was a half-breed. Not that his background concerned Helen; she was measuring him as a man, and he came up with a high mark.

"I shall be happy to call you Hawk, and I would be delighted to have you share my supper with me, if you have nothing better to do. It's nothing fancy, but I would enjoy your company."

"Well, Mrs. Clayton, I'm honored. I accept your invitation," Hawk told her.

So he shared her supper, and they enjoyed chatting for another hour afterward before he finally took his leave to go home. When he finally told her goodnight, he made a point of reminding her that if she should need him, he would be there.

"It is very comforting for me to know that, Hawk. I will let you know immediately if I need anything," Helen said as she walked to the door with him.

It had been a most pleasant evening for Helen, and she had found Joe Hawk a very nice young man. He had made her forget, for a few hours, the horrible night that had just passed.

During the next two days, Helen helped make arrangements for the funeral, which she suspected Melba would not have wanted. Helen wanted to keep it simple, but the city was already making Melba a martyr. A simple graveside service would have been more to Helen's liking.

Since she had no family, it was Melba's lawyer who greeted the mourners. Arthur and Billy had come together, and sat beside Helen. Afterward, they accompanied her back to Gillian's house, and she was pleased to hear that both of them had gotten jobs with the railroad.

While the three of them were sitting in the kitchen, there was fierce rapping on the front door. Helen, wondering who it could be, opened the door, to find a panic-stricken young Barry standing there. He had just come back into town from his brother's and discovered the burned-out ruins of the inn.

The young boy was in a state of shock. Everything he possessed, though it wasn't a lot, was gone, for he had left his belongings in his quarters above the inn's stables.

When he saw Helen he gasped, "Oh, thank goodness you're here, Miss Helen! Wha—what happened to the inn?"

Helen brought him into the kitchen. "There was a terrible fire, Barry. Arthur and Billy are here. We've all just attended Miss Melba's funeral . . . she was killed in the fire."

Barry sat down with the other two young men, and they told him what had happened. "I guess I'll have to get back to my brother's ranch, then. I won't have a job now, or a place to stay," he declared, with a desolate look on his face.

Helen felt sorry for the young lad. He was still in his teens, and she knew both his parents were dead. The only family he had was his brother, who had a small place just outside the city.

"Barry, you're welcome to stay here, until you can manage to get back to your brother's. I'm sure Miss Gillian would have no objections to that," Helen told him kindly.

"Well, as long as you don't think she'd mind, 'cause I sure wouldn't want to get you in trouble with her," Barry said.

Later, when Arthur and Billy had left and just Helen and Barry were left at the house, he roamed around the kitchen restlessly. When she prepared to cook them some supper, he volunteered to set the table.

"I think I'll get up early in the morning, Miss Helen, and look around town to see if I can find some kind of a job. I don't really want to go back to my brother's place—I don't think his wife much likes having me around."

Helen assured him that it would not disturb her if he got up early. She had already decided to help the young man, for she'd seen the small bundle he carried under his arm when he arrived at the front door, and she knew it was probably all he had left.

After they had finished the tasty meal Helen had prepared, Barry told her about that last afternoon, when he'd taken Miss Melba to the jewelry store. "She was awfully nice to me that day. She told me to take a few days off, and to leave that day, which I did. She even handed me a couple of dollars when I helped her out of the buggy. Why, it was almost like she knew she wasn't going to see me again. And she said goodbye to me, instead of good afternoon as usual."

Barry's revelation confirmed to Helen that Melba had indeed cleverly plotted the destruction of the inn and herself, and that she had carried it out to perfection. Helen could almost envision her now, sitting with a smug smile on her face, wherever she might be.

Part Three

Bittersweet Summer

Chapter Twenty-seven

The next day, Helen went to the bank to make her deposit, as she had always done on payday. She was careful not to put in one cent more than usual. She stopped by the store on the way back to the house to pick up a few things that were getting low in Gillian's pantry. She had been using the supplies and groceries left there by Gillian, so she felt it was only right that she restock the shelves.

As she went by the little bakery shop, the wonderful aroma urged her to go inside. She bought a loaf of raisin bread, and it made her recall how she used to sell her own loaves of raisin and carrot bread to the Old Pueblo Inn. It was how she and Melba Jackson had met, when Helen was married to that shiftless Kent Clayton. On an impulse, as Helen was about to leave the little bakery she asked the clerk, "Would you need some extra help here in the bakery? I'm very good with pastries and breads."

The lady asked her, "What is your name?"

"Helen Clayton."

"Well I'm Ruth Crawford, and I own this little bakery. If you are as good as you say, yes, I could use some help here in the afternoons, a few days a week. I don't need anyone full time, and I'm learning the hard way that it's easier to find someone for full time than for just a part time shift."

"I would like to try it, if you are willing. I think I could please you."

"Shall we say Mondays, Wednesdays, and Fridays, for four hours each day?"

They agreed on the wages Helen would get for those four hours, and she left having promised to be there at one on Monday afternoon.

She was smiling as she walked to Gillian's house, for she had not been looking for a job when she'd left the house this morning. It felt good to have one now, though, and at least it was something to start her new life with. She just hoped that young Barry would be as lucky.

Helen had been home for almost three hours, and had got a fat hen stewing on the stove when young Barry came rushing through the door like a whirlwind. Excitedly he announced to her that he had hit the jackpot. "Got myself a job, as well as living quarters, Miss Helen. Golly, I can't believe it! It must be my lucky day."

"Well, sit down here and tell me about it." She smiled, glad that they would both have something to celebrate this evening.

He was breathless, for he had been so eager to announce his good news to her that he'd run from the livery, which was a short distance away from the inn.

"Well, I just walked into Parson's Livery and told him I'd lost my job when the inn burned. I told him I'd been working for Miss Melba for the last two years, and he said that told him all he needed to be told. He fired the man who'd been working for him a week ago, and he wants me to start tomorrow—so I'll impose on you one more night, if that's all right."

"It's more than all right, Barry. I'm so happy for you," she said, and then told him about her good luck in finding a part-time job.

Then Helen got up from the table to go into the bedroom, and when she returned she laid some bills on the table. "That's for you, Barry. Now you go to the mercantile store and get yourself a couple of shirts and some pants, and whatever else a young man like you must need after his things have burned."

He shook his head and his eyes looked up at her warmly. "Ah, now Miss Helen, I—I can't do that! I surely do appreciate you being so nice, but I can't accept the money."

"Don't you argue with me, young man! You just go do it, then get yourself back here, 'cause we're going to have a feast of chicken and dumplings. I'll have it ready by the time you get back."

"My, that does sound good!" A broad grin came to his face, for he'd eaten nothing since breakfast. As his hand clutched the bills he thought that Miss Helen had to be the most generous lady he'd ever known. He vowed right then and there that he'd never forget her kind act this afternoon. If she ever needed him, he would certainly be there to help her.

251

"I'll be back soon, Miss Helen," he promised as he rushed out of the kitchen.

An hour later, Barry had returned with a huge package in his arms. It was filled with things he was certainly in dire need of—underwear, socks, two cotton shirts, and a couple of pairs of dark-colored twill pants. But besides the huge bundle of clothing for himself was a wicker basket, hung over one of his arms. "I got this for you, Miss Helen. I thought it would be handy for you to put your needlepoint in. I saw you working on it last night." He took the basket off his arm and handed it to her.

"Now, Barry, I meant you to spend all that money on yourself, but it tells me what a thoughtful lad you are. I will certainly enjoy using it, and I'll think of you every time I do. Thank you."

Helen was finding herself feeling very motherly toward this young man, who could, after all have been her son. She told him that by the time he had put his things in his room she would have the chicken and dumplings on the table and ready to eat.

She had never seen a young man eat with such a ravenous appetite as Barry. He positively devoured the chicken and dumplings, and the flaky biscuits. It dawned on her that he probably had not eaten all day, and he confessed to her as they were doing the dishes together that he hadn't.

"That had to be the very best chicken and dumplings I ever ate. No wonder you ran Miss Melba's kitchen and dining room. You sure are one fine cook, Miss Helen," he declared.

"Well, thank you, Barry!" She laughed. It was always nice to be appreciated.

Barry went to bed very early that evening, and Helen sat there alone for another two hours, just enjoying the quiet of Gillian's parlor and working on her needle-point. It was the first time she'd been able to indulge herself doing something like that for longer than she could remember. Evenings like this were impossible to have at the Old Pueblo Inn.

She found herself feeling very sorry for poor Melba, who she knew had died a very lonely lady. The glamour and excitement the inn had once generated for her had disappeared, and Melba must have found she could no longer cope with the various problems the inn was facing. Helen felt sad that Melba's life had ended that way.

Gillian's letter was a wonderful surprise for Hawk when he returned home from work. He was pleased to hear that Mrs. Foster had improved, for he was very fond of her. She'd always been very gracious to him, which was more than he could say for a lot of people in Maricopa County. Because he was a half-breed, he had to live with prejudice.

But Gillian made no mention in her letter of when she was planning on returning to Tucson. Hawk realized that she was going to be away longer than he'd anticipated. The thought of being separated from her for many weeks was enough to dampen his spirits. After the thrilling nights they'd spent together just before she'd left, he felt great depths of yearning for her. The nights were very lonely without her.

*   *   *

Helen did not get her letter until two days after Hawk received his, because Gillian had addressed it to the inn. Like Hawk, she was thrilled to hear from Gillian and to read the encouraging news about Nancy. She had no doubt that Gillian's arrival had been a tonic for her sister.

That night, Helen sat down at the kitchen table after she'd eaten supper and finished doing the dishes to write a letter to Gillian. It was difficult to write the news she had to tell Gillian. Her letter would not be as happy as Gillian's had been for her to read, but she knew that Gillian would be glad to know that she and Barry were safe, and that young Barry had found another job and place to live. Helen knew Gillian was very fond of the young lad.

She also told Gillian about the part-time job she'd found in the bakery a short distance from the house. At least, she thought as she closed the letter, there were a few good things to tell Gillian about.

The next afternoon she mailed the letter on her way to the bakery. She and Ruth Crawford got along just fine, and Helen could tell at once that Ruth was very pleased about how Helen handled herself around the bakery. Ruth decided after a couple of hours that if she wanted to take off an entire day sometimes, Helen was quite capable of running the shop. It would be a nice change for her, Ruth thought, after all this time being solely responsible for her bakery.

In fact, the only thing that bothered Ruth was whether she would be able to get Helen to stay there. It was obvious to Ruth, who had run the bakery for several years, that Helen was an experienced cook and baker. She moved with confidence and assurance, and

Ruth had to give her no instructions about baking. Helen's raisin bread was sheer perfection.

Helen left the bakery at five to go back to Gillian's house, and on the way home she reflected that the four hours' work had not left her at all tired. Even if she had been working there daily, it would not be like the long, weary hours she had labored at the inn.

However, since she didn't have to work tomorrow she decided to walk over to the livery the next day to see how young Barry was doing in his new job, and to invite him to dinner when he could manage it.

A light shower of rain fell during the night, and Helen woke up very early when the bright sunshine came streaming through the windows. As soon as she was dressed and had drunk a couple of cups of coffee, she went out to the garden to pull up some weeds she'd noticed sprouting up there. She knew they would pull up easily after the rainshower.

After she'd done that, she picked a bouquet of huge, colorful zinnias to take into the house. The birds were singing sweetly, and when she took the flowers into the house she gathered up some bread left over from the night before to toss out for the birds.

Helen was very conscious of all these simple pleasures she was enjoying, as she had not been able to for so very long. Life seemed wonderful.

A few hours later, she took a leisurely stroll toward the livery. When she arrived and young Barry looked up to see her entering through the wide-open doors, his face broke into a broad smile. "Miss Helen, it's so good to see you!" he exclaimed, rushing toward her.

"It's good to see you too, Barry. You look like you're doing just fine," she said warmly.

"Oh, I am. Mr. Parsons is one nice fellow. Come on and let me introduce you to him," he said, taking hold of her arm to lead her back into the building, where he had been talking with Jack Parsons when she'd arrived.

Jack Parsons knew this lady must be the one young Barry constantly talked about, and who had been so kind to him. When he saw that Barry was bringing her back to meet him, he took the kerchief from around his neck to wipe his soiled hands and rub the sweat from his brow.

"Miss Helen, this is Mr. Parsons," he told her, when they had joined the gray-haired man. Helen judged him to be in his fifties, and she detected that he had probably already developed a liking for young Barry the way his brown eyes twinkled when they looked his way.

"Nice to meet you, Miss Helen. I'm afraid my hands are too dirty to shake your hand," he apologized.

But Helen held out her hand. "A little dirt never hurt anybody, Mr. Parsons," she told him as she shook his hand, which was not only soiled but weathered and rough.

He chuckled. "I guess you're right, Miss Helen."

"Well, I certainly didn't come here to disrupt your work. I just wanted to see that Barry was doing all right, and it looks like he is," she explained.

"Oh, you're not disrupting anything, ma'am. And I think you could say me and young Barry are getting along just fine, aren't we, son?"

"Yes, sir, we sure are!"

"Barry here has sure been a help to me. I'm not as young as I used to be, and he's working so hard I'm not having to spend as many hours around here."

"Well, I don't want to interrupt, so I'm going to be on my way. It was nice to meet you, Mr. Parsons, and Barry, you come to see me when you can. I'll fix you some more of that chicken and dumplings you liked so well." She smiled, glancing up to see a grin on Parsons's face.

"Anytime you say, Miss Helen," Barry declared eagerly.

"Well, then, what about tomorrow night?" Helen grinned at his enthusiasm.

"Yes ma'am—I'll be there," he said quickly.

Helen bid them both farewell and turned to leave. As Barry and Jack Parsons went back to work, Parsons commented, "She sure is a nice lady, Barry. A mighty nice lady!"

What he didn't add was that he found Miss Helen a very pretty lady, with her trim figure neatly dressed in a sprigged muslin frock. He even liked the way she wore her light brown hair, which was streaked with gray, in two neat coils on the back of her head.

Jack didn't find attractive the overpainted ladies he saw roaming the streets of Tucson or coming to his livery, and nor did he approve of their fancy gowns, with all the frills and flounces and low-plunging necklines. But everything about Miss Helen was just the way a lady should be.

Chapter Twenty-eight

Helen returned to Gillian's house feeling very good about young Barry, for Jack Parsons had a fatherly air about him, it seemed to her. The next evening, when she and Barry were sharing the pot of chicken and dumplings, Barry told her that Mr. Parsons was like them: he was alone. His wife had died a few years ago.

Hearing this, Helen felt sorry that she had not invited him, too, to share the chicken and dumplings with them this evening. When Barry was about to leave a couple of hours later, Helen inquired, "Well, shall we say that you have another invitation next week, Barry? Next Tuesday night, if you can come, I'll fix you a big skillet of fried chicken—and you might just ask Mr. Parsons to come too, if he'd like to."

"Oh, golly—he'd like that, Miss Helen. I'll be sure and tell him," Barry replied as he went out the door.

"I'll be expecting the two of you, then," she called to him as he walked across the porch.

Helen went back into the house, thinking that Jack Parsons was probably enjoying the company of young

Barry, being a lonely man. She hoped Barry did bring him to dinner next week. He seemed a very kind gentleman, of the sort it had been her misfortune to know only rarely. Her brother-in-law, John Foster, was like that, and Hawk also seemed to possess a kind, generous heart.

On the other hand, Helen had never been that convinced about the handsome Steve Lafferty when he'd marched into Gillian's life. Oh, he had a winning way about him, and a devilishly charming smile that could make any young girl swoon when he was around her. Gillian had lost her heart quickly as soon as she met him, but Helen was convinced that before Steve had been swept to his death at sea, he had not given her the wonderful life she'd anticipated. She understood that Gillian had spent a lot of lonely hours in Ireland.

In any case, Helen was not imagining it that Gillian had been relieved to get back here to Arizona after her stay in Ireland.

On this wonderful, early summer day, Gillian was happy to be taking the Fosters' little mare out for a good ride, as John had suggested the night before. She had to confess that she was ready to get out of the house, after two weeks of working long and hard to get Nancy back on her feet.

She was glad that Nancy was so much better, and was happy to be in the house alone while John went about his chores and Gillian had her ride.

As she rode, she wondered about Hawk. She was yearning to see him after these last two long weeks in Rock Springs.

She had ridden only a short distance from the ranch when she spotted another rider galloping toward her. She wondered who it could be as he came closer, and he was almost up with her before she saw that it was Zack Morrison. He raised his hand to greet her, and called, "Hey, Miss Gillian. I was just coming over your way."

"Hello, Zack. Were you heading for the Fosters'?" Gillian asked as she pulled up on the reins.

"Yes, I thought it was time I paid a call on you all to see how everything was going, and Ma had me bring over these vegetables. Her garden is outdoing itself this year, and she didn't know whether John had had a chance to plant anything," he said.

"Well, that's very kind of your mother, Zack. I'm happy to tell you that everything is going along fine. Mother Foster is up and about more and more all the time," she told him.

Zack fell silent. He felt awkward around Gillian, for she was so beautiful, and he always secretly wished she could have been his girl. But when she was sixteen and he was eighteen, he'd been too shy to ride over to try to court her, as he had wanted to do.

Now that he was almost twenty-three, he still felt somewhat shy around her. She was like no other girl he'd ever met here in Maricopa County.

This afternoon, he had come all this way not so much to bring the vegetables to the Fosters as to come to call on her. He didn't know how to enlighten her about this, though. She still seemed like the untouchable goddess that he had to worship from afar. Unable to let her know how he felt, he merely listened in silence as she told him that he would find Nancy up and about when he arrived at the house.

"Well, I'm—I'm sure glad I got to see you for a moment, Miss Gillian. I guess I nearly missed you today," he declared.

"Oh, I'm glad to see you, too, Zack, and I know the Fosters will be, too. Give your folks my regards," she said, and spurred the roan to move on.

She had no inkling that he watched her ride on until he could no longer see her, just as she had no idea that Zack was a secret admirer of hers.

With the bright sun shining down on her, Gillian was in no hurry to get back to the ranch. She intended to take a long, leisurely ride this afternoon. She felt as if a giant magnet was drawing her to the mountain trail, and she surrendered to the impulse to go up to Hawk's mountain cabin, even though she knew it would be empty. There was an enchantment there that Gillian could not have explained, but she knew how she felt when she was in that cabin.

As she rode up the trail through the pine trees, she could hear the calls of the creatures of the woods in the serene quiet. A gentle breeze rustled through the branches of the trees, making a pleasing melody for her to hear.

She came to the last bend in the trail before the cabin thinking that even though Solange was many miles away, the essence of that loving lady was still there at her little cabin. Gillian could feel it as she dismounted and walked up the pathway, stopping to view all the lovely blooming flowers that Solange had so devotedly planted.

It surprised her to see the front door ajar, but since Hawk had told her that Troy came over every few days she figured that he must have failed to secure it the last

261

time he was here.

But since the door was open, she could not resist entering. She found it hard to believe that the cabin was not being lived in, for it seemed so alive. Gillian could have sworn that there were fresh branches of Solange's herbs hanging from the rafters in the kitchen. But she knew that it must be her imagination, and she started to go back toward the front door to leave.

As she was about to open it, she heard lilting laughter that could only belong to one person. She wondered if she was hallucinating. Slowly, almost cautiously, she opened the door.

Coming up the path were the laughing Solange and her huge French-Canadian husband, Gaston, carrying a nice line of fish he'd just caught in the mountain stream.

"Gillian! *Oh, chèrie!*" Solange shrieked excitedly, rushing toward Gillian. The two of them locked in a long, affectionate embrace, while Gaston stood smiling at them, for he knew how dear this young lady was to his Solange.

He also knew that she was often in Solange's thoughts, even though it had not been her son Gillian had married. This fact had been more evidence for Gaston of what a marvelous, understanding lady his wife was.

They had been married for over a year now, and it had been all he had hoped for in the years he'd waited and hoped for love. Solange Touraine was a lady who had many intriguing sides to her character. Back here, where he had first met her, she was like a child of nature, in love with the woods and the mountain where she loved to grow her flowers and herbs. Seeing this love, he understood how this petite French lady could have existed so many years up here with her half-breed son, Hawk, and raised him to be a fine young man. Few women could have done that.

And during the last year, he'd watched her in his more sophisticated world up in Canada, where as his wife she had played the role of hostess to his many friends and business acquaintances and their wives. She charmed them all, and she was always the most elegant lady in any soirée they attended.

After Solange and Gillian finally broke their embrace, Gaston inquired with a twinkle in his eyes, "Well, may I have a kiss and a hug, too?"

Gillian laughed. "Of course you can, Gaston. Oh, this is such a wonderful surprise!"

His huge arm reached around her tiny waist, for the other hand held the line of fish. He gave her a big bear hug, then suggested that the three of them go into the house so that he could relieve himself of the fish. He also invited Gillian to stay and enjoy their feast with them.

"Oh, I wish I could, Gaston, but the Fosters would be worried about what had happened to me," she told him.

But she did stay there to talk with them for an hour before she left, and then it was most reluctantly that she took her leave.

Solange told her in parting, "Hawk doesn't even know we are here yet. We decided to come a month earlier than I'd written to tell him we would come."

Solange had enjoyed hearing Gillian telling her about her son, and how the two of them had been spending time together. She had never been able to convince herself, even though Gillian had married Steve Lafferty, that her son and this girl were not destined to share their lives. She was elated to hear that they had found one another again. Perhaps fate would be kinder to them this time.

When Gillian finally departed from the cabin, Solange turned to look at Gaston. He was smiling down at her, for he knew how happy she was to have been reunited with Gillian.

"Oh, *mon cher,* she and Hawk will find that they were meant to be together. I feel it here, so very deep in my heart," she declared.

"I can believe that, *ma petite,* for your heart never seems to lie to you." His huge arms reached out to draw her to him.

Solange reveled in the infinite comfort of his arms holding her. She was so glad they'd decided to return to her mountain cabin earlier than they'd planned. Now, her happiness would be complete if she could only spy her handsome son riding up that mountain trail. But it wasn't likely, for Hawk was not expecting them yet. She had just written to her son of their arrival, and Gaston had ridden into Rock Springs yesterday to send off her letter.

She also realized that even if Hawk did know, he might not be able to get away from his job. She hoped he would be able to come, but if not, there was nothing to keep them from traveling to Tucson to see Hawk before they returned to Canada.

Chapter Twenty-nine

Gillian was in a very happy mood when she rode back to the Fosters' ranch. Being with Solange and Gaston had been the most delightful surprise for her. How glad she was to have taken that impulsive decision to ride up the mountain, otherwise she would not have known they were there, and nor would they have known about her being back in Maricopa County.

But now, as she was approaching the ranch, she could spot John Foster in the barnyard doing the evening chores. She had probably been gone too long, and she would feel awfully bad if Mother Foster had tried to do too much while she was away.

But at least, when she rode in, John Foster gave her a warm greeting. When she had been living there and arrived back home late after going out for a ride, he used to make his disapproval clear.

"Hello there," she called to him. "I'm sorry I'm so late, but I rode up the mountain this afternoon and found that Solange and her husband, Gaston, had returned for a visit." She dismounted when she reached the yard.

"Well, what a nice surprise for you, Gillian. I know how close you always were to Hawk's mother."

Gillian was about to lead the roan into the barn, but John took the reins, telling her that he'd attend to the mare and she could get on into the house. "That wife of mine has been just fine, though. She's enjoyed fixing up a big pot of beans and ham this afternoon."

Gillian laughed. "Well, I'll get in there and get the rest done if she's been that busy." She rushed to the house and dashed through the kitchen door to find Nancy setting the table. Immediately, she insisted on taking over.

"You trying to boss me in my own kitchen, missy?" Nancy grinned goodnaturedly as she sat down and allowed Gillian to have her way. As she busily whipped up batter for cornbread, she told Nancy about her ride this afternoon and finding Solange and Gaston at the cabin. "Hawk could not have known they would be here, or he would have mentioned it to me when we were together," Gillian remarked, pouring the batter into the greased pan to put it into the hot oven.

"It will be a big disappointment to that young man if he doesn't get to see them while they're here. Hawk was very close to his ma, and admired her as he should have. I was always sorry I never got to know her better," Nancy confessed regretfully.

"Yes, the two of you could be very good friends, I think, Mother Foster," Gillian told her.

A short time later, John came in from the barn and the three of them sat at the table to enjoy hefty helpings of beans and ham, along with the cornbread. Over dinner, John announced that he was going into Rock Springs in the morning to pick up the mail, and he suggested to Nancy and Gillian that they make him a list of anything they wished him to purchase while he was in town.

For the first time in the three weeks that Gillian had been at the ranch, she slept far later than usual the next morning. By the time she had dressed and brushed her hair, she could hear that Nancy was already bustling around in the kitchen.

When she entered the kitchen she saw that Nancy had prepared John's breakfast and he had obviously already left for town.

"Well, I guess we can assume you're feeling better, Mother Foster," she said, giving Nancy an affectionate hug.

"Honey, I feel like my old self again, and lordy, that's a good feeling. You know what I'm going to do today?" Nancy went over to sit down as she wiped her hands on her apron. "I'm going to write that sister of mine, and tell her just how good I'm feeling."

"Oh, she'll be happy to get a letter from you—although I wrote her about a week ago and said you were improving," Gillian told her.

At that moment John came in through the kitchen door. His trip to town had taken him less than two hours, and his arms were full of the goods he had bought. After greeting them both, he announced to Gillian, "You got a letter, dear."

Eagerly, Gillian took it, thinking that it might be from Hawk. She wasted no time opening it, and felt a little disappointed to find that it was from Helen, not Hawk.

As she read, Nancy and John noticed that the expression on Gillian's face had become very tense and sober. Alarmed, Nancy asked, "Is something wrong, Gillian? Is anything wrong with Helen?"

Gillian stammered, "Oh, no, Mother Foster, Helen is fine. It's—it's the inn. It burned down, and Miss Melba died in the fire." Nancy saw tears in Gillian's eyes, and she went over to give her a consoling embrace.

"Thank God Helen was staying at my house. Oh, thank God for that!" Gillian sighed, thinking about all the other people who worked at the inn, most of whom she knew. What a trauma for everyone! The inn was home to a lot of them, as well as their livelihood.

For the rest of the day Gillian could think of nothing but that devastating fire. It was hard to imagine Melba Jackson dead.

The Fosters understood her quiet mood that day, and they also understood why she went to the quiet of her room shortly after the evening meal was over and the dishes were done.

But what they could not know was what was going on in Gillian's mind. After reading Helen's letter, she felt like a moth drawn to a flame. Tucson was the flame, and she wanted desperately to return there. Mother Foster was certainly recovered now, and Gillian wanted to be in her own little house. She also wanted very much to see Hawk.

It would not be a bad time to leave, since Nancy was so much better, and John had also gotten caught up with the many things he'd had to leave undone while Nancy was so ill.

She said nothing to either of the Fosters that evening about her decision to leave, but quietly started to pack her things. She regretted that she would not be able to make another trip to see Solange and Gaston again, but her mind was made up.

It was a shock to John and Nancy when Gillian announced at breakfast next morning that she would be leaving to return to Tucson. They both knew that it had been Helen's letter that inspired her decision, and they understood, but it wasn't easy for them to accept.

"Did you hear what she said, John? She said she needed to get back home," Nancy had pointed out to her husband. "This used to be home for her, but I guess she doesn't feel that way now."

"Well, we were lucky to have her stay this long, Nancy. Look on the bright side, though. You're well again, and we're going to keep you that way."

"Oh I'm going to stay well, John Foster! I've never been so miserable in my whole life as when I was laid up in that bed."

It seemed no time at all before Gillian was gone, for there was a stagecoach headed for Tucson that afternoon, and she managed to be ready in time. John and Nancy found it lonely without her at the table with them that first evening.

The next day, Zack Morrison finally gathered up the courage to ride over to the Fosters' ranch to call on Gillian. He'd dressed in his best pants and shirt, his boots had a high shine on them, and his unruly mop of hair was slicked down when he mounted his horse to ride over there at about three in the afternoon.

It was a crestfallen Zack who rode back to his father's ranch that evening, having been told by the Fosters that Gillian had returned to Tucson. As he rode home, he faced the truth that the beautiful Miss Gillian would never have been his girl, and he might as well settle for one of the nice ranchers' daughters here in Maricopa County.

A month later, Zack Morrison took himself a wife, and Nancy and John attended the festivities.

The closer she got to Tucson, the more excited Gillian became. She wondered just how much longer she would have stayed at the ranch if she had not received Helen's letter. Time had begun to hang very heavy once Nancy was up and able to work around her house.

Finally, she could see the outskirts of Tucson in the distance, and they were a welcome sight to see. She would be arriving before sunset, fortunately, so she would still have time to get to her house before dark. She thought how nice it would be if Hawk was there to see her home this afternoon, but he had no way of knowing she was on her way.

However, there was someone she knew at the station. Jake Harmon was preparing to board his buggy, and the sight of the little auburn-haired beauty, Gillian Lafferty, was more than he had bargained for. What a waste it would have been, he thought, if she, too, had perished in that fire. It had been two or three days after the fire that word had come to his father's ranch, and old Sam had taken the news about Melba Jackson very hard, for they'd known one another so long and not parted on the best of terms.

Even Jake had to admit that it seemed strange to come to Tucson, as he had today, and not see that old, sprawling inn where it had stood for years.

As he approached Gillian, he wondered where the pretty little thing had been, for he saw the two pieces of luggage by her feet.

"Well, good afternoon, Gillian Lafferty. Remember me?" he asked, a confident grin on his face.

Gillian turned to see the tall, sandy-haired Jake Harmon smiling down at her. "Good afternoon, Jake," she replied coolly.

He gave a husky laugh. "Well, at least you do remember me. I know—I know I acted like a damned fool, but I guess I can apologize for that. I hope you'll accept my apology."

"I do accept your apology, but you're going to have to excuse me now, for I've got to get on home."

"Have you got a ride?"

"No, but I'll get one," she replied firmly.

"Look, Gillian—I'll take you home, to make up for my being such an idiot. I promise to be the absolute gentleman. After all, it's broad daylight. Come on, Gillian, you look tired."

Gillian did feel weary, and the sooner she got to her little house the happier she would be. As he'd said, it was still daylight, and whatever else his faults, Jake was no fool.

"Look, Gillian, let me help you into the buggy. I'll have you home in just a few minutes," he promised her. He held out his hand to her, sensing that she was ready to accept his offer.

The thought of getting home quickly was tempting

271

enough that she accepted, but she warned him, "I want to go straight home, Jake Harmon. I am weary as you said, for I've come all the way from Rock Springs."

He nodded his head as he helped her climb up into the buggy's seat, then he lifted a piece of her luggage in each hand. After he'd put the luggage into the buggy, he climbed into the seat and immediately urged the bay to start moving.

As they were traveling along the street, Jake told her how sad he'd been to hear about Miss Melba and the inn. "It sure stunned my father. I don't know if he has really accepted it yet."

"Well, I still find it hard to believe. I had left Tucson when it happened, so I just found out about it recently."

"So you weren't here when the fire happened?"

"No, I wasn't."

"Well, when I take you to your house you've got a shock coming. It's eerie to look in that direction and not see the old building inside the walled grounds," Jake told her. It was only a few minutes later that Gillian got her first startling view of the site where the inn had once stood. Jake had been right about the shock she'd feel.

"Oh, my Lord!" she gasped, as her hands went up to cover her mouth.

"I wanted to prepare you, Gillian, but I guess that would have been impossible when you face the stark reality of something like this," Jake Harmon said gently.

"No, you could never have prepared me for this, Jake."

In another minute or two, Jake halted the buggy and

Gillian could enjoy the sight of her little house. He took her luggage to the front door, but didn't try to get himself invited in. No, he played the perfect gentleman, in the hope of getting back into her good graces. Gillian appreciated Jake's good behavior.

With a devious grin on his face he pointed out, "You see, I brought you straight home. Now maybe you'll realize that my apology was sincere and from the heart, Miss Gillian Lafferty."

"I do realize, and I thank you, Jake. Now, I must get inside, for I am tired," she told him as she opened her front door.

"I understand, Gillian. Here, just let me set these inside, and I'll be going on my way." He lifted the two pieces of luggage through the door, then Jake raised his hat and bid her goodbye. "I'll be seeing you soon, I hope, Gillian."

Gillian smiled, but said nothing as she stepped through the front door. All she could think about was how glad she was to be back in this little house.

Serenity flooded through her as she roamed through the rooms, noticing how nice and neat Helen had kept the house. Since she wasn't there, Gillian assumed Helen was at her part-time job at the bakery.

She went directly to her bedroom to stretch out and rest awhile, before Helen came home. She wasn't this weary when she'd arrived at the Fosters' ranch, but the trip back to Tucson had exhausted her, it seemed. Or maybe she was just feeling the effects of the hard work she'd put in at the ranch.

Jake rode back to the new hotel thinking to himself

that he found it very easy to be a gentleman around a lady like Gillian Lafferty. She seemed to bring out the best in him, and he knew by now that she was not like most of the women he'd known. Gillian was not the kind of woman a man could have for a few nights of pleasure and then walk away from. No, she was the type of lady a man wanted as his wife, and to be the mother of his children.

Chapter Thirty

How deceptive an observation could be! Hawk's black eyes had only to spot his beautiful, auburn-haired Gillian sitting beside a good-looking young fellow in a buggy for all kinds of wild imaginings to take place. They certainly seemed engrossed in conversation. Hawk hadn't even known she was back in town—for she had carefully not let him know, he told himself.

He tugged on the reins and turned Tache around to follow them as they traveled toward Gillian's house. When Harmon's buggy turned down the side road, Hawk followed a short distance behind them. At the corner, he slowed Tache's pace as he watched the young man help Gillian down from the buggy. What he didn't stay to see was Jake taking the luggage out of the buggy. If he had, he would have known that Gillian had just arrived back from Rock Springs. Maybe that would have mellowed the savage rage within him as he turned Tache around.

By the time he arrived at his house, after riding

Tache at a furious gallop, he had begun to think that Gillian was some elusive dream he had chased but never quite caught. But, he told himself, he had not dreamed those torrid nights of making love to her.

He wanted to go to her house and confront her with what he'd observed that afternoon, but Hawk was a very proud man. Instead, he stayed at home and wallowed in the miserable torment his jealousy was stirring within him.

That evening was far more pleasant for Gillian. She enjoyed a refreshing nap before Helen came home from the bakery, and was awakened by the pleasant aroma of the raisin and carrot bread that Helen had brought home from the bakery.

The two women had a joyous reunion when Gillian came out of her bedroom. They spent the next hour just talking, for Gillian had so much to tell Helen about her sister and how well she was doing when Gillian left Rock Springs.

"Oh, Gillian, it's so good to have you back!" Helen declared.

They drank the coffee Helen had brewed, and continued to talk, for Helen had many things to tell her about all that had happened since she'd left Tucson. Gillian was glad to know that young Barry had found himself a place at Parsons' Livery. Helen decided she was not ready to tell Gillian about her new friendship with the man young Barry was working for. When he'd come to the house with Barry to have dinner, Helen had found herself liking Jack Parsons very much. She could also tell that he found her attractive. It had been a long, long time since Helen Clayton had felt about a man as she did about the kind-hearted Parsons.

It was wonderful to feel this way again. The truth was, Helen couldn't remember when she had been so happy. As she and Gillian worked in the kitchen together that evening, preparing themselves some dinner, Gillian made her happiness complete by telling her, "Now Helen, you must consider this your home for as long as you want."

"Oh, Gillian, thank you! I don't know what I would have done if I hadn't had your house as my haven when everything happened."

"I'm glad it was here for you, Helen."

They enjoyed the meal they'd prepared, and later they sat in the parlor to talk the evening away. Helen excused herself for a moment to get the little box Melba had requested that she give to Gillian. Gillian was very moved by the gift, and she could not hold back the tears that sprang to her eyes when she saw the beautiful sapphire earrings.

"It seems very strange to me, Helen, that Melba could not have gotten out of there, too," Gillian declared.

"Well, I believe she didn't want to, Gillian. Oh, I'd never say this to anyone but you. But some things that happened there in the last two or three days before it happened have me convinced that Melba set fire to the inn herself, and that she chose to stay there to go up in flames with it."

"Oh, Helen!" Gillian gasped, shocked.

But by the time Helen told her about how Melba had paid her the share of profits that had been overdue for months, Gillian was finding herself intrigued, especially about the gifts of exquisite jewelry. There was also the incident young Barry had told Helen about, and the tale Arthur had told about Melba's sending him home early.

"That doesn't sound like Melba at all, Helen."

"Well, it wasn't—unless she knew exactly what she was going to do. She made sure that I was gone, and that Barry had left to go to his brother's. All the kitchen help was gone, so she went to the desk to shoo Arthur out of the inn. Only one wing of the inn was occupied, so she must have started the fire in the other wing, knowing that all the guests would have time to get out."

"Oh, Helen—she planned it so carefully! I always knew she was a clever woman."

Helen certainly agreed with her about that. She knew that it had to have been Melba who went down the hallway to knock on the doors and warn the guests about the fire. She'd heard them talking the next day, and nobody was sure who had alerted them. But Helen was able to put all the pieces to the puzzle.

"It eased the sadness for me, Gillian, because I know beyond a shadow of a doubt that this was what Melba wanted. She could not have existed without her inn, nor could it have run without her."

"No, that's true," Gillian agreed.

"Business had fallen off drastically in those last four weeks. The railroad has brought so many new people into the city that new places are being established everywhere, and they were draining the inn, slowly but surely. Melba saw this, and no longer had the strength to fight, as she might once have done."

"Then wherever she is, she must be happy and content about her decision. I think you are absolutely right, Helen," Gillian told her.

It was late by now, and both women were ready to seek the comfort of their beds after the long hours of talking.

Gillian's sleep was sound and deep. She was looking forward to seeing Hawk the next day. As soon as she was up and dressed, she planned to walk over to the railroad office to surprise him.

She was also going to have the joy of telling him that his mother and Gaston were at the cabin, and that she had seen them.

It was late when she finally woke up, and Helen was gone from the house when Gillian came out of her bedroom and went into the kitchen to pour herself a cup of coffee.

As soon as she had drunk it, she rushed to the bedroom to start dressing. She took special care to make herself look pretty for when she and Hawk would meet after all these long weeks apart. She tied her auburn hair back from her face with a blue ribbon that matched the bright blue tunic she was wearing with her dark blue twill riding skirt. She was eagerly anticipating a ride on Fuego.

As she left the house to walk to the office, the sun seemed unusually warm, so she walked in the shade of the trees lining one side of the street when she could.

As it happened, when she arrived at the office Warner was just arriving back from an errand he'd gone on. "Well, Miss Gillian, how nice to see you again. Did you just get back to Tucson?" he asked her, with a friendly smile on his face.

"Yes, sir. Hawk doesn't know yet, so I thought I'd just come over here to tell him that I was back, and that

I'd seen his mother while I was in Rock Springs." By now, she and Warner were walking up the steps toward the front door.

"Well, Hawk will be happy to see you. I think that young man's been moping with you out of Tucson for so long," Warner said with a chuckle.

Gillian replied playfully, "Well, I should hope so. I'd like to think I was missed."

Hawk stopped work to listen to the voices he heard outside. Suddenly the door opened and Warner and Gillian came in, still laughing. "Look who I found outside, Hawk!" Warner announced.

There she stood, looking as beautiful as ever, or perhaps even more so. Hawk stared directly at her. It was not easy for him to force himself to smile or pretend nothing was wrong, but Warner was watching him.

"Well, Gillian, it's good to see you back!"

Gillian was expecting him to rush around the desk and take her eagerly in his arms, but since Mr. Barstow was there, she understood why he was so reserved.

"Well, it's wonderful to be back. I just arrived late yesterday afternoon," she replied excitedly.

"Yesterday afternoon?" he echoed.

"Yes, Hawk, and guess what? I got to see Solange and Gaston. They've arrived early."

"Mother and Gaston are at the cabin?" Hawk's black eyes flashed brightly when he heard that surprising news.

"Yes, it was a surprise for me, too, Hawk."

Hawk was filled with mixed emotions after the miserable night he'd spent last night. Now here she was, standing in the office talking to him. It was obvious that she had no inkling that he'd seen her in the company of another man yesterday, or of the rage that had brewed within him for hours afterward.

But how could he explain to himself why she had walked to the office to see him, if she was so interested in that handsome fellow he'd seen her with late yesterday afternoon?

In that childlike way of hers, with her eyes sparkling brilliantly, she asked him, "Could I take Tache, Hawk, like I did before? I'd like to go over to see Fuego today."

Hawk told her to go ahead, for he could hardly say anything else with Warner right there in the office with them. Hawk knew that his boss highly approved of Miss Gillian Lafferty. As she was turning jauntily to go out the door, having declared that she'd disturbed their work long enough, Warner called out to her, "Miss Gillian, don't worry about riding all the way back to the office at five. I'll run Hawk home when we close up."

"Why, thank you, Mr. Barstow—that's mighty sweet of you," she replied, flashing him a smile as she went on out the door.

Warner turned to Hawk and declared, "Lord Almighty, she is the prettiest little thing—but then, I don't have to tell you that!"

Once again, Hawk was forced to smile as he responded, "No, you don't have to tell me." Turning to go back to his desk, he wanted to lose himself in his work. Right now he was in a quandary where Gillian was concerned. He was hoping his work would take his mind off her, but that proved impossible.

*   *   *

As Gillian rode Tache over to Hawk's house, she was puzzling over Hawk's manner when she was in the office. He had made no effort to go outside with her to assist her up on Tache, as he had before. He could have kissed her if he'd come to the hitching post, for Warner would have been back in the office. How she had been looking forward to that kiss!

By the time she reached his house, Gillian had concluded that it was not her imagination that Hawk had been aloof toward her. She could not get it off her mind, even when she'd taken the ride on Fuego.

When she got back, she didn't feel as comfortable in Hawk's house as she had the last time she'd been there to await him coming home from work. She had been planning that the two of them would share dinner together this evening, and that later Hawk would take her in his arms, as he had the night before she'd left for Rock Springs. Now she wasn't even sure she should stay.

But as she sat resting in the parlor, she decided to quit speculating about Hawk. He would be home soon, and then she would know one way or the other. But she made no effort to go into his kitchen and prepare a meal for them. Somehow, she didn't feel free to do that, as she had before.

When Hawk arrived at his house, leaped out of the buggy, and bid Warner goodnight, he wondered if he would find Gillian still there. He'd seen a questioning look in her blue eyes when she'd left the office. Gillian was a very perceptive person, and he thought she had sensed that something was gnawing at him.

He felt even more sure about this when he opened the front door and there was no aroma of dinner being

282

cooked. Gillian was sitting over in the corner, looking at him as he stepped through the door. Hawk had always found Gillian to be the one person he could always talk to with ease and comfort, but this afternoon, he did not find it so easy.

Feeling awkward, he did not rush over to her to take her into his arms, as he had yearned to do for weeks now. Instead, he sank down into a chair in the parlor and talked to her about things like the fire at the inn, and how she had found his mother and Gaston.

Gillian decided to treat him in the same casual manner as he obviously wanted to treat her. She had her own pride, and she was confused by Hawk's mood. She tried to think of some way to get them both out of their misery. By now a half hour had gone by since Hawk had entered the door, and he was yet to invite her to stay to dinner. She was feeling unwelcome.

"Well, Hawk, I think you must be tired from your day's work, and I guess I should be getting back to my house. Did I tell you Helen is staying at my house?"

"Yes, you did. She was lucky to have your place to stay in after the fire. So, you—you want to go home, then?" He watched her get up from the chair and start to walk toward him.

"I probably shouldn't have come to your office today."

"Well, I was glad to know you'd got back, Gillian," he answered. "What time did you come in yesterday?"

"It was about five, I guess," she replied, going back to pick up the reticule she'd left in the chair. She hung the drawstrings around her wrist.

"Well, I guess I'll go get Tache, Gillian," he mumbled, and ambled out the door.

Gillian watched him go, and yearned to cry out to him that she truly didn't want to leave. She wanted to ask him if he loved her, as he'd told her he did. Perhaps he'd met someone while she was gone all those weeks.

The thought of that made tears form in her blue eyes, but she quickly wiped them away when she heard Hawk coming back up the front steps. She lifted her chin proudly. She wanted him to see no tears in her eyes if he'd found himself a new love!

Chapter Thirty-one

To have Gillian's soft, warm body pressing against him as they rode Tache toward her house was sheer agony. The closer they got to her house, the more intense the anguish became, until at last he was so intoxicated with his longing for her that he forgot about his stupid male pride.

He gave a sudden yank on the reins and Tache came to a halt. Gillian suddenly found herself being grasped and turned just enough for his lips to meet with hers in a searing kiss. His strong arms enclosed her tightly and pressed her firmly against him.

He kissed her so fiercely that when he finally released her she was breathless. She gasped, "My Lord, Hawk!"

He, too, was panting. Staring down at her face, he announced, "I'm not taking you home. I don't want to take you home, Gillian."

She was still trying to get her breath, but she stammered, "Well, you—you could have fooled me, Hawk. I thought you didn't want me at your house, and you didn't act too happy to see me when I came to your office today."

He had already turned Tache around to go back the way they'd come. "It's not that I wasn't glad to see you, Gillian; something else is bothering me."

"Well, I feel I have the right to know what it is, Hawk," she declared.

"And I'll tell you, as soon as we get back to the house," he promised her, urging Tache into a canter.

When they arrived, Hawk leaped down and raised his arms up to her. She allowed herself to be lifted down to the ground.

"I'll see you in a minute, Gillian. I'm going to get Tache settled in for the night," he told her, and started to lead his horse toward the stable.

This time, Gillian felt much better as she entered Hawk's house. Soon as she was sitting in one of the parlor chairs yanking off her boots, which were beginning to hurt her feet, she heard Hawk come in the kitchen door.

He stood watching her until she had them removed. Then he walked over to where she was sitting and effortlessly picked her up, then sat down with her in his lap. "Now, Gillian, I've a confession to make to you. I've been crazy with jealousy because I saw you riding in a buggy with a good-looking fellow late yesterday. I went into a rage, and spent a miserable night worrying about it."

She gave him a loving, understanding smile, and her hands stroked his cheeks. "Oh, Hawk—my dear, dear Hawk! You had no reason to be jealous. Jake Harmon only gave me a ride to my house. He happened to be at the station when I arrived, and I was very grateful to get the offer, since I had two pieces of luggage."

"I was beginning to think I must have been wrong today, when you appeared at the office, but I guess I can't quite forget that I lost you once to another man, Gillian."

She bent close to assure him that it would not happen again, and her lips took his in a kiss. His hands pressed against her back to press her closer to him. "Oh, Gillian, losing you again would drive me mad!"

"You'll never lose me, Hawk!" she vowed.

Holding her cradled in his arms, he rose up from the chair to take her to his bedroom. He swore to himself that Gillian was one person with whom he'd never again allow pride to get in his way.

Right now, he was only interested in loving her, as he'd yearned to do for weeks, and it pleased him to find out that she was just as eager to make love to him. That was all Hawk needed to know as he lowered her down on the bed. They wasted no time in removing their clothing for they wanted to feel the satiny softness of her flesh against the muscular firmness of his. His huge hands were gentle as they caressed her. It had always amazed Gillian what tenderness he had when they made love—and how forceful was the surge of his thrust when he filled her, passion churning savagely within him.

And so it was again this evening, as they soared to their wonderful lofty pinnacle again. For golden moments they stayed there, atop that sensual summit, their entwined bodies shuddering until they both felt the climax engulfing them.

Afterward Gillian sighed with pleasure, and Hawk gave a deep, husky moan as he pressed her closer against him. When he thought that he had almost denied himself this wonderful felicity because of his stupid pride, Hawk swore that he'd never make that mistake again. If he'd kept riding on toward Gillian's house, he would have returned here on his own and been very lonely. And Gillian would have felt the same way.

Eventually they shared a very late supper. Gillian had no desire to leave Hawk that night, nor did he want her to go, so they slept together in Hawk's bed. Gillian did not get back to her house until seven o'clock next morning, which gave Hawk enough time to get over to his office after he left her at her front door.

Helen did not hear her come in, for she was still sleeping, but she had found a note Gillian had left her yesterday, so she wasn't concerned when Gillian had not returned from Hawk's house by the time she had retired last night.

Gillian tiptoed through the parlor and took a look in the back bedroom to see that Helen was still asleep, then went on quietly to her bedroom, got undressed, and slipped into her nightgown so that she could enjoy another few hours of sleep.

Gillian was still asleep when Helen quietly left the house to go to work at the bakery. When she finally woke up it was a little past noon, and Gillian told herself that the hours she was keeping now were as crazy as the hours she had kept when she was working at the inn.

When she was dressed, she spent a few hours working around the grounds of her house, weeding the flower beds and vegetable garden. She thought that she could pick some of the vegetables in her garden today, and have a nice meal prepared for Helen when she came home from work at the bakery.

So she went in to get her basket, then went back out to the yard to see what was ready to be picked. That was where Jake Harmon found her when he stopped by her house. She was a most fetching sight as he approached the backyard, and for a moment he just stood there, observing her shapely form bent over.

"Good afternoon, Gillian," he finally called out to her.

Gillian stood up and saw Jake standing there with a bundle cradled in his arms. "Good afternoon to you, Jake."

"I've brought you something. Compliments of the Harmon ranch—one of Pa's cured hams. He wanted me to bring it to you. They're the best you'll ever eat, I'll swear," he told her cockily.

She smiled and thanked him. "You didn't need to do that, but you give your father my thanks for me."

She picked up her basket and went up to join him. Courtesy demanded that she take the ham and invite him into the house for a cup of coffee, so she did just that. Jake was more than eager to accept her invitation. As he followed her into the kitchen, he told her, "You've got yourself a nice little place here, Gillian."

"I like it," she replied, placing the basket of vegetables over on the kitchen counter.

"Do you miss working at the inn?" Jake asked, as he straddled one of the kitchen chairs and took his wide-brimmed hat off his head.

Gillian was thinking, as she fired up the cookstove with some kindling, that she didn't remember him ever being this charming. In her candid way she replied,

"No, I can't say I miss working there, Jake. I miss the sight of the old inn, and I miss being able to go see Miss Melba. But I found the work denied me any other life, after I had worked there several weeks."

"You sure were the attraction there, in case you didn't know it. I guess that's why the first time I saw you I went absolutely loco. I apologize again for that."

"Once is enough, Jake." She smiled at him. Now that the coffee pot was on the stove and the fire was going, she sat down at the table with him.

"You're a very gracious lady, Gillian—you truly are!" His face and manner, along with that mane of sandy-colored hair, reminded her very much of Steve Lafferty. There was a cocky way about him when he spoke or moved that was very reminiscent of the Irishman she'd once loved so intensely.

As they shared the pot of coffee, Gillian had to admit that regardless of what Helen had told her about Jake Harmon, he was a perfect gentleman today, as he had been when he brought her home from the station.

When he got up to leave he told her, "I'd like to come by here again sometime, if I might, Gillian. It can get kinda lonely out there on that ranch sometimes."

Gillian smiled. "Now, Jake, I heard you were quite the man about town. How do you have time to be lonely?"

"Gillian, I know all about those tales, and most of them are, pardon me, a lot of bull! Most of my time is spent at the ranch working my tail off, but when I do come to town, being Sam Harmon's son makes me a hellraiser."

Gillian figured that either he was telling her the truth, or he was a most convincing liar.

A twinkle came to his eye. "Now, I'll tell you who the *real* hellraiser was: it was old Sam!"

Gillian laughed. She could certainly believe that, from what she'd observed when she was at the inn and had watched him drink his liquor during the evening.

By the time Jake finally said goodbye and went out her front door, Gillian was amazed to look at the clock and see just how long he'd stayed there. Helen would be leaving the bakery any time now, and she hadn't even started dinner. Gillian immediately filled the kettle with water to cook some of the vegetables from her garden. They would have some of Jake's ham with their supper—and with many suppers to come.

Gillian worked busily in the kitchen, cleaning green onions and slicing one of the huge tomatoes from her vines. Tender ears of corn steamed in one pot on the stove, and new potatoes were simmering in another.

At five-thirty Helen came through the door to find a grand meal awaiting her. The loaf of potato bread she'd brought from the bakery would be all they needed to make it a feast.

A while before Helen had turned down the side street where Gillian's little frame house was situated, Hawk had been riding Tache along the main street on his way home. He could not resist glancing down that side street where Gillian lived, and where he'd dropped her off early this morning.

When he spied that familiar buggy there by her gate, he found it very difficult to shrug it aside. It was certainly the same buggy, for it was very distinctive, and Hawk knew it was the same young man's buggy as

291

he'd seen bringing her to her house the evening she'd returned to Tucson.

Last night he'd tossed aside his pride, but now he questioned how far his faith in Gillian would sustain him. He wanted to believe her—God knew, he wanted to! But Hawk was a very practical man, and he knew from past experience that Gillian could give way to an impulse if her heart told her to.

She'd left him once before to rush off and marry another man, and Hawk had no intentions of allowing that to happen to him again. Not even Gillian was worth that pain and hurt!

This morning, when he'd taken her back to her house, he had been thinking that it was time he asked her for the second time to be his wife.

But this evening he wasn't so sure. Something told him to give it more time.

Chapter Thirty-two

There must have been something in the air that night, for both Helen and Gillian wanted to have a very confidential talk as they shared the evening together. Gillian's vegetables and generous slices of Jake's cured ham, with the potato bread Helen had brought from the bakery, made a most delicious meal. As they were cleaning the dishes together, Helen started to talk about the nice man she'd met. She told Gillian how she had invited him, along with Barry, to the house for dinner.

"I'm glad you did, and you must invite them here again, Helen," Gillian told her.

"I was hoping you would say that, Gillian. I'd like you to meet Jack Parsons. I think he's a mighty fine man, and he's been awfully good to Barry."

"I'd be happy to meet him," Gillian told her.

"He . . . likes me, Gillian, if you know what I mean," Helen said, with a blush on her face.

"And why not, Helen? You're a very nice-looking lady. I think it is absolutely wonderful that you and

293

Mr. Parsons find that you like one another," Gillian declared, in that very straightforward way of hers.

"Do you really feel that way, Gillian?"

"I certainly do!"

Helen gave a pleased smile, for she respected Gillian's opinion. It washed away some of her fears that she was just being a silly woman, past middle age, suddenly feeling as romantic again as when she was sixteen and had the misfortune to meet Kent Clayton. For the next thirty years she'd regretted that she'd lost her heart to him, for he'd used her, and used her sorely.

With Jack Parsons, it was so different. He had come with young Barry to dinner, and by the time the evening was over she found herself talking easily to this nice, kind-hearted gentleman. Twice after that, Jack had come by to see her alone, and it had been nice for them both to have some company. She realized that he was as lonely as she was for someone her own age to talk to and be with.

At first she'd thought of him as just a very nice man and a friend. He told her about his wife, and she found it easy to speak to him about Kent. But there came an evening when he suggested they take a stroll after dinner, and as they'd walked down the street his weathered, rough hand had taken hers. After a while, he'd looked over at her with the warmest look in his dark eyes, and said, "This is nice, Helen. I like just holding your hand like this."

Helen knew what he meant, and she agreed that it was a nice feeling.

As he bid her goodnight that night, he told her, "You know, Helen, I think there are many loves one can have in a lifetime. All of them can be just as exciting.

Tonight, I feel twenty years younger, and all I've done is hold that tiny little hand of yours in mine. It sure was a good feeling. I'd—I'd like to think that you share this feeling I have. We could give each other a lot of happiness in these later years of our lives. What do you think?"

Helen had answered softly, "I think we could too, Jack." And she had meant it, but to hear Gillian say what she had tonight had swept away any shadows of doubt she had harbored.

After the night when they had held hands and Jack had voiced his sentiments, he had come to take her for a ride to the house where he had lived since he had come to Tucson. He'd told her he knew it was far more space than he needed, being alone, but he could not bring himself to part with the place because he loved it so much.

"Then you shouldn't, Jack," Helen had told him.

She'd seen from the expression on his face that it pleased him to hear her say this. Things had not yet progressed any further, but Helen felt good to have confided in her friend.

Now it was Gillian's turn to confess to Helen how she felt about Hawk. She also told Helen that she had spent the night with Hawk, several times. While Helen was amazed for a moment by this candid confession, she had no doubt that Hawk loved Gillian, and that he had for a long time.

"Maybe it should have been Hawk you married, Gillian, instead of Steve. But you were so young, and the heart can play such crazy tricks. I should know, for it happened to me," Helen said ruefully.

"I know that too, Helen. But it won't happen to me

again. I was so naive, but when I found myself expecting Steve's baby, Hawk was willing to marry me, even though I told him the truth. I didn't know if Steve was going to return here."

"Well, I think that was a good test of Hawk's love for you, Gillian."

"I know that, Helen. But Steve *did* return, and that was all that mattered to me at the time, so I rushed away with him and deserted Hawk. I've often wondered if that was why I found only brief happiness with Steve, and why I lost my baby. Steve was gone most of the time, and I was lonely. I don't think my life would ever have been happy, with the kind of life that Steve lived. Even if the baby had not been lost, I would not have been a happy woman."

"I thought that was how you felt, Gillian," Helen told her.

"Well, you were right. You see, I learned quickly that, as passionately as Steve loved me, he also loved his ship and the sea. How could I possibly have fought that?"

"I guess there was no way you could, Gillian. It can't be a very happy life for a sea captain's wife, with the man gone from home for such long stretches."

"No, and I had begun to realize that. I thought about it when I was considering having another baby, after I lost the first one. I thought at first that it would help, but then I realized that I would have had the responsibility of raising that baby on my own, most of the time."

It was nice for Gillian to be able to talk with Helen this openly. It reminded her of the many talks she'd had with Hawk's mother. It was strange that, as close as she and Mother Foster had always been, she could never have talked to her as she was talking with Helen.

"No, Helen, it just was not meant for me to be a sea captain's wife," Gillian confessed sadly.

"Well, Gillian, you're so young. You'll find the life you need to make you happy—and the love," Helen told her kindly.

"And I suspect that you will too, Helen." Gillian smiled. There was a rosy flush on Helen's face, for she felt Jack Parsons might provide that love. They still had time to share some wonderful years together, as Jack had told her the other night.

Both Helen and Gillian were amazed to hear the clock chiming midnight, and soon thereafter they dimmed the lamps in the parlor, and retired.

Hawk came face to face with the arrogant, cocky Jake Harmon the day after he'd spied his buggy in front of Gillian's house. At first, he didn't know who the angry young man was, as he came rushing through the office door as he and Barstow were working at their desks.

"Barstow, your railroad is going to pay for the damage done to the supplies we shipped here. I'm not accepting that pile of junk they just unloaded. My father's going to be madder than hell, I can tell you right now."

Warner got up slowly from his desk and removed his glasses. In that slow drawl of his he urged Jake, "Now, just simmer down, young Jake. I've known Sam Harmon a lot of years, and I've always found him a reasonable man. Let me just go down there with you, and take a look at what you're talking about." He turned to Hawk to tell him he'd be gone awhile. "By the way, Jake, this is Joe Hawk. Hawk, meet Jake Harmon."

They mumbled greetings to one another. Jake was too angry right then to care about the big half-breed sitting at the desk. Hawk formed an instant dislike, knowing that this was the upstart vying with him for Gillian's attention. His black eyes scrutinized Jake carefully as he stood there, and Jake found that he didn't care for the way the half-breed was staring at him.

Warner, being the sensitive fellow he was, urged Jake to come along with him. Somehow, he could see, the two young bucks seemed not to take to one another. Warner knew Jake could be obnoxious from time to time, and he didn't want him saying anything to Hawk while he was in this disgruntled mood. It would be best to get him out of the office and try to soothe his ruffled feathers quickly.

Warner was gone for almost an hour, but when he returned he had a smile on his face. Looking up from the papers he'd been working on, Hawk asked him, "Did you get it all worked out with Harmon?"

Just the way he spoke the name told Warner that Hawk wasn't impressed by young Jake. "Oh, Jake's a lot of bluster, and his bark is worse than his bite," Warner laughed.

"Were the supplies damaged badly?"

"Yeah, they were damaged, but not as badly as he was trying to make out. I told him we'd store them in the warehouse and let his pa tell us which he was going to accept and what he would want to reject. I'd rather deal with Sam than Jake any day."

Hawk asked no more questions, but turned his attention back to his work. For the rest of the afternoon, though, all he could think about was that he didn't want that fellow hanging around Gillian. Oh, he knew Gillian had told him that this Jake Harmon had just offered her a ride home that afternoon, and he'd accepted her explanation. But it didn't explain why he'd seen Harmon's buggy at her house a second time. Maybe his guileless Gillian thought Harmon was just being nice and polite, but Hawk knew there were other things he had in mind where Gillian was concerned.

As always, Hawk intended to protect her from the likes of Jake Harmon.

After he left the office today, he was going to make a point of going over to her house to have a talk with her. He rode there as soon as he left work, but when he arrived no one answered the door. He walked around to the back to see if she might be in the backyard, but there was no sign of her.

He fought what was springing unbidden into his mind, but he could not help wondering if Harmon was taking her for a ride in his buggy.

But Jake had not gone by Gillian's house after he'd left Warner, earlier that afternoon; he'd ridden directly to the ranch to report to his father about their supplies.

Gillian had gone out after Helen had left for her job at the bakery. It was a glorious day, and she wanted to walk along the wall of the courtyard garden of the Old Pueblo Inn. If she could, she also intended to go through the gate and walk around the grounds.

But when she arrived at the old iron gate, she found it had been padlocked, so she could not enter. She stood looking at the grounds through the iron railings of the gate. Nothing was left of the huge, spacious building. It was the first time that Gillian had really surveyed the grounds, and she was wondering as she stood there just what would happen to the place. Who did the property belong to now that Melba Jackson was dead?

After her talk with Helen last night, Gillian had also decided to walk over to the livery and seek out young Barry. There was no denying that she was most curious to see this Jack Parsons Barry was working for, and whom Helen had become so fond of in such a short time.

Jack's keen eyes spied the young lady coming through the doors of the livery before Barry did, for he was busy tending to the horses in the stalls. Her long hair was the color of flaming fire, with the bright rays of the sun reflecting down on it. Her simple little blue sprigged muslin gown molded to her petite body, displaying a fine figure. She had such a tiny waistline that Jack figured his huge hands could have spanned it.

Barry came out of the stall, and he saw her coming into the livery just as she saw him. He put down the pail in his hand and rushed to greet her. "Miss Gillian—you're back!"

She gave him a warm hug. "I just got back, Barry, and I wanted to come and see you. Helen told me you had yourself a good job—I was so happy to hear that."

"I got myself a much better job than I had at the inn, Miss Gillian, and I'm a lot happier working for Mr. Parsons. You've got to meet him. He's back there reading his paper, I think," he told her.

"How wonderful, Barry. I would be delighted to meet Mr. Parsons," she declared, as he took her hand to lead her back to the far end of the livery, where Jack was sitting in an old oak straight-backed chair.

He was a hefty man, with a thick mop of gray hair and long sideburns. He already had a warm, friendly smile on his face as the two of them came up to where he was sitting.

He rose and wiped his hands on the sides of his pants. "Now, Barry, you don't have to tell me that this is that Miss Gillian I've heard so much about!" He gave a chuckle as he extended his hand to Gillian. "Jack Parsons, Miss Gillian."

"I'm very pleased to meet you, Mr. Parsons. I must tell you, I'm so happy Barry came your way—or I should say, you came his way," she told him.

Jack gave Barry's unruly dark hair a playful tousle and told Gillian, "Well, I'm glad he came my way, too. I've got myself a hardworking young fellow here. Me and Barry—well, we're good buddies, aren't we son?"

"Yes, we sure are buddies, sir," Barry replied with boyish enthusiasm.

Gillian smiled at Barry, and her eyes glanced over to see the affectionate look on Parsons's face. "Well, I just wanted to come by to say hello to you. Now that I'm back I can fix that dinner I promised you, Barry. That invitation includes you, too, Mr. Parsons."

"We'll come, Miss Gillian," Barry was quick to respond.

"That's mighty nice of you, Miss Gillian," Jack put in.

"Just call me Gillian, Mr. Parsons," she told him, as she turned to leave the livery. "How about tomorrow night?"

They both promised her they would be there. Gillian

smiled as she left the livery, for she was sure her invitation would meet with Helen's approval.

Being in a carefree mood, Gillian suddenly decided that she wasn't ready to go back to the house, so she decided to go to the bakery, since it was almost time for Helen to get off from work. She'd tell her about her visit to the livery and her invitation to Mr. Parsons and Barry to come over for supper tomorrow night.

On the way home, they could stop by the meat market to pick a nice beef roast, which she knew young Barry would enjoy.

Hawk missed seeing her walking from the livery toward the bakery by a few short seconds.

Chapter Thirty-three

Jack Parsons had already made up his mind that he was going to ask Helen Clayton to marry him, and he had also been thinking about something else. If she was willing, and he felt she would be, he was going to suggest that they take young Barry into their lives as their son. He was already envisioning how nice it would be to have Helen and Barry sharing his rambling old house with him. It would be a good life the three of them could share. He loved that young lad!

Barry could keep helping him there at the livery and maybe someday, he might just turn the whole thing over to the young man to run for him, as the years went by. He had a nice home to offer both Helen and Barry, and he figured they needed him as much as he needed them. At his age, Jack figured, it was time to enjoy every precious moment of life, and he intended to do just that!

It was a pleasant surprise for Helen to see Gillian

breezing through the bakery door. She looked very pretty in her simple little muslin gown, and with her long hair curling around her shoulders. But it was her eyes, sparkling so brilliantly, and the smile on her face that made Gillian especially beautiful this afternoon. Helen didn't have to be told that she was feeling lighthearted and gay.

"I thought I'd come by and walk home with you, Helen," she announced as she walked up to the counter where Helen was busily stacking fresh loaves of bread that would be sold before the day ended tomorrow.

She'd already put one of them aside to take home with her for their supper tonight. "Well, that was a good idea. I'm glad you could come by and see where I work. It's a nice little place here, Gillian. I certainly don't put in the long hours I used to at the inn. I've run things all by myself this afternoon, for the owner had some errands to do."

By the time Helen had removed her apron and checked the back door to see that it was locked, the clock was chiming five. She gathered up the loaf of bread, and the two of them went out the door, with Helen pausing to lock it. "Let's go home," she said, and smiled at Gillian.

"I also paid a visit to the livery to see Barry, and I met your Mr. Parsons, Helen. I have to tell you that I found him very nice."

"Oh, isn't he, Gillian!" Helen gushed like a school girl talking about her beau.

"I was sure you wouldn't mind if I invited him and Barry to dinner tomorrow night. I thought I'd stop in at Dawson's Meat Market to get us a nice beef roast. I can get it prepared tomorrow while you are working. What

304

do you think? Will your Jack like that?"

Helen laughed, "I think he likes anything that's a good home-cooked meal, Gillian. But you've forgotten that I only work every other day, so I'll be able to help you."

The brief stop at the meat market did not take long, and Gillian purchased a fine rump roast. She was thinking that it would have been nice if she had some way to invite Hawk to dinner, too, but tomorrow was his day off, so she couldn't speak to him at the office.

Hawk had only just ridden out of sight of Gillian's house when the two of them walked through the gate of Gillian's cottage. Again, he missed Gillian by a few seconds.

By the time the two of them had eaten their supper and cleaned up the kitchen, the patter of raindrops had started to pelt the window panes in the kitchen. Helen remarked that she'd not seen a cloud in the sky when they had been walking home. "A sudden summer storm, I guess."

Gillian laughed. "Well, it will be a good night to sleep, since we talked so late last night."

"Yes, but it was a good talk we had, Gillian, and I enjoyed it. I needed to talk to someone about Jack."

"Well, I'm glad you talked to me. I guess I needed to do a little talking myself, last night."

But tonight, neither of them lingered long in the parlor after dinner. The light rain outside was enough to make them want to get cozy in their beds and sleep.

A few miles away, Hawk had arrived home to attend to his evening chores. When they were finished, his supper was easily fixed, for he fried himself a few slices of bacon from a slab Warner had brought him the other day, and with them four fresh eggs from his basket.

He was just leaving his kitchen when he heard the rain starting to fall outside. He lit the lamp in the parlor, sat down, and took out the letter he'd received today from his mother.

It made him yearn to go and join her and Gaston up at the cabin. He would have enjoyed catching fish with Gaston. No one could cook fish like his mother, with all those special herbs she sprinkled on them.

He knew that Little Bear must be a happy animal, with Solange back to give him her affection. He could picture that big, brown dog dutifully following her wherever she roamed. No one could take Solange's place as far as Little Bear was concerned, for it was she who had taken him as a pup and raised him, after Troy had brought him to her.

Just reading her letter had a calming effect on Hawk, and he felt less irritated than he had been when he'd gone by Gillian's house to find her not at home. He certainly wasn't as tense as he'd been in the early afternoon, when Jake Harmon had come bursting through the office door.

But Jake Harmon was forgotten now, and as far as Gillian was concerned, Hawk promised himself that tomorrow he would stop by her house again on his way home. Surely he would find her there tomorrow.

Jake Harmon might have been forgotten by Hawk, but Hawk wasn't forgotten by Jake Harmon. Harmon wasn't used to a half-breed staring at him with such arrogance as Hawk had this afternoon.

That evening he rode back into Tucson to join his old friend, Kurt Hoffman, as he often did, to go out on a night of carousing. Jake planned to ask him about this Joe Hawk.

Kurt was a young lawyer who had just returned to Tucson a few months ago, after attending college back East. Now he was just starting to establish his law practice in the offices of his father and his partner.

He was a very striking young man, with the features of his German heritage: golden blond hair, and very keen, intense blue eyes. He possessed a cunning, shrewd mind, which would take him far as a lawyer.

His association with Jake went back to the time when they were in their teens. But for the last few years, while Kurt was away in the East and Jake had remained out on his father's ranch, back here in Tucson, they had not been around one another too often.

Jake's ways were no longer Kurt's ways, for college had changed him, but he still found Jake a fun-loving fellow to be around occasionally. Jake's rambunctious air was a contrast to Kurt's more dignified manner and they were truly a most unlikely pair to be friends—but friends they were.

Jake had the ability to make Kurt relax, and have some laughs when they went to their favorite taverns for a few drinks, as they were going to tonight.

When Jake arrived at the tavern he spotted Kurt at once. It was never hard to find Kurt, with that fair head of hair of his.

He sauntered back into the dark corner where Kurt

307

always seemed to like to sit. Jake took a seat, more than eager to get a drink served to him. The young waitress knew what Jake Harmon always drank, so she didn't wait for him to order it. Indeed, she was carrying it on a tray to his table the minute he sat down to greet his friend.

For a few minutes, while he had a few gulps of his favorite whiskey, Jake spoke in his usual, casual way. But Kurt, with that sharp mind, knew that Jake had something gnawing at him this evening. Kurt figured maybe he and old Sam had locked horns, as they often did out on the ranch.

He wasn't exactly prepared when Jake started to quiz him about Joe Hawk. "What do you know about him? It's obvious he's a damned half-breed, so what the hell would make Barstow have him working there in the office?" Jake asked Kurt.

Kurt set his glass down on the table, and his piercing blue eyes looked directly at Jake. The tone of his voice was as it might have been in a courtroom if he was trying to drive a point home to a judge or jury. "Wait up just a minute, Jake. Let me enlighten you about something. You'd better watch that tongue of yours when you talk about Joe Hawk. Yes, he's a half-breed, as you say, but he is not your ordinary Apache buck. A lot of people in Tucson think very highly of him, and Warner Barstow is one of them."

"Well, that don't mean a damn to me, Kurt," Jake told him, sounding surly.

Kurt hoped it was the whiskey making Jake talk like this, for Jake would have met his match and more if he ever tackled Joe Hawk, who he knew was a powerfully built man. In Kurt's opinion, Hawk would whip

Jake easily with one hand tied behind him.

"What's Joe Hawk done to you, Jake?" Kurt asked.

"It's—it's the way he acted when I was in the office with Barstow. I didn't like it one bit. He's got too cocky a way about him for a damned half-breed."

Kurt could think of nothing to do but fill Jake in on some facts he knew about Hawk. He'd never met him but he had seen him, and he was obviously a proud, spirited man. Knowing that wealth and riches impressed Jake Harmon, he told him, "Hawk's stepfather happens to be a very wealthy industrialist, with holdings in Canada and here. His mother is a very beautiful French lady, so I've been told. The truth is, Jake, from one friend to another, I have to tell you that Gaston Dion could buy and sell your father a couple or three times."

This was enough to grasp Jake's attention. He sat up straight at the table. "Well, now—I don't know whether you're my friend or not, Kurt Hoffman."

"Oh, yes you do, and you know I would not speak anything but the truth. I just don't want you to go throwing your weight around, thinking that Joe Hawk is your ordinary Apache half-breed, for if you do you'll be in for big trouble, my friend." Kurt spoke with a very sober look on his finely chiseled face.

Because he credited Kurt Hoffman with being one of the sharpest, smartest men he knew, Jake absorbed everything he'd heard him say. But it still didn't mean he was not going to put that half-breed in his place before he was through with him. He decided to drop the subject of Joe Hawk for the rest of the evening.

Kurt had the impression that he had succeeded in convincing Jake not to allow that hot-tempered nature of his to lead him into something rash. He was glad that Jake seemed to get his mind on other things as the evening went on. Kurt had to call an end to the evening at midnight, for he had an early-morning appointment.

Reluctantly, Jake followed Kurt out of the tavern. Kurt watched him mount up on his horse and ride toward the outskirts of the city, before he drove his buggy toward his home.

Kurt was thinking, as he guided his buggy down the dark, deserted street, that the time might be coming when he would have to sever his friendship with Jake, for his own best interests.

His life was completely different from Jake's now, and the people in it would have nothing in common with Jake Harmon, even though he was the son of the wealthy rancher, Sam Harmon.

And Kurt had no intention of allowing a friendship of yesteryear to jeopardize his career.

Chapter Thirty-four

The light rain that started to fall in the evening continued through the night and into the next morning. Gillian was glad it was starting to let up, because Helen was ready to go out and run some errands.

When Helen left, Gillian began preparing the roast for their evening meal. She puttered around the house during the afternoon, cleaning and putting things in order. She gathered enough of the flowers blooming in her yard to have a colorful bouquet in the parlor, as well as one in the center of the table.

She wanted everything to be nice for Mr. Parsons and their little friend Barry this evening. But what a shame it was that she could not get word to Hawk to come share this evening with her and her friends.

When Helen returned, she didn't have to be told how busy Gillian had been while she'd been out. The house looked so nice and festive with the pretty bouquets, and everything looking clean and tidy. The aroma of the roast and its rich brown juices whetted her appetite, and when she lifted the lid to see the roast surrounded by new potatoes, tender baby carrots and quartered onions, Helen knew that Jack and Barry were surely going to enjoy themselves tonight.

As if that wasn't enough, Gillian had baked a cake and made two pies. Helen felt she was contributing very little with the two loaves of bread she'd stopped in at the bakery to pick up.

Even after doing all this, Gillian, dressed in a pretty pale pink frock with her hair pulled back with a pink ribbon, looked as beautiful as the pink rosebuds she'd cut for the bouquet in the parlor.

Helen rushed to change from the simple dress she was wearing to the blue frock with the lace collar, which she knew Jack thought was so flattering on her. When she was dressed and her hair was neatly combed and pinned into two thick coils, she went out to the parlor to join Gillian.

At the appointed hour, Jack and Barry arrived, and after a little chatting they sat down to dinner. Gillian had never seen a young man stuff himself as young Barry on her roast. It delighted her to see him eating with such relish, and she was amused when he asked her, "Did you really cook all this, Miss Gillian?"

"Most assuredly. Did you not expect that I could cook?"

He smiled sheepishly. "I guess I never thought about you cooking, Miss Gillian. I always saw you in those fancy gowns, going and coming from the inn."

All of them laughed—it was a very happy evening they enjoyed in Gillian's kitchen. Barry told Gillian that he would help her clear up, which she thought was a sweet gesture. "I'd be very pleased to have you help me, Barry. Helen, you and Jack could go for a nice evening stroll, if you'd like. Barry and I will finish up in here," she told them.

They seemed eager to accept her offer. They were gone for a long time, and when they returned to the house, Gillian and Barry had done the dishes and were sitting out on the front step, for it was a lovely night. There was a full moon shining down on them, and Gillian found it very relaxing to be sitting there after the busy day she'd had. She'd removed her slippers, and it felt good to sit there in her bare feet. She decided she must have been as guilty as Barry of eating too much, for her gown felt too snug.

Barry had laughed when she made that confession to him. He had been dreaming as he sat there in the moonlight that one day he would be sitting like this with some young lady his own age, and he wanted her to look just like Miss Gillian.

When Jack and Helen returned to the house to find Gillian and Barry sitting there on the front steps, they clasped hands and announced that they were going to get married.

Gillian and Barry were thrilled, and when many embraces and good wishes had been exchanged, Jack made another announcement, which brought tears to Gillian's eyes. She knew she would never forget Jack's words. "Barry, me and Helen can't ever have ourselves a son, but we both care for you so much that we want you to be our son, and share our home with us. Would you want to be our son? We sure want you!"

Barry was too overcome with emotion to say anything; he just rushed into Jack's arms, tears flowing freely. Jack held him close, for he understood what it meant to Barry to be wanted and loved.

Helen was still in a state of shock herself. She'd never known a man like Jack Parsons, who had such a kind, generous heart. She went to Gillian and embraced her emotionally.

Gillian felt privileged to be able to share this special moment. To know that Helen was to have a good, loving husband and her own home again was enough to make Gillian happy, but to think also that Barry was going to share their home and their lives was absolutely wonderful!

Later, after Jack and Barry had left, Helen and Gillian sat in the parlor, too excited to think of going to bed. Helen sighed happily. "Gillian, I would never have believed that a man like Jack existed."

"I think they must be few and far between, Helen—I'm just glad the two of you found one another."

Later, as Gillian was lying in bed and staring out the window at the full moon, still shining up there in the dark sky, she thought about where her own life was going. Was it to be a life with Hawk? She reminded herself that Hawk had not made an offer of marriage to her, despite his professions of love and their increasingly passionate physical relationship.

She wondered why Hawk had not come by her home since the morning he'd brought her from his house. She had expected him to come over the next evening, and had been disappointed when he'd made no appearance at her front door. Hawk knew that she had no way to get to his house.

If only she had her own means of transportation. Hawk had very generously bought Fuego for her, and she appreciated his gift, but the horse was only hers when she went to Hawk's. Suddenly she was struck with the idea of asking Jack if she could keep Fuego at his livery so that she could ride him whenever she wished. Then she would be able to ride him to Hawk's whenever she liked.

The next day she went to speak to Jack about Fuego, and he was very quick to tell her that she was welcome to keep her horse there for as long as she needed to. The generous man even offered her more. "I've always a horse you can use until you get your horse over here," he volunteered.

"I appreciate that, Mr. Parsons," she told him. After a moment's thought, she added that she might just take him up on his offer of a horse tomorrow. "I've an errand I need to go on," she told him, although it was not exactly an errand she had in mind. If Hawk didn't show up at her house this evening, then she was going to find him.

It had not been Hawk's intention to neglect Gillian—he was more eager to see her than she could know—but some unexpected problems had developed at the railroad office that demanded his attention. He had had to cancel his day off and work, but otherwise he would have been at Gillian's door the night Barry and Jack Parsons had come to dinner.

Unfortunately, however, he was on the train traveling up to Phoenix early the next morning, so he wouldn't be able to stop by her house, as he'd planned. He had only just managed to make arrangements with his neighbor's boy to take care of Tache and Fuego, in

315

case he had to be gone for a couple of days.

Gillian stopped by the livery next day to borrow one of Jack's horses. Although it was not far, she rode to the railroad office, where she learned from Warner that Hawk was out of town. He told her, "I can't say just how long he'll be gone, because I don't know. Hawk has to get this thing straightened out, though, before he comes back. It could be a day or it could be a week."

"Well, tell him I came by, will you, Mr. Barstow?"

"Sure will, ma'am."

Gillian was pouting as she rode away from the office. He might at least have come by her house to tell her he was leaving, she grumbled to herself. But then she thought, just because Hawk was gone, it should not keep her from going over to his house to get Fuego. After all, Hawk had told her the horse was hers, and now she did have a place to keep him. What better time to do it than now, when she had Jack's horse for the afternoon?

Yes, she decided, she would do just that. When she arrived at Hawk's, she unceremoniously entered the unlocked door of Hawk's house, helped herself to a piece of paper from his desk drawer, and scribbled him a note to tell him what she had done. Then she went to the barn to saddle Fuego.

A few minutes later she was on her way back to the city, riding Fuego and leading Jack's mare. It never dawned on her what a furor she would be raising by her act.

When she arrived back at the livery on the handsome stallion, Jack Parsons was very impressed by the fine beast. "Oh, Miss Gillian—this is one fine horse! What a magnificent coat he has! I'll almost feel nervous about keeping him here." In fact, the more he thought about it, the more he felt compelled to suggest to Gillian that he stable Fuego at his place. She could always ride one of his horses out there when she wanted to ride him.

"You know, Miss Gillian, a high-spirited fellow like him needs a place to run and kick his heels up. I've got the space out there to give him that kind of freedom. What do you say?"

"Well, if you think that would be better, Mr. Parsons, I trust your judgment," she told him.

"I think he would like it better. He ain't going to be too happy in a stall all day long, and you won't be riding him all that often," he pointed out. Gillian had not thought about that when she'd decided to bring him here to the livery, and Parsons had had no idea she was talking about such a mettlesome creature as Fuego when she had asked if she could keep him there.

So Jack took Fuego home with him that night when he left the livery. As he was leaving, he told Barry to gather his belongings together that night, for he was going to move into Jack's house with him the next evening. "We don't have to wait until me and Miss Helen get married. I'll get your bedroom ready for you to move into tomorrow night, son. You are going to come home with me."

"I'll be ready to go tomorrow night, Mr. Parsons," Barry assured him. All evening he found himself curious about Mr. Parsons's home. What would it be like? Barry had found the little room at the back of the livery very comfortable, and he'd been grateful to have it as his living quarters. But living in Mr. Parsons's house would be something else! He'd never expected to find life as rewarding as it had been to him the last several weeks.

Helen recognized immediately that Gillian was not in the best of moods that evening, when she returned from the bakery. She waited until after supper to say anything to her about it, for she kept thinking that Gillian might explain why she was so remote and quiet. But she didn't say a word.

"Are you not feeling well tonight, Gillian?" Helen finally asked her.

"I'm just a little out of patience with Hawk, Helen. I went by Hawk's office this afternoon, only to find that he had left town without so much as coming by to tell me."

"Maybe he just didn't have time, Gillian," Helen said, trying to soothe her.

"It wouldn't have taken that long, Helen," Gillian retorted. Helen could not argue with her about that, so instead, she asked Gillian how long he would be gone.

"Warner Barstow couldn't tell me that. He said he didn't know. Hawk could be gone a day or two, maybe a week."

Helen decided that it was best to speak no more about Hawk tonight. She felt that it was one of those nights when Gillian might like to be alone, so she retired to her room early, pretending that she had some letters to write before she went to bed.

Gillian went to sit out on the front steps after Helen had gone to her bedroom. She was beginning to think she would never find happiness and hold on to it. She knew that part of her gloomy mood was due to learning that Hawk was out of town, but that wasn't really the cause of this new wave of discontent. She didn't exactly know what was.

Perhaps she envied women like Solange and Helen, for they seemed to have found happiness. She wanted to believe that Hawk would bring her that same kind of bliss. When they were together she was sure of it, but when they were apart there were moments of doubt, like she was feeling tonight.

Was it her own fault that she could not hold on to happiness, once it was hers? Her joy with Steve had been so very brief, and was swept away so quickly. Since then, she'd found these moods of discontent washing over her every so often. It seemed like the places where she'd once known happiness and contentment could not hold her restless heart anymore.

Was happiness to be an elusive thing that she would never be able to grasp? Would she be forever filled with a wanderlust to seek new places and new surroundings?

Oh, she felt so unsettled!

She stared up at the starlit sky above her and asked where her happiness lay. She truly did not know where to search for it.

The weeks she'd spent nursing Mother Foster back to health had firmly convinced her that their ranch could never provide happiness for her. She had been eager to get back to her little house here in Tucson, and for a while she did find herself happy to be back.

But today, she realized, that same overwhelming feeling of discontent had come over her once again. She really could fault no one but herself for it. It was true she was slightly vexed with Hawk, but it wasn't his fault that she felt the way she did tonight.

No, she knew that it was within herself that she must find the answer. This was what was bothering her so much. Not even the people like Hawk or Helen, who loved her, could solve this for her. She had to do it herself!

Chapter Thirty-five

After Hawk had worked out all the problems for the railroad, he found himself in Maricopa County. He was close to the mountain cabin he loved so dearly, and he could not resist giving himself a few extra days and going up there, before traveling back to Tucson. He figured that no one would be any the wiser, but even if it would have cost him his job, he could not have resisted the temptation, knowing that his mother and Gaston were up there in the cabin.

The afternoon he arrived, Solange was there by herself, so she and her son were sharing a happy reunion when Gaston returned to the cottage. He had been trekking through the dense woods surrounding the cabin to determine whether the wildlife was still as plentiful as ever. After all, that was what his fur trading business depended upon.

When he entered the cabin and his dark eyes spied Hawk, he rushed to give him a warm embrace, for Gaston was a very demonstrative man with those he loved.

"Mon dieu, it's good to see you, Hawk. So good to see you," Gaston declared, giving him another big bear hug.

Everything about Gaston reflected the powerful, forceful man he was. His thick, unruly mane of gray hair and his sharp, distinctive features could make him look very formidable. But Solange and Hawk knew him to be a gentle, loving man, who possessed a rare compassion and tenderness.

It always pleased Solange to see the camaraderie her son and husband shared. When Gaston had come into her life so late, she'd feared that Hawk would resent him, but Gaston had seen to it that this didn't happen. Her Gaston had understood, as many men would not have been able to, why she and Hawk had such a close relationship. He respected their bond.

As for Hawk, he found the two of them remarkable —a perfect pair! Like Solange, Gaston had a wonderful zest for living, and wasted not one precious moment.

Tonight the little cabin resounded with laughter and gaiety, as the three of them dined on the delectable meal Solange prepared and the good wine Gaston had cooled in the mountain spring. They told Hawk about what had been happening during the last few months in Canada, and what their plans were when they returned to spend the winter months there.

Hawk told them in turn what had been happening in his life, and in doing that he naturally mentioned Gillian. Solange told him about the delightful surprise of having her for a brief visit at the cottage.

"Gillian has not had an easy year, from what she told me, Hawk. If you still love her as I know you once did,

322

my son, then don't allow her to slip away from you again," Solange cautioned him.

"I don't intend to, Mother. I would have been willing to marry her as soon as she returned to Arizona, but Gillian seemed to need some time to sort things out after all that had happened to her."

"She has not had time to do that yet?"

"I'm not exactly sure if she has or not. For a while she seemed very happy, and content with her job at the inn. But she quit just before the inn burned down, and I thank God that she was here at the Fosters' the night it happened. I guess what troubles me is that I've never quite been able to figure out why Gillian bought herself a house, when she knew I owned a house and property in Tucson. It was as if she was telling me she still wanted to be on her own," Hawk confessed to Solange and Gaston.

"You have let her know how you feel about her?" Gaston asked him. "More to the point, have you asked her to marry you?"

"No, I haven't exactly come right out and asked her, but she surely knows what I have in mind," Hawk responded quickly.

Solange gave a soft little laugh and reached over to pat her son's hand. "Oh, my darling son—never assume that a pretty lady knows what is in your mind. You must tell her, Hawk." With a twinkle in her eyes, she suggested to him that he waste no more time.

Gaston laughed. "Hawk, women as beautiful as your mother and Gillian are enough to tempt the very souls of men, and there are plenty around ready to whisk them away. Why, I keep my eagle eyes on your mother constantly!"

"Oh, Gaston!" Solange laughed, playfully tousling his thick hair.

"It is true, *ma chère*. At any soirée we attend, your mother is always the center of attraction, and the men gather around her like bees after honey, Hawk. I swear it."

Hawk smiled, for he thought it was wonderful that the two of them were so completely in love with one another. Their eyes could not meet without filling with warmth, it seemed to him.

He didn't take lightly what they had said that afternoon, and after thinking about it, Hawk decided that he wasn't going to stay here any longer, but would head back to Tucson and Gillian.

It didn't surprise Gaston when Hawk announced to him later that evening that he was going to get started back to Tucson tomorrow.

While the two of them were alone, Gaston told him how much he could use Hawk's knowledge of these woods and the animals living there. "You wouldn't have to come to Canada. You could live right here on the mountain and represent me in the state. If you should ever tire of the railroad and Tucson, you could be worth your weight in gold to me and my company. Just keep that in mind, Hawk."

In bed that night, Gaston told Solange about the bait he'd thrown out to Hawk. "I don't think he is truly happy with his job with the railroad. Hawk was never meant to sit in an office, Solange. We both know that. He needs more freedom, as he's always had up here, to roam through the woods or ride Tache on all these mountain trails. He could do that for me and gather information that would be very valuable. He could set his boundaries as he wished."

"And you told him all this?"

"Yes, I told him so that he might start thinking about it. I even have another plan in mind, *ma petite.*" He chuckled as he snuggled up closer to her.

She gave a soft giggle. "Oh, Gaston, you are such a wonderful devil! Tell me what you are conjuring up now."

"Well, I am going to speak to Troy and this friend of his about building a few extra rooms on this cabin. Should Hawk take Gillian as his bride, then this little cottage would need to expand, would you not say, *ma petite?*"

"Oh, Gaston, you think of everything, *n'est-ce pas?* I've never known a man like you." She sighed happily.

"And I can assure you that you never will, either. That's what makes me so lovable—*oui?*"

"It surely must be, Gaston Dion, for I do love you!"

"Do you *really* love me, *chèrie?*" he growled teasingly, his lips planting featherlike kisses on her cheek. "If you do, then you must convince me of this."

A knowing smile was on Solange's lovely face as she pressed closer to him. It was a pleasure to convince her husky Gaston just how much she loved him.

Hawk left the next day to go back to Tucson, although if it had not been for Gillian he would have had no incentive to leave the mountain at all.

The tall pines were so verdant, and as he rode down the trail the woods had such a pleasant aroma. Everything about the air up here seemed so fresh and clean, when he compared it to the air in Tucson. The crystal clear waters of the springs and creeks up here were the most delicious he'd ever drunk, and Gaston's trout were so good and tasty.

Hawk liked the fact that Gaston never fished for sport or shot an animal that wasn't eaten. He didn't believe in killing anything just for the sport of it. Hawk had resented, over the years, the few ranchers who came to the mountain to just enjoy killing the animals. In some way it seemed to swell their egos, and he was glad it was only a few men that liked to engage in this folly.

Gaston's offer had certainly given him something to think about while he traveled back to Tucson. He knew the French Canadian well enough by now to be sure that he didn't say anything he didn't mean. When he'd first offered him a job, a year ago, Hawk had figured it was just because he was marrying his mother, and Hawk had refused his offer.

But this time he felt differently. Hawk understood now how he could be of service to Gaston. No one knew the vast acres of woods like Hawk did, and certainly no man Gaston could send down from Canada to gather information could do as good a job as Hawk would.

It would mean a lot to Hawk to return to that cottage where he'd lived most of his life. Now the only question he had to ask himself as he got closer and closer to Tucson was whether Gillian would be happy to share a life with him in the mountains.

Somehow, he felt it might just be the place where Gillian could find serenity and contentment as his own mother had—for they were very much alike in a lot of ways. She had not been happy in Ireland or at the inn,

326

and Hawk suspected that Gillian, like him, did not find Tucson the most peaceful place to live.

Hawk allowed his thoughts to roam back to when he had first seen the beautiful auburn-haired girl of sixteen, riding Foster's mare down in the canyon while he sat up there on a high plateau watching her.

Her lovely hair had looked like flaming fire, and he'd never seen anyone more enchantingly beautiful. And the blazing passion and desire he'd felt for her that day had only intensified since then. He wanted her, and he meant to have her!

Chapter Thirty-six

Dusk was gathering over the city of Tucson by the time Hawk arrived at his house. As he rode up the drive toward the barn, he spotted Charlie Christy coming out of his barn, obviously just finishing the chores.

Hawk called out to him as he dismounted from the horse he'd borrowed to ride home. Charlie walked up to the fence to meet him, feeling nervous about the news he had to tell him. When he'd found Fuego gone from the barn, Charlie had been petrified, and for hours he had searched for the stallion, stopping to inquire of the various neighbors if they'd seen him.

Of course, Charlie never went into Hawk's house when he was away, for he had no reason to. Little did he know that all his hours of worry and searching would not have been necessary if he'd gone into Hawk's kitchen and found Gillian's note on the kitchen table.

So as soon as the two of them met there by the fence, Charlie didn't hesitate to tell him about Fuego. "I—I feel so bad about it, Hawk. I've looked high and low for that stallion, and I've not come up with one clue. But I do know that he was taken out of the stall, for the gate was closed by whoever it was that took him. The horse didn't break out."

The news stunned Hawk, and he said nothing for a moment. But then he noticed the expression on the boy's face, and he said, "Don't blame yourself, Charlie. It was nothing you could help, and I appreciate all the effort you went to trying to find him."

He urged Charlie to go on home and have his supper. "I'll give it some thought, and tomorrow I'll see what I can do to locate Fuego. I'll find him, though. Don't you worry about that for a minute. There's a very distinct look about Fuego, and somebody must have seen him."

When the boy had gone and Hawk had stabled the borrowed horse, he walked pensively up to his front door. It was now dark, so he paused long enough in the parlor to light the lamp before he went on into the bedroom to toss his luggage on the bed. The unpacking could come later. Right now, he was ready for some food, and he wasted no time in going to his kitchen and lighting the lamp in there.

The first thing he did was check the pantry to see what he could fix up fast, for he was famished. The simplest meal would be some eggs and a few slices of cured ham, he decided, so he carried the basket of eggs and the shank of ham over to the kitchen table. It was then that he saw the sheet of paper and picked it up to see that it was a note from Gillian. His first reaction was to be happy that she had come to see him, not knowing that he was out of town because he had not had a chance to tell her. But by the time he had read her note he was furious, and angrily tore up the paper.

As he slammed the kindling into the cookstove and started the fire he swelled with resentment that she would take Fuego without even waiting to speak to him about it.

Her act was as impulsive as she had proved herself to be in the past. True, the horse was hers; he had told her that when they'd left Rock Springs together to come back to Tucson. But when he thought of all the worry she'd caused poor Charlie, and of the many hours he had put in looking for the stallion, he got even angrier.

And by the time he had four eggs and some slices of ham sizzling in the skillet, he had begun to wonder just where in the hell she was quartering a fine stallion at her little cottage.

He gulped down the food hurriedly, partly because he was famished and partly because he was so vexed at the woman he loved. If she had been there right now, he would have been tempted to turn her over his lap and spank her soundly. If she acted like a child, she should be treated like one.

Hawk gathered up the dishes but he didn't start washing them, for he had to ease Charlie's mind about the horse. He owed him that much. So he went to the barn, saddled up Tache and rode over to Charlie's father's place. It was embarrassing for Hawk to have to confess that it was Gillian who had taken Fuego, and he apologized to Charlie for all the trouble it had caused him.

Charlie, however, was relieved that the horse had not been stolen as he feared, and he was actually happy to hear that Hawk's lady friend had the stallion.

Glad to have the mystery cleared up, at least, Hawk said goodnight and headed back to his house to tackle

330

the dishes waiting for him, as well as unpacking his luggage.

After his kitchen was in order and his luggage was unpacked, Hawk finally had a moment to sort out the papers he wanted to take with him to the office the next morning. By the time he finally got to bed, it was late. Well, he had Gillian to thank for that.

The next morning Hawk was still in a disgruntled mood as he rode Tache to the office, but he tried not to let it show once he was with Warner.

Hawk must have seemed normal, for Warner had no inkling of the feelings churning within him as they worked together all day. There was a lot of talking to be done, for Hawk filled him in about the problem areas he had been sent to check. Warner was pleased to hear how Hawk had gone about correcting most of them.

"It will take a few weeks to see if my other suggestions work, Warner," Hawk cautioned.

"Well, it sounds like you did your usual good job, Hawk. It was a busy few days. Oh, by the way, your Miss Gillian came to the office while you were gone, and I told her you were out of town. She wanted to know how long you'd be gone, but I couldn't tell her."

Hawk strolled back to his desk and sat down, commenting that he was sorry she'd had the long walk for nothing, and explaining that he hadn't had time to tell her he was leaving town.

"Oh, she hadn't walked. She was riding a horse. I happened to see her riding away," Warner told him, and turned his attention back to his own work.

Warner's remark had given Hawk something else to wonder about. Who had given her the loan of a horse to ride over here?

His first thought was that Jake Harmon must have lent her the horse. That really riled him, and when he left the office at five, he knew exactly where he was heading.

As he was approaching Gillian's house he spotted the auburn-haired beauty strolling between the flowerbeds in her front yard. Before she was aware that he was riding up to the gate, he watched her picking a bouquet of purple and pink phlox in full bloom. He was reminded of the times he'd watched her picking wildflowers there in the Fosters' meadow. She could have still been fourteen.

When she happened to turn, and saw him, her face beamed radiantly and she exclaimed, "Hawk—you're back!" She rushed to the gate to greet him, and as she opened the gate for him it was impossible for Hawk's arm not to enclose her, for she almost flung herself against him.

But too much emotion churned in Hawk for his kiss to be as warm as usual. Gillian sensed this instantly and slowly backed away from him to stare up into his face. In her very straightforward, candid way, she asked, "Hawk? Hawk, is something wrong?"

"I'm not sure, Gillian. You'll have to tell me that. Where is Fuego?" His bronzed face wore a solemn look.

"Is that why you came over? You didn't come to see me, but to find out about Fuego?" Her blue eyes were flashing with irritation.

"No, I came to see you, Gillian—but you can't keep him here," he said.

"Is Fuego mine, or did I misunderstand that, Hawk?" Her fingers played nervously with the flowers

332

she was holding.

"He is yours. I told you that weeks ago."

"Well, Fuego is being well cared for. I got tired of never having a horse to ride, and of having to walk over to your office if I wanted to see you, since you didn't seem to have the time to come by here too often," she declared, her head held high and defiant.

But before he could reply to this, two other riders arrived by the gate. It was Barry and Jack Parsons arriving to have dinner. This evening Helen was preparing the meal, which was why Gillian was out in the yard, picking a bouquet to take in to the house before her guests arrived.

She turned from Hawk to greet them as they came through the gate and in turn introduced Hawk to Jack and Barry. Then she said to Hawk, "Hawk, you must join us for some of Helen's delicious fried chicken for dinner. Oh, by the way, Mr. Parsons, here, is allowing me to stable Fuego out at his place, and he kindly allows me to ride one of the horses from his livery there any time I want to go out on Fuego. It's worked out very nicely, because the livery is just a short distance away."

At this Hawk's mood began to mellow, but now it was Gillian who was feeling vexed. Hawk could read the signs, and he began to feel a little guilty that he'd allowed himself to get so angry at her.

He knew that it would not be right for him to share the evening with Gillian and her friends when there was this tension between them. The two of them needed time to be alone, but it could not be tonight.

So he stammered out an excuse that he had a lot of paperwork to get done to turn over to Warner Barstow

333

in the morning. "I'd like nothing better than to join you for some of Miss Helen's chicken, but I've got to get home now, Gillian. I'll come over tomorrow night to see you." His black eyes gazed at her face to watch the expression on it, but he could not read her mood. He turned next to Jack Parsons and Barry, to tell them it was nice to meet them both. "I'm glad Fuego is in such good hands, Mr. Parsons."

"Ah, that's one fine stallion, but then I don't have to tell you that. You picked a fine horse in that one, Mr. Hawk," Parsons told him.

"Yes, I think he is one of the finest horses I've ever seen," Hawk agreed. Everyone found Jack Parsons a likable fellow, and Hawk was no exception.

He didn't know how Gillian would react when he sought to take her hand in his, but he dared to test her. He was encouraged that she allowed him to hold her hand as he said goodbye. "I'll be by tomorrow evening, Gillian."

"I'll be here, Hawk," she told him, and her blue eyes watched his tall figure move through the gate and mount up on Tache. She was glad that Jack and Barry had moved on up the pathway ahead of her.

Well, it had obviously not pleased Hawk that she had taken Fuego while he was gone. She had to admit to herself as she walked into the house that perhaps she had been wrong to do it.

Tomorrow night, she would tell him that, and apologize.

When Gillian went to bed that night, she lay there thinking about Hawk, and anticipating their seeing each other the next evening. It was good to have him back in Tucson. Just knowing that he was in the city was comforting to her. When Hawk was near, Gillian always felt protected, and there was a good feeling washing over her as she fell asleep.

A few miles away, Hawk, too, lay in bed. He was thinking of many things, but especially of Gillian. And thinking of Gillian also made him think of Gaston's intriguing offer. He was convinced that, of all the places he knew about, it was there in Maricopa County on that mountaintop that he and Gillian were destined to be together.

These thoughts were soothing, and Hawk drifted off into a peaceful, deep sleep. He was not going to wait any longer to ask Gillian to marry him. It would be the second time he'd asked that little minx to marry him, but this time, it would happen!

Chapter Thirty-seven

Gaston Dion was a man of action, and once he made his mind up about something, he wanted to do it. While other men wasted time thinking and pondering, Gaston immediately got busy. It was the reason he'd been such a successful businessman when a lot of his competitors in the fur trading business had failed.

The day Hawk left, Gaston hiked over to Troy's cabin to offer him the job of building on the extra rooms at Solange's cottage. Before he'd left, he had drawn a sketch of what he'd planned so that she could approve the plans before he went any further. She liked his plans; her cozy parlor and spacious kitchen would remain the same, and the addition would be at the back of the house. Mischief twinkled in his eyes as he pointed out to her, "There'll be a nice spacious bedroom for us when we come to visit after Hawk and Gillian are married, and an extra room for the grandchildren we shall enjoy, *ma petite!*"

"Oh, Gaston, you are a hopeless romantic!" She laughed indulgently, and kissed him.

"Oui, I admit to that! You approve?"

"I approve, Gaston, so be on your way to Troy's," she urged him, knowing how eager he was to get started on this new project. Their time was growing short, and soon they would be leaving to return to Canada.

He gave her one of his big bear hugs and a kiss on the cheek before he strode out the kitchen door. "See you in a couple of hours," he called back to her as he disappeared down the steps.

The minute Gaston had left, the huge brown dog, Little Bear, came into the kitchen, seeming to sense that now was his time to get attention from Solange. He had been curled up on the rug in front of the hearth in the parlor all morning, sleeping soundly.

Solange smiled down at him, knowing what he wanted, and sat down in an armchair. Little Bear put his huge head on her lap and her nimble fingers ran through his thick brown hair. She watched his eyes shut, for now he was completely contented.

Finally she gave him a pat on the head, declaring that she could hardly sit there all morning. "I think I've got you spoiled, Little Bear."

Little Bear looked up at her, wagging his tail as she rose from the chair. She wished it had worked out for her to have kept him in Canada with her, but at least she never worried that he was not given good care by Troy.

Time had gone by too quickly for Solange since they had arrived here. It didn't seem possible that six weeks had almost gone by. And as it had turned out, because of their coming earlier than they'd planned, Hawk had not been able to share as much of the time with her as she had hoped.

But Solange would never have complained to Gaston, for she knew he had had to work many extra hours to enable them to be away from Canada this long. And he would be doing the same thing for the first two weeks after they returned.

They longer she was married to her French-Canadian husband, the more she realized what an amazing man he was. He seemed to have endless energy for a man his age, and she didn't think Gaston had been ill a day of his life. The only time she'd ever known him to be laid low was the time he caught his foot in an animal trap and was injured. That was when they'd first met, for he had managed to drag himself to her cabin, which was near where he had been hurt. By the time Solange had nursed him for the next few days, they were very much in love with one another. When he left the cabin he'd got her promise to marry him; Solange had never regretted that decision.

It did not take Gaston two hours to set the wheels in motion for the job he wanted Troy and his friend Homer to do for him. Troy had promised that they would be over there in the morning to stake out where Gaston wanted rooms built on.

Like Hawk, Troy was a half-breed, and he made a very meager living for himself in the woods doing various jobs. He'd never married, though, so he had only himself to worry about. The hunting and fishing in the woods were good, and he grew all his own vegetables, so he needed to buy few supplies in Rock Springs.

Gaston, knowing the state of Troy's finances, had

338

told him, "Since I won't be here when you buy the supplies and lumber, I'm going to turn over the funds you'll need today." He had reached into the pocket of his pants to pull out a roll of bills the size of which almost made Troy stagger. He'd never seen such riches. Troy actually felt nervous holding that much money, and Gaston realized it as he saw him staring down at the money in the palm of his hand.

He chuckled. "That will go fast, Troy, when you pay for that first wagonload of supplies. You'll realize it isn't so much."

Troy gave him an uneasy grin. "I guess that's true. I usually just cut my own trees down for the timbers I needed for my cabin."

Gaston was pleased to know, as he walked back to Solange's cabin, that the next time they came here the two extra rooms would be finished. Then it would be up to Solange to see to furnishings, if Hawk had not yet brought Gillian here as his bride.

And Gaston would be sadly disappointed if that had not happened.

Hawk had not had a ring for Gillian the first time he asked her to marry him. He had planned to buy her one when they had gone back to Tucson together. But they never did return to Tucson together, for Steve Lafferty had suddenly appeared at the Fosters' ranch.

No, Hawk had ridden to Tucson with no wife by his side. The only thing that had consoled Hawk that day was knowing that Gillian was so happy, for he knew she had married the man she truly loved.

But this time, when he asked her to marry him he

would be able to put a ring on her finger if she agreed. He vowed that where Steve Lafferty had failed to make her happy, he would succeed. Gillian and he would find their happiness together.

Their home would be warm with love, and echo with the gay laughter of them and their children. It would be a good life they would share, and Hawk felt very strongly that the place that should be their haven was the cabin up there on the mountain.

That day Hawk took a long midday break from the office, explaining to Warner he had an errand to run. He felt a little awkward as he entered the jewelry shop, for he'd never purchased a fine ring or a gem before. He decided to allow his instinct to guide him on the right ring for Gillian. He had no intention of allowing the clerk to choose the ring he would purchase.

He looked at many rings, displayed in velvet trays, but he saw nothing he felt was right. He tried to ignore the clerk's constant quizzing about what he had in mind, or what stones he was interested in. He just mumbled that he would know the ring when he saw it, so the clerk pulled out one tray after another, becoming a little impatient with this difficult young man.

Several trays later, Hawk declared, "That one there—the one with the little diamonds all around it. I'd like to see it."

"Ah, so you like sapphires? That is a very fine cut of the stone."

Hawk's huge hand took the ring, and his black eyes surveyed the sparkle and glimmer of the stone as the light reflected on it. He knew immediately that it was the ring he wished to purchase, so he asked the clerk how much it was.

It amazed Hawk that a little ring could cost as much as a fine horse, but then this was his first time buying a ring, whereas he'd bought horses before. Still, he didn't hesitate to pay the price.

A few minutes later, he was riding Tache back toward the railroad office with the ring in his pocket. When he entered the office Warner was back at work, and looked up only long enough to ask Hawk if he had got his errands done.

"Yes, sir, I sure did," Hawk replied as he went to his desk. He said nothing more about it to Warner.

The afternoon seemed to drag, for Hawk was eager to finish for the day and be on his way to see Gillian. He was constantly looking up at the clock on the wall during the last long hour.

As the clock was chiming five, Hawk saw Warner push back from his desk, and he was delighted to do the same. He quickly put his desk in order, preparing to leave. Together, the two of them left the office at a few minutes after five.

Warner drove his buggy toward his home, and Hawk reined Tache in the direction of Gillian's house.

Jake Harmon always rode by the small acreage of land belonging to Jack Parsons when he went into Tucson, and he'd known old Jack for years. But he'd never spotted the fine-looking stallion in the small pasture before, and he pulled up the reins of the horse he was riding to admire the fiery animal he saw. Its flaring nostrils and wildly swishing tail told Jake that this was a spirited horse that he'd like to own. That was a magnificently built stallion. Harmon was curious

341

how Parsons had acquired him, for an animal like that didn't come cheap.

The minute he arrived in Tucson he went directly to the livery to talk to Parsons about the red stallion. But when he arrived there, Parsons was quick to tell him, "Fuego isn't mine. I'm merely keeping him there for Miss Gillian."

"Are you talking about Gillian Lafferty? *She* owns that horse?" Harmon frowned. He was just as curious how she'd acquired such a fine stallion as he had been when he'd thought it belonged to Parsons.

"Well, I guess she's the one I'll have to talk to, then," Jake remarked, and he turned to walk away.

"I don't think you'll have any luck there, Jake. I don't think you'd get her to part with Fuego," Jack called after him.

Jake turned back to flash a smile. "Oh, Jack, if the price is right you can get a person to part with anything, in my experience."

Parsons didn't argue with the young man, but he knew how Miss Gillian felt about the horse. Money would never urge her to part with that stallion.

Gillian was very busy in her kitchen when Jake Harmon knocked on her front door. She was in the middle of putting a pie in the oven to bake for dinner. All day long she had been excited that Hawk had said he would be over tonight. She felt sure he would come over as soon as he left the office, so when she heard the knock she rushed to the front door, wondering if he might have left the office early. Helen had not arrived home yet, for today she and Ruth were going to stay late to clean the ovens.

But it wasn't Hawk standing there when she opened the door, it was Jake Harmon. She wondered why he would be coming by at this time of the day.

"Jake! I—I didn't expect to see you," she stammered. Darn it, she thought—of all the times for him to show up at her door! Hawk could be riding up at any time.

So instead of inviting him into her parlor, she walked outside onto the porch. Jake gave her a dramatic pout and said teasingly, "You mean I'm not invited in, Gillian? Oh, my feelings are hurt."

"Well, it's a bad time for me. I'm having dinner guests tonight, Jake, and I'm in the middle of cooking."

"Then I'll make it brief and to the point, Gillian. I spotted that red stallion in Parsons's pasture when I rode to town today. When I went by the livery, Parsons told me you own it. I must say that took me by surprise, but that's why I'm here. Name your price, because I'd like to own him."

Gillian gave a laugh and shook her head. "Oh, no, Jake—Fuego isn't for sale."

But Jake refused to accept that as the final answer. "Now, Gillian, you mean to tell me that if I offered you a price that was ridiculous, and far more than the horse was worth, you wouldn't sell him? As I told Parsons, anything can be bought, if the price is right."

Inevitably, as he was talking Hawk rode up, but this time he didn't turn Tache around and ride away. Instead, he leaped off his horse and marched through the gate, striding up the pathway.

Before Gillian could reply to Jake, he heard footsteps approaching and turned around to see who it was. Gillian, unaware that they had met in the railroad office, attempted to introduce them.

Jake told her curtly, "We've met. How are you, Hawk?"

"Fine, Harmon," Hawk retorted, just as cooly.

Gillian looked into Hawk's black eyes and saw that he didn't like Jake Harmon. Jake's face was reflecting similar feelings, so she quickly remarked, "Jake saw Fuego, and was interested in buying him."

"Oh?"

"That's right, Hawk," Jake put in.

"Of course, I told him he is not for sale."

Hawk's eyes moved away from Gillian and he glared at Harmon. "Guess you have your answer, eh, Harmon? Fuego is not for sale!"

That bastard was too damned arrogant for a half-breed, Jake was thinking as he shrugged his shoulders and prepared to take his leave. He'd have liked to slam that redskin face with his fist, but he was no fool. The half-breed towered over him, and he noticed those firm-muscled arms.

Instead, he walked jauntily toward the gate, then paused there with a smirk on his face. "I've always found that anything is for sale, Hawk, if the price is right," he called back as he went through the gate.

"No, not anything, Harmon. And definitely not Fuego!" Hawk assured him.

Jake Harmon wasn't used to being spoken to this way, and Hawk made himself an enemy at that moment.

Chapter Thirty-eight

The incident with Jake Harmon was forgotten as soon as he left, for Hawk was determined that nothing was going to stand in the way of his doing what he had come here to do this evening.

Gillian was happy to see that he wasn't going to become sullen, after he'd arrived to find Jake there on her front porch. She gave him a grateful, loving smile and invited him to come on in. "Jake interrupted my cooking, but it won't take me long to finish up." She urged him to have a seat in the parlor while she checked the food she had simmering in the pot.

He replied, eyes twinkling, "Only if you'll hurry back in here."

She was back very quickly, asking, "There, was that fast enough?"

"Come here, Gillian." He held out his arms to her and she did as he requested. Hawk's hands took her by the waist and lifted her into his lap. His dark eyes looked into hers and he took a deep breath. "Gillian: I want you to marry me—no more delays and no more waiting. I've waited long enough. Tell me you want to marry me too—you must know by now."

A slow smile came to her face, and she replied, "I thought you were *never* going to ask me, Hawk!"

They both began to laugh. Hawk kissed her tenderly and murmured softly in her ear, "Gillian, I can't remember a time when I didn't want to have you as my own and take care of you. Since you were fourteen I've felt this way."

"Oh, Hawk, I've been unsure of so many things about the two of us. I should always have known it was you I was meant to be with. I should have known."

"Well, that doesn't matter now, Gillian. All that matters now is the rest of our lives, and that we will share them together."

Gillian was overwhelmed by the happiness engulfing her as she sat there on Hawk's lap. She forgot all about the dinner she was cooking and that Helen would be arriving home soon.

Hawk took a precious moment to slip the ring on Gillian's finger. It fitted perfectly. "This time I have a ring, Gillian," he said with a sheepish smile on his face.

Gillian gazed at the ring he had chosen for her. It was so beautiful she felt like crying, but she didn't. Instead, she recalled the first wedding she and Hawk had planned, to save her from shame when she found herself pregnant with Lafferty's child.

"Oh, Hawk—we've shared so much, been through so many things together. With you, I can laugh about them now, but at the time they were not so funny."

He pulled her closer to him, and took her dainty hand to look at the ring on her finger. He was pleased to see that it looked so perfect on her. He'd watched the expression on Gillian's lovely face as he'd slipped the ring on her finger, and he knew that she was overwhelmed by it. It was well worth the price he'd paid.

Helen had arrived home a few moments earlier and come upon the sentimental scene as she was entering the front door. Silently, she'd backed off, to let them enjoy the moment without her intrusion. Then, with a sly smile on her face, she had decided that they were so engrossed in one another that they would never hear her if she went quietly to the back door and slipped in through the kitchen.

She was right, for neither of them was aware that she had entered the kitchen door. The minute she was in the kitchen she removed her shoes and tiptoed into her bedroom.

She was glad that she had managed not to spoil the lovers' interlude by coming through the front door at exactly the wrong moment. She was also happy to see the two of them not at odds with one another, as they had been so much recently.

After changing out of her work clothes, Helen decided that she had better go back into the kitchen to check the pots on the stove. She was glad she had thought of it, for Gillian's well-planned dinner was about ready to burn. When she checked the oven, Helen found that the pie was almost ready to be removed from the oven.

Gillian had lost track of time, sitting there on Hawk's lap and looking at the exquisite ring on her finger. She was entranced by the realization that Hawk loved her so deeply and devotedly that he'd asked her a second time to be his wife. How many women were blessed with a man loving them that much?

But she did finally come out of her reverie when she suddenly realized that her dinner might be burning. She leaped up quickly and announced, "Oh, my Lord, Hawk—I bet I've ruined our dinner!"

Hawk watched her dash into the kitchen, smiling as he watched her desert him. Then he heard laughter coming from the kitchen, and went in there to discover Helen and Gillian standing there giggling like two schoolgirls.

When Hawk came sauntering into the kitchen, Helen confessed how she had slipped into the house through the back door.

The three of them enjoyed their dinner, and afterward Helen insisted that they take a nice evening stroll while she cleaned up the kitchen. Gillian and Hawk accepted her offer willingly.

By the time Hawk took his leave from Gillian that night, to ride back toward his own home, he was a very happy man. His ring was now on the finger of the lady he loved, and she had accepted his offer of marriage.

Hawk had loved seeing the stars twinkling in Gillian's eyes tonight when he kissed her goodnight. He could think of nothing more beautiful. And what had made him even happier was her saying she agreed with him that there was no place she could imagine being happier than up on the mountain, in that cabin that had always held so much enchantment for her.

Hawk felt like he owned the whole world tonight; everything seemed to be going right in his life.

Jake Harmon had left Gillian's house and rode

directly to one of his favorite haunts, Trixie's Tavern. Three hours later he was still sitting there drinking by himself. His pal, Kurt, wasn't with him tonight, although it would have been better if he had been there. He could cheer Jake up as much as anyone could, when he was in one of his bad moods.

Jake had it stuck in his mind that he was going to own that red stallion, one way or another. When he decided he wanted something, he would figure out some way to have it.

The other thing on his mind was that smart-mouthed half-breed, Hawk. That bastard would regret talking to him the way he had a few hours ago. He wasn't stupid enough to tangle with the guy himself, but he knew a couple of dudes who could handle Hawk. They hated Apaches as much as he did, and that included half-breeds.

In a way, he was glad that he was here at Trixie's alone tonight, for Kurt would have tried to talk him out of his plan.

He figured the chances were, the two burly hired hands from Cutter's ranch would be coming into town this evening, as they often did after their day's work was over. He saw the two of them in here often.

And he was not to be disappointed. At about eight, the rough, rugged-looking pair came swaggering in through the tavern's swinging doors and looked around.

He beckoned them over to his table. "How you doing, boys? Cutter working you hard?"

"Hard enough," Jess Marcy replied as he took a seat. His pal, Artie, sat down too.

"Buy you two a drink?" Jake asked them.

"I got no objections," Jess told him, lighting up a cigarette.

Jake called the waiter over to order a bottle of whiskey. He allowed them to drink most of it as he made small talk with them.

With a crooked grin on his face, he finally looked over in Artie's direction and casually asked him, "You still hate them Apaches as much as you used to, Artie?"

"Hate them 'til the day I die, Harmon!"

"Yeah, you and me both," Jake agreed.

"At least there ain't many of them around these parts any more," Jess chimed in.

"But we're still left with a bunch of damned half-breeds," Harmon remarked, as he took a sip of his whiskey. He motioned to the waiter to bring another bottle for them.

"You two interested in taking care of a half-breed for me, and making a little money while you're enjoying yourselves, too?" Jake asked them.

"How much, Harmon?" Jess wanted to know.

Jake told them the price he would pay, and the two exchanged looks. Jess looked back at Harmon. "This half-breed must have really rubbed you the wrong way. I heard you were pretty handy with your fists, Harmon. Why do you need me and Artie?"

"I'm damned good with my fists, but this dude is a big son of a bitch!"

"Who is this buck?"

"I'll tell you that if we make a deal," Harmon replied.

"Well, what do you say, Artie?"

"I say all right. You willing, Jess?"

"Hell, I'm ready."

"All right, we got ourselves a deal. I want it done at

night. He gets home from the office where he works at five-thirty. That ought to work out with you two, since you're through at the ranch and in here by eight. Figure by ten he's in bed, and could be caught with his guard down. Now I don't want him killed, Artie—just a good beating. You understand?"

"I understand you, Harmon."

Jake told them exactly where they'd find Hawk's house, and that he wanted it done tomorrow night or the one after. Jake wanted to be sure he wasn't in Tucson when the incident happened.

"I'll show up here with your money in a couple of nights. How's that?"

They were satisfied with that, and Jake decided that it was best that he leave Trixie's, for he didn't want to be seen in their company for too long tonight—or any other night.

Jess and Artie remained there at the table and finished the whiskey before they rode back to the Cutter ranch. Both were thinking about the money they'd make from the job for Harmon. It would be enough to have themselves some good times for a while, they figured.

Jake rode home with a smug grin on his face, for he'd seen the results of a beating those two could inflict. After they were through with Hawk, he wouldn't be mouthing off to anyone for a while.

Now, the next thing he had to figure out was how he could convince Gillian Lafferty to sell him that red stallion. Tomorrow, he'd think about that!

Chapter Thirty-nine

Hawk was still blissfully happy the next morning when he went to the office. It was always pleasant for Warner Barstow to see Hawk in a jovial mood, for usually he was a very serious young man. Oh, it wasn't that Hawk couldn't join in a joke, but he wasn't as lighthearted as most young men his age.

But Warner didn't mind that, for he'd never had anyone as conscientious as Hawk work for him. He hoped that Hawk would find himself a nice young lady to marry, and he liked to think it would be Gillian Lafferty. They certainly made a handsome couple.

A minor problem developed late in the afternoon, and Warner and Hawk both had to stay at the office for an extra couple of hours, so it was after seven by the time Hawk was galloping Tache up his drive. It had been a long day for both of them, and Tache was as glad to get into his stall as Hawk was to get to the house.

By the time he had fixed himself some supper, eaten it, and finally dimmed the light in his kitchen, it was almost nine o'clock. Hawk knew that he would be hitting that comfortable bed of his shortly, for the long day had tired him.

He sat down in his favorite chair in the parlor and removed his boots, stretching out his long legs. He read for a little while, but his eyes kept drooping, and he saw no reason to fight the tiredness.

He dimmed the parlor lamp and went into his bedroom. A few seconds later he was in bed, and as soon as his head hit the pillow he fell asleep.

Jess and Artie had arrived at Trixie's Tavern at about the usual time, and fortified themselves with three quick rounds of whiskey. Artie ordered a fourth drink, but Jess looked at the clock behind the bar, saw the time, and said, "We'd better get started, Artie."

Artie hastily downed his drink, and followed Jess out of the tavern. Few people were left in the streets as they rode toward the outskirts of the city. Jess was careful to follow the directions Harmon had given them, because he didn't want to go to the wrong place.

But he knew they were going to the right place for there was no other house on the west side of the road for the last mile they'd ridden. It had to be the right place and it was situated back off the road with a drive leading up to the house and a fenced barnyard.

When they got there, Jess couldn't have seen what the hands of his pocket watch said, for it was a dark night and with a new moon, but he figured it was about ten, or a little after.

Since Hawk had never gotten into the habit of locking his door, it proved to be no problem for Jess and Artie to get into the house. The two huge men bumped into the kitchen table in the center of the room, but Hawk's usually keen ears did not hear the slight noise because he was so soundly asleep.

As they were moving cautiously through the parlor, Artie came in contact with one of Hawk's boots lying on the floor. He picked it up, for he knew from experience that a swinging boot could do a lot of damage.

They knew when they had found the right room, because although it was shrouded in darkness, they could make out the massive bulk of Hawk's body, lying in the bed.

"Let me take the first swing at him with this," Artie whispered to Jess, and he moved forward.

Jess didn't try to stop him, so Artie moved to the side of the bed and swung back his hand to slam the boot's heel against Hawk's head. By sheer luck, Hawk's head moved slightly, and thus he was spared the brutal blow to the head. The boot only slightly grazed the side of his head, but the blow was sharp enough to bring Hawk very much awake and alert. Like a mountain lion, he leaped out of bed and grabbed at the intruder. He didn't know that there was another man on the other side of his bed.

The boot Artie was holding was suddenly yanked from his hand and Hawk's huge fist struck his gut. Artie gasped. Now Hawk had the boot in his hand and swinging it dangerously.

Jess dashed around the bed to come to the aid of his partner. He saw the swinging boot strike Artie and heard his groan. Then Jess's powerful fist made contact with Hawk's face. But Jess could see why Harmon had not wanted to tackle this dude by himself. He was a giant of a man, and barely flinched at the blow.

Now Jess managed to slightly stun Hawk with two more fierce punches, and he took advantage of the situation. He gave his hand to Artie to pull him up, knowing that he would be more than ready to get his revenge on Hawk.

He aimed his foot at Hawk's groin and kicked, and as strong as Hawk was, he bent over, a sickening agony consuming him. Weakened by this, Hawk felt punishing blows from two pairs of fists pummeling his face and head. Finally he lay limp on the floor, and Jess and Artie, satisfied that they'd done a good job for Harmon, turned to rush out of the house.

Jess was left with aching, skinned knuckles from slamming so hard into Hawk's face, but Artie was to discover that blood was coming from his mouth as well as from the side of his head. During the fight in the dark room he had not been aware of it, but now that he and Jess were riding back to the ranch, he felt dampness on the side of his head and knew it was blood. It was not until they got back to the ranch that Artie discovered Hawk's boot had broken his front teeth.

By God, he figured, he had earned Harmon's fee after all!

Hawk finally came to, but found himself in too much pain to stand up, so he started to crawl toward the kitchen. He knew he needed some cool water on his face, which was already swelling.

It took all the willpower he could muster, once he reached his kitchen, to raise himself up off the floor and stand there for a moment to dip some water from the pail and put it in a pan. When he had soaked some cloths in the water he covered his face with them, flinching from the pain.

Slowly, he managed to get over to one of the kitchen chairs and sink into it. He sat holding the damp cloth against his face and head.

His head throbbed miserably, and it was hard to even try to think. What was this all about? Were the two men robbers? That was the only explanation he could think of. One thing he did know, though, and it was that from this night on, his doors would be locked. This was not the peaceful mountain cabin.

After a while he rose from his chair, went directly to the back door, and locked it. From there he walked through the dark parlor to lock the front door. This took great effort for him.

When he got back into his bedroom, he lit the lamp to survey the room for some clue. The money in his pouch, lying in plain view on the high chest, had not been touched, so it was not to rob him that those two had come to his house. He noticed spots of blood on the bottom of his coverlet, and there also was a stain of blood on the heel of his boot. That gave him a degree of satisfaction, at least.

By now the cloths had lost their coolness so he went back into the kitchen to dampen them again. He dimmed the lamp and slowly made his way back into the bedroom, then lay his exhausted body across the bed, the cool cloths draped over his face. He found himself too exhausted to sit back up and dim the lamp on the nightstand, so it burned for the rest of the night.

The next morning as the sun rose, its bright rays

streamed through the window to shine on Hawk's face. His sleep had been restless, and when he reluctantly opened his eyes he saw the lamp still burning. He knew immediately that the pain was going to settle in on him today. He wondered if he was going to be able to make it into the office and, if he did, whether he could last the day.

There was one thing certain in Hawk's mind: he was going to make someone pay for what had happened last night. Since the men hadn't robbed him, he figured he must have an enemy he didn't know about.

His face looked terrible, but that didn't matter to Hawk. It was the blows to his groin and body that really made movement painful. But a strong-brewed pot of coffee made him feel a little more human. Dressing took longer than usual, but he managed it.

When he left his house to go to the barn, he locked his kitchen door behind him. A thought struck him as he was walking to the barn, which had not even occurred to him last night: what if they'd stolen Tache? But he soon discovered that this had not happened. No, they were not robbers, drifting through the countryside to gather themselves some bounty. Hawk was firmly convinced of that this morning.

It wasn't an easy ride to the office, and Hawk was glad that it wasn't further.

Warner was shocked at the sight of the young man coming through the door. "Holy Christ, Hawk, what happened to you?" He leaped to his feet, concerned.

"I look like a freight train hit me, I know, but that wasn't what did it." Hawk told him everything that had happened last night, and how he was baffled that he had such an enemy. "They didn't come to rob me,

357

Warner. That was the first idea that struck me. At first I figured they were a couple of drifters riding through Tucson who needed a fast few bucks to take them on their way. But my money was handy for them to have grabbed, and it wasn't touched."

"But who would want to do this to you, son? You haven't argued with anyone, have you?" the older man asked Hawk. But this young man kept so much to himself that Warner found it hard to believe this was possible.

"No, and I can't imagine who it might be, Warner," Hawk told him. Warner felt great compassion for Hawk as he looked at his face. He knew the young man had made a great effort this morning just to get here to the office.

"Why don't you just take the day off, Hawk? Go home and take it easy. I can handle things here," he suggested.

"No, time might hang heavier at home than it would here, Warner. I'll see if I can work; if not, I might just take your suggestion."

Warner moved around to take his seat at the desk. "Well, you'll have to be the judge of that, Hawk, but you know how I feel."

Hawk gave him a nod and walked slowly around to sit down at his desk. He found that concentrating on the paperwork there helped him forget the aches and pains of his body. But the throbbing headache remained with him.

At midday, Warner asked him how he was doing. He insisted that Hawk share the fried chicken and biscuits his wife had packed for him. "That little wife of mine is the reason I'm so fat. She's too good a cook, and far

358

too generous with these lunches she packs for me," he said, hoping to cheer Hawk up.

"Well, I can't resist your wife's chicken, Warner," Hawk confessed, accepting Warner's offer.

A few minutes later the two of them had devoured every piece, and all the biscuits. Hawk gave a pleased sigh, and declared that Warner's wife's was the best chicken he'd ever eaten. Warner laughed, telling Hawk that she would be very happy to hear it.

The good food had made Hawk feel better, and he and Warner were preparing to get back to work when the door opened and Jake Harmon came sauntering in. He announced to Warner that his father had sent him to check on what the railroad had done about the damaged goods.

"The claim's in, Jake, but I've had no word back. It's too soon. I'd have figured Sam would realize that," Warner told Jake.

Of course, it had not been Sam's idea at all for Jake to come to the office. Jake wanted to see if his men had taken care of Hawk. He was more than pleased to see the bruised, swollen face on the half-breed. The two men had done a good job!

Hawk's sharp black eyes were surveying Harmon carefully. His instinct told him that Jake Harmon was interested in his battered face—so why didn't he ask what had happened? Hawk could have sworn that there was a hint of a conceited smile on Harmon's face.

Jake prepared to leave the office, for he'd seen what he came to see. But he couldn't resist taunting Hawk before he left. "Looks like you must have tangled with the wrong man, Hawk."

"Make it two men, Harmon, sent by one lily-livered

bastard! But when I get through with them, they're going to look worse than I do," Hawk promised, his voice level.

Warner sat observing all this, and saw the strange look on young Harmon's face. For whatever reason, Jake didn't care for Hawk, and as he glanced over to see Hawk's piercing eyes on Harmon, he realized that the feeling was mutual.

Hawk managed to stay at the office for the day. By the time he left to go home, he had figured out that it had to be Jake Harmon who'd been responsible for what happened to him last night. Oh, he had not dirtied his hands to do the job, but he'd hired the two cowhands to beat him up, and Hawk thought he knew why, now.

Part Four

Autumn's Bounty

Chapter Forty

As Hawk rode home he found that his body did not ache quite as badly as it had that morning. He concentrated on the last twenty-four hours, weighing each and every little incident. He knew that the men invading his house had come to do him harm. He also recalled the strong odor of liquor on their breaths when he had fought with them.

Hawk had to figure that one of the men had certainly suffered from the blow of the boot in his face. The blood he'd found on the heel and the bottom of the coverlet told Hawk that.

Still, the room had been too dark for Hawk to see the faces of the men. All he had to identify them by was that they were two husky fellows. When he arrived at his house and put Tache in the corral so that he could kick up his heels for a while before dark, Hawk felt like a man obsessed. He *had* to find the bastards who invaded his home last night.

Right now he could not even think about Gillian, for all his thoughts were on the revenge he must have. He had a light supper, and by the time he was leaving his kitchen the sun was beginning to sink in the western sky. Now that summer had come, the evenings were longer. He sat down in his parlor and stared out the window, deep in thought. Gillian would be expecting him to come by her house this evening, since he hadn't gone there last night. But he would not be good company for her tonight, and he didn't want her to see him looking like this. Hawk knew that he would not be able to rest until he found the men who'd done this to him. He figured their kind would be found in the evenings at one of the city's taverns. Hawk wasn't a drinking man, so he didn't frequent the taverns as a lot of young men his age did, but tonight he might just make the rounds of a few of them, he decided.

Once his mind was made up, Hawk wasted no time in going to the barn to put the saddle back on Tache and going back into the city. Hawk did not find sauntering into a tavern to his liking, but he forced himself to go in the first one he came to and survey the place without sitting down at a table or ordering a drink.

He knew that he was hunting for a needle in a haystack, and it was probably futile, but he went through the same routine in five or six taverns. Some of them were crowded; others had only a few fellows sitting around at the tables.

Hawk was wondering what they found so interesting at these places. It seemed like a very dull atmosphere to him in the foul-smelling rooms that were filled with smoke. He felt like he was walking into a fog when he'd entered the places. Yet there was raucous laughter resounding in some of the taverns, and the men did seem to be enjoying themselves. Hawk could not imagine what was so entertaining.

He told himself he would try one more place before he gave up. It had been a long day, and he was going to have himself a good night's sleep tonight, behind locked doors.

Something caught Hawk's eye as soon as he rode Tache up to this last tavern. It was a buggy that Hawk recognized instantly as belonging to Jake Harmon. Now what was Harmon doing at a place like Trixie's Tavern?

Well, he would find out. Seeing the buggy was enough for Hawk to start feeling that this evening was going to pay off for him, after all. When he had dismounted from Tache he didn't go into the tavern, but stood outside the swinging door to look inside the room. At once Hawk spotted Jake Harmon, sitting at a table with two ruffians, who Hawk knew instinctively were the ones who'd beat him up last night.

He would have been very pleased to know the damage he'd done to one of the men. Jake had found it hard to suppress an amused grin earlier, when Artie had grumbled about the two teeth he'd lost last night. Still, the money he'd put in Artie's palm had seemed to pacify him.

Jake didn't want to stay at Trixie's too long with the two men. He'd paid the debt he owed them, and bought them a couple of drinks, so he figured that score was settled. Now he was ready to take his leave and get back to the ranch. He'd had his gratification this afternoon, seeing Hawk's face, but he also remembered Hawk's words as he'd left the office. That half-breed made him leery, and he could not just shrug aside his remarks. It was as if he had been giving him a warning, and Jake

365

was ready to leave Trixie's and get back to the ranch, where he knew he would be safe.

For a while, Jake figured, he'd better stay close to home. He had no desire to have an encounter with Hawk. He had only to remember the fierce look in Hawk's black eyes this afternoon, when he was in Warner Barstow's office, to know that the man would be a very formidable foe.

Hawk watched as Jake rose from the table, and moved away from the door, back into the shadows of darkness. Before he went to mount Tache, he took one last look at the two fellows in the tavern. He observed the angry-looking cut on the side of the face of the one called Artie, and knew the heel of his boot had done that. Hawk watched Jake get into his buggy and start moving down the street. He allowed him to travel for a short distance before he urged Tache into motion.

As the buggy reached the outskirts of the city, Hawk spurred Tache into a canter. Hawk had no doubt in his mind that he was about to have his revenge when he rode ahead of the buggy, forcing Harmon to stop.

Jake cursed fluently. "Wha—what the hell?" he cried. The blackness of the night made it impossible for him to recognize Hawk, but Hawk wanted him to know who was beating him up. He leaped off Tache, going around to the side of the buggy to yank Jake off the seat. Jake broke loose and fell heavily to the ground.

"Your men did a good job on me last night, Harmon, so I figure I'll do a good job on you tonight," Hawk told him, and reached down to yank him up by the collar. His mighty fist slammed into Jake's face, and Harmon let out a moan of anguish and pain. Hawk's long leg tensed as he brought his knee upward to pound into Jake's groin.

But as Jake went down to the ground, moaning with pain, Hawk showed him more mercy than he'd been shown—he didn't kick him as Artie had done him.

It was not Hawk's nature to be sadistic, and he'd had his revenge. He figured that Jake's face was going to look a little like his by the morning.

"You can give your men the message that they are next on my list, Harmon," Hawk spat out, before he turned to mount Tache.

As he rode off toward his house, Jake began to struggle to his feet and board his buggy. It took a seemingly endless effort to finally get on the seat, and the ride on to the ranch was sheer hell.

He wondered later how he had ever managed to get the bay into the stall and hobble into the house to his room. Once inside, he managed to pour some water into the wash basin and dampen a cloth to put to the side of his face, without lighting the lamp.

Old Sam was a light sleeper, and Jake certainly didn't want an encounter with him tonight. Sam would not have approved of him hiring two heavies to beat Hawk up, although he was not adverse to a good fight when two fellows had a difference to settle.

No, Jake would have to come up with a good lie to explain his appearance. But right now, he was hurting too bad to think straight.

It never dawned on Hawk as he went homeward that he'd done what no other man in Tucson would have dared to do: he'd tangled with the son of Sam Harmon.

Giving Jake the beating he deserved might well cause all kinds of troubles for him, but Hawk slept peacefully that night, in blissful ignorance.

Riding to work the next morning, he found he was not half as sore and aching as he had been the day before. But his face still looked as bad, and he knew it was going to take a few days for that to change.

When he arrived at the office, Warner noticed immediately that Hawk did not walk so stiffly. "Did you get a good night's sleep?"

"Sure did, sir. I feel much better this morning."

"Well, I'm glad! Damn, Hawk, I have to tell you, I've thought about what happened to you last night and it makes no sense to me. Are you *sure* you haven't riled someone here in Tucson?"

"Well, yesterday, I would have told you I hadn't, but this morning I have to correct that. There's one person, although I wouldn't have expected it to bring out such a reaction. It was Jake Harmon."

"Jake Harmon? My God, man, it isn't good to bring out the wrath of the Harmons. How did you manage to do that?" Warner sank down in the chair at his desk with a look of grave concern on his face.

Hawk told him about Jake becoming determined to purchase Fuego from Gillian, and how he'd happened to arrive at Gillian's the day Jake had gone there. "Jake wouldn't take no for an answer, so I answered for Gillian. I told him Fuego wasn't for sale. As you know, I bought that stallion for Gillian, and the likes of Harmon will never own him," Hawk declared firmly to Warner. Warner understood that Hawk had a right to feel as he did, but he also knew Jake Harmon.

"Oh, Hawk, promise me you won't do anything

crazy," Warner cautioned him.

"I'm afraid it's too late for me to take that wise advice, Warner," Hawk said simply, and went to sit down at his desk.

"What are you telling me, Hawk?"

Hawk explained his deduction yesterday, and what had happened last night. Warner listened to everything he said with intense interest. His mind was whirling with ideas about how he might help Hawk if it became necessary—and he feared that it might.

Warner had a sober look on his face when he spoke. "Hawk, who knows about that mountain cabin where you and your mother lived, besides me and Miss Gillian?"

Warner's question struck Hawk as strange, but he hesitated and thought for a moment before he replied, "No one here in Tucson, besides you and Gillian. Oh, Miss Helen knows that I come from Maricopa County, but she doesn't know where the cabin is located."

"Wonderful! Look, I'm advising you as I would if you were my son. I want you to leave Tucson today. Don't even take the time to see Gillian. I'll go and tell her why you've left. Go to your mountain cabin and stay there, until I send word to Rock Springs that everything is all right. Sam Harmon will have the law on you before the day is over, if I know him as I think I do, and I don't want you to take that chance. You can't compete with the power of the Harmons, and you'll just land in jail."

Hawk seemed about to voice a protest, but Warner cut in. "Sam's temper will cool after a while, and I can give you the perfect alibi. I can say I've sent you out on an inspection route and have no idea where you might be. Listen to me, son, for I'm telling you right."

Hawk had never questioned Warner's wisdom. In fact, he knew no one he respected more, other than the wise Solange. "I'll do it, sir, if you think that's what I should do."

"I surely do, Hawk. I'll write you in care of the Rock Springs station and keep you informed. Do it, Hawk. Leave the office, right now."

Hawk could not take lightly the seriousness of Warner's manner and the intense concern on his face. He had to appreciate that Barstow cared enough to urge him to take time off and leave Tucson.

Hawk walked around the corner of his desk and Warner gave him a comradely embrace. He cautioned Hawk, "Remember, don't try to see Miss Gillian, Hawk. I will ensure that she is told about everything. You shouldn't stay here that long. You don't know Sam Harmon like I do, and if you land in jail, my hands will be tied."

So Hawk did exactly as Warner advised him. It did not take him long to throw a few things together and saddle up Tache, ready to leave his house. He was glad now that Fuego was over at Parsons's place, for he had only to lock the doors of his house before he rode out of the drive.

His only regret as he headed north was that he was leaving Gillian alone in Tucson.

Chapter Forty-one

Jake Harmon had delayed making an appearance downstairs for as long as he could the next morning, for he had only to look at his once-good looking face in the mirror to see that his father would have a few questions for him.

He figured he had concocted a good story that old Sam would accept, otherwise he would not have dared to venture out of his bedroom. But when he encountered his father in the dining room, having his cup of coffee and reading a journal as he did daily, all his well-laid plans went awry because of Sam's reaction when he saw Jake's face.

Being a light sleeper, Sam had heard him coming into the house late last night. The slow shuffle of Jake's footsteps had convinced Sam that he was coming in dog drunk. He was already in a foul mood with his son this morning.

When he looked up from his journal and saw the awful mess Jake presented as he sauntered up to the table, he spoke with a curt tone in his voice. "I've told you time and again that carousing you and Kurt are always doing would catch up with you one night. Well, it looks like I was right."

Jake sat down in his chair and their mestizo housekeeper, Zola, immediately served him a cup of coffee. Then she went over to the sideboard to fill his plate with eggs, sausages, ham, and biscuits, brought it back to the table and placed it before him.

Jake took a couple of bites of the food before he realized how sore his jaw was. "Kurt and I weren't carousing, Father. I had a disagreement with another man."

"Well, I'd say he must have won that disagreement, as you call it, Jake."

By now, Jake was beginning to get riled, as he often did, with his father's lordly manner. His pride was being battered, but he knew he should be cautious. Sam Harmon felt a fierce pride about his family.

Jake decided that he had better tell his father a believable story, so he made some quick changes in the tale he had prepared.

"I'm sure I don't have to refresh your memory about the beautiful Miss Gillian Lafferty. Well, the other day I spotted a magnificent red stallion out in the pasture at Jack Parsons's place, so I stopped at the livery to ask Jack about him. I found that it belongs to Gillian Lafferty, and I went by her house to make her an offer. But while I'm there, talking and dealing with her, this half-breed, Hawk, that works for Warner Barstow, arrives and throws his weight around. Tells me that this stallion is not for sale. Now what do you think of that, Father?"

"I'd say he was very cocky."

372

"Well, it was as if he was taking charge of the horse, and of Gillian. Now I found that interesting, since Miss Gillian Lafferty didn't have the time of day for the son of Sam Harmon, but then she allows a half-breed Apache to take charge and speak for her."

Sam shrugged his shoulders and asked impatiently, "So, she does. What are you getting at, Jake? She refused to sell the stallion to you. What does that have to do with the way you look this morning?"

"The son of a bitch waylaid me last night when I left Trixie's."

Sam sat still for a moment to consider everything his son had told him. Finally he spoke. "You let me take care of this, Jake, and keep your ass right here at the ranch for the next few days. Do you understand?" Sam's piercing eyes glared across the table at him.

"Yes, sir. I will."

Sam said nothing more, but got up from his chair at the dining table and left the room. Jake sat there with a smile on his face, for he knew that the revised story he'd told his father had been a good one.

Jake felt very satisfied later that day when he saw Sam ride away from the ranch. He knew that his father was riding into Tucson to seek justice for the wrong that had been done to the Harmon family. And Jake was right, for the first place Sam went was to the office of Warner Barstow.

He looked like a storm cloud when he entered the office to confront Warner. Warner knew he had been right to advise Hawk to leave Tucson when he looked up to see the towering figure of Sam Harmon standing there glaring down at him. "Where's that half-breed Apache that works for you, Warner?" he snapped.

"You inquiring about Hawk, Sam?" asked Warner casually.

"You know damned well I am!"

"Well, he rode out at the crack of dawn to go on an inspection tour for the railroad. Can I be of service to you?"

"You're not the one who beat the hell out of my son last night. That Apache bastard did, and he's going to pay for daring to lay hands on a Harmon."

Warner stood up at his desk and, in a cool, calm manner, told Sam, "Well, Sam, if you're going to get carried away doing justice for your son, you'd better know that Hawk was beaten up bad the night before by some lowlife characters. You might ask your son about that. And I might add that there are some people here in Tucson, myself included, that hold that Apache bastard in high esteem! Hawk is not a man to start trouble, Sam."

Warner's remarks were enough to make an impact on Sam. He had always respected Warner Barstow as a true gentleman, so he could not take lightly what he had just said. He left Warner's office without saying another word.

But as he rode back to the ranch, he knew he had a lot of questions to ask Jake when he got back. Warner Barstow was a truthful, honest man, and would not lie. Sam didn't doubt that Jake would.

After Sam left his office, Warner took off his glasses and rubbed his weary eyes. He hoped that Hawk was already far away from Tucson, and he knew that he had advised him wisely. He also hoped that Sam went directly to his ranch and shot some questions at Jake. Then maybe this thing would die down and go away.

When he left the office at five he decided to satisfy himself that Hawk had left the city. He arrived at Hawk's house to find it locked up, and no one answered his knock. He went through the barnyard gate to check the stall, and Tache was not there, so Barstow left the place feeling greatly relieved.

Tomorrow, he would pay a call on Gillian Lafferty and let her know what had happened.

Barstow's buggy pulled out of Hawk's drive and he'd traveled about a half mile on down the road when he saw two riders ahead of him. Something about their looks caught Warner's attention, and he realized that they fit Hawk's description of the pair that beat him up. If he had not been so far away by then from Hawk's place, he would have halted his buggy to see if they turned into Hawk's drive.

But if it was them it didn't matter. They wouldn't find Hawk at home, so Warner didn't fret about it. In fact, he went home and spent a very relaxed evening with his wife.

He was already starting to realize that Hawk's absence was going to put more work on him, so he went to bed early, planning to get to the office about an hour earlier than he normally did.

The extra hour he put in the next day enabled Warner to leave the office at the usual hour, so he headed his buggy toward Gillian's house. When she opened the door to see Warner Barstow standing there, she felt like she was going to stop breathing. She just knew something had happened to Hawk—that was why he hadn't been by the house for the last two nights. She'd decided this afternoon that if he didn't come tonight she was going to ride over to the office first thing in the morning.

As soon as she'd greeted Warner and invited him into her parlor, she asked if something was wrong with Hawk.

"No, Hawk is fine, but he did have to leave town in a hurry. That's why I came by to explain it to you, Miss Gillian."

"Please, have a seat, Mr. Barstow," she urged him. She offered him a cup of coffee, which he politely refused.

He told her everything that had happened to Hawk the night after he'd been to Gillian's. He watched the emotions displayed on her face as he spoke, and he told her that it was his idea that Hawk leave town for a while, until all this died down. Sensing that she and Hawk might be lovers, he also felt the need to caution her about something. "Miss Gillian, I suggest that you don't try to leave Tucson to join him. You could be followed by Jake or some of his men. Hawk told me that you and I are the only ones here in Tucson that know about the cabin, so we don't want to give away its location."

"I understand, Mr. Barstow. Dear God, poor Hawk! I'd—I'd do nothing to put Hawk in any kind of danger, I promise you," Gillian assured him.

"I know you wouldn't. Hopefully, this thing will run its course shortly—but knowing Jake Harmon, it could also fester for a while. He's not used to someone standing up to him like Hawk did. And he's not used to being refused anything he wants, as you did when you refused to let him buy Fuego," Warner told her.

"Well, Hawk and I are a lot alike when it comes to being stubborn. Jake Harmon will never have that stallion, so he isn't going to get his way about that," Gillian vowed to him.

"Well, young lady, now that you know everything, I'm going to be on my way. I'll keep in touch with you. If you should need me for any reason, you know you have only to come to the office to see me," Warner told her, as he rose from the chair.

"Thank you very much, Mr. Barstow. I have been wondering about Hawk so at least now I know why he's not been over," she said, as she walked with him to the door.

Warner had just urged the bay into motion when Helen turned the corner on her way home from the bakery shop. Like Gillian, when she saw him leaving her first thought was that something had happened to Hawk, and that he'd come to the house to inform Gillian.

But when she walked into the parlor to see Gillian sitting there with a thoughtful look on her face, and with no tears streaming down her pretty cheeks, Helen's fears eased.

Gillian informed her about everything Warner Barstow had told her. "Well, I'm glad Hawk has such a fine gentleman as Mr. Barstow as his good friend, Gillian. There is no denying that this city still steams with a lot of prejudice where half-breeds are concerned. It never dawns on me when I'm around Hawk that he is a half-breed, but people like the Harmons would feel differently," Helen said.

377

A faraway look was in Gillian's blue eyes as she told Helen, "Oh, I wish I could go to him, Helen. I wish I could leave first thing in the morning, but I know Mr. Barstow is right, so I won't."

"No, Gillian—he is right. Just be patient, at least for a while," Helen advised her.

Gillian gave her a smile, and suggested they turn their attention to getting themselves some supper.

Chapter Forty-two

Jake Harmon had felt vindicated when he'd gone to Barstow's office and seen the damage to Hawk's face, but now he had another ax to grind with that half-breed for daring to be so bold as to attack him. It also kindled more hate in him when Sam returned to the ranch and started an inquisition.

"I went to the railroad office to have a talk with this Hawk you said beat you up. I didn't get to talk to him, but I did have a very interesting talk with Warner Barstow. And before you say one word, Jake, let me tell you something. I've known Warner a lot of years, and that man doesn't lie."

Before Sam left him alone he had the truth. There was no way Jake could wriggle out of it, after what Sam had learned from Barstow.

But it also ignited anew his vendetta against Hawk. Jake knew he would not rest until he settled this new score with Hawk.

That night, after supper, he left the house to ride into town, not caring that his face was still a mess. He hoped

379

that he might meet up at Trixie's with Jess and Artie, to see if they'd like to take another turn with Hawk. And this time he didn't give a damn if they did kill him.

He did indeed meet up with them, and they willingly agreed to do another job on the half-breed when Jake doubled the fee he would pay them. He told them, "Hurt the bastard worse this time. He didn't learn his lesson the last time, and when he figured out it had to be me who'd sent you two after him, he came after me."

"Just how bad do you want him hurt, Harmon? He's as strong as a bull," Jess told Jake.

"I don't give a damn, now," Jake said.

"You be here tomorrow night, Harmon, with the money?" Artie wanted to know.

"Will you two be here?"

"We'll be here, won't we, Jess?"

"Yeah, we'll be here and ready to collect that money, Harmon," Jess agreed.

A short time later, the three of them left the tavern together. Jake rode back to the ranch. He knew where they were heading.

When he arrived at the ranch house, Jake slipped in quietly so he would not alert old Sam. He didn't want another lecture from him tonight.

Once he was in his room and undressed, he stretched out in his bed, smiling as he thought that about now, Hawk would be receiving another dose of punishment from those two rugged ranch hands.

But instead, Jess and Artie were riding away from Hawk's place, disappointed that a fat roll of bills would not be in their hands tomorrow night. The doors had both been locked when they tried them. They managed to break one door down, but there was no one inside the house, nor was there a horse in the barn. Hawk was definitely gone.

So the only thing left for them to do was ride back to the Cutter ranch and get themselves some sleep.

Hawk would have enjoyed a laugh about that, had he known it. He was enjoying a pleasant, peaceful evening up in his mountain cabin. He yearned for only one thing to make his happiness complete, and that was for Gillian to be there by his side.

Solange and Gaston had departed by the time he arrived, but as she always did when she left the cabin, Solange had left a note for Hawk to read the next time he got up there. This time, her note explained what Gaston had put in motion before they left, and that Troy and his friend would be doing the work there, adding the two extra rooms.

Hawk read the note, and an amused smile came to his face. That Gaston—he was a most unusual man! He, as well as Solange, was lucky that he'd come into their lives. Hawk was thinking how proud he would have been to boast that Gaston Dion was his father. Unfortunately he couldn't do that, but he was certainly proud to have him as a stepfather.

It was uncanny, but Gaston seemed somehow to know that this was the place Hawk dreamed about having as his and Gillian's home. That must be why he'd put Troy to work building on the two extra rooms.

*   *   *

Gillian's days and nights seemed endless now that she knew Hawk was not in Tucson. She tried to keep herself busy around the house and yard, but it was not enough to occupy all the hours of the day. Helen was gone most afternoons at her job at the bakery, but at least she had company in the evenings, especially now that Jack and Barry came over a couple of times a week for dinner.

She had said nothing to Helen about Jake Harmon coming to the house once again to offer her an astronomical price for Fuego. This time she did not have Hawk to back her up but she figured she had handled him very calmly. Now that she knew what he was like, she had recognized a fury in Jake's intense eyes when she'd flatly turned down his offer and he'd walked off her front porch.

She also now knew what Jake was capable of to get his own way. Gillian did not doubt for a minute that Jake could steal her handsome Fuego out of Parsons's pasture while he was in town at the livery. She just had to hope it didn't happen.

Gillian had a lot of time on her hands to think, and she knew that Warner must have no news of Hawk, or he would have contacted her. After two long weeks, Gillian's pretty head was full of all kinds of crazy ideas that she had not dared voice to Helen or discuss with Warner Barstow. But she had convinced herself that she was about to try one of her ideas, for she wanted desperately to be with the man she loved, and there was nothing holding her here in Tucson.

Her little house seemed to have become a prison, and she was no longer enchanted with it. She remembered Warner's warning that she should not try to leave Tucson to join Hawk, so she felt trapped in Tucson.

But Gillian had been possessed by an idea for the last few days that she was convinced would get her and Fuego out of Tucson without anyone knowing about her departure. She was just about ready to attempt it.

After what she'd observed this afternoon, she was convinced that she needed to get away from Tucson as soon as possible. She could have sworn that Jake Harmon was watching her house, and she wondered if he was expecting Hawk to make an appearance, after all this time. From her parlor windows, she watched as his horse walked slowly up and down the road two or three times.

She knew that she could not keep living like this. Only one thing occupied her thoughts, and that was that she needed desperately to get to Hawk—to be with Hawk. Jake Harmon made her nervous. One never knew what to expect from a man like him. For Fuego's sake, as well as her own, she needed to get to Hawk. She was glad that Jack and Barry were coming to dinner tonight, because she had to have their help to carry out her plan. She knew that they would help her.

Helen had also been keeping some things from Gillian since all this had happened. Jack had been anxious for them to set a date for their wedding, but Helen had persuaded him that they should delay it, because she did not want to move out and leave Gillian alone in the house. Reluctantly, Jack had agreed, even though he was eager to have Helen as his wife and move her into his home.

Young Barry was already very comfortably settled in

out there, and all that was lacking was Helen. Jack saw no reason to delay, until Helen told him what had happened with Hawk. He knew how devoted Helen was to Gillian, so he understood her feelings.

Gillian was so sure about what she was going to do that she had gone to her bedroom and packed the belongings she was going to take when she left. She had no need of any fancy gowns, and she knew she had to pack light, so only certain things were tossed in the bag, including a change of riding skirts and tunics. In her velvet pouch, with the jewelry she'd acquired during her time at the inn, were the sapphire earrings Melba had left to her.

By the time Helen got home, Gillian was dressed in her pink frock and had her hair pulled back from her face and tied with a pink ribbon, for it was a very hot summer evening. The steaming pots on the stove only increased the heat in the kitchen.

She knew that her announcement was going to shock them all this evening, so she waited until they had had an opportunity to enjoy the meal and the dessert.

When the four of them were pleasantly sated by the meal, she finally told them about her plans.

"Now, please don't try to talk me out of it, for my mind is made up. I've done some very careful planning for this venture. I well remember that Warner cautioned me that I could lead them to Hawk, but I won't be taking a train. I will ride Fuego, and leave in the dead of night." She went on to tell them how she had purchased a pair of twill pants and a faded blue shirt, very much like those young Barry wore all the time. She had also bought a cap so that she could tuck her long tresses out of sight.

"So you see, I will look like a young fellow instead of a girl."

"Oh, Gillian, you will still look like a young lady, even with all your disguises," Helen declared skeptically.

"No, you just wait and see, Helen, for I've already tried it out. I was amazed myself. I'll be riding during the night and I'll hide away and get my sleep during the day."

"Oh, Gillian, what if you meet up with the wrong sort?" Helen asked her. Jack said nothing, for he knew that nothing he or Helen could say was going to stop her. Privately, he had to admire her spunk and the clever plans she'd made. There was no denying that she might encounter the wrong sort, but at least the trail would be more deserted during the night than it would during the day.

This was exactly what she was now telling Helen. "I won't concern myself after the first night out, Helen. By then I'll be far enough away from Tucson that it'll be safer. Jake Harmon and his father will have no idea that I've left Tucson until I'm probably already in Maricopa County."

Helen had to confess that she made it sound very convincing. Gillian was certainly no naive little ranch girl anymore—she'd traveled all the way across the ocean from Ireland by herself.

"Well, I guess there's nothing more to ask you, Gillian, except when do you plan to leave?" Helen asked her.

"Tomorrow night, Helen."

Jack Parsons finally spoke up. "What can I do to help you, Miss Gillian?" He suggested that he could

385

have Barry lead Fuego from the ranch late tomorrow night.

"Oh, no, Mr. Parsons! No, I wouldn't want that. I don't want Fuego brought into town at all. But I would be grateful if I might come over before you close the livery, and use one of your horses to come back home to wait until it got dark. Then I would ride to your place to get Fuego and exchange horses with you."

"All right, ma'am—that's the way we'll do it. I'll have Fuego in the stall and ready for you. About what time?"

"I'm going to plan to leave the house about ten, so I'd be at your place around a quarter after ten," Gillian told him.

Young Barry had been listening intensely to every word she'd spoken. It all sounded very exciting to him. Admiring her as he always had, he found this cross-country venture very intriguing, and he wished that he could be traveling with her.

Jack thought he and Barry should be leaving, but he did have a few moments alone with Helen before they boarded his buggy to go home.

He told her, "Helen, there is no reason to delay our wedding plans any longer, with Miss Gillian leaving. There's no need for you to be here all by yourself when you can be with me and Barry."

She gave him a loving smile as she agreed whole-heartedly with him. "No reason at all."

"That's all I needed to hear you say, Helen. I'll go tell Reverend Johnson we'll have need of his services, this Saturday evening."

Helen gave him a nod of her head and waved her hand to Barry, who was already sitting in the buggy waiting for Jack.

As Helen walked back into the house, she understood how Gillian felt about wanting to be with the man she loved, for Helen felt the same way about Jack Parsons.

It would be nice not to have to say goodbye to him every evening as he left to go home.

Chapter Forty-three

Helen and Gillian spent a wonderful day together, knowing that it would be the last one they would share for a long time. They shopped for a pretty dress for Helen to wear when she and Jack got married on Saturday night. It was a simple gown of pale blue, trimmed with delicate lace around the collar and sleeves. Helen also purchased herself a new pair of white leather slippers.

As Helen was shopping for a few other things she needed, Gillian had a chance to purchase a wedding gift for the couple. She gave it to Helen, but told her that they couldn't open it until the night of their wedding.

They even treated themselves to a light lunch in one of the new tearooms. It was a pleasant little place, decorated in cool shades of green and white, and a perfect retreat from the hot summer sun.

Pots of massive ferns sat on stands at various spots in the room, and each table had a small vase of colorful summer blossoms, which gave a pleasant atmosphere.

The place was crowded with people, and Gillian realized why Melba had lost so many of her lunch crowd to this place.

"Oh, I wish I was going to be here to see you and Mr. Parsons married," Gillian sighed, as they sat there enjoying their leisurely lunch.

"I wish you were too, honey. You know, I think I'll wear that beautiful brooch Melba gave me, Gillian. I think this will be a good occasion to wear it, and there won't be many times I can."

"I think you should, Helen. I'll have to tell Mother Foster about your getting married. She'll be happy for you."

"I hadn't thought about that, Gillian. Oh, yes, tell her! You also tell her that me and Jack are going to come out there one of these days. I want Nancy and John to meet him. They'll like him, the way they never liked Kent."

After they'd finished their lunch, Helen happened to glance up at the clock on the wall. "Oh, Lord, Gillian you've got a long, long night ahead of you. We've got to get home, honey, so you can get yourself some rest."

Gillian knew that what she said was true, but she rather doubted that she would sleep, for she was too excited to relax.

But when they arrived back at the house and she had checked over the things she had packed, finding everything ready for her departure, she did lie down on the bed. Lying there so still and quiet, Gillian looked like a child to Helen, who had tiptoed to the door to see if she was sleeping. Helen could not help being concerned about what Gillian was going to do, but she knew she could do nothing about it except send up a lot of prayers for her.

It amazed Gillian to find she had slept for over two hours. By the time she was dressed in a riding skirt and tunic, it was time for her to go to the livery to get ᵗhe horse she was going to borrow from Jack.

In less than a half hour, Gillian was riding back to her house. Now the endless wait really began for Gillian. Try as she might, she found it hard to eat the dinner Helen had prepared as she sat there at the table.

"Try to eat *some*thing, Gillian," Helen urged her. "You'll be sorry later if you don't."

She did try, but she just wasn't hungry. Helen noticed how she kept checking the clock on the kitchen wall.

For the next two hours they talked of many things, and Helen assured her that even though she'd be living at Jack's place, she'd make a weekly check on her little house. "I haven't decided yet what I'm going to do about the job at the bakery, Gillian. Jack says it's up to me whether I want to keep working for Ruth. I guess I will for a while, and see how it goes." Helen was sure that Gillian was absorbing little of what she'd been saying.

As soon as the clock struck nine, Gillian leaped out of her chair and went into the bedroom to change into the boy's pants and shirt. Before she walked back into the parlor, where Helen was sitting working on her needlepoint, she sat at the little dressing table to tuck all that thick, auburn hair of hers into the dark blue cap. When it was exactly as she wanted it, she sashayed back into the parlor.

"Well, Helen, what do you think?" she said, with an impish grin on her face.

Helen dropped her canvas. "Well, mercy me! Dear Lord, Gillian—I see what you were talking about last night! I wouldn't have believed it if I hadn't seen it, I have to tell you."

Someone would have had to look awfully close to detect that she was a young lady instead of a young man. With the cover of darkness, it would not be possible.

Promptly at ten, Gillian left her house, after she and Helen had embraced one another farewell. Carrying the little leather bag that held the few belongings she was carrying with her, she walked down the pathway to mount the horse she'd borrowed from Parsons's livery.

The streets were dark and deserted, as Gillian had hoped they would be, and she made a point of following a route out of town that would take her by no taverns. Shortly, she was at the outskirts of the city, and feeling very confident that her plan had been the right one to get her away from Tucson secretly.

As he'd promised, Jack Parsons was waiting in his barn with a lantern lit. Fuego was saddled up, and prancing as though he sensed that he was going to be allowed to exercise that free spirit of his.

Without wasting any time, Gillian leaped down from Jack's horse. She saw that the look on his face was like the expression that had been on Helen's. "Well, I'll be damned!" he gasped as he got a full view of her. Gillian could not suppress a giggle.

He gave her a big hug before she mounted up on Fuego. "God go with you, child," he told her, watching her settle on the huge stallion.

"I'll be with you in spirit on Saturday night, Mr. Parsons," she said, as she spurred Fuego forward.

Jack threw his hand up to give her a farewell wave, and started to go back to the house. That young lady would be all right. She'd get to Maricopa County and her man, Jack felt sure. She was a pretty smart little filly, he realized after he'd seen her tonight. She really could have passed as a young gent instead of a lady.

Fuego liked the idea of the late-night gallop across the countryside. His strong, long legs carried her swiftly, and Gillian gave him his head. They rode for over two hours before she finally urged him to slow down so that they might stop by a stream of water and rest for a while. They both enjoyed a fresh drink of water from the stream, which flowed down from the Picacho Mountains.

Gillian figured that once she reached those mountains she would have no further cause for concern, for she would be far enough away from Tucson that the Harmons would no longer pose a threat.

By four in the morning, they had reached the mountains, and Gillian found herself completely exhausted. She reined into a little side trail surrounded by tall pines. When she found a spot that satisfied her, she secured the fiery horse's bridle to a strong pine, and removed his saddle. Taking the blanket she'd draped across his back under the saddle to cover herself with, she propped herself up against the saddle and tried to get some rest.

It was cool there in the mountains, even though it was the hottest part of the summer in Arizona. Gillian tucked the blanket around her and felt very cozy as she lay against the saddle. Sleep came swiftly, and she slept for over six hours before waking up in the dense forest.

Once she had the saddle back on the stallion and her blanket folded she was ready to ride again. It was a grand feeling to know that she had now entered Maricopa County, even though there were still a lot of miles to cover before she was to reach Hawk. But she truly felt she could relax now, and decided there was no reason to wear that miserable cap. She discarded it by the side of the trail, allowing her long hair to flow loose and free. She also realized that she had planned to ride only at night, but she felt safe enough now to continue in broad daylight.

At the first little hamlet she came to, she stopped to buy food for both herself and Fuego. She and her horse had never spent this much time together, and she found that her affection for him had heightened during their journey. Fuego seemed to sense this, and he would lean over to nudge her whenever she was standing by him.

During the rest of the day they kept traveling toward Rock Springs, but since night was falling when they came to the small town of Guadalupe, and she was very tired, Gillian decided to give herself and Fuego the luxury of a night in pleasant lodgings. She had spied a sign in front of a two-story white frame house, which said SMITH'S LODGING AND LIVERY. She went inside and made arrangements for a night's lodging for herself and a comfortable stable for Fuego.

The young mestizo lad who took charge of Fuego was obviously impressed by her stallion, and he kept muttering his name. "Ah, Fuego—he is certainly that, miss! He is fire!"

"Well, you take very good care of him, and I will see that you are rewarded for your care in the morning before I leave. What is your name?" Gillian asked the young lad.

"My name is Paco, miss, and I shall take very good care of Fuego, I promise you," he told her, with a most infectious smile on his face.

Gillian left then to go back to the inn. Once she was in the room assigned to her, she enjoyed the luxury of a warm refreshing bath, after ridding herself of the clothing she'd been wearing since she left Tucson. After her bath she dressed in the deep blue twill divided skirt and light blue tunic she'd packed.

She had even taken the time to wipe off the dust soiling her fine, black leather boots before she left the room later, to go downstairs to the dining room and enjoy a hearty meal with the rest of the guests.

Needless to say, when she entered the dining room its occupants all turned to admire the auburn-haired young lady. There were those who wondered about such a pretty young lady traveling alone. Gillian aroused the curiosity of the two elderly couples sitting there, as well as a middle-aged lady and a couple of the single gentlemen who were staying at the inn that night.

However, the two elderly couples found Gillian a most enchanting young lady, and they immediately warmed to her because she was so friendly and polite. The middle-aged lady was a little more reserved, and resentful that Gillian was the center of attraction. The two single gentlemen had both been mesmerized from the moment she'd strolled into the room. Gillian was well aware of the attention she was drawing from them but neither of them was particularly pleasant. Still, she tried to be gracious when they directed their conversation to her.

When the meal was over it did not surprise Gillian that one of the single gentlemen invited her to have a stroll with him. Politely, she refused his invitation, telling him, "I will be leaving very early in the morning, so I must get some sleep, Mr. Cardwell." With that, she went upstairs with the two older couples.

Gillian was looking forward to a comfortable bed tonight after sleeping on the ground last night, and before long she was lying between the sheets.

Having gone to bed so early, she was awake and ready to get out of bed at sunrise. She had a delicious breakfast in the dining room, and as soon as she had finished eating she went to pay her bill before going to the livery for Fuego.

Young Paco was there to greet her when she came through the wide doors. "Fuego and I rested very well, miss. He has a full belly, too."

"Well, thank you for looking after him, Paco. Here, this is for you." She smiled down at the young boy and saw his dark eyes light up when he saw how much she'd paid him.

"Oh, thank you, miss! Thank you very much!" He hurried to get Fuego saddled for her.

Finally, she was ready to go. Sitting atop Fuego, she smiled down at Paco and said, "It was nice meeting you, Paco."

"Safe journey, miss. I—I sure like your horse."

"So do I," she called back, as she and Fuego rode away.

She was glad to see a clear blue sky above her, without a cloud in sight. With any luck, she would be at her destination before nightfall.

So she would not be going into Rock Springs, but instead would take the dirt road out of New River and ride eastward to get to the trail that led up to the cabin.

An excited smile came to her face when she thought how surprised Hawk would be when he saw her standing at his door!

Chapter Forty-four

Helen didn't sleep too well after Gillian left the house, but the next day she didn't have time to dwell on Gillian, for she had her own packing to do. Jack had come by that morning to see how she was.

"She'll be fine, Helen. I saw her off, and I figure by this time she may be not too far away from where she was heading. She said it would be two or three days' ride. Now, you just spend the day getting your things packed, because I'm going to come by here after I shut down the livery. You're coming to the house to eat supper with me and Barry this evening."

Such a dear, thoughtful man he was. Helen had not been looking forward to eating here alone tonight.

There was a twinkle in his eye as he told her, "I'll bring you back here after supper, but it's the last time I'll be doing it, Helen Clayton. Tomorrow night you'll be my wife. I'm taking myself a holiday tomorrow, and Barry's going to run the livery for me."

What he did not tell Helen was that some old friends of his who lived nearby were coming to his house tomorrow to prepare a feast for their wedding dinner. His old friend, James, was going to fix a side of beef out in a pit in Jack's backyard, and his wife, Rebecca, was baking them a wedding cake. Both of them were very happy about Jack taking himself a wife, for they'd met Helen and liked her.

By the time Jack arrived at Gillian's house shortly after five, Jack was feeling both excited and nervous about being a bridegroom. It had been many a year since he'd stood up in front of a preacher to take the vows of marriage.

His buggy was fully packed by the time he and Helen pulled away to go to his house. When they arrived there, while Jack and Barry were outside unloading her belongings, she had time to wander around the parlor. She found herself moved, knowing how hard the two of them had surely been working around here, to make everything clean and neat for her arrival tomorrow night after the ceremony at six.

A huge vase of flowers sat on one of the tables in the parlor, and she saw how the organ sitting over in the corner had been given a high shine. She wondered if Jack played the organ. There were many things she knew she would be learning about him as time went by. But the most important thing she already knew, and that was that he was the kindest, most generous man she'd ever known.

Later, as the three of them were sitting in the dining room eating the meal Jack and Barry had prepared, Jack commented, "You know, Helen, your woman's touch will be making this old house a lot nicer."

"Well, I was just about to tell you and Barry how very nice it looks tonight." She smiled at the two of them.

They exchanged glances and grinned. To tease them, she said, "Now, I allowed the two of you to have your way tonight and take charge in the kitchen, but I won't put up with that after we're married, Jack. I'm going to be the one shooing you two out of there when I'm fixing supper."

"That's all right with me, Miss Helen. Can't say I like cooking," Barry quickly told her.

Jack laughed. "And I will be happy to just sit here in the parlor, with my feet propped up on the footstool, and read my paper while you cook, Helen my dear."

"Well, I'm glad we have that settled," Helen declared, and laughed gaily.

An hour later, Jack took her back to Gillian's house, wishing he did not have to do so. But he knew a lady had to dress herself pretty before her wedding, and do all the special little things a lady had to do.

When they arrived back at Gillian's house, he saw her inside the parlor and lit the lamp for her, before he turned to say goodnight and leave.

"It's going to be a long twenty-one hours for me, Helen, dear, but I'll try to endure it." He grinned. "I'm not going to linger, because I've a few last-minute things to attend to myself."

"I'll be ready when you come tomorrow. Just think, Jack, this is the last night we'll be parted," she told him.

"I know, and I've never been happier in my whole life, Helen. I never expected to feel this happy again, and I bless the day I met you, Helen Clayton. This time tomorrow night, you'll be Mrs. Jack Parsons!"

They embraced tenderly and then Jack prepared to go out the door. "I'll be here at five-thirty, Helen."

She gave him a smile and a nod of her head, and she closed the door behind him.

It was a glorious August day, and Gillian's garden was filled with a bounty of beautiful flowers, so Helen had an array of flowers to cut for her bouquet for this evening. It was the stately white and pink gladioli she decided to cut, for their blossoms were so profuse and beautiful.

She had spent a part of the day preparing Gillian's house to be left unattended, since she would not be there daily. She took two baskets and picked all the vegetables in the garden that were ripe. Being a frugal person, Helen felt it would be a shame for them to go to waste.

Her new blue dress was laid across the bed, and Melba's diamond brooch was pinned to its white lace collar. Her new white shoes and stockings were also waiting on the bed. One remaining valise was left open, partially packed and ready to receive the last-minute articles. She picked up for a moment a bottle of sweet-smelling jasmine toilet water, which Melba had given to her when she'd first come to the inn to work for her. This evening she was going to dab it behind her ears and on her wrists.

Finally, the time came for her to start getting dressed, and an hour later she was ready and waiting nervously for Jack to arrive.

Helen would never have been considered a beautiful woman, but when Jack saw her standing there in her new blue dress, he thought she was the prettiest thing he'd ever seen. Helen had hoped to look her best this evening, and the admiration gleaming in Jack's eyes was enough to make her exceedingly happy.

When the baskets of vegetables and Helen's valise were loaded into the buggy, Jack then took his bride-to-be by the hand and helped her up into her seat.

It was a very simple and moving service the preacher performed, and there were only two other people present. Reverend Johnson's wife, Sadie, played the organ, and young Barry sat in the preacher's parlor to witness Miss Helen and Mr. Parsons saying their wedding vows.

A few minutes later, the three of them were heading for Jack's house, Jack and his bride in the buggy and Barry riding his horse, Corkie, behind them.

Helen kept looking at the gold wedding band on her finger and telling herself she was truly married to Jack. Getting married was something she'd never expected to do again after she and Kent Clayton had parted, since she'd lived more than half her life with him.

When they pulled into the drive of Jack's place, Helen smelled the most delicious aroma. She looked over at Jack inquiringly. He smiled as he told her that his friends had insisted on fixing a wedding dinner for them. "You'll be eating the best beef you've ever had in your life—even at that fancy inn where you worked."

And what Jack said proved to be true. It was a most tasty dinner his friends had prepared for them, and Helen was very touched by their thoughtfulness.

She was thinking, as she sat in the yard with her new husband what an absolutely perfect wedding she had had. She and Jack were both past fifty, but tonight she felt younger than springtime. For the first time in her life she felt secure in her love. Life with Jack Parsons would be happier than any time she'd known in the twenty-five years she had been married to Kent Clayton.

The only thing she was grateful for from that marriage was her beautiful daughter, Melissa—but she rarely got to see her, now that she was married and lived so far away.

To have young Barry living here with them pleased Helen. He would be the son she'd always yearned to have, and he was such a nice lad. She'd found it very sweet that he'd bought her a gift, a little music box made of teakwood and inlaid mother-of-pearl. She and Jack had also opened Gillian's gift to them, which was a beautiful, tall vase. There were tears in Helen's eyes as she thought of the flowers in Gillian's garden, and the happy times they had spent together.

Helen could not imagine how any woman could be happier than she was tonight. Her thoughts strayed to Gillian, and she prayed that she was now with the man she loved.

If only she could have known that for sure, it would have been a perfect evening for Helen.

The remainder of Gillian's journey was uneventful, and she encountered very few people as she rode further into Maricopa County.

In fact, as she approached the mountain ahead of her, it dawned on her just how few riders she had seen on the road. Not one rider had gone by her the night she rode out of Tucson, or the day she ended in Guadalupe. Today a couple had gone by her in a flatbed wagon, and once she'd had a lone rider come up behind her.

She had not at all liked the way he looked or how he'd given her a wolfish grin. But luckily for her, a small town had been right ahead, and she figured the fellow had stopped in the town, for she'd not seen him again. The feelings of apprehension he'd fostered had faded by midafternoon.

Now, she was so close to the cabin where she'd find Hawk that she was feeling giddy with happiness.

Already, the air seemed fresher to her. She had never been over this side of the mountain before, because the Fosters' ranch lay in the opposite direction.

Wildflowers were blooming profusely by the sides of the road, and Gillian had to agree with Solange that no flowers were more beautiful than the wildflowers in these mountains. Even the ones growing in her garden back in Tucson could not compare to these.

Since this was a new trail for her, she thoroughly enjoyed discovering the scenic beauty surrounding her. She came across no other cottages along the trail—it was isolated up here.

It did occur to her that this way must be a lot longer, for she kept rounding bends without any sight of Hawk's cabin. Still, she knew she was going in the right direction, for there had been no side roads off this main dirt road. It was frustrating, though, for the many hours she had put in were beginning to take their toll on her. She was feeling very anxious to see that cottage and finally be with Hawk.

Maybe she had been wrong to come up this side of the mountain. Perhaps she should have taken the trail she was familiar with—but to travel that near to the Fosters' ranch and not stop there would have made her feel guilty.

Suddenly, as she rode around another turn in the track, she spied the welcome sight of the cabin, and a relieved and happy smile broke on her face. She urged Fuego into a trot.

When she arrived at the wooden gate, she quickly dismounted and dashed up the pathway to the front porch. After she anxiously knocked on the wooden door, she stood with a grin on her face, anticipating seeing her handsome Hawk's stunned expression.

But no one came to the door. She turned the knob to find the door unlocked, as it always was, so she walked into the cozy parlor. After calling out Hawk's name she realized that he was not there. The cottage was silent.

When she was wandering through the kitchen she saw that changes were taking place. It was obvious that Hawk was expanding the cabin. Since there was no sign of Hawk on the grounds, she figured he was probably paying a visit over at Troy's cottage. She had no doubt that he and Troy had been spending a lot of time together since Hawk had returned here.

She went back to the gate to get Fuego, for she knew that he was as weary as she was. When she had him comfortable in the barn and his saddle was put away, she went back to the cottage. With Fuego's needs taken care of, she just wanted to collapse in one of those comfortable, overstuffed chairs in the parlor.

It hit her how exhausted she was when she sank into the chair. She hardly had the strength to remove her boots, but it was a divine feeling to be rid of them and rub her stockinged feet against the plank floor.

Wearily laying her auburn head back against the chair, Gillian fell asleep.

Chapter Forty-five

Hawk had been pitching in daily to help Troy and his friend Homer on the addition Gaston had designed. This afternoon, however, Hawk had suggested that they give themselves a break and go over to the stream to catch themselves some fish. Their catch had been a good one, and when they left the stream, Troy and Homer taking the trail toward Troy's place and Hawk going toward his cottage, they were each carrying four nice-sized fish to fry for their supper that evening.

Troy told him they'd be over bright and early the next morning. "We're going to finish up the framework by this time tomorrow, while the weather's holding up so good," he told Hawk as he began to walk away.

The sun was already sinking low when Hawk got to the cottage. He was trying to remember which of the herbs Solange grew out in her gardens she always used on fish. Darned if he could remember which was the one, though!

He went around to leave the fish out on the back porch as he went into the kitchen to get a pan. As he picked up the pan and took a glance toward the parlor, his black eyes caught sight of two feet propped up on the little footstool. A curious look came over his face, and slowly he put the pan back down on the counter so that he could go and see who those feet belonged to.

With astonishment he saw that the sleeping beauty in his parlor was his beautiful Gillian! She was sleeping so soundly that she didn't even know he had entered the house. She was obviously exhausted from the long journey she'd made from Tucson, although it didn't dawn on Hawk that she could have ridden all the way here on Fuego.

So he let her rest, resisting the overwhelming urge to bend down and kiss her sweet lips. Instead, he went back to the kitchen to get his pan and went out on the porch to clean the fish.

When they were gutted, scaled and washed clean, Hawk took them into the kitchen, trying to move quietly. He didn't find that too easy to do with his boots on, so he sat down in one of the kitchen chairs and removed them.

Tiptoeing back into the parlor to check on Gillian, he found her still sleeping soundly, so he went back into the kitchen, picking up his boots as he went out the back door. He sat down and yanked on his boots before going to the barn to do the evening chores. Tache would be waiting for his feed.

When he got to the barn and found that Fuego was also there, Hawk realized that Gillian had ridden all the way from Tucson on the stallion. Now it was obvious to him why she was so completely exhausted. Oh, that little daredevil!

Naturally it thrilled him that she had come to him,

but he was also aware of the risks she had taken to ride that long way by herself. But that was his Gillian. When she decided to do something, nothing could stop her!

Well, at least she had arrived here safely; that was all that mattered to him. And now that she was here, he was determined to keep her with him!

When the chores were done and he got back to the house, he paused once again to take his boots off before he entered the house.

By now the house was dark, so he lit the lamp in the kitchen, then went into the parlor to check on Gillian. Still she slept!

Hawk found it impossible to move around the kitchen silently, but he tried his best as he set the table and fired up his cookstove ready to fry the fish.

He did manage to whip up a pan of cornbread and get it in the oven without waking her up, or at least, he thought he had. But Gillian had awakened from her deep sleep, and knowing it was Hawk she heard in the kitchen, she quietly got up out of her chair, still in her stockinged feet. The sight meeting her blue eyes when she peeked through the kitchen door was enough to cause an impish grin to come to her face. There he sat in a kitchen chair, with his boots off, busily peeling a pan of potatoes. She knew it was a sight she'd never forget, as long as she lived.

She slipped cautiously up behind him, and his keen ears did not detect that she was behind him until she was bending down to kiss his cheek. "Hello, Hawk," she purred softly in his ear.

A broad smile creased his face. He put down the pan of potatoes and leaped up from the chair to put his two huge hands on her tiny waist. Gillian found herself whirled around before Hawk sat back down in the chair, placing her on his lap.

"Well, hello to you! You little imp, I should throw you over my lap and spank you soundly for traveling all this way by yourself. But I'm so damned happy to see you, I won't do it."

His black eyes looked lovingly into hers before his lips claimed hers in a long, lingering kiss. When he finally released her, he announced, in his deep, husky voice, "Gillian—we're not going to part again. I won't allow it! Tell me—tell me you're going to stay here with me."

"I'm never going to leave you again, Hawk, I promise you." She smiled into his bronzed face, delighted to be with him again.

"That's all I needed to hear!" He lifted her up from his lap and announced that she could now help him get their supper prepared while she told him all about her journey.

The little cottage glowed with the happiness that it had known so many times, first with Solange and Hawk, and later with Solange and Gaston. And now Gillian was there to create that wonderful atmosphere of enchantment, Hawk told himself, as the two of them talked and laughed.

Soon they were enjoying a delicious meal, and Hawk watched Gillian devouring the food like a hungry little wolf, realizing she must have been famished.

After such a fine meal, and that wonderful two hours of sleep, she felt very refreshed despite the long day behind her.

As they left the kitchen together after the dishes were

done, she asked where Little Bear was. Hawk grinned, "Well, Little Bear hasn't had much time for me or Troy in the last day or two. It seems Little Bear has found himself a lady friend. Homer's collie caught his eye, and neither me nor Troy could get him to come home with us, so Homer told us to let him be."

"So Little Bear is in love?" Gillian smiled.

"There ought to be some beautiful pups. Homer's collie is a pretty thing," Hawk told her.

"Well, it will thrill Solange when she next returns to find that Little Bear has become a father. You know how she adores him," Gillian remarked, as she made herself comfortable in an armchair.

"I expect it will be a few months before they'll be able to return for their next visit, though." Hawk sat down and decided he had waited long enough to hear about what had happened since he left Tucson.

"Did Jake Harmon come to your house again, trying to buy Fuego?"

"Once, but I flatly refused him, and I had no problem afterward. But enough about that: I've some happy news to tell you, Hawk. Jack and Helen are getting married! In fact, by now they *are* married, and they have taken young Barry into their home as their son. Isn't that wonderful news?"

"Yes, it is! I liked Parsons the first time I met him. He's a good man, and Miss Helen and Barry will have themselves a good home."

"That was my only regret about leaving Tucson, I must admit. I would have loved to be with them when they got married."

"Was that really your only regret, Gillian? You don't feel like you will miss your life in Tucson? I—I want you to feel very sure of that, Gillian. This mountain is an isolated place, and it takes a certain kind of person to find happiness here, as I and my mother did for so many years."

"I can't imagine ever being lonely up here, as long as you are with me, Hawk," she told him. "That was the reason I decided to wait no longer to come here. Warner had warned me not to try to leave Tucson in case I led the Harmons to you, if they were still out for revenge. I didn't even think about doing that, at first. But then I got to thinking that if I left late at night and rode Fuego, instead of traveling here on the stage-coach, I could do it. No one but Helen, Jack, and Barry knew about my plans."

"And you did it!" he smiled at her.

"Yes, I did it, and I'm glad, for this way Fuego is with us and not back in Tucson."

As she spoke, Hawk saw once again that childlike quality in Gillian. But he also knew there was a side of her that could be very shrewd. She could be a brave little miss when she had to be! He would have to remember this about the beguiling little lady he adored so much.

Suddenly he could no longer stand sitting so far away from her. He got up and walked, still barefoot, to where she was sitting.

He crouched beside her and kissed her, then he murmured softly, "I'm glad you and Fuego are both here, where you belong, Gillian. As I told you, I don't intend to be parted from you again."

Her hands went up to caress and encircle his neck, and her blue eyes warmed with love as she told him, "I'm where I want to be. I know now that I was always destined to be here, Hawk. I should have known it that day so long ago when my horse threw me and you brought me here. I've never understood it, and I don't try to, but whatever happened that day between the two of us and Solange too, has always remained within me."

"I know what you're saying, Gillian. That feeling you are talking about was there about you with mother and me, too." He reached down to pick her up, as he did so often, and held her cradled in his arms. He was so strong, and she was so small, that he did it as easily as if she were a feather.

His black eyes were looking seriously at her as he told her, "Gillian, I've become a very impatient man. I want us to marry, and soon!"

"I know nothing that should stop us," she told him with a pert look on her face.

A broad grin came to his face. "Nor do I!"

His next kiss was enough to tell Gillian that passion was throbbing through him, and it stirred a wild sensation of desire that surged through her.

She found herself being carried to his bed. There he undressed them both and joined her on the bed.

Once again his huge arms were claiming her, his huge hands gently caressing her, and she felt the powerful force of him pressing against her body. She pressed closer to him. A wildfire of passion was flooding Hawk, and he shifted to plunge himself into the satiny softness of her thighs.

The two of them clung together, feeling like they were soaring to a peak loftier than this mountaintop. They were soaring through the skies on the wings of eagles. For a few glorious moments they stayed at the summit, where lovers set themselves apart from the rest of the world.

It was a wonderful feeling for Hawk to hold his beloved Gillian in his arms, and they fell asleep pleasantly exhausted.

Now that Gillian was here with him, as Hawk was drifting off to sleep he made a decision.

As much as he liked Warner Barstow, he wasn't going back to Tucson to work for the railroad. That wasn't where he belonged. This was where he would stay!

Chapter Forty-six

Troy arrived far too early for Hawk, and he tried to release his arms from Gillian without disturbing her, feeling that she needed her sleep. Wanting to stop Troy from starting his hammering, he slipped into his pants and dashed out through the back door to call to Troy, "No, Troy! Hold up!"

A quizzical frown appeared on Troy's face as he asked, "What's the matter, Hawk?"

"Gillian's here, and she's still sleeping. You and Homer shouldn't do any hammering for a while."

"Gillian's here?" Troy repeated.

"That's right. Give me some time to dress and we'll sit and have some coffee for a while," Hawk told him.

Homer and Troy exchanged glances as they laid down their hammers. Hawk went back into the house to throw on a shirt, and he closed the bedroom door behind which Gillian still lay sleeping.

Once a pot of coffee was brewed, the three of them sat in the kitchen drinking it. By the time they were finishing their second cup, a sleepy-eyed Gillian came strolling into the kitchen, not expecting to find Troy and another man sitting there. She was glad she had put the wrapper over her gown before she'd left the bedroom.

"Good morning, gentlemen," she greeted them.

"Good morning to you, Gillian—and welcome back," Troy answered.

Hawk thought she looked very beautiful this morning, standing there in her pale blue wrapper with her eyes still heavy from her deep sleep. He rose from his chair, led her over to the table, and introduced her to Homer Crow, Troy's friend. Then he turned to go to the stove to pour her a cup of coffee.

Looking at Gillian, it wasn't hard for Troy to understand why Hawk could never have truly become involved with his cousin, Shawna, even after Gillian had married Steve Lafferty and left Maricopa County. Married she might have been, but Hawk's stubborn nature would not accept it, and he never got her out of his mind. That's why little Shawna had never had a chance to win his love, try as she might.

Gillian sat down, and as she sipped her coffee she spoke of casual things with Troy. A certain way about her reminded Troy of Solange, and he had to wonder if this was what had attracted Hawk to Gillian. He knew how enamored of this young lady Hawk had been since the day he'd first seen her.

Looking over at Hawk, Troy thought he'd never seen his friend looking happier than he did this morning. It was obvious that it was Gillian who was responsible. He hoped that the two of them would finally marry, for he was very fond of Hawk and wanted him to be united with the woman he had loved for so long.

414

After a while, in that most gracious way of hers, Gillian excused herself from the table, declaring, "I'll leave you gentlemen now, so that you can get on with whatever you were doing."

When she had left the room, Troy looked over at Hawk to inquire, "Can we get busy now?"

Hawk laughed. "Yes, Troy! Now you can hammer as much as you want."

So Troy and Homer went outside, leaving Hawk alone in the kitchen. He sat there, musing idly that his old friend, Troy, approved of his lady, and that Homer had seemed mesmerized by her beauty.

By the time he finally left his kitchen to go to the bedroom, Gillian was already dressed in her divided skirt and tunic. She announced to him that she was riding to the Fosters' today. "When shall I tell them the wedding will be, Hawk?"

"As soon as I can get the preacher to do it. I want it to be as soon as possible."

"All right, Hawk," she responded simply.

"While you ride to the Fosters', I will be going into Rock Springs. I've some things to attend to for our wedding day," he told her, with a sly grin on his face.

They left the cottage together. Gillian sat astride her huge red stallion, and Hawk rode by her side atop Tache, until they came to the base of the mountain. She parted with him, then, to go into the valley, and Hawk rode in the opposite direction toward Rock Springs.

Rock Springs was a small town, and it didn't have big enough stores or shops to provide a selection of the things Hawk would have liked to purchase for his bride. He was well aware that she had left Tucson traveling very light, and that many of her things had been left behind.

But the one dress shop in town did have a very pretty bright blue frock, which Hawk thought would be most attractive on Gillian. It reminded him both of the loveliness of her eyes, and of the cornflowers she used to pick in the Fosters' pastureland, as he watched her from that high plateau on the mountain.

Before he got out of the shop, Hawk had purchased many more things than he had intended when he walked in there. He'd bought the lovely blue gown, lacy undergarments, slippers, and a couple of lovely sheer nightgowns in lavender and pink shades that reminded Hawk of the beautiful flowers blooming around the cottage.

By the time he left town he was feeling very happy about the things he'd purchased for Gillian. He looked forward to showing them to her.

Ironically, Gillian was disappointed as she rode toward the valley that she wasn't going to be the beautiful bride she'd like to be when she married Hawk, for she had none of her lovely gowns here with her. But it suddenly dawned on her that she might have left one or two of her little muslin gowns back at the Fosters' house when she'd left to go to Tucson. At least one of those dresses would be nicer than the divided riding skirts she'd brought with her from Tucson.

John Foster's eyes widened in delight when he spotted her riding up toward the house on that magnificent red stallion, with her auburn hair flying wildly around her shoulders. He knew at once that she had come from the mountain and Hawk's cabin. He wondered if she and Hawk had got married in Tucson, and had returned to his cabin to live here. If so, it would be enough to delight him—and how very pleased it would make Nancy.

A broad smile lit up his face as he waved to her and called out a greeting. She smiled and waved back.

"Ah, what a wonderful sight you are, Gillian, my dear," John told her, as he rushed around to help her off the huge stallion.

"Oh, it's good to see you, too. I trust Mother Foster is still doing fine?"

"She sure is, and she's going to really be delighted by this unexpected visit from you."

As the two of them walked into the kitchen, Nancy Foster almost let the pan of peas she was shelling fall from her lap as she leaped out of her chair to embrace Gillian. "Lord, I was just sitting here thinking about you! We were worrying a little, 'cause it had been a while since we'd had a letter from you."

"I know, Mother Foster." As she sat down in the chair to explain, she was bubbling over to tell them that she and Hawk were going to get married. But first she wanted to tell them the good news about Helen.

"Do you like him, Gillian, this man she married?" Nancy wanted to know.

"He's wonderful, Mother Foster. Helen will be very happy," Gillian told her. She also told them about young Barry, and how he would be making his home with them.

John remarked, "Well, now, I'd say I like the sound of that Parsons."

"She told me to tell you that they would be coming up this way one of these days."

"Now that sounds wonderful to me, and I'll certainly

look forward to it," Nancy told her, with a pleased expression on her face. For almost an hour they sat there in the kitchen, listening to Gillian tell them about everything that had happened to her since she'd left to go back to Tucson.

Gillian realized, when she heard the clock chiming, that she had to get started back up the mountain soon. A shy smile came to her face as she informed them that there was going to be another wedding in a day or two. "Hawk and I are getting married, very privately. But we shall expect the two of you to come help us celebrate the occasion! Would you come to our cottage for a festive evening? I'll send word to tell you when."

"Oh, you know we will, Gillian! We're so happy for you and Hawk. Now, does that mean you will be living here, or going back to Tucson?" John Foster was quick to ask.

"I think you can count on us living right up there on the mountain." She laughed softly. "You know how Hawk loves that place—but then, so do I."

Nancy left no doubt about how she felt when she declared, "That's where the two of you belong. I truly believe that, Gillian. I think maybe it should have been this way in the very beginning, now that we know what we know."

"Yes, I think maybe you are right, Mother Foster. But now I've got to get started back home. Oh, I've got to ask you though—did I happen to leave any dresses here, since I left Tucson with only what I could manage to fit in one small bag?"

"Well, let's you and me just go back to your room and see. I think there were a couple or three frocks, and I think there were a few things left in the drawers of the

418

chest," Nancy told her, as she got up from the table.

A short time later Gillian told them farewell, and was very pleased to be taking back to Hawk's cabin a simple but pretty sprigged blue muslin frock that she could be married in. She carried it in a flour sack Nancy had found for her, along with a couple of other cotton dresses. There were also a few undergarments and a batiste nightgown.

"I'll see you both very soon," she called back to them, as she and Fuego rode away from the ranch.

Nancy couldn't have been happier to know that her dear Gillian was going to be living so near to them. It had also been wonderful to hear the news about her sister, Helen. To know that she had herself a good man and a home meant everything to Nancy Foster.

When John looked over at her and saw how radiant she looked he, too, was happy. "It's turned out to be a wonderful summer after all, hasn't it, Nancy? I'm already anticipating a glorious autumn," he told her, as his arm went around her waist. The best blessing for him was that Nancy had got well and gained back all the weight she'd lost over the last three months. She was as hale and hearty as ever.

Hawk arrived back from Rock Springs long before Gillian returned from the Fosters' ranch. With boyish enthusiasm, he had laid out all his purchases for her on the bed, and now he was anxious for her to arrive so he could see her eyes light up with excitement when she saw everything.

To calm the impatience gnawing at him, he went out to see what Troy and Homer had accomplished during their day's work. Things were taking shape on the long extension, which ran across the entire length of the cottage. All the framework was up, and the plank floor was laid in across the studding.

Hawk went back into the kitchen and put some kindling into the cookstove, for he felt like having a cup of coffee. When it was brewed and he had poured himself a cup, he looked up at the clock to see the time. Gillian should be on her way back by now, surely, he told himself.

When he looked out the window a while later and saw that the sun was starting to sink in the west, he became anxious about her. Knowing she would be completely oblivious about the time when she got to talking with the Fosters, he just had to hope that she wouldn't stay there so long she would be riding up the mountain trail after dark.

By the time he had finished the cup of coffee and walked out on the front porch to see if he could see her coming up the road, he decided to ride Tache down the mountain to either meet her or see what was detaining her. But as he was on his way to the barn to get Tache, he saw the red stallion, carrying his woman with her hair of fire, galloping up the mountain trail.

The sight of her made Hawk heave a sigh of relief. How magnificent the two of them looked as they came toward the cottage!

He'd never seen a woman who looked grander on a horse than his Gillian. Fuego was perfect for her, and it was obvious to Hawk that the stallion adored his mistress. Most women could never have handled such a fiery, spirited animal as Fuego. Gillian, of course, had accomplished it very easily.

Chapter Forty-seven

Hawk was there when she leaped off the stallion to grab her in his arms and welcome her with a kiss. She was in a capricious mood and she teased him. "Was I missed, Hawk?"

"Darn right you were! I was just about ready to ride out to come get you," he confessed to her.

Holding hands, they walked up the path to the front steps, and she chattered like a magpie, telling him about the Fosters and their delight at her announcement that they were to be married. "They're very happy for us, Hawk. Oh, and thank God, I had a few clothes over there. As you know, I've brought precious little with me." She sighed deeply.

"I know, Gillian, but we'll take care of that eventually," he assured her, as he led her through the front door.

"Did you get all your business attended to in Rock Springs, Hawk?" she asked him.

"Sure did. Are you ready for a wedding here at our own cottage the day after tomorrow? The preacher and his wife are traveling this way out of Rock Springs to go to their daughter's place, a few miles away from here. Reverend Holcombe said if he could be here about six and perform the ceremony, they could still get to their daughter's place before dark."

Gillian gave a soft laugh. "Well, I guess so. But you don't give a lady much time to prepare, do you?"

Hawk wrapped her in his arms as he told her, "There is no preparation for us, Gillian. It will just be a confirmation of something that happened long, long ago. We were bound together long before we ever encountered one another in this mountain's woods."

"You're right. I know that now, even though I think I fought it for the longest time," Gillian confessed to him.

"And I always understood why." He led her over to the settee and sat down beside her, for he felt that it was time he made a confession to her. "I want to tell you something that I've harbored deep within me for a lot of years. You know that Cochise sired me when he took my mother captive, and you know how she escaped from his Apache camp, fled to these woods, and met up with the woodsman who offered her and her baby son refuge here in this cottage. You also know that this woodsman died a few years later. She and I continued to live here, and I grew into a young man. Mother and I never knew how Cochise found out about us living here, but he came here to claim me as his son. I guess he wanted to initiate me as an Apache. This is difficult for me to say, Gillian: He took me on the raid that claimed your parents' lives."

Gillian, although stunned, saw the emotion playing on Hawk's face, and she understood that he had needed o tell her this to cleanse his soul.

"It sickened me, and Cochise realized I could never be an Apache. But as we were riding away, I saw the Fosters riding up in their wagon to rescue a beautiful auburn-haired young girl who was hiding underneath one of the wagons. It was you, Gillian."

He paused, and Gillian squeezed his hand wordlessly.

"I used to ride up to the plateau and watch you wading in the creek when you'd gone on a ride on that little mare of Foster's. I felt I should protect you long before I fell so hopelessly in love with you."

She leaned over to give him a soft kiss. Her voice purred with tenderness when she told him, "You had no choice about going on the raiding party, Hawk. You should feel no guilt. But you know, now it looks like you're going to have to spend your life taking care of me and protecting me. Are you sure you want to take that on?"

He grinned. "What do you think?" He had not intended to have such a serious conversation this evening, but somehow the time had seemed right. Gillian had cheered him up, though. Suddenly he realized that he still had not taken her to see what he had purchased for her while he was in town today.

He leaped up from the settee, taking her hand to pull her along with him. "I've got a surprise for you." He smiled mysteriously at her as he led her into his bedroom.

"A surprise, Hawk—for me?"

"That's right, Gillian," he declared, and led her through the door. Immediately she saw the clothing lying on the bed, and she was overwhelmed with

423

emotion as she rushed to pick up the lovely blue dress he'd got for her. She also saw the fancy lacy undergarments and nightgowns, and it flashed into her mind that she would have never imagined Hawk picking out ladies' apparel.

She turned and exclaimed, "Well, Hawk, you absolutely amaze me! They're all just beautiful! I see that I've much to learn about you." There was a twinkle in her blue eyes as her arms reached up around his neck. "I will look beautiful for you, after all, with all those pretty things to wear when we get married."

"Oh, you always look beautiful to me, Gillian." His arms encircled her waist as he pulled her close to him.

It was late when they finally got around to eating that evening, but it didn't matter to them. No longer did Gillian worry about the past haunting her if she surrendered herself to Hawk completely. It was not his fault that it had been Apaches who'd killed her parents. Obviously, from what he'd told her this evening, it had repulsed him so much that he'd ridden away from the band of Apaches Cochise had forced him to ride with that day.

No, there was great gentleness in Hawk. He was no savage, like the Apaches she'd always hated with such passion. The passion she felt for Hawk was love.

Gillian had puttered around in the kitchen all morning, baking a cake, and putting in the oven the young turkey that Hawk and Troy had caught the afternoon before.

Hawk thought it hardly seemed right that a bride-to-be should be doing all this on the morning of her

424

wedding, but Gillian laughed, "Well, we aren't exactly having a conventional wedding, are we? But we must have a cake to cut, and since it is to be only us and the Fosters here, with the minister and his wife, I felt that we should have a meal to serve them before they leave to be on their way."

"I suppose you're right about that—but we'll make up for it, Gillian. I promise you that."

"I know we will, Hawk. You know, I was thinking: it would be nice to have Troy here for our marriage this evening, as well as the Fosters. Why don't you go over and invite him? Maybe you might get him to give you some of his nice ears of corn for our dinner tonight."

Hawk grinned. "Well, I can tell you are trying to shoo me out of here, so I'll go over to Troy's while you're so busy here in the kitchen. But I warn you, when I get back I'm going to make you relax for a while, before our wedding!"

"We'll see." She turned around to flash him an innocent smile.

As soon as Hawk was gone, she went to the cupboard to see if any of Gaston's wine was left from their last visit here. To her delight she found several bottles, and she took two of them and dashed out of the cottage to place them in the spring to chill.

Her next chore to accomplish before Hawk returned was gathering a massive bouquet of flowers for the parlor, and one small arrangement for the kitchen table.

She was pleased, as she looked around the parlor when she had adorned it, to see that it was going to make a very pretty setting for their marriage.

The wedding cake was baked, and her turkey and dressing were roasting slowly in the oven, so now she could relax. She flopped down in a chair.

Suddenly, Little Bear appeared at the front door, which Gillian had flung open because the day was warm, and the oven had heated up the house. The huge brown dog looked very weary, and he came and curled up at her feet. She smiled as she patted his head. "Well, Little Bear—you finally decided to come home, eh?"

She suspected that he was going to be very contented to sleep there by the hearth for a long time. His few days of wandering with his lady friend had obviously tired him out.

When Hawk returned to the house he found both Gillian and Little Bear having a nap, and he did not disturb them as he went on into the kitchen to clean the corn Troy had given him. Troy was delighted that Gillian had sent Hawk over to invite him to the ceremony this evening and to enjoy the dinner later. "I'll gladly swap some corn for some of Gillian's turkey and dressing. You've got yourself a real lady there, Hawk."

Hawk gave him no argument about that as he prepared to leave. "See you at six, Troy," he called back to him as he rode away.

As Gillian had figured when she'd seen Little Bear come through the door, his roaming was over now, but Hawk imagined he must be hungry, so he filled generously the empty bowl on the kitchen floor. It seemed that he must have smelled the food, because Little Bear suddenly woke up from his nap, came into the kitchen, and ate every bite of it. When he had finished he did not linger, but went back to his favorite spot to curl up again and sleep.

Gillian knew nothing about Hawk's return, or that he'd fed Little Bear and cleaned the ears of corn. Hawk figured that he would allow her to sleep for another hour if she needed to.

Now that the time was drawing so close, Hawk found himself beginning to feel nervous. To occupy himself, he moved his pants and shirt to the back bedroom, so that Gillian could attend to her dressing and preparations in his bedroom, where all her new things were hanging. Hawk also had an awareness of a lady's need for a leisurely bath before an important occasion, so he put two teakettles of water to heat on the cookstove. He set the tub up in the bedroom along with a towel, and some lavender-scented soap that his mother had left behind.

The clock chiming four brought Gillian wide awake, and she leaped out of the chair mumbling, "Oh, Lord, I'll never have time to heat the water!"

She heard Hawk's deep laugh, and he called out to her, "You've got two kettles of steaming hot water, so relax!"

"Oh, Hawk—what would I do without you?" she cried.

"I honestly don't know," he teased. "Now, you just go and make yourself beautiful for me. I've taken my things to the other bedroom."

"Oh, thank you, Hawk," she said, still feeling heavy from sleep. She trailed behind him as he carried the two kettles of hot water to pour in the tub, and returned a few minutes later with a pail of cold water to add to it.

"There, young lady. Your bath awaits you!"

"Well, I must say that you are a handy man to have

around," Gillian told him, as he emptied some of the cold water into the tub.

"I'm glad you realize that," he laughed. He was in a most lighthearted mood, thinking that Gillian was to be his wife in less than two hours, now. To Hawk, it seemed he had waited for this to happen most of his life.

"Well, you go make yourself very handsome for me, and I will be joining you soon so that we can greet the reverend together," she said, sweetly dismissing him.

An hour later, Gillian had enjoyed a warm, lavender-scented bath and dressed herself in the lacy undergarments Hawk had purchased for her. She thought about putting up her auburn hair, but in the end she knew that Hawk would prefer it loose and free, lying in soft waves around her shoulders.

But she did brush it until it glowed like highly polished copper, and when she was pleased with the way it looked, she slipped into the new blue dress, with its scooped neckline and soft, puffed sleeves.

She liked the way the full gathered skirt swished when she walked back and forth in the room, turning to observe herself in the mirror. Suddenly, she was reminded of the sapphire earrings Melba had left to her, and she got out the small velvet pouch she'd brought with her from Tucson. It was a fitting occasion to wear them, just as Helen had worn Melba's diamond brooch on her wedding night.

The twinkling diamonds and sapphires in the teardrop earrings gave a very elegant touch to the blue gown, and Gillian was glad that the gown had no lace on it to detract from the jewelry.

She did look like a bride, she thought, as she took the

final look in the mirror and dabbed some toilet water behind her ears and at her throat.

When she entered the parlor, Hawk was already sitting there in his best slate-gray pants and white linen shirt. He could not bring himself to wear the coat he'd bought in Tucson for wearing to places like the Old Pueblo Inn with Warner.

When he saw her appear with the exquisite earrings dangling on her ears, sparking with their white and blue fire, he took a deep breath and he murmured, "Dear God, Gillian—you take my breath away! I know the gown is not that fancy, for I had little to pick from, but I've never seen you look so beautiful!"

"Well, it's how I should look when I marry the man I love," she told him, feeling very pleased that he found her so beautiful.

She told him the story behind the beautiful earrings she wore tonight. "She is here with me in spirit, I figure." She told him that Melba had given Helen a diamond brooch which she had worn when she married Jack.

Suddenly a startled look came to her face, when she remembered the huge pan in the oven containing her turkey and dressing. "Oh, Hawk, would you take that turkey out of the oven for me? I'd just die if I soiled this pretty gown."

"Well, we don't want you dying," he declared, as he went to the kitchen to remove their feast from the oven. As he was doing it he heard someone at the front door, and as he expected, it was Troy, arriving early as he usually did. Gillian went to the door to greet him, and Hawk saw Troy give her a wildflower bouquet that he had gathered along the way through the woods.

429

"Well, this will be my bridal bouquet, Troy, and I thank you kindly for being so thoughtful. I love wildflowers more than any other."

Troy beamed, glad that he had pleased her. "You sure look mighty pretty this evening, Gillian."

"All brides look pretty, Troy," she said modestly.

"But few are as pretty as you," Troy told her.

"Oh, did you hear that, Hawk. You're just a flatterer, Troy, that's what it is."

Reverend Holcombe's wife was a little leery about their coming by this mountain cottage for him to perform a wedding, but all that changed when they entered the cottage. Immediately, she fell under its spell, as most people did when they entered the cottage, and she felt the warmth and love in this enchanted cabin and the people there.

She was also charmed by the handsome young couple her husband was about to join together as husband and wife. It was always nice to see a young couple as much in love as these two clearly were.

She was only sorry that they could not have stayed to share dinner with them, but her husband had politely declined, telling them that they wanted to get on to their daughter's ranch before dark.

But Eunice Holcombe knew that she was going to remember this simple little wedding for a long, long time, as well as the people she'd met. She could never remember her husband marrying a lovelier bride than Gillian Lafferty Hawk!

Chapter Forty-eight

"Well, shall we all go inside and enjoy dinner?" Gillian asked Hawk, Troy and the Fosters, as the Holcombes' buggy moved out of sight. She suddenly remembered that she had placed the wine in the spring early this afternoon, so she asked Troy if he would fetch them for her while Hawk helped her get the huge pan containing their turkey on the table.

They spent a very festive hour in the kitchen eating the wedding dinner Gillian had prepared. Nancy praised Gillian's turkey and wanted to know which herbs were in the dressing. The cake was cut and a wish made, but none of them ate a piece, since they'd all eaten too much turkey, dressing, and corn.

Gillian was teased by Hawk about helping herself to Gaston's wine, but she quickly retorted, "Gaston would be the first to tell me to take all I wanted."

Hawk watched his beautiful wife, amused, for he knew that she was sipping the wine too fast. He and Troy exchanged glances as they both observed her, and Hawk hoped the Fosters would not notice, for he didn't think they approved of drink.

Before long, John and Nancy rose from the table to say goodnight. They felt the rest of the evening should belong to the newlyweds, and they had a long ride home. Troy said he would head out with them.

"One more toast to me and Hawk, then, before you leave," Gillian requested.

Hawk saw Nancy Foster glance at her husband with a worried expression. Obviously, they *had* noticed that Gillian was getting a little carried away. But Troy just laughed.

"All right, Gillian—just one more toast, but we don't need any more wine. Any more and none of us will make it home tonight!" After the toast, Nancy hugged Gillian, and Hawk walked to the door with Troy and John Foster.

"We were glad you could all share the evening with us," Hawk said, shaking their hands.

"We wouldn't have missed it for the world. We're very happy for you and Gillian, Hawk," John Foster replied. He stepped outside to wait for his wife, and Troy said quietly to Hawk, "Well, this is the first time I've seen Gillian a bit tipsy. She's very happy tonight, Hawk, and I'm happy for the two of you. I know how much you love that little lady in there."

"Yes, you're right, Troy. Now, I guess I'd better get back in there and see if I can persuade Mrs. Foster to join her husband!"

But Hawk met Nancy Foster on her way out, dabbing at her eyes with her handkerchief. She had told Gillian that she and Hawk would be welcome at the ranch any time, and she hated to leave, but she knew John was waiting for her.

After bidding her goodnight, Hawk turned to go back into the house. Gillian had managed to clear away the dishes, but she was struggling with the big turkey, hampered by Little Bear, who was fussing around her feet, wanting his share of the turkey.

Suddenly she swayed, and Hawk rushed forward to catch her. She fumed at the huge brown dog, "Darn, Little Bear, you almost made me fall!" Hawk was finding it hard to suppress his laughter, for he knew it was hardly Little Bear causing her to be so clumsy.

"Here, honey, let me put this bird away and give Little Bear some to fill his belly," Hawk suggested.

"Think I'll let you," she told him. She went out of the kitchen and Hawk watched her go to the parlor. He only turned his attention away from her when he saw that she was safely into the chair there.

He pulled some hunks of turkey off the carcass and took them out on the back porch, with Little Bear eagerly following him, then returned to the kitchen. When the turkey was stored away he dimmed the lamp, deciding that no dishes need be done tonight.

Entering the parlor, he went over to sit down in the chair opposite Gillian, by the hearth. "You were a very beautiful bride, Gillian, and the dinner was wonderful. I'm just sorry the Holcombes could not have stayed longer."

"Yes it was a wonderful night, wasn't it, Hawk? I felt that all the people we love were here with us, either in body or in spirit. Didn't you feel that too?"

"I sure did! It would have been good to have my mother and Gaston here, but in a way they're always here in the cabin."

Gillian smiled at him, lovingly and a little blearily.

Then, taking his large hand in her small one, she rose up from her chair, announcing that she would enjoy a stroll in the moonlight with her new husband. Hawk was more than eager to oblige.

There was a bright full moon in the dark sky, and as they walked Hawk was thinking what a much happier autumn this was going to be for him. Last autumn, Gillian had been far, far away in Ireland. It hardly seemed possible that she walked by his side now as his wife.

Gillian looked up to the sky, where millions of stars were twinkling. "All those stars are shining just for us tonight, Hawk."

"Of course they are. That is why they're so bright. That's also why that moon is so full and brilliant," he told her, grinning down at her beautiful upturned face.

"And the night-blooming flowers smell so wonderful when you stroll around in the evening like this. Listen, Hawk—do you hear that night bird calling?"

"I hear him. He's lonely for his mate. It's no good being lonely for the one you love and want to be with," he declared, for he knew that feeling well.

"Oh, I'm glad I'm not lonely anymore, Hawk. I feel so completely happy now that it almost scares me."

"Oh, don't you be afraid ever, little Gillian. I'm always going to be with you, because I don't want to be lonely again, either," his deep voice replied.

As they were walking around the back of the house, they spied Little Bear cozily curled up on the back porch, and they laughed, knowing he was pleasantly sated with the turkey he'd devoured.

When they had almost come back to the front of the house, Gillian asked Hawk, "We *are* going to live here, aren't we, Hawk? We're not going back to Tucson, are we?"

"No, we're home, Gillian. Nowhere else could be home for us. I sent off a letter of resignation to Warner the day I went into Rock Springs and bought your dress for you."

"Oh, Hawk, it makes me so happy to hear that! This is where I want to be." Saying this was the nicest wedding gift she could have given Hawk, for it convinced him that she truly wanted to live on his mountain.

He swept his bride up in his arms, so easily that she could have been a rag doll. She giggled. "Hawk! I wasn't expecting that!"

"Well, I just remembered that Troy had piled some lumber over here on this side of the cottage. I don't want you to fall." He straddled the timbers easily, and then headed toward the front door.

Once they were inside the cabin, Gillian suggested that he let her down, but instead he bent his head to kiss her soft lips. When he released her, Gillian murmured breathlessly, "It's time your bride got into something more comfortable, I think."

"Well, I would agree to that." Still, he did not put her down, but ambled on toward the bedroom, with her still cradled in his arms. Gillian suddenly realized that she was not going to be wearing her pretty nightgown, for Hawk's gentle hands were firmly ridding her of her blue dress.

"I find you even more temptingly beautiful out of your clothes than in them. I worship everything about you," he told her, his voice husky with the mounting passion beginning to consume him. His touch on her

435

naked flesh made her more giddy than all the wine she'd consumed.

Gillian had never known such ecstasy as she came to in Hawk's arms on their wedding night. He left no part of her untouched or unfulfilled. She felt she was surely as satisfied and pleasured as it was possible to be.

Later, as Hawk held her in his strong arms and she was drifting off to sleep, he felt sure that his unspoken wish would be granted: there would be a son or daughter to remind them always of their wedding night.

Languorously, Gillian nestled in Hawk's firm-muscled arms, a lovely smile on her face as she felt Hawk's gentle fingers brushing back her damp hair from her face. Never had anything been as difficult for Gillian as keeping her secret to herself since she'd arrived at the cottage.

She had experienced moments of anxiety that she'd been foolhardy to take such a long ride when she suspected she was carrying Hawk's child. And yet, it had seemed all the more reason to leave Tucson and come to him. She'd dared to try it, and she had made it here, so now she did not regret taking that chance.

There was no doubt in her mind about her condition. She had felt like this when she'd been pregnant with Steve Lafferty's child, which she'd lost. But this baby, she would not lose. She was determined to bear Hawk's child.

It was a golden autumn in Maricopa County, but it lasted for only a brief time before the chilling air of winter began to settle over the mountain. Nancy and

John were able, however, to make the trip to see Gillian and Hawk a few weeks before the first snowfall.

They were happy to see that Gillian was radiant and glowing with happiness. It was obvious that she was expecting a baby. Her tiny waist was just beginning to thicken, and at once they understood why Gillian had not been riding down the mountain to visit them.

Gillian laughed. "I fear my little visits will have to wait for a while now."

But Nancy told her, "The timing is perfect, because in late spring, Helen and Jack are going to visit us!"

Seeing them again was something Gillian would anticipate with great joy in the weeks that followed. Nancy warned her that it would be difficult for them to make the trip up to the cabin once the snows came to the mountain, but Gillian assured her that she understood. The trail up the mountain could be very treacherous.

Hawk had already begun to prepare for the harsh winter months by going to cut wood daily, so that they would always have a warm fire in their parlor and wood for the cookstove.

Twice he had taken Troy's flatbed wagon into Rock Springs and come back with it loaded high with supplies. And with typical thoughtfulness, not only had he purchased the things he and Gillian would need, but he had bought all they would need for their firstborn child. He didn't know whether Gillian had thought about it, but he certainly had.

He knew he would be the one delivering their son or daughter, and he could not deny that the thought made him nervous. But he and Gillian had talked about it, and he knew she trusted that he would manage fine when her time came.

Gillian kept herself very occupied, keeping house, cooking, and stitching curtains for the windows of the now-completed addition. The new space became their bedroom, with its adjoining room slowly taking shape as a nursery. Their good friend Troy took great pride in his woodworking skills, and he worked for weeks to make their baby a cradle. When he gave it to them, it brought tears to Gillian's eyes. She thought it was the finest cradle she had ever seen.

By the time the holidays were over, Gillian was growing heavy with her baby, and both Hawk and Troy were her doting slaves. She told Hawk one night, as they sat in front of the hearth, "Hawk, if we have a son, let's name him Troy—for our friend seems unlikely to have a son."

Her remark took Hawk by surprise, but he thought it was a wonderful idea. "Why, old Troy would bust the buttons off his shirt, he'd be so proud."

"He's your dearest friend, and he's been so thoughtful to me. Why, he's like a mother hen when you're not around," she told him.

Hawk laughed. "Well, our son will be named Troy. But what if it's a girl?"

"I haven't thought about that yet." But that wasn't quite true, for in the recent days she had been thinking about a name for a daughter, even though she was so sure the baby was going to be a boy. She liked Hawk's mother's name, and knew that Solange would be thrilled for their daughter to be named after her.

The winter proceeded, and by the end of February, Gillian had begun to sense that her capable, robust husband was beginning to feel pangs of fear about his role as midwife. She also knew that his challenge was going to come very soon, for the baby had sunk lower in the last day or two. She probably should have been frightened, but she wasn't. She never doubted for a minute that Hawk would take care of her, as he always had.

By the time March was into its second week Gillian was wishing the time would come. She was able to move around the house to do a few chores, but everything was difficult. Hawk was never away from the cottage for any length of time, and he had made all the preparations he could think of for the birth.

Gillian felt that she was going to suddenly wake up and find herself in labor, but night after night went by without it happening.

Hawk was becoming as perplexed as Gillian, but he tried to keep his mood lighthearted for her sake. He even jested with her, "I think I'm going to take you for a ride on Fuego to get this stubborn baby of ours on the way."

But Gillian laughed softly. "As strong as you are, Hawk, you'd never be able to get me up on Fuego!"

Chapter Forty-nine

It was the third week of March, and Gillian had decided that it was useless to fret, as she had been doing. All day she'd been restless. Hawk announced to her as he was banking up the fire for the evening that he thought they were going to have a new fall of snow tonight.

When he had carried in another armful of wood for the cookstove, and had a fire going there, he left to go to the barn and do the chores. The first wave of pain struck Gillian, and she moaned as she grabbed the back of the kitchen chair.

When the pain had eased she tried to carry on preparing dinner, but another ten minutes were enough to urge her to forget about the evening meal. She went into their bedroom to remove her dress, thinking that now that their little angel had decided to make an entrance into the world, it might be a speedy one.

When Hawk came back into the kitchen a half hour later he found the kitchen deserted, but Gillian's anguished moans came to his ears. He muttered, "Oh,

God, this is it! And God, you're going to have to help me, or I'll never make it!" He quickly washed his hands before he went in to see her.

He did all the things he could to comfort her, but he soon realized he could do nothing but hold her hand and rub her back. She would get a brief moment free of pain before each new wave washed over her. He'd wipe her forehead and pull the hair away from her face, feeling helpless that he couldn't share the pain she was suffering to get their child into the world.

One hour passed, and then another. It was during one of her periods of calm between contractions that he heard the clock chiming nine, and knew she had been in labor a little over three hours.

Another two hours would go by before Gillian let out a wild scream and gasped, "Oh, I—I think, Hawk—" She could say no more, for the pain was too severe.

He flung the covers aside and he knew he was seeing a new life trying to emerge. "Bear down, Gillian! Bear down, as hard as you can!"

He knew it was so near, but not quite enough. "Bear down, Gillian—harder!"

"Damnit, I *am!*" She gritted her teeth to push with all the strength she had left.

"One more time, Gillian! One more time!" His hands were already there, and suddenly he found them filled with a brand new, tiny little piece of humanity. "Oh, Gillian, you did it!" Hawk had no hand free to wipe his sweating brow as he immediately laid the wee babe on a table by the bed, cleaned it, and wrapped it in a blanket. Gillian had given him a son.

He heard his wife weakly asking him about the baby

and he told her it was a boy. "Oh, wonderful!" Hawk was relieved that her pain had subsided. He was amazed at how tiny the baby was, for Gillian had seemed so huge. This little tyke could not weigh over six pounds, if he was any judge.

Gillian lay quiet as Hawk tied and cut their son's cord and carefully wrapped him again in the soft blanket. He was crying lustily, and Hawk was thrilled at the sound.

He was about to take their son over to Gillian when he heard her give a sharp gasp. He laid the baby in the cradle and went anxiously to his wife's side.

A startled look was on Gillian's face as she stammered, "Hawk—c—could we be having two? I feel—I feel like it's happening again!"

Hawk had only to examine her to see that it was true. About a half hour after their son's arrival, a daughter arrived. The huge baby Hawk had feared his wife was going to have to bear proved to be two small babies, each weighing five pounds and a few ounces.

It was past midnight before Hawk had his wife's and their babies' needs attended to. He had cleared up the room and made everyone comfortable, and he'd never been so pleasantly exhausted as he was this March night. There were not two cradles, so he emptied a drawer from the chest and lined it with sheets to make a bed for their unexpected daughter. Old Troy was going to have to get busy making another cradle, he thought gleefully.

When Gillian had fed both babies and drifted into an exhausted sleep, he brewed himself a pot of coffee and sat in the kitchen for another hour, just drinking his coffee and trying to unwind his frazzled nerves.

Eventually, fatigue overcoming his excitement, he slipped quietly into bed beside Gillian.

Their son was named Troy, and their daughter, Solange. It took a few weeks to adjust to having two small, hungry babies in the cottage, but Gillian and Hawk adored their little angels. Gillian made a quick recovery, with her adoring husband and the doting Troy helping her. As Hawk had predicted, Troy was overcome with emotion that they had named their son for him. He had immediately begun working on the extra cradle that was needed, and although it took all his spare time to have it ready, he took it over to Gillian a week after the babies were born.

A month later, the Fosters came to the mountain. To see Gillian glowing and radiant as a new mother of twins was well worth the trip. Nancy also announced that Helen and Jack were coming to their ranch at the end of the month. Gillian told her, "Then we shall have our long-delayed celebration in the last week in April."

Nancy, always the mother hen, inquired if she would be up to such a celebration, but Gillian was quick to tell her she felt wonderful.

It was a wonderful afternoon the Fosters spent with Gillian and Hawk. Those adorable babies were enough to bring tears to Nancy's eyes. They were not identical twins; little Troy's hair was as black as a raven's wing, and while all newborn babies' eyes are blue, his were a much darker blue than his sister's. His eyes would clearly be black, like Hawk's. But Solange's eyes would be blue like Gillian's, and her hair, neither black nor auburn, was a warm chestnut brown.

The Fosters left reluctantly to return to their ranch, with the promise they would return with Helen and Jack for Gillian's party. But Nancy firmly demanded that Gillian allow her to bring all the pies and cakes, and Gillian, grinning, agreed.

The day approached when their friends would be gathering to celebrate with Gillian and Hawk. Gillian, laughing, told Hawk, "There is so much more to celebrate now than our wedding. There are the twins, and Helen and Jack's marriage. I only wish Solange and Gaston could have been here, Hawk."

"I do too, Gillian. But I guess we can't have everything. They will be here very soon, I'll bet. They usually come in May."

"But how perfect it would have been if they could have come." She smiled wistfully.

The night before the party, Gillian prepared a simple supper, knowing that tomorrow night was going to be such a long evening. There was a delicious aroma from the chunks of beef, potatoes and onions she had steaming in the large pot. She had helped herself to some of the dried herbs Solange had hung in the kitchen. She'd added a touch of dill and marjoram, along with savory. Solange had taught Gillian long ago how to enhance the flavor of food.

After the pan of cornbread was in the oven, she set the table. Her two angels slept soundly and she was glad that she and Hawk would be able to eat without interruption, and enjoy their dinner.

Going to the parlor, she lit the lamps, thinking that she wished she could have flowers for their festive occasion tomorrow night. This afternoon she had gathered armfuls of green holly with red berries, and boughs of pine, and Hawk had complimented her on the urns she had filled with them.

By the time Hawk returned from the barn, she was removing the cornbread from the oven and was ready to serve the stew. For once, they got to enjoy their evening meal without an outburst of crying from the nursery.

Hawk's black eyes sparkled. "What magic did you work on them to allow us this wonderful quiet meal?"

"I fed them very late so they would sleep," she answered, with a laugh.

While Gillian was gathering up the dishes from the table, Hawk went in to check on the two little cherubs. He found them still asleep, but he also heard a commotion outside his house.

He went softly to the front door and ran out excitedly. Gillian was puttering in the kitchen, unaware of the arrival of Gaston and Solange.

Hawk gave them an enthusiastic welcome, unable to resist telling them that he was the proud father of twins. But he decided to let Gillian announce what they had named their children. He insisted that they linger back behind him as he went into the kitchen, crying, "Gillian—you got your wish!"

It was then that Gaston and Solange rushed into the kitchen, and exuberant greetings were exchanged all around. They had a happy hour to visit, before Gillian and Hawk were summoned by cries from the nursery. It was then that Solange and Gaston got to meet the delightful babies, as Hawk carried his son, and Gillian her daughter, into the parlor.

Gillian made the announcement that the baby Hawk held was Troy. "And our little girl, here, is our baby Solange."

Rarely had Hawk seen his mother cry, but tonight he saw her give way to a flood of tears, overcome by her emotions. Even Gaston's comforting arms around her could not stop the torrent.

Gillian walked over to place her namesake in her arms, and Solange's tearstained eyes gazed at Gillian. Now she understood why she'd always felt so close to this young girl, who was now Hawk's wife and the mother of his children. For all the hardships Solange had endured when she'd first come to this country, she felt she had received a bountiful reward in the golden autumn of her life. She had found the wonderful love of Gaston Dion, and she had lived to see her beloved son, Hawk, married to Gillian, whom she had always adored. But the most wonderful blessing of all was these two grandchildren. To have one named for her was beyond anything she could have hoped for.

By the time the guests started to arrive the next evening, everything was ready. Those attending Gillian and Hawk's celebration were to go home later knowing it was something they would remember for the rest of their lives.

Gillian wore her blue wedding dress with Melba's sapphire earrings, and she was pleased to notice that Helen wore the diamond brooch on her dress.

The meal was a feast and everyone ate their fill.

There was much news to be exchanged, and Gaston's fine wines were certainly an enhancement to the delicious fish, ham, and roast beef. Afterward, music was provided by Homer, Troy, and John Foster.

It was an evening Gillian would never forget. When the hour grew late, and all their friends had left, she was filled with the knowledge that she had never been happier in her life than she was tonight.

The house was quiet. Solange and Gaston had retired, the babies were asleep, only Gillian and Hawk remained in the parlor. Hawk took her on his lap and she laid her head on his shoulder. "I hope you're not too tired from all this, Gillian. You're suddenly so quiet."

She smiled at him. "I am tired, but delightfully tired. I am so happy tonight, and maybe a little reflective. All the people I love so dearly have found the happiness I would have wished for them. To have had them all here with us tonight was so wonderful!"

"It was a night I don't think any of us will ever forget, Gillian." Hawk held her in his lap as if she was a child, but he of all people knew she was certainly no little girl. He thought of the night when she had given birth to their twins. He wondered if he would ever be able to tell her how scared he'd been, for she had never given him the impression that she had been frightened.

And yet, he had to admit that nothing could bring him more pride than the fact that he had delivered their babies all alone. Never had he done anything that had given him more satisfaction than helping to bring his son and daughter into this world.

Gillian sat pensively on his lap, and Hawk saw once again the childlike quality about her that he had always loved. She remarked in her honest way, "Oh, Hawk—we're so very lucky that we found one another again, after we almost lost our chance to be together."

"I know, Gillian. I know, and the thought of losing you scared me. It scared me almost as much the night the twins were born," he suddenly confessed to her, before he realized it.

"You were scared that night, Hawk?" she asked, pushing herself back so she could look at him more clearly.

"I was scared to death!"

She gave a gale of laughter as she encircled his neck with her arms and planted a kiss on his lips. "Oh, Hawk—you were my strength that night! I never doubted for a minute that you would take care of me. You've always protected me, Hawk, for almost as long as I can remember."

And he promised, "And I always will, Gillian."

It was a vow he was to keep, and Gillian would always know he would be there by her side to love and cherish her. Hawk gave himself completely and unselfishly to her, and in return Gillian adored him with all her being.